The Oracle and the Pearl

The Oracle and the Pearl

By Nikki Pison

Little Heart Press
Rosendale, NEW YORK

This book is dedicated to my mother:

Karen Peone Cathers

A Wild Woman who has changed the destiny of everyone who has crossed her path. She's still at it, Goddess bless her!

Author's Note

When I was a teenager, my mother sent me to a friend of hers to have a "Rebirthing/Past-life Regression." I was skeptical, but I had already had some experiences that made me question the limits of our human vehicles to house the soul across the bounds of time. Not only did I see the moments of my own birth during this session, but I was taken back even further to revisit a life in a time period and place that I later identified as the medieval landscape appearing in this book. What was compelling about this experience were glimpses into a life that was filled with pain, poverty, and lack of renown: an anonymous life. If I had seen myself as Cleopatra or a wealthy noble it would not have been so convincing. Still, as curious as it was, I thought little of what could only be described as "memory" until I had a dream in 2014. I had just finished publishing two books and was not sure if I would ever write another. In the dream, I was holding a book, the title of which was: *The Oracle and the Pearl*. I did not recognize the phrase, but I knew I had written the book. When I awoke, I wondered what the phrase could mean, and what such a book could be about. My mind flashed back to my experiences being regressed to another life when I was a teenager.

This book takes key moments of the life that I "remembered" and fills in stories in between to link the memories. As such, it is fabrication. However, as a clinical psychologist, I have learned that all memories are a kind of fabrication: the mythology we create has only moments of truth woven in and is mostly an invented product. This does not make it less valuable. To the contrary, the lore we create about our lives is truly the most fascinating thing about us, and often reveals our underlying psyche better than if we recounted memories as accurately as film. Family stories that get retold and passed on are always part history and part fantasy. So are folktales and legends that seem too mystical to have ever happened. It is in this spirit that I offer to you the story of Jaelle, an incarnation of the Wild Woman archetype—the one who can't be tamed—who embodies the Outsider in all of us. In this tale, we see both the freedom and sacrifice that comes with following one's own path.

Part One

Chapter One: The Oracle

The night air is cold: so cold it hurts my lungs. I can see the bright pearl of the moon, plump in the sky, through the opening at the top of my tent. My animals are breathing, leaning together in their sleeping mass on the other side of the cloth. I can smell their earthy presence. As always, it comforts me to have them so close–my true family–the ones who have stayed with me through all life's journeys. Even when I was a child, my animals brought me comfort.

∞

I was on the mountain with the goats on the day the Rroma came for me. I remember them arriving in what seemed like an impossible swarm, their dark clothes and strange voices blanketing the hillside. I was very small, but I went out every day with the herd. It was just me and Mama, but Mama did not get up anymore. The Clan surrounded me and the herd, tying ropes around the necks of the yelling animals. A very tall woman scooped me up. I was not used to people in general, but she seemed terribly exotic to me, with strong narrow features, big dark eyes, and long black hair. There was a scar across her cheekbone. She did not look unkind, but she did not smile, and the big scar frightened me. She held me up and looked at me as if she were regarding a bundle of turnips at the market. Then in one movement, I felt myself being wrapped in a long cloak and tucked under her arm.

I think I might have shrieked for a second, but I was either so stunned or already so defeated by my short life that I quickly quieted. I settled into the rocking movement of being carried. I think I may have fallen asleep. That night I refused to sleep under the tents in the encampment by the river and instead bedded down with the goats. I had another name, but I soon forgot it. The Clan called me Jaelle, which means "mountain goat." For years after I joined them, they affectionately called me "Sixth Goat," a reference to the small herd that was part of my acquisition when they found me in the foothills of the Carpathian Mountains.

In the early dawn, I felt myself being lifted into a cart filled with a mishmash of straw, iron pots, and leather bags of tools. I don't recall if I even protested. An old woman came over and inspected how I was packed in with the supplies.

"Mama?" I inquired.

In her thick accent, she replied: "Mama is gone. She told us to care for you. I'm your mama now."

I thought I misunderstood her words. How could this crumpled old lady be my Mama? I repeated, a little quieter: "Mama?"

"You're right. I am too old to be your mother. You may call me Baba."

Everyone else called her Baba, too. She was a grandmother to the tribe, but in time she would serve the role of mother to me. Her daughter was the tall woman who had scooped me up. She was Ankah, who became my sister. I grew to love the Clan, but I resented them at first for taking me from my Mama. I believed they had stolen me and my animals. Later, I found out that my mother had paid them with the goats to take care of me as she lay dying.

Ironically, life was easier wandering with my new family than it had ever been in the small mountain shack where I was born. There, I had been lonely and hungry. Mama, although loving toward me, was mostly sick and unable to care for me. I had survived by browsing on berries and fallen apples. Now I was always surrounded by laughter and the smells of cooking, someone was always within arms' reach. There were no other young children in the Clan when I was adopted, but I had never been around children anyway. It took a long time to figure out the complex relationships in our family unit, but all were related by blood or marriage: 22 in all.

Baba was the oldest. Her husband had been Chief before he passed on. He was one of countless victims of the sickness that had swept through the country. We knew it as the *Pestilence* then, but I have since heard it referred to as the time of the Black Death. The plague had wiped out half of the family, including the oldest and all the children, so there were holes and painful grimaces of loss where family members had been. Because significant pieces of the puzzle were missing or mixed up, it made it hard to figure out how everyone was related. For instance, one young man and woman were always close together, so I assumed they were married. I found out later that they were brother and sister, but both had lost spouses and young babies to the illness. This may have been why the family was so kind to me. At the time, I was the only child they had.

Although ravaged, the Tribe was still strong. When we were not on the move, someone was always singing, cooking, telling a story. They all spoke the language of the Country to communicate with the Gentle Folk to trade or barter. Amongst ourselves, we spoke Rromani. I learned the new language quickly. People I met later in life said I have the accent of a *Cigany*.

Although I missed my mother at first, I guiltily found that I loved my Clan. The best part was that someone was always touching me. I had been starved for human contact. Now, my head was always in someone's lap, my shoulder touching someone else's, a hand was always stroking my cheek or hair. Even before I could understand their words, this is what won me over. This was why I never cried to go home after that first request for Mama. Ankah was my savior, although she was aloof at first. She was still a teenager when they took me, but she seemed so old and stern to me. Maybe it was the scar, or her stone expression, frozen with grief that made her old before her time.

Ankah had lost a young sister. She kept her distance from me at first. She was strict, and impatient when I didn't understand words or instructions. I was expected to help with everything, but I didn't know the language or basic things, like how to fold a blanket or wash out a pot with wood ash from the fire. I had fed myself on the mountain by grazing, eating what the goats ate. Under Ankah's tutelage, I learned to chop onions without crying and to wash clothes in a stream. I followed her like a puppy, hoping to get the smallest nod of approval. While she didn't smile and fuss over me like the others, I knew she finally loved me when she sat me down between her knees and detangled my wild nest of hair.

I was like a stray kitten to them. They took me in, fattened me up, and brushed out my fur. They all teased me about my golden hair and green eyes. Most of them were dark, so I stood out. I learned to respond to the suspicious looks of the Gentle Folk by speaking loudly in Rromani so that they could see that I belonged with my Clan. Although I'm sure many of them thought as I did at first–that I was stolen–nobody ever questioned why I was with the tribe.

I have often wished to go back to the simplicity of those times. We moved around a lot, but it was more of a home than I had ever had. My belly was always full and I was cherished. I didn't know what had happened to my real mother or if I had any family. I suspected that my mother died soon after I left. If anyone wondered what became of the wild goat child on the hill, or if relatives or neighbors came looking for me, I would not know until much later.

∞

Ankah was severe, but I soon learned her subtle manners. I clowned for her, pretending to be the snooty ladies at the market by sticking my nose in the air and pushing out my derriere while examining merchandise. She never laughed, but if I could make the little muscle in her cheek with the scar twitch, I knew I got her. I would hold out an embroidered dress with two fingers and say, "Miss! Miss! Don't you have anything that looks more expensive, but for *much* cheaper?" They were funny, the Gentle Folk, always trying to appear to be something they were not. My People did not care what anyone thought of them. We wore any old rags stitched together, so long as they were sturdy and warm, and cared more about one another than about any physical thing.

Not that the Tribe didn't have its revered objects: Baba's pot, for example. Baba had a giant black pot that had been handed down to her from her mother and her mother before. It had three legs and a handle so that it could be hung over the cooking fire and Baba spoke to it constantly as if it were a person. We ate from that pot almost every night. If I had to say where I grew up, our home was around that pot. Everything else changed: the town, the scenery, the dialects, but the pot was always at the center of our universe. It was always the same, the orange glow of the fire spilling over laughing faces, the dark pot holding our evening meal, steam curling up into the vast starry expanse above.

The nights were all the same and the mornings, too. In the dark that happens before even the first hint of day, the silent movement would begin. It was a sweet way to awaken, a gentle awareness of the people you love, alert and shifting quietly through blackness. Their hands knew the ritual so well they could roll bedding and pack the carts with no light at all. I would lie there, savoring the warmth until sleep receded and just the dimmest gray would appear outlining the encampment and moving forms. The first soft bleats of the goats would nudge me out of my roll.

We were piled into the carts as the birds gave their first sleepy greetings and shapes became more themselves and less shadow. Sometimes we would just be going to the market to set up for the day, sometimes we had more of a journey ahead. It was a somewhat tenuous dance, trying to be close enough to town to do business, but far enough away not to alarm the Gentles. More than once we were chased off farmland that we thought was remote enough not to bother anyone. Many Rroma families traveled by foot with no carts or animals, just the wares on their backs. They had an easier time finding places to camp without drawing attention. We traveled with a skinny brown nag, two mules, and of course, my goats. Whereas a farmer might overlook a sleeping group of *Ciganyok*, he was more likely to be wary of carts making tracks in the mud and animals grazing on his land.

Baba or one of the elders would usually persuade them by offering to fix a pot or repair a bent farm tool. Metal was our specialty. The women were experts at getting dents out of a cherished pan, and the men could forge and smith practically anything with just a fire and the equipment we carried in leather bundles and rolls. To this day, I find the soft clink of metal against metal comforting.

A few of the younger women were talented embroiderers, but Ankah was the best. Women in the market would drool over her swirls and tendrils, florets and paisley. While others would laugh and talk into the night, she would be hunched over near the fire, concentrating on the garment in her lap. Her eyesight was going from the close work. I once asked her if she was mad at me because she had been glaring at me so intensely across the market. She replied, "I'm practically blind, Jaelle. I was probably just trying to figure out if it was you."

While Ankah had trouble seeing the physical world, she could see the spirit world easily. Baba's mother had the Sight, but it had skipped over Baba and gone straight to Ankah. "They look like swirls of light," she told me when I asked what spirits look like. They talked to her all the time, whispering secrets about the people she passed in the market, giving her advice about what to throw into the soup or how to stitch her thread properly. Maybe that was why she was so quiet: her mind was already full of the dialogue of the dead.

"Who are they?" I asked her.

"Oh, lots of people. They walk with the living, sometimes even hold their hands. When we're in the market it's the busiest because they cluster around their living kin. Sometimes they try to get my attention to convince me to give their family members messages."

"Like what?"

"Like where they hid their money or to stop drinking so much. Mostly common things. Last week a granny wanted me to tell her grandchild to stop picking her nose."

"And you never pass on the messages?"

"No, not anymore. I made that mistake once," she absently stroked the scar on her cheek.

"What happened?"

"It was after Gildi died." It was the first time I had heard her say her little sister's name, though others in the Tribe talked of her often. "I had been very ill. I wanted to die, too. That's when I started hearing the voices. First, it was just the Woman, I hear her all the time. It's not like a human voice. I don't know how to describe it . . . it's the voice of the earth and the universe and the sky. She doesn't speak in words, really, but I know when she has a message for me. Sometimes she points things out to me or tells me how to do something."

"Like a spirit guide?"

"In a way, but she doesn't belong to me alone. She's in everything. I see the way a tree is bending or how sunlight filters through a leaf or the shadow of a rock and it means something. I know what she's telling me. I don't know how else to explain it."

"What does she tell you?"

"She says we're all connected, that we're made of the same material: the blood in a caterpillar and the stars in the sky are the same. You and I, we just have different bodies. I'm the same as any stranger, any animal, the moon, the wind."

My young mind tried to grasp what Ankah was saying. "How do you know that's what she means?"

"I just do. She tells me things I need to know. When I was sick, she told me that I couldn't die yet–that I had work to do. When I started seeing the spirits, she told me that I would learn to live with them, that the dead and the living walk together. I didn't know what to do. It was confusing. They all talk at once and they're all so . . . nervous. Later I realized only the ones who are distraught stick around. The ones who are at peace move on quickly. The peaceful ones only come back if they are summoned or have an important message.

"It made me crazy at first, the anxious ones would pull at my sleeves and point to their loved ones, try to get me to help them. I didn't know what to do. There was this young woman. She told me she'd been poisoned. She wanted me to tell her lover not to marry her best friend, the girl who had poisoned her. She was so persistent. She led me to him and I said her name. He looked like he had seen a ghost when I spoke his true love's name. I told him that she wanted him to know that the woman he was about to marry had poisoned her.

"He listened to me and went to break off the engagement. His new fiancé, the murderess, found me in the market. She screamed 'Witch!' and came at me with a knife. Uncle Jarani and the other men pulled her off of me, but not before she cut me."

"Oh." I had always wondered about the scar, but I had been afraid to ask.

"I never passed on the messages again, at least not directly. Sometimes I'll be kinder to strangers because I know their stories. I'll sell a dress for less because I'll see a girl's mother standing behind her worrying that she won't eat enough if she spends too much on clothes."

"Are there any spirits here now?" I was hoping there might be word from my mother.

Ankah easily read my intention. "No, but I have seen your mother–after you first came with us."

"Really? What did she say?"

"Nothing. She was just checking up on you. Making sure we kept our promise."

"What was the promise?"

"To take care of you. She was so ill. She couldn't even get up. She died that night after we brought you with us. We were just in time."

"How did you know to go there?"

"The Woman told me."

"The voice that you hear?"

"The Mother of Everything. She led me to the cabin. I knew we had business there, I just didn't know what it was until we knocked on the door. Your mother begged us to take you. She told us where to find you, grazing with the goats. She said we could keep the goats if only we would care for her little girl."

"So, you did it for the goats?" I was hurt.

8

"No, silly!" Ankah ruffled my hair and pulled me close to her in a rare embrace. "We took you because you were meant to be with us. You were part of our family, but we just didn't know it yet. I knew I needed to go to the mountain, but I didn't know why. We came for *you*. The goats were more of a burden than a gift. I came to get my little sister."

She had never called me that before.

"It took me a while to realize who you were," she said. "I knew we were supposed to bring you with us. That was clear. You barely protested and after a few days clinging to the goats, you fit right in. You even learned our language quickly. One night I noticed that your hair was a complete matted mess. I thought it would need to be shaved off. It took me forever to get the tangles out."

"I remember."

"As I was combing, I realized that you would have been born right about when Gildi died. That's when I knew. I knew in my heart, with you there between my knees that my sister had come home."

"You think *I'm* Gildi?"

"No, you're Jaelle, my little mountain goat. But I always thought it was strange that Gildi never came to me, even after all the spirits started to appear to me. Some of our other family did, to give me messages or to say goodbye before moving on to the spirit world or to be reincarnated. Gildi never did. I think it's because she didn't stay around. She was reborn in a little mountain cabin waiting for us to find her again."

I didn't know how to take this information. It felt strange to think Ankah's love for me might be based on the fact that she thought I was Gildi, and even stranger to think that she might be right. How could I fill the hole where Gildi had been in Ankah's heart? After that conversation, I worked even harder to please Ankah. I peeled potatoes faster, brought thread to her at night, watching to anticipate what color she might need next. I worried that if she stopped thinking I was Gildi she might stop loving me. Looking around at the Clan, I began to wonder if they all thought I was Gildi, too. I had always felt like I belonged until Ankah told me that she believed I truly did. Then I felt like an imposter who was adopted on a pretense. I still accepted the Tribe as my family, but I began to wonder if I was really one of them.

As winter approached, we moved to the foothills of the mountains near Brașov. After traveling about for the warmer months, we needed shelter from the snowy weather that was encroaching. I had seen other families like ours. We encountered them frequently in towns and cities. Baba always knew them or knew people they were related to, and many were distant relatives of ours. We camped together when we were in the same area, and even traveled together for a few days sometimes. Now the families converged and headed for sanctuary from the cold. The families gathered every five years to winter together, intermarry, and share the long nights.

Our destination was a sprawling old castle, Vár Buceci, built and abandoned by the Teutonic Knights a dozen generations prior in their efforts to guard agains the encroaching Cumans. The fortress had been strategically placed to defend from invaders coming through the mountain pass. There was a lake below it. The crumbling stone was barely habitable in many places, but some chambers and sections remained intact. For people like us, who were used to living under the sky in rain or blistering sun, the castle was luxurious. The families settled in, choosing areas and setting up living quarters, practically on top of one another without argument. Everywhere, greetings of reunion, singing and laughing prevailed, as if it were a great celebration. There were hundreds of us, and I was amazed to learn that the numbers were greatly reduced from previous years. The Pestilence had killed more than half of the Tribe, as it had killed half our small clan. There were very few children my age, and only a few babies. Now, the families gathered to re-formulate.

Everywhere, conversations were happening about marriage and re-marriage for those who had lost partners. Ankah was nervous. I had never seen her like that. She was always so serious and composed, but now she moved around quickly, shaking out blankets and rugs, organizing the cooking utensils, and cleaning the silver. I watched her move a pitcher from one shelf to another, and back again. Cousin Milosh watched her and explained, "Ankah will have a husband soon!" Milosh was great and round and jolly, and his wife, Lala was a tiny slip of a woman never far from his side. They were one of the few intact couples.

"Yes, finally our dearest Ankah will marry!" said Lala, glowing.

"Who?" I said, suddenly concerned. "Who will she marry?"

"We'll see," said Milosh. "I'm sure Baba will find her a wonderful husband."

Baba had made herself scarce since arriving. I saw her fleetingly, deep in conversations with other old Babas.

"Poor Ankah," said Lala. "She was all set to marry that sweet Tobar before the nasty Pestilence took hold. It killed him and his brother, who would have been another good match. Then she got so sick. Now finally she'll be able to be a real woman, a wife! Just in time, too. She's practically an old stick of wood."

"So, we'll have a new brother with us!" I observed.

Lala and Milosh exchanged looks. "No, Lyuba, little love," said Lala. The family called me "Lyuba" often, meaning *beloved* or *favorite*. Lala continued: "Ankah will go with his family."

I felt as if I had been stabbed in the heart. "Well, then I will go with her!" I blurted out. I couldn't imagine life without Ankah.

"We'll see," said Lala and Milosh together.

I was Ankah's shadow anyway, but now I clung even closer. I tried to help her arrange our belongings, but she finally shooed me away, annoyed with me for being underfoot. I decided to spy on Baba and sought her out. She was having tea with a large woman with a headdress. The woman wore a big gold necklace and rings on every finger.

"Yes, the Badi would be a wonderful family for my Ankah," I heard Baba saying. "You know she has the Sight?"

"Of course, I know, but that scar! It's so big! Poor thing. I hope it won't bother my Mihai," said the lady. She had so many colors on her skirts it made me dizzy.

"Oh, Violca! Don't be silly! Scars don't stop babies from being made!" The two laughed and clinked their tea glasses.

∞

So it was that Ankah and Mihai were to be married. Once it was decided, the mothers saw no reason to delay. The wedding was set for the next week, on the Winter Solstice, when several other unions would also be sanctified. Baba said this would be perfect. Ankah would go live with Mihai's family in their section of the castle, but we would still be able to see her until the families parted ways in the spring. "With any luck," she said, "Ankah will be with child when she leaves with the Badi Clan!"

Mihai came to visit Ankah, first with his mother present, but then he came every day just to sit with her. Ankah served him food and sat across from him, shyly watching him eat but taking nothing herself. Mihai was quiet like Ankah, a solemn, but gentle-looking young man about Ankah's age with big dark eyes. It was said that he had been married before, but his wife and small child died during the plague. Baba said it was very fortunate for Ankah to find a man her age who was a widower. Mihai was polite and complimented Ankah's cooking.

Ankah, who was usually so hard-edged and forthright, became demure and quiet around Mihai. I didn't know what to think of the new Ankah. Even when Mihai was not there, Ankah had a look that was a million miles away and barely acknowledged me. If pressed, she answered my questions, but she was distracted. All her attention went to Mihai when he was visiting, and when he was gone, she was busy sewing. It was a wedding dress. Baba must have bartered with another family for the fabric because it was a quality I had never seen before. It was thick green silk and Ankah was embroidering a panel of goldenrod yellow down the front with vines of white flowers and heart-shaped leaves. I was torn between being dazzled by the dress and terrified of what was to come.

One day, I couldn't wonder any longer. "When you go to live with Mihai, can I go, too?"

Ankah looked up, startled. "No."

"But why, Ankah?"

"You belong with Baba and the Clan."

"I belong with you! You said so yourself. You found me!"

"When a woman marries, she goes to her new family alone."

"But I want to stay with you! Mihai's family could be my family, too."

"It doesn't work like that," she said. "I've been waiting a long time, Jaelle. I didn't think I would ever find a husband, especially . . ." she fingered her scar. "It's time for me to be a real woman." The conversation was over.

I was heartbroken. I knew I couldn't live without Ankah, and I didn't understand how she could live without me. I wanted to hate Mihai, but I couldn't. He was too nice. He brought me a sesame candy one day. When I refused it, he looked so hurt that I felt bad for the rest of the day. He was gentle and sweet and had lovely manners. Everyone said so. All of the Badi were performers of some type, and Mihai was a dancer and juggler. He had graceful hands and looked like he was moving underwater when he was only reaching for a cup. I could see why Ankah was enchanted.

The preparations for the wedding continued. There were multiple weddings planned to happen during the same celebration, with new couples joining together from different families. Many who had been widowed were remarrying. My cousins, who had both lost spouses, were marrying siblings from the Dalca Clan. The sister would go to them, and the brother's new bride would come with us. I seemed to be the only one who was not happy.

Baba chided me, "Why the sad face, Lyuba? Your sister is finally getting married!"

"I don't want her to go with Mihai. Can he come with us instead, Baba?"

Baba laughed, "No, little one. It doesn't work like that."

Down toward the lake side of the castle were old stables where all the animals were kept. It was noisy and smelly and I loved it. I found solace in the stall where my little herd was locked. I decided to take them out onto the hillside overlooking the icy lake. It was cold, but there were patches where there was no snow, and the goats rummaged through dead leaf litter to eat pine needles. I was feeling sorry for myself, lonely and abandoned. Suddenly, I heard a noise behind me and turned to see a girl somewhat older than me approaching with a horse on a lead.

"We had the same idea," she said. "Let them eat a little while they can still graze."

"Yes," I was not used to speaking to anyone outside my clan, much less another child.

"You're Ankah's sister, aren't you?"

I nodded.

"I'm Isa. Mihai is my cousin."

"Oh."

"You look different. Are you Rrom?"

"Of course!"

"Hmmm. I've never seen hair like yours on a Rrom." She reached out and fingered my golden locks. "And your eyes are different, too."

"I'm adopted."

"Oh."

We sat in silence for a while. Isa stood while her mare poked her nose around in what was left of the brittle grass. "Nice goats," she finally said. "Are they bred?"

"No."

"Are you going to breed them this winter?"

"I don't know."

"You should breed them. Then you'll have babies and milk in the spring. My brother has goats. His does are already bred for the year. I'm sure he'd let you put his buck in with your herd."

The idea somewhat horrified me. "Thank you."

"Aren't you excited about the wedding?"

"I guess so."

"What do you mean? You're not happy for your sister?"

"No, it's not that. I . . . I'll just miss her."

"Oh, I see. Well, you never know. You may end up a Badi, too."

Isa could see from the expression on my face that I didn't understand what she was saying. "I mean, in a few years you'll be married," she said. This had never crossed my mind. She continued, "Maybe you'll be married to a Badi and then you'll be closer to Ankah. Who knows, maybe you'll even marry my brother!"

My mind began spinning. Could I actually end up closer to her? The idea of marriage was repulsive to me, but if it allowed me to stay with Ankah, I might be willing to give it a try. For the first time in days, I felt hopeful.

Back in the castle, I went to look for Baba. "Baba, how old does someone have to be to get married?"

"Why, my Lyuba, did you find yourself a husband?" She asked with a twinkle in her eye.

"No, I'm just wondering."

"Everything is changing. Before the Pestilence, we started to make plans for marriage well before the tenth year. Sometimes the actual wedding might not happen for a few years more, but there was usually a match made well before a young lady's first moon blood. Ankah was already a little late when she was engaged the first time. The Pestilence changed everything. It was starting to spread, and everyone kept to themselves. Most marriageable young ones were just wiped out. People who were married before may have lost a spouse, as I did. I'm too old to remarry, but many are remarrying, which makes it even harder to find a match these days. Your sister is very lucky. In the old days, she would have had many children by now and would probably be starting to make plans for their weddings! She is very fortunate that Mihai's family will have her."

"How old am I, Baba?"

"Your mother told Ankah you were born just at the end of the plague—you were a 'child of hope,' she said—so I would think you should be almost ten now. Ah, my little goat! Are you sure you don't have someone in mind?" She laughed me right out of the room.

The day of the wedding came before I knew it, and everyone was swept up in the preparations. The smell of cooking and smoke filled the air and the castle was a cacophony of clanging pans, laughter, and singing. After being sent to fill pails of water for the cooking for most of the morning, I was forgotten in all the activity. My head was ringing from the noise, so I escaped to the stables. The cold air was refreshing after the stuffy, smoky air in the chambers. The muffled sounds from inside the castle were remote and reassuring. I re-filled the water bucket and got fresh straw from the communal mound. My goats were noisy and restless, and I assumed as annoyed as I was by all of the chaos. There was a slaughterhouse connected to the stables outside, with meat hanging in the cold rafters. Many more animals than usual had been butchered in the days leading up to the wedding, and I wondered if that had something to do with their loud complaints. We ate goat meat regularly, but when Baba asked me about making stew, I always fiercely defended my goats.

I tried to settle my restless herd with stale breadcrumbs from the pockets of my apron, but they snorted and jumped around anyway.

"They have the heat," a voice behind me said authoritatively, and I turned to see a tall boy with dark hair.

"What?"

"Your goats—they're ready to breed," he said.

"How . . . how do you know?"

"You can tell, the way they're bleating. See how they're jumping on one another? They smell the bucks. It's put them into heat. Haven't you ever bred them before?"

"No."

"So, they give no milk? Are they for meat?"

"No!"

"Oh, so then you'll want to breed them." I was not sure how to take the conviction in his voice. "I'm Sasha," he said. "I'm Isa's brother. She told me about you. You're Ankah's sister, the adopted one."

"I'm Ankah's only sister," I said, a little sharply.

"Yes, well, I have a herd, too. I only have four females and a male. Next year, we may keep some females and butcher the males, so I'll have a bigger herd. Do you want to see them?"

Curiosity filled me. "Yes."

I followed him to a stall at the end and peeked over the edge to see earnest caprine faces looking up. They yelled greetings to him.

"The buck is called King," he said pointing out an impressively large animal with long white fur and big horns. "That's Honey, she's the light amber one over there. Then over there is Marigold, Amaranth, and Pebbles. Pebbles is the small speckled one. I got her from a Jewish family all the way out in Moldavia. I traded a gold ring for her—she's very valuable. You don't see that kind of color around here."

It hadn't occurred to me that anyone took pride in their animals, loved them as I did. Sasha jumped over the stall wall and the goats crowded around him, nibbling at his jacket, nudging his back. For the first time, I noticed the delicate lines of Sasha's face, his graceful arms. I tried not to let him know that I was watching him and uttered a few appreciative words about the goats.

"The females are already bred for the season. We can put King in with yours if you want."

"Will he . . . hurt them?" The white giant looked so massive.

Sasha laughed, "No, of course not. It's natural. It's what animals do. Breed and make babies. It's the way the Mother intended it. Don't you want lots of beautiful baby goats? You would probably have ten by spring."

"Ten! That's a lot. Baba would not be happy with that. She already complains that they are expensive to keep because I won't let anyone eat them."

"Well, half will probably be boys, so that's meat for the family or to sell. The other half you can sell when they get big enough, or maybe keep one or two. You'll have milk and cheese to sell, too. That would help to pay their keep."

I hadn't thought of that. Maybe if I learned to make cheese Baba would be happy with the goats. I often wondered how long she would let my herd tag along with us when they were clearly a burden. The requests for goat stew were becoming less of a joke recently.

"Alright, I guess it makes sense."

Sasha led King out of the stall and down to the enclosure where my goats were held. I watched, fascinated, as the does yelled and scuttled around the pen, and King proficiently attended to each.

"See," said Sasha. "It's natural. They know what to do. He won't hurt them."

I nodded.

"Now we're family!" Sasha smiled at me and my heart flipped in an unfamiliar way.

Chapter Two: The Wedding

All the clans gathered in the Great Hall. Crumbling and cold as it was, it quickly warmed with the presence of the masses. Lanterns and torches threw long shadows across the stone, dancing with the movement of hundreds of bodies packed closely together. The families made a long row for the fourteen couples who were marrying. The Elders stood at the beginning of the row. As each couple came forward with their hands clasped, the grandparents or oldest kin of each family wound a long leather cord around their entwined hands. They were carefully "fastened" together, symbolizing their eternal bond.

I was placed in the front of the long corridor on the floor across from Isa. As some of the youngest, we held the broom low across the line for the couples to step over after each was hand-fasted. This would complete the union and make it official in the eyes of the Ancestors and the community. I looked down the row to try to get a glimpse of Ankah's shining face over the crowd. As each couple passed over the broom, a loud shout went up in celebration.

As they got closer, I saw Mihai's eyes. They always seemed so large and sad to me, but tonight they were sparkling in torchlight as he looked at his bride and stepped over the threshold into marriage. I had never seen Ankah look so beautiful. She was always so stern, but now she glowed and smiled, her scar invisible in her happiness. The dress she had worked on so tirelessly sparkled in the fire's light.

The simple ceremony was over quickly, and the feasting began as each couple was swept into the throngs of their enmeshed families. Food overflowed on lavishly set tables. Music and laughter clashed and jangled together. The feasting and celebrating went on all night. I only saw flashes of Ankah and Mihai. As was the tradition, the couples were embraced by their families, surrounded and adored. Each time they tried to slip off, someone would grab them.

"Have another drink, Mihai!" they would say, or grabbing Ankah's sleeve, "Let me see that dress close up!" It was a joke to keep the couple from escaping to the privacy of their marriage night as long as possible. I couldn't even get close to my sister. Finally, when I had eaten too much of the lavish food and felt my head spinning from the smoke and music, I escaped to the stables to check on my herd.

I was surprised to see Sasha leaning on the stall door. We had left King in with my goats, just to make sure they were bred properly, and Sasha was talking to him. I startled him and he seemed embarrassed to be caught conversing with his buck.

"I was making sure he's doing his job," he said.

"Thank you," I said.

"He'll give you nice babies in the spring."

"How can I repay you?" I wondered out loud.

"It's alright. It costs me nothing and King is happy to serve. Besides, by next year your sister will probably give me a new cousin!"

I blanched. The idea of Mihai attending to Ankah in such an intimate way made me queasy. Even worse, the thought of Ankah with a baby, cradling and loving someone more than me made me sick. I felt the rich food churning in my stomach and turned to vomit. I felt a hand on my back and jumped a little but the food kept coming up. Sasha gently rubbed my back and held me steady as my gut emptied.

"So much for the curried goat," he observed. That made me wretch again, although there was nothing left. As the convulsions wracked my whole body, I resolved to never eat goat again, no matter how hungry I was.

Sasha pulled a small leather flask from his waistband. "Here, just a little sip." The taste was sweet and sharp at once but got the sour flavor out of my mouth. "It's mead, I made it myself."

"Thank you."

Sasha took a sip of mead himself.

"How did you learn to make mead?" I asked.

"My father taught me. It's easy. I make cheese, too. Isa milks the goats. That's woman's work, but I make the best cheese around."

"Could you teach me?"

"Of course. I think Johan has some goats in milk, those dark brown ones a few stalls down. We could borrow some milk and I could teach you tomorrow."

"Thank you." I seemed to be racking up a lot of debt to Sasha.

"It's no trouble, Jaelle." Something about the way he said my name made my heart flip in that unusual way again. I thought it might be my stomach again, so I reached for his flask. Sasha smiled and graciously allowed me another sip. The sweet, strong fluid calmed my stomach and nerves like a balm. "It's good medicine," he said. "Too much can make you sick, but when you're not feeling well, a little bit can help. I put herbs from the side of the mountain in it. Mother taught me that. She's a very skilled healer."

"I don't think I've met her yet."

"She's quite famous. She was a trapeze artist in the Circ before she had me and Isa. She stays closer to the ground now."

"Do you perform?"

"Of course. Every Badi has a Circ skill. I'm mostly a tumbler and juggler, but I'm training with fire. I hope to be famous someday."

I looked at his beautiful face and could see adoring fans coming miles to see him perform. "I'm sure you will be."

He smiled.

The next day, Sasha followed through on his promise and showed me how to heat the milk and stir in a small amount of mead at just the right point. We borrowed a small piece of linen and poured the clumpy liquid through the mixture, catching the whey in another pot. The little pouch was tied with twine and hung from a nail with the pot underneath to catch more of the yellowish water. Later, we walked with Isa along the edge of the mountain and they showed me the herbs that were sleeping, still green, just below the dead leaf clutter. Isa said her mother had taught her how to speak to the spirits of the plants to find just the right ones. We took the fragrant leaves and crushed them along with a few grains of precious salt and mixed them with the curds in a wooden bowl. Cousin Milosh said it was the best cheese he had ever tasted. Baba nodded approval and poured the whey into the big pot to simmer with the rest of our supper.

One day as the cold encroached, men on horseback came and demanded to see our papers. They were sent by the Lord of the estate in which the castle lay. The Lord, Domn Alexandru, took up residence in a fine house on the edge of a town many miles on the other side of the mountain, but he owned everything in the district. The men were well-dressed and armed and scared me. Nobody else seemed alarmed. They just swiftly went to find Baba, who hobbled up and greeted the noblemen politely while reaching in to pull out the cord and small leather satchel that she always wore around her neck. I had seen her pull it out a few times in tense negotiations when we visited an unfamiliar town seeking a quiet night in a field. We were usually only confronted harshly by locals when there had been recent sickness, crimes, or unexplained deaths in the area. They were wary of any occurrence they could speculate resulted from our presence or witchcraft. Although the Rromani had long adopted the ruse of pretending to be Christian pilgrims for safety, if anything went wrong, they were the first to be blamed for practicing sorcery.

Inside Baba's small bag was the Clan's most valuable possession: it was a letter guaranteeing safe passage, officially stamped with the seal of an important aristocrat. He was long dead, but the fraying page still held its power. Most people we encountered could not read at all and had no clue what was written there. Still, once seeing the impressive marks, nobody had ever questioned us further. Their original scorn never seemed to prevent them from hiring us to repair a harness or from buying our beautifully embellished cloth.

These men seemed even more interested than usual in the page and exchanged looks with one another. "Why, this is the mark of the Lord's grandfather!" the oldest among them exclaimed.

"Yes, I knew the gentleman in our youth," said Baba. "He was a very kind man and was a great friend to my husband. Sadly, neither walk with us any longer." The men looked skeptical, apparently unable to imagine how the Lord's grandfather had befriended a Cigany.

"And what of the others?" he inquired. "This guarantees your family's safe passage, but what of all of the . . . other people here?"

"Respectfully sir, they are all my family," Baba smiled.

"All of them?"

"Yes, sir. We have come here every fifth year for many generations, to over-winter in this very castle. The Lord's grandfather, and his father, too, have always welcomed us, although I must say the buildings were more habitable in years past. We will be happy to bring gifts in the spring before we depart, to show our gratitude. We have livestock and fine cloth and can repair anything that the Lord needs fixed. We are many strong, and can reduce the troubles of the Lord's household with our skills. He needs only to bring us his broken wares and we'll mend all of it for no charge."

"Hmmmm . . ." the elder statesman considered this. "I will have to consult with him. I'll be back. Prepare to leave if the Lord wishes it so."

"Of course," said Baba. "We would never stay where we are not welcomed."

A few days later, the Lord himself arrived with a small entourage of armed men. He spoke to Baba personally, and his henchmen gasped when Baba touched his shoulder and talked to him tenderly. After he left, Baba said that she remembered him as a little boy. The Lord said that he recalled Tata Vornic, Baba's husband, coming to the estate to conduct business. He said Tata

Vornic had made the harness for his first horse. After that, nobody bothered us for the rest of the winter. They did, however, drop off an occasional item to repair.

I saw very little of Ankah. She had set up house with Mihai's family and any time I wandered by, she was earnestly scrubbing something or preparing a meal with his mother. She was always happy to see me, but as I watched her laugh and converse with her new family, I felt that she was a different person than the sister who had quietly untangled my knotted hair. I took refuge with my goats. I would sit for hours in their little stall, soaking in their warmth and unconditional regard for me. With them, I was the most important entity. I understood the language of their soft bleats and whispery soft kisses. Since they had practically raised me, I wondered if I owned them, or if they owned me. Perhaps they believed I was their kid, another member of the herd.

I didn't understand the people around me: the customs, the nuances, the history. I had no idea how I fit in there or how I could continue to make my life make sense after Ankah left. I did not have to worry about how I fit with my goats. I knew I belonged to them and they belonged to me. The funny thing was that I knew Sasha felt the same way about his goats. More than once I had caught him talking to them as if they were having a deep conversation. His ease around them was so familiar to me. Very quickly, he became familiar to me, like the goats, as if he were just an extension of his herd and my herd.

"I think Jaelle has found a husband," teased Cousin Rodica, the new wife of my cousin Hadrian. She was talkative and a busy-body, and I didn't particularly like her or her mother, who was always nearby. "Jaelle and Sasha are making *cheese* together," Rodica fake-whispered to her mother and Lala. Lala could see it bothered me and drew me close to her, "And who would not love our little Lyuba, the light of our family?" The word "family" felt foreign to me, and I didn't even know what it meant anymore without Ankah. Everything had changed. With the new unions, we had different people like Rodica and her mother milling around, as if they had always been there, cooking with our pots and eating our food.

Baba was making a blanket. It was a marriage blanket for Ankah to take with her to her new life. She had been working on it for some time. It was deep blue like the sky and she was embroidering golden stars across it. Her eyes were not what they used to be, so the effort was slow, but her hands remembered the work and she could feel the raised surface to find where she had missed a stitch. "Come here, Lyuba," she said softly. "Do you like this boy?" She didn't look up from the cloth in her lap.

"What boy, Baba?"

Baba raised her eyes and just looked at me.

"Um . . . I like his goats."

She paused. "You know, we had a puppy once. It was a sweet little dog with silky soft long ears. It absolutely adored Tata Vornic—would not leave his side. When Tata died, the poor thing just cried and cried. She looked for him everywhere and got sadder and sadder. Finally, that puppy—she just lay down one day and died!"

I looked at Baba, unsure of her meaning.

"You are kind of like that puppy, Lyuba. Since Ankah got married, you just mope around, sadder and sadder. I wonder if you might die without her?"

I let out my breath. I hadn't realized I'd been holding it, but Baba's words went straight to my core as if she had verbalized what I'd been feeling for weeks. Before I knew it, I was sobbing with my head on Baba's lap. "There, there, little one. Baba knows how you feel. I felt just like that puppy when Tata left this world, only I couldn't lie down and die. I had to become Tata, to take care of the Clan. Ankah is not just your sister, she's part of your soul. Do you know that she was the one who brought us to find you?" I nodded, wiping my nose on my sleeve. "Don't worry, Lyuba. The Divine Earth Mother knows what She is doing and will bring you to your destiny." I didn't know what she meant, since the theology of the Clan was still elusive to me, but her words comforted me.

The next day, Baba disappeared for several hours. When she came back, she was smiling and gave me a quick kiss on the forehead. "*She* knows, Lyuba," she said. "*She* knows what *She* is doing."

"Your Baba came to see my mother," Isa told me later as we walked around the lake, poking sticks at the crystals of ice forming around the edge.

"Oh?"

"Yes, they drank tea for hours. She's never visited before."

"Maybe they are old friends?"

"Maybe." She tossed her head and pushed a strand of black hair back under her headscarf. I admired Isa; She was so confident. It was as if she knew exactly where she fit into the world. "You know," she said, "Sasha is going to be a great acrobat, like my parents. He's very good already. Anyone would be lucky to have him as a husband."

"Yes, I'm sure," I agreed.

"Would you like it if he were your husband?"

"Me? Why would he marry me?"

"Well, families decide these things, you know."

"Yes, but why me?"

"Sasha likes you, and you're a hard worker, and you like goats," she said. "And, there aren't a lot of young people now, you know. There will be babies again soon, but the Clan is still small from the Pestilence."

"That's true."

"Would you like to be Badi? Maybe you can be a performer, too?"

"Oh no, I don't think so."

"Really? Do you dance?"

"No."

"What do you do best?"

"I'm not sure. Take care of my goats, I suppose." I had never tried to do anything else.

"Well, maybe you can train them to do tricks? Some people have animals that can jump through hoops or stand on top of each other to make a tower. Maybe something like that?"

"I'm . . . not sure."

"Well, you'll figure it out. Everyone has a skill. If you come to the Badi, you'll find a way to fit in to the Circ."

"Why do you think I'd come with the Badi?"

"I heard my mother talking about it. They think you and Sasha might be a match."

A few days later, Baba confirmed that when the clans broke up in the spring, I would go with the Badi, with Sasha's family to live until we were old enough to marry. More importantly, I would stay with Ankah! My heart swelled and I felt dizzy and flushed all the time, but also wracked with nerves at what might be expected of me by my new family. Baba saw me looking dazed and staring into the fire one day.

"Don't worry, little one. You have been a flash of gold for us, a ray of sunlight. You'll be a ray of light wherever you go."

Sasha found me with the goats. Without speaking, he went to fill the water bucket, then began to feed my goats carrot nubs from his pockets.

"It will be a much bigger herd now," he said without looking at me.

"Yes."

"Don't worry, Jaelle. King will protect them all."

∞

The rest of the winter passed in the slowed-down, sped-up way of short days of cooking and chatter and long nights of fireside stories, music, and dancing. On one of the first days of real sun, with all the snow receding on the ground to expose patches of brown vegetation, I took the herd into the woods to browse. There had been an ice storm the night before and every branch in the forest was encased in sparkling crystal. Light reflected in a million glittering drops off the

23

forked black wands. I was dazzled by the spectacle, and the cold, wet thrum of the dripping waterfall from the trees muffled all other sounds. I didn't hear someone approaching, but the goats did. They scampered away, then swarmed back to form a close bundle behind me. It was the Lord of the estate, but this time alone on horseback.

He pulled up the reins on his prancing bay stallion and looked down at me while the horse danced sideways, snorting at the goats. I looked down at the ground, unsure if I should curtsy or say something reverent. When I dared look up, his head was tilted, regarding me. He was not very old, I noticed, but had a severe cast to his expression that made him look ancient, as if his skin were sculpted over metal. His eyes looked metallic, too, a light gray that made him seem not quite of this world. He did not say anything, just looked at me, as if he were trying to figure out who I was, or even more strangely, *what* I was.

"My lord," I finally found words and lowered my head.

He pulled his fur-lined cape around him and turned his horse. He looked at me once more over his shoulder, still seeming to be puzzling something out, and with a quick nod, nudged his horse into a gallop down the narrow trail.

The day of leaving our mountain retreat came soon after, and the clansfolk made repairs to their wagons, wrapped their tools and pots in leather, and packed all their worldly goods. Some of the carts had canvas tented sides so that a family member or two could sit in out of the weather. I was to huddle in one of these with Isa and my new mother while Sasha herded our goats in the caravan. Ankah would be traveling in the Badi caravan, too, alongside her new family. As Baba had predicted, she was with child.

I found Baba giving orders to the younger men and ladies and grabbed her tightly around her waist. I buried my head in her chest and felt the lump of the leather pouch where she kept the Letter of Safe Passage, knobby against my forehead. "Lyuba! You're going to upend me!" She cried. I loosened my grasp but did not pull away.

"Maybe I should stay with you, Baba," the tears were coming now. "Maybe I should go with you and we can visit Ankah when the baby comes. Maybe I belong with you!"

"Oh, sweet starlight, child! Of course you belong with me! You belong in my heart, but that will not change no matter where you are. I am old, Jaelle, and getting older. I am no mother for an active young girl. You need to be around people of your age. You need company more than just some old folks and your goats, people who can teach you more than scrubbing a pot and putting together a meal. The Badi are a lively bunch. It's for the best, Jaelle."

I protested, but Baba wiped away my tears, dug in her apron, and pulled out a red string. She tied two knots: one on each end. "See, now you and I will always be connected, just as close as the other end of the string. Now say goodbye to Lala and Milosh. They're waiting to say goodbye and we all have much more work to do." I turned and crumpled into Lala's arms and against Milosh's great soft stomach as they ruffled my hair and kissed my forehead, and then passed me along to the next family members.

I clutched the red string in my hand and unconsciously wiped tears with it until it was soaked and I had made all the rounds. Then Isa was grabbing my arm and pulling me toward the departing caravan. As the horses began picking their hooves up carefully over the uneven ground and our carts drove away, I waved the soggy string out from the canvas flap window. All were too busy to notice or wave back. The last I saw of Baba was her nodding head, calling out instructions to a new wife of the Clan, who was herself shedding tears and embracing her mother.

I tried to calm the sobs in my chest as we put the sprawling ruins of Vár Buceci behind us on our journey to Udvarhely in the North, where the Circ would find their summer employment. I sat up straight and shamed next to Isa and her mother, struggling to breathe normally. Selene was very beautiful. From what Isa had told me, she was kind, but I had never spoken to her. She barely looked at me now in the cart. An hour or so passed, and the bumpy uneven tracks lulled me to sleep. In sleep, I dreamed a great mountain lioness was coming down the mountain, chasing our cart, hungry and snarling. She wanted to eat me, specifically, because of my golden hair. Like a warrior, Selene jumped gracefully from the cart and wrestled the lioness to the ground, holding her mouth closed. She looked up at me from where she lay in the dirt, holding the mouth of the vanquished beast, smiled, and winked!

A jolt of the cart woke me. I had unknowingly been resting my head on Selene's shoulder and pulled back now, startled, to look at her. She smiled down at me. It was the same calm smile from my dream. From the other side of her, Isa reached across her lap and took my hand. Selene put an arm around each of us, and said, "Now I have *two* girls!" For some reason, this made us laugh, and the three of us were caught up with giggles. Isa's father, Iosef, walked forward from where he had been trailing behind with Sasha and the animals to see what the noise was about. He seemed pleased to find us in such a state, and called back to Sasha, "When the women of the family are happy, we may all have peace!"

The Badi were different from my tribe, I found. They laughed more, sang more, and were louder; they teased and played tricks on each other. They were performers by nature, and all was conducted with drama and fanfare. The Chief, Nandu, was a great bearded man with a thunderous laugh you could hear from anywhere in the caravan. Most different, though, was that there were just so many of them! I was used to our small group, where we could all fit around one fire at night. This camp required multiple sites, many cooking pots, and needed at least a great hillside to house us all. There were not many children. Like other clans, the Badi had lost great numbers. Isa and Sasha were some of the only remaining young ones.

At dusk, we would stop and begin the process of setting up for the evening meal and making camp. I would go to visit Ankah, but she was always busy cooking with her new mother-in-law, and I often felt underfoot, so I would not stay long. Still, it was comforting to know she was nearby. I tried to make myself useful with the skills I had learned from Ankah, but I found I was still inept at many tasks. Isa was quicker and knew what to do, whereas I had to ask or stand and watch before I could figure out how to help unless I was given instruction. Selene was quiet and hardly asked for help, but Isa would let me know what needed to be done and point out ways to get things done quicker. She was an efficient girl, and clearly in command of her household. It puzzled me at first, but Isa later told me that her mother had episodes that gripped her for weeks at a time. During those times, Selene barely spoke. Isa had learned to take charge.

"It was the accident," Isa explained. Selene had fallen from a high rope during an act and had barely survived. Before that, she had been one of the most famous trapeze artists alive. "This was before she had me and Sasha. After the fall, she never performed again." Despite how gentle she was toward me, I was a little shy of Selene. I was also confused by her. The Selene in my dream had seemed so real: she was fierce and dynamic. I had trouble reconciling that lingering impression with the woman who barely spoke.

Closer to Udvarhely, the scenery changed, and more towns and villages cropped up. We were such a large group that we attracted a lot of attention. Unlike my clan, who tried to remain inconspicuous and polite about asking for passage, the Badi were rambunctious and flamboyantly pronounced their presence. When entering a town, they blew horn trumpets and the jugglers began juggling, twirlers twirled, and others sang, performed tricks, and clowned to put the people at ease. The Gentlefolk were at once entranced and wary, mothers holding their wide-eyed children tight so that they might not get stolen or seduced. The Circ was famous, so it was a novelty to have them flood through a town, but no one wanted the little ones to get too close.

Most of the time, the routine worked, and we passed with ease. Other times, loud and angry men chased us with raised fists or even hatchets, crowds threw rotten vegetables, and we were cursed and pushed out of town. In these episodes, the character of the Badi impressed me. Even in the direst circumstances, they wore perfect smiles and gracefully spun out of the way of upraised tools, deflected blows with a twirl to safety, as if it were all just part of their elaborate act. None seemed especially troubled by it. Due to their composure and artful handling of even the tensest situations, we avoided any truly dangerous skirmishes.

Several weeks after we started our journey, we got to the main valley where the Badi performed for most of the year. We made camp by a river, and preparations for the Circ season began. Nandu sent ambassadors to nearby towns to meet with key stakeholders to negotiate fees and taxes to be paid so that we could plan our summer performance route. Everyone settled in, repairing costumes and working on their acts. My goats were happy to graze with their new herd along the hillside and I stayed with them and watched Sasha as he worked with Tata Iosef to perfect tumbles and practice juggling. Isa wanted me to join her on the high wire, or to learn along with a small group of women who coordinated lively and daring routines. That made my stomach turn, and so I politely declined.

I wished I had a skill to share as I watched the talents of my new clan. Each seemed so confident in their abilities. I left my herd to visit Ankah, with her small moon of a belly beginning to show under her skirts. "Ankah, what will you do when the Circ performs?" I asked.

Ankah looked uncomfortable and glanced around, as if to see if anyone was nearby to listen. "Mama Violca says I must be a Seer," she confessed. "It's because I have the Sight, and I'm with child and can't do much else." I could see how unhappy this made her.

"Really? Will you share the voices of the spirits?"

Ankah sighed. "I will never make that mistake again. I told Mama Violca that, but she insisted. She said it does not matter if I tell Gentles the truth or not, that they are ignorant and superstitious, and will believe anything a Cigany Seer tells them. So now I have to tell pretty lies and make up stories that they will want to hear."

"I'm sorry, Ankah."

"Don't be sorry, Jaelle. I have what I've always wanted: a husband and a child. It's a minor inconvenience. I need to contribute somehow. I just wish I could go back to embroidering dresses instead of tales!" We laughed.

"I'm worried, Ankah. What if I can't find something to do and they don't want me anymore? I'm not a tumbler, I can't dance, and I really don't think I can train my goats to do tricks. What if I can't earn my keep and they make me leave?"

"Jaelle, you are a magical child. You just don't know it yet. You have spirits protecting you and you bring light wherever you go. Nobody would ever make you leave." She pulled me into an embrace, and I felt the strain in my body seep away into the earth. I had no idea what she meant, but Ankah was not one for superficial praise. I trusted her and her words settled my churning nerves and fluttering heart.

Chapter Three: The Circ

Life with the Circ was a whirlwind: a new town every few days, elaborate preparations for performances, and noisy throngs of people. There was the ever-present risk of drawing in the Gentles without threatening them to violence. It was a dance, to intrigue and fascinate them, without making them fear for their lives or their purse. The Badi did it well. Their brilliant smiles and larger-than-life personalities made the audiences fall in love with them, if just for an hour. They could be caught up in the dazzling motion of bodies twirling, get lost in dangerous feats as the Ciganyok swung from ropes or walked across the torch-lit night sky on a single cord. The men could imagine themselves entwined in the dark arms of a dancer, children imagined they could swing from the stars and pile onto towers of people, part of a contorted living sculpture. The Badi's livelihood was built on these fantasies. They were fragile things that needed to be carefully constructed, then disappear in a puff of smoke overnight, leaving just an empty lot as the caravan moved on. Children would run through and search for a discarded bead or ribbon and hold onto it, destined to wait a year or two when the Circ might return.

I tried to make myself useful to my new family, taking over the responsibilities with our blended herd, and often attending to Mama Selene. At first, as I was trying to make sense of her, I thought she might be crazy. She would say something strange, like: "Jaelle, please move that bundle of herbs. The pot does not like it there." It was true that sometimes my new mother would slump into a vegetative trance, her eyes almost closed, but staring straight ahead for hours at a time. I took the lead from Sasha and Isa and just walked around her, ignoring her strange half-sleep. Just when you would almost forget she was even there she would pop up with a directive. "We will eat dandelion stew tonight. Isa, get my bowl."

Other times, she would just disappear. When Isa noticed she was missing, she'd say: "Jaelle, can you find Mama Selene? She's probably at the edge of the forest." When I would go to look, there Selene would be, standing and facing a tree, her head tilted forward as if listening.

When Selene noticed me, she would turn back to the tree quickly. In an apologetic tone, she'd say: "I have to go now," before walking toward me and following me back to the campsite. From Selene's sometimes odd behavior, it was easy to believe that the family catered to her because she was disturbed or fragile. I soon realized that they were not just placating her: she was gifted. The Tribe knew it, too. Women came for counsel and Selene would rummage through small bottles and pouches. She would ask them to hold one in each hand and was able to tell which one was the best remedy for their particular malady. She'd send them away with a bundle of dried leaves or flowers or would make them tea on the spot. I was surprised one day to see Ankah come to visit Selene. They sat for a short time, with Selene mostly listening as Ankah spoke to her. I knew I shouldn't intrude, but my curiosity kept me close by to see what this could mean.

Selene reached into a box and pulled something out that I couldn't see, putting it into Ankah's hand and giving her an instruction. Ankah kissed Selene's hand and left. Later, I found Ankah rinsing clothes out in the stream and asked her what it had been about. "The spirits know Selene well," she said. "She gives good counsel."

"But what did she give you?" I asked.

"This." She took something small out of her apron pocket and showed me. At first it looked like a piece of glass, but it was actually a small roundish crystal with points on both ends.

"What is it for?"

"For my dreams."

"To give you dreams?"

"No, to make them stop. I've been having strange dreams that wake me up, disturbing dreams, and I can't get back to sleep. Selene told me to put them into this crystal."

"How can you put dreams into a crystal?"

"Selene says it will hold them for me so that they don't wake me up."

"How does she know that?"

"It's like what happened to me. Selene lives in both worlds . . . because of her accident, I'm sure you know about it." I nodded. "She has one foot on either side of the wall between the living and the dead. You might even say she's half in the spirit world herself."

"So, do they talk to her like they talk to you?"

"I don't think so. No, it's more like she's already one of them."

"You mean, she's a *ghost*?"

"Not exactly, no."

"Then, what?"

"She just lives between the veils. There are these shifting–I don't know how to explain them–curtains? Like walls, but they move–they're always moving. Most of us live on one side or the other. Selene . . . she lives *in* them." My expression must have shown that I was not following her at all. "She can speak to the spirits in objects and she can talk to people far away who give her advice. She is able to see things: how to fix things, how to heal."

"So, she's a medicine woman."

"Sort of, but more than that. I know the Badi come to her for everything. They know she has a talent. They say that when the Pestilence hit their tribe, Selene wrapped her children's heads with wet leaves and fed them tea and soup made with stones all day. They say it's why her children survived when so many others died."

"She made soup with stones?"

"That's what they say," Ankah said, and turned back to wringing out her laundry.

∞

My goats were getting rounder, but Sasha's goats were so fat they looked comical. I knew I should stop thinking of them as mine and his, since he told me: "They're all *ours* now," whenever I made this distinction. I spent a lot of time with the extended herd, and always took them to the hillside in the morning. We kept them close to the fires of the caravan at night, to discourage the wolves from coming after them.

It was still early in the year, and the nights were chilly. One cold morning I heard a strange shriek and I ran to see if there was something hurting the goats. I found two glistening white babies and Honey licking them, with the other goats bleating and poking their curious noses toward the new members of the herd. Within a few minutes, the babies were up and nursing. I was amazed that both they and Honey knew exactly what to do. A few hours later, they were standing and even trying to jump and pronk about. Sasha was proud of the two new babies, both boys that would be meat and leather for the clan, but he did not want to hold and play with them the way Isa and I did. "They're impure," he said, regarding them from a distance with crossed arms. Men were restricted from touching newborns of any kind.

Late that afternoon, two more cream-colored babies were born, and a big speckled baby was born to the colorful doe, Pebbles, the next morning. "They all had the heat at the same time," Sasha explained. He came by to inspect the new kids, but kept his distance, as did the other men. Isa explained that not only were men not supposed to touch babies: they felt birth was unclean and unlucky to be around. The women were delighted with the babies and came to admire and hold them. By the following morning, Sasha's last doe had kidded with another set of twins, and then there were seven tiny babies wobbling around.

I had always liked goats more than humans anyway, but now I felt even more drawn to the herd. The other members of the herd–my goats and even King–were gentle and patient with the babies, and were careful not to trample them. Isa told me that by eating the placentas, the mothers learned the smell of their babies and this created a permanent bond to their newborns. I spent hours watching them, fascinated how the mothers spoke to their babies in soft bleats. The tones they directed toward their kids were distinct from the sounds they made toward other goats, like human mothers change their tones when talking to their infants. The kids would answer back, and all seemed to know their own mother's voice. I was amazed that these tiny newborns could find their mother's teats among all the others and know how to nurse, and the mothers knew exactly how to care for them. It was as if the seed of all they needed to know was already contained in their tiny bodies and minds and was growing with every moment.

I saw how the babies and mothers were intimately connected, as if they were one unit, knowing each other from the second of birth. The tiny ones were so dependent on their mothers, who found them by smell and voice and nudged them back toward their udders. Isa told me that they had a baby goat the year before whose mother had been killed by a lynx. They tried to get another doe to nurse it, but the other mothers nudged it away and only nursed it if they held one hoof up to give the little one a sip. They were able to give it enough milk to survive that way, but without that critical connection, without the soft bleats and loving nudges, the baby goat died. "Human babies will die, too," Isa said knowledgably, "if their mothers pass on."

"Why is that?" I wondered.

"Well the father will not hold it, of course. Men will not go anywhere near birth or babies if they can help it. It's impure and will poison their manhood. Unless a motherless baby has someone who will hold and love it like their own, it would surely die. Babies need to be with their mothers. It's the way of the world." I saw that she was right about the magical connection between the creatures of the world and their mothers. I did not quite believe, though, that a child would die without a mother. I lost my mother, but I survived. Still, I had my goats–and Ankah and Baba–so maybe that was all the love I needed to keep me tied to life after losing my Mama.

The nights were full of activity for the Badi. Whereas my former tribe had been early morning risers, the Badi did not get into full swing until after the midday meal. There were always rushed preparations for that evening's performance, and people running to and fro, getting ready for visitors and making sure the ropes were safely secured to the trees high above. After dusk, the townspeople would arrive, following a row of lit torches to the hillside where a natural arena would be set up in advance. This way, even the littlest viewer would have a good vantage point to see the performance. I could do little more than sell small trinkets, help guide people to seats, or direct curious or lovesick Gentles to Ankah's small tent to have their fortunes told before the show. Once the performance started, I was as dazzled as the audience as I watched from the edges of the dark. I was mesmerized by the flaming lights and thrumming of the drums and instruments accompanying the dancers and acrobats. Hordes of performers in dizzyingly bright costumes came spinning and tumbling down the rows of the amphitheater to the torchlit circle where Nandu would stand.

Proud and impressive, Nandu would bellow an opening greeting: "Do not be afraid, fair guests!" he would say. "We have come from the far corners of this land to entertain you, and it is our greatest pleasure to have your company this evening. What you are about to see will amaze you! We have the most talented performers who have trained their whole life in dangerous and death-defying feats for your enjoyment. Relax and wonder at their courage, be amazed at their skill, and do not be alarmed by the risks they take. It is all for your enjoyment!"

With that, the crowd would shush, and the dancers would swirl in, circling in pulsing waves that contracted and expanded. Acrobats would descend from the ropes hung above, appearing out of the dark sky like magic, twirling and spinning through the air, to join the performers below. All of a sudden, the music would stop, and the dense nucleus of the dancers would part to reveal Nandu's tiny wife: Tatiana, the most gifted dancer, would stand glistening before the crowd. A collective inhaling of breath would arise from the audience, men who were instantly filled with longing, and mothers who would shield their children's eyes at Tatiana's revealing garb, brightly adorned with tiny gems of sparkling glass that caught the light. The music would resume in a slow and melancholy wail, as Tatiana's flexible body would begin to transform. She would assume unnatural shapes, demonstrating inhuman balance and control, punctuated by the sparkle of firelight reflecting from her costume. Once they had gotten over their alarm at her dress, the women were entranced, too, and children stared open-mouthed at the wonder of her form twisting in ways they had never imagined possible.

Just as quickly, she was picked up under the arms and whisked off by two strong acrobats and replaced with men spinning small torches and juggling small painted leather balls. The audience was never left to grow fatigued. The pace was frenetic and the performers and music changed every few minutes. My favorite part of the performance each night was watching Sasha and his father, making the audience gasp and applaud with their routine. Sasha would stand on his father's shoulders, where fire jugglers tossed him torches flaming at both ends. He would throw them into the air, jump and flip backwards only to land again safely on Tata Iosef's strong back. The fire sticks spun up so fast and so high into the dark night that they created circles of flame, but Sasha always caught them, making the whole maneuver look effortless. I was impressed with Sasha's ability to tolerate all eyes upon him without it distracting him from his hazardous purpose. My heart would flip along with him, and a glowing sense of pride and ownership would spread across my chest and face as I thought that this strong and graceful boy-man somehow inexplicably belonged to me.

The final act was the high wire, which was suspended high above, but only visible once lights reflected from polished bowls were aimed upward. Isa had begun her training in the sky arts, following after her mother despite the tragedy that stopped Selene's Circ career. She was as daring and confident in the air as she was on the ground. I always held my breath when Isa performed, willing the air around her to hold her steady. I loved my new sister and could not bear to think of her being hurt. She never faltered, and after she reached the other end of the rope: a spin, several dips and jumps that stopped the heart, and a tumble later, and then the show was almost over. The last dancers and acrobats would jump and flip, allowing the audience to let out their breaths, relax shoulders they didn't even know they had tensed watching the precarious caper above, and refocus on their family members sitting next to them. Nandu would again retake the center of the grassy stage to give thanks and closing remarks in his resonant voice, and I would have to go to collect a few extra coins in a basket from the dazed audience as they came back to earth.

After the crowd dispersed and a quick cleanup of the area, Nandu would gather the tribe together, all sitting in the amphitheater where the audience had sat and congratulate and give pointers for the next show. I loved those times, with Nandu at our helm, laughing while replaying the audience's key moments—a boy who wet his pants because he didn't want to leave the show to relieve himself, or the stoic-faced Gentle men who had become pliant with intoxicated smiles watching Tatiana's undulant graces. Nandu always made us laugh and generously handed out compliments to the performers. Even when he gave feedback on the performance and ideas for the next one, it was so gracious that everyone just wanted to improve to make him and the Tribe proud. The after-show gathering was where the plans for the next performance were made. It changed a bit every night, so even those who came back night after night got a different show. The clan was such a cohesive, functioning system, and the Badi such professionals at their craft, that only one discussion was needed to determine the entire content of the next presentation.

Then the families would retreat to their respective cooking pots, blending into clumps and small groups for the evening meal. The last night in any location, animals were butchered, and the meal would be shared as a large group. It was a rowdy feast to celebrate the final night of the show and moving on. In some areas, depending on what "tithings" had been worked out with the civic officials in that territory, the Circ would perform one or two nights a week for many weeks in a row before moving on. Sometimes we settled into a place so well that it seemed sad to be leaving the familiar trees and stones and to have to uproot all of our tents and belongings to travel on. It was always with an air of excitement, though, that seemed to be inborn for the Badi. It was as if their thirst for newness and adventure was infused into who they were as a people. It was infectious. Despite any yearning for a pretty hillside or a quiet stream where I had sat watching the goats, I was always swept up in the perpetual movement of the Tribe and quickly became eager to move on with them to see what the next town held.

The clan did not even seem to blink with the addition of me and Ankah. They treated us as if we had always been there and were a natural part of the extended family. After a few curious questions about my golden hair and light eyes, I was accepted and treated as another of Selene and Iosef's children. I missed Baba and my old Clan, but I barely had time to reflect on that, with all the activity of my new family. No one catered to me or called me their "Little Light," but things were really too busy to notice.

∞

Ankah was getting closer to giving birth, and I could no longer pretend that my life being Ankah's first priority hadn't changed. I'd gotten used to her being nearby but preoccupied with her tasks, attending to her duties to her husband and Mama Violca. One night, Selene called to me and roused me from a dead sleep.

"It's time—Ankah needs us."

I followed her and Isa, who was already awake, through the night that was illuminated almost like daylight by a giant white moon sitting low in the barren slate sky. We walked to the tent where Mihai was pacing outside, biting a finger. Violca was there, but as soon as she saw Selene coming, she let out a relieved sound and backed her large form out of the tent to make room for the healer. Ankah was in pain. I could tell by the rigid grimace on her face. Her flashing eyes, like a wild animal, dashed around and landed on me. She reached up and grabbed my hand.

"Jaelle—my little mountain goat," she said, and perspiration coated her brow.

"Come, Ankah," said Selene, urging her up. "Time to stand. Babies need to come out facing the Earth Mother. She will help to pull her out of you. Your waters have not even broken yet! There is more work to do."

Ankah protested, but Selene and I helped her to a standing position. Soon Ankah was crouching in agony and making sounds that frightened me, like a wild boar grunting and groaning. I was scared, but took my lead from Selene, who seemed possessed with calm. She and even Isa, who stood back, did not seem concerned by Ankah's muttering and gasping, her lowing groans. Selene's eyes glazed-over, as if she was not seeing Ankah, but listening. Suddenly, she tilted her head up quickly, as if hearing something far away. Selene then gave instructions to Isa, who ran off to boil water and get the requested herbs.

Time stood still, and each moment watching Ankah transformed by pain was terrible and frightening. Selene had her stand and walk and then crouch again when she would feel the pressure. Ankah was shaking her head and exhausted, resisting Selene's directions and then finally always complying once the pain became too intense. How did women do this all the time? The goats just seemed to pop babies out, with a little yell and some blood, but this seemed to be a much bigger ordeal. Isa returned with tea and hot water, and Selene held the tea to Ankah's lips and made her drink, even though Ankah made a face at the smell and would only take tiny mouthfuls.

"It's too hot in here." Ankah suddenly stood up and started pulling her clothes over her head until she was naked. I was a bit shocked, as I'd never seen Ankah completely nude. Her giant glowing belly and tightly stretched skin seemed vulgar and made me think of a piece of fruit that was ripe to the point of bursting. Isa and Selene seemed unfazed by her nudity and went about dipping rags into the boiled water and wiping down Ankah's swollen body.

"Jaelle," Ankah suddenly pulled me close to her and whispered to me: "There's someone here. They're waiting for me."

I looked where she was staring at a dark corner.

"Who is it?"

"They'll wait. They must wait!"

Ankah became frantic and Selene came close and stroked her hair, and spoke into Ankah's ear something I could not hear. Ankah nodded and then crouched and with a great uttered groan, a giant flood of water gushed out of her. The tent filled with the smell of something salty and overpowering. Selene had Ankah lay back on the bedding and gently pushed her legs apart, looking directly into Ankah's womanhood, inspecting her closely. I was embarrassed and looked away, but Selene called me and Isa to look, too.

"Look girls! That is Ankah's baby. Ankah, her head is arriving. Your baby is coming!"

Once I saw the dark curls and small circle of head pushing through from inside of Ankah, I swooned and dizzily collapsed beside Ankah, taking deep breaths. She reached out and took my hand and Isa went to her other side and continued to wipe down her forehead. Ankah seemed to get her strength back now, becoming calm and focused. Selene, who remained between Ankah's legs, began singing. I didn't recognize the words or the melody, it was high and lilting and in a strange cadence that was not like the songs I knew. It was not Rromani. It sounded ancient but somehow familiar, like something I could almost remember or should be able to understand.

Ankah's quick breathing became deeper and she emitted what sounded like a low roar, like a wild beast. Selene nodded and continued singing, but a little louder and faster. I peeked over the angle of Ankah's leg and saw a whole head emerging there.

"She's coming!" I told Ankah excitedly. "Her head is out!" I had unconsciously adopted Selene's language, calling the baby "she" without question.

One more giant groan from Ankah and the baby swooshed out in a tide of blood and fluid. Selene never stopped singing. In one smooth motion, she caught the babe in her trajectory and made the most graceful arc, like dancing to place her gently upon Ankah's chest. Ankah held her and looking down, laughed as Selene wiped the baby's face and body and we could see the evidence of her sex. The baby made a few gasping cries, but then quieted and looked up at her mother, eyes wide and blinking and dark like Ankah's, staring up into her mother's eyes.

It was a blur after that, Selene helping the baby to the breast and assisting with the delivery of the placenta. Soon Ankah was sitting up and modestly covered again so that the baby could be introduced to the rest of her family. Isa went to fetch Mama Violca and Mihai while Selene tied the flaps of the tent wide open.

Mihai came, looking relieved and eager, but stood way back, adhering to the custom dictating that birth is unclean and not suitable territory for men. Violca poked her head in, and harrumphing about being given only a granddaughter, soon ambled away. Mihai stood for a few moments and after uttering a few awkward encouraging words to Ankah, soon departed also.

"She's beautiful," I told Ankah, who nodded and smiled without looking away from her daughter. She had confided in me many months ago what the baby's *True Name* would be, but that name would be private, never spoken out loud so that dangerous spirits could not have access to her. She would have a given name that would fool the bad spirits who might harm her if they knew her secret name. "What will you call her?"

Ankah looked up, as if it had not occurred to her. The bright pearly disk of moon was finally sinking, but was still high above the far mountain, illuminating the whole landscape. Wisps of clouds traced like spools of spun wool against a sky melting dark blue into the inky receding night.

"Perla," she said.

Chapter Four: The Pearl

Selene made Ankah drink more of the bitter tea. Then, after she and Isa cleaned up, they departed to sleep a wink before the sun rose. I sat dazed. It did not even occur to me to offer to help. I could not take my eyes off the tiny human who had only moments before been only an idea. When the others left, I sat for a while, then realized that Ankah might want to be alone with her newborn. Surprisingly, the possessiveness and jealousy that I had throughout Ankah's pregnancy had completely disappeared.

"I'll leave you two now," I said, and began to rise.

"No, wait!" Ankah said urgently. I sat back down on the bedroll next to her. "I need to tell you something: it's very important."

I nodded.

"You're a *Bibi* now, an auntie. It's a big responsibility."

Again, I nodded, still speechless.

"I need you to promise you'll always take care of Perla. No matter what happens to me, do you understand?"

"Of course," I mumbled. "I promise."

"Jaelle!" It was sharp and I was startled. Ankah rarely raised her voice. "This is important. I need to make sure you understand that you must always protect her. She needs you."

Seeing the small bundle sleeping peacefully against Ankah's breast, I could not understand how she might need me, but I nodded anyway.

"After me, *you* are her true family."

"Yes, I understand."

Ankah sighed and lay back against the pile of blankets propped behind her. Her hair spilled out over her shoulders and although she had circles under her eyes, she still looked radiant.

"I need rest. I'm so, so tired." I rose and kissed Ankah's forehead, and in an impulsive moment, reached out and stroked a finger over Perla's small fist. I backed out of her tent and began to walk toward my own. "Thank you, Gildi." I heard the words follow behind me. At first I thought I imagined them, but they echoed through my mind all the way back to my bedroll and haunted me as I sunk into unconsciousness.

It felt like only minutes later, but it could have been hours. I was sitting up, without realizing I had awoken, and I couldn't breathe. I gasped in great shuddering intakes of air, my heart pounding throughout my body, the blood rushing through my head and resounding in my ears. I stood up and rushed out into the night air. It was still mostly dark, but the sky was edged with a crisp pale line across the far mountain. Still gasping, I breathed, cooling my overheated body with the chilled air as I tried to calm my raging heart. Something was not right. I ran to Ankah's tent. Mihai had a separate tent set up far enough away to avoid becoming tainted. The flaps of Ankah's tent were still tied open. I stood in the opening and my shadow fell across Ankah and the baby. I adjusted my body out of the dim light, and saw Ankah, laying back against the bedding, her hair still splayed out, and a beatific smile upon her lips. The baby was sleeping upon her bared breast.

I sighed and began to untie the cords binding the tent flaps open so that she could have privacy once the others awoke. As I shook out the fabric, I noticed it was wet at the bottom, and I stepped back to avoid a pool of liquid. Spilled tea? No, it was thick. Bells pealed in my head as I recognized the fluid as blood. I jumped back then, and with fire in my veins, I rushed in, stepping widely over the dark puddle. It came from Ankah. The whole bedroll was soaked.

I grabbed her wrist, which was slightly stiff and hard to pull from her body. She was cold. There was no pulse there and none at her throat. Terror overcame me and I backed against the tent wall, staring at my dead sister and her very living infant. My hearing was amplified, and I could hear the baby's tiny breaths against the stillness of the night. Suddenly, through my horror, Ankah's words rang out in my mind: to protect Perla and take care of her no matter what happened. What would become of Perla here with these people? Her father would not even touch her–and Violca? What kind of nurturance would she get from her?

And what would become of me? My whole life until that point became shallow, like a one-dimensional line pointing only to Ankah: Ankah finding me on the mountainside; Ankah caring for me; Ankah teaching me how to be Rrom. Ankah leaving our Clan and going to the Badi and me following her, even compelling me to consider marriage, despite my apprehension. Now what? Should I try to take over caring for Perla? Would Violca even let me? Did I still need to marry Sasha? Should I try to be Badi, just so I could watch over Perla?

A flash of pure reason stilled my mind. I knew what I needed to do. Quickly, I grabbed a blanket that had not been soaked in the wide ocean of blood. It was the marriage blanket that Baba had made for Ankah. I folded it into a long strip and tied it diagonally across my shoulders. Trying not to look at Ankah's face, I picked up Perla, gently, such as I had done with the newborn goat kids. She squirmed but did not open her eyes as I arranged her against my chest, tucked in with the folds to support her fragile, impossibly small form.

I looked around and then made myself look at Ankah one more time. Now I saw the pale cast to her face and body, all life having run out onto the ground. Her midsection and bedding were soaked in blood. I had seen dead bodies before–they were common in traveling. With my first family, we would often come upon a farming accident or a sickness arriving swiftly to take a newborns and elders in a town we were passing through. We would find parents crying pitifully, children or widows throwing themselves upon a wrapped corpse on a cart being hauled off to be buried. We had even found a dead urchin once under a bridge as we looked for a place to find shelter from the rain.

Seeing Ankah–the first love of my life after my long-dead Mama–cold and still and no longer alive, seemed like a strange dream. It was as if in a dream that I moved, kissed her cold hand, and found the half-closed tent doorway, stepping around the blood to leave. I practically bumped into Selene. She stood, tall and imposing before me. I had never seen her stand so erect: she was usually sitting or rushing with her head bent over her cooking, curled over her herbs and bottles and teas. I gasped as I looked up at her, feeling so incredibly small and captured, like a criminal, in the act of something unspeakable. I held the bundled baby close against me, sure she would be taken. I would be severely punished, probably expelled from the Tribe and shunned forever.

I waited for her to yell at me, grab the baby from my arms, sound the alarm, but she did not speak. Instead, she pushed something toward me . . . a bundle.

"You will need some things," she said. I could not speak. I just silently reached out for the package that was offered to me. It had a neat loop that I put across my free shoulder. I waited, sure she had more instructions for me as it sank in that she was not going to turn me over to the Elders. "You will know what to do, and you won't be alone." I still waited. She sighed, seeming suddenly impatient, as if I had interrupted her as she was shelling nuts. She made a shooing motion with her arms, and turning, walked back to our tents. I stood for a moment, then rotated on my heels and walked swiftly toward the mountain, passing tents of the late-sleeping Badi. I glanced back, but saw only the fabric of Selene's tent swooshing closed.

At the edge of the encampment by the river, *our* goats were sprawled out in piles of babies and mamas, some sleepy lifted heads chewing endless cud as the morning approached. Despite the goats becoming one herd, they still slept in two clusters, in their primary arrangements. With one exception: Pebbles, Sasha's speckled doe, and her look-alike doeling had been adopted by my small herd. Pebbles was the smallest of Sasha's goats, and the other members of her initial herd had mercilessly bullied her until she had her singleton kid. Once her baby came, they just ignored her, but she was always pushed to the outskirts. She had found solace in the tight circle of my timid ladies. Pebbles' head rested on the neck of my queen doe and her baby nestled within the pile of my first herd, all of them now almost as round as the moon as they awaited the arrival of their kids.

I clucked at them, the signal to get up and drive. My girls struggled up, lifting the enormous weight of their bellies, and followed me. Pebbles and her baby followed right along with them. Sasha's other goats stood, but they didn't follow. King rose up, and made a loud, intimidating snort, pawing at me as I walked past with my train. For a moment, I thought he was going to try to stop me. Given that he probably outweighed me, I was not sure how that would go. I tensed as I walked past and he lowered his head as if to butt me with his massive horns. I flinched, but he just pushed his head into my hand, asking for a nice scratch. "Oh, you're such a good boy, King," I whispered to him. "Thank you for caring for my women-folk." I continued to the rocky trail and the goats came easily along, waddling and looking back occasionally to utter a parting bleat to their friends. Sasha's herd stood stationary, with King at the helm, and called back and forth to my herd–not in distress, but as if wishing them a safe journey.

∞

I walked briskly, regularly glancing behind me and expecting to see the Badi menfolk chasing after me at any second. I rushed through the open plains and into the forest. My obedient goats followed me, reaching down for snippets of spring grass and shrubs and then rushing to keep up. I hurried along into the morning until the sun was high in the sky. I would have kept running, but I felt the wetness of the babe seeping through the cloth that bound her to my chest and she began to wail. I sat by the edge of a stream, and while my goats drank, I unwound Perla and prepared to rip some cloth from the hem of my dress. I suddenly recalled the bundle Selene had given me. Opening it, I found several small bags of herbs and roots, some dried food and a small pot, and a quantity of folded cloths. I washed Perla off with cold stream water, making her cry even harder. I secured a small cloth package to her bottom the best I could while she continued to scream. The cries reverberated across the whole valley; they were so loud for such a tiny child, I thought, if anyone was near by she would lead them right to us. I picked her up and rocked her, desperate to figure out how to make her stop crying.

I noticed Pebbles' speckled doeling, whose head was shoved under mother's belly to nurse from her swollen udder. I had seen the kid trying futilely to take sips as we had ambled around all morning, but now she was finally getting to drink her fill. Inspired, I sat and pulled Pebbles close to me by the small rope collar Sasha had affixed to each member of our herd. Hoping for the best and uttering calming words, I rested Perla on my knee under Pebbles, willing her not to kick or hurt the baby. It took a few tries, while Perla still yelled, but Pebbles was as cooperative as could be and I finally got Perla to latch. She gulped a large amount of milk and sputtered, and I had to remove her before she drowned. I put my hand around the teat so I could control the flow of milk better, and supported Perla's head with the other hand. In this way, she got a suitable amount of milk.

When Perla was done, I tucked her right inside my blouse, against my skin, and tied the fabric to support her tiny shape. With one hand supporting her, I tied the dirty blanket to my queen doe, who only protested for a moment about having to carry it, and we went on our way. When the sun began to dip, Perla started to squirm and make little unhappy sounds, so I knew I needed to stop and feed her more. This time, it went easier. Pebbles accommodated by squatting slightly, and I held Perla under her. Perla's round dark eyes looked up at me as she suckled, and I felt something deep inside me shift and fall into place. She drank until she fell off the udder, back asleep again. I switched out her wet swaddling cloth for dry as she slept, and then set her gently on some fabric on a bed of moss while I cleaned up.

I knew I could keep going. I was used to walking a full day, and I was still so terrified of the Badi catching up to us that I could probably walk all night, too. I looked at the plump, placid goats resting their wide girths on the mossy stream bank, and realized they were exhausted. Instead of pushing them, I washed the dirty blanket and hung it on a tree, then lay down next to Perla. After eating a few morsels from Selene's pack, I fell fast asleep. Waking to Perla crying in the night, I called to Pebbles, and miraculously she was close by to feed her, as if she was now aware that this small one was also her responsibility. I fell back to sleep, but when the moon rose, still full in the sky, I heard the wolves begin to howl. Quickly, I fastened the damp blanket to my herd queen and tucked Perla into my blouse before rushing back onto the trail. The goats were not used to traveling at night, but I knew we would not be able to fight off a pack of wolves. I'd have to be more careful and make a fire next time, which would be our only defense if the wolves found us.

We walked until after the sun rose and into the late morning, stopping only to let the goats graze or drink, and for Perla to suckle upon Pebbles. I was quite depleted by this time, and after Perla drank, I also drank my full, milking Pebbles into Selene's small pot. There seemed to be plenty for all of us, since Pebbles' kid bounced happily along and even began to nurse on Pebbles' other side whenever I fed Perla. We stopped earlier that night so I could build a big fire, positioning my herd against a rocky outcrop with the fire between us and the night. Although I heard the wolves nearby again, attracted by the smell of goats and babies, thankfully they did not like the odor of the smoke, so they stayed away.

We traveled like this for many days until we came to the foot of the mountains. I think I knew deep down what my plan was already, but my only instinct had been to flee and put as much distance as possibly between us and the Badi who might be pursuing us. Now, as the mountains towered above us, dark peaks cancelling out the surrounding landscape, I knew where we would go: the ruins of Vár Buceci would be empty and safe, visited only once every five years by the converging tribes. I was taking Perla home.

Chapter Five: The Castle

It had only been a few months since I had left Baba and the others to go with the Badi, yet Vár Buceci looked completely foreign. The crumbling walls and broken stone seemed in so much worse condition without the people milling about, cooking and laughing, without the warmth of other bodies and life. I settled the goats into the biggest stall in the barn attached to the castle and took the rooms closest to them inside the castle walls. I went through the rooms, finding useful things that had been discarded in the haste to leave, items that were broken or not worth carrying, to equip our home. There was still dried hay left in the barn, but with spring upon us, there was plenty for the goats to eat on the steep mountainside by the lake.

We arrived just in time. The second morning, all my goats began to kid. By that night, we had eleven more babies, two to each of my does, except triplets to my queen. All were some shade of cream or gold, mostly male, many looking white and giant like their father. With Pebbles' friendly speckled doeling, there were soon twelve jumping unwieldy goat kids following me everywhere. How different these babies were from Perla! They were active and lively, from the first day. Perla, on the other hand, mostly slept tied close to my chest. As long as I made sure she was dry and had milk, she rarely stayed awake for more than a few minutes. In those moments, she would gaze up at me, and I felt the deep loss of Ankah in those dark, sullen eyes.

The days were busy as I cared for Perla, cleaned our area of the castle, and gathered food and firewood. In the quiet evenings, I spent a lot of time dwelling on what had happened after I left. I wondered if Selene had told the Clan anything, or if they had even come after me. Was Mihai devastated? This would be his second wife lost, his second child gone. I ached to know what Isa and Sasha thought. Isa was losing a sister and a friend, but Sasha was losing a future wife. I was sure he must be furious. And how had Selene known what had happened to Ankah? Why was she willing to help me to leave, when it would also mean losing a daughter-in-law and a wife for her son. It was puzzling, and now I yearned for two clans I had lost.

Of course, nothing hurt more than the loss of Ankah. My heart felt as though it were crying all the time, but I had not shed any tears since losing my sister. I had been too distracted by the horror of finding her stone dead and by the frightening journey. Now I was immersed in the duties of caring for an infant and setting up a house. My grief was lightened by the inherent joy of watching twelve goat kids frisk and play. When I lay Perla down on the grass and changed her swaddling cloth, when I held her to Pebbles' udder to drink, I heard Ankah's last request resound through my head. I desperately hoped this was what she had meant.

∞

The weeks and months passed quickly, and throughout the lush summer, I collected food and herbs, prepared our dwelling, and dried tall grasses for the goats to eat when snow came. On a bright day, I sat on the inclined grass above the lake with Perla on my knee, watching the babies play while the mama goats munched and soaked in the sun. I was smiling as one little one jumped to land on his mother's back, then leaped off to spar with his brother. Out of the corner of my eye, I saw Perla's face change, and I glanced down. She was always watching my face, staring into my eyes. This time, she was smiling! I smiled down at her and felt the warmth spread through my whole body. It was the first time I knew for sure that I was more to her than a nanny to change and feed her.

I made a funny face, and she made a sound like a gurgle. I moved my face close to hers and made silly sounds. Each time I came close, she gasped in a tiny giggle, her smile lingering and eyes watching for what I would do next. I realized that like the baby goats, Perla needed to play. Since she could do no more than lay there and look at me, I must be her playmate. After that, I spent a lot more time talking to her, playing games by clapping my hands and singing to her, touching her soft belly to make that wonderful, gurgling laugh escape her tiny mouth.

When the sun was too hot, I would sometimes take Perla to sit in the dappled light of the forest above the lake while the goats browsed on ferns in the cool shade. On one such day, as I watching the moving shadows on Perla's perfect face as she looked up at me in fascination, it occurred to me that she had no memory of her true mother. She had barely entered the world before Ankah harshly left it, and the only thing she knew was me. To her, I was her mother. It stunned me, this realization. I had been thinking of Perla as Ankah's daughter, as my niece that I must care for. I had always had the distinct sense that I was just watching Perla until Ankah returned, even though I knew this was not true. After it occurred to me that Perla would have no other mother in this life except me, my feelings toward her changed. I grew to love her as my child, the way the goat mamas loved their kids and had special voices and bleats they used just for speaking to their children.

My devotion to her grew as the autumn approached and I prepared to shutter in the castle for the winter. I tied lake grasses into long bundles to layer across the floors and insulate from the icy stone. I had found lots of leftover rags and spare cloth tucked into corners of the abandoned living quarters. I used anything that was destroyed to stuff the cracks in the stone to keep the cold at bay. With the better pieces, I began to sew baby clothes, dresses and swaddles for Perla. They were a mish-mash of colors and patterns, being born from the leftover edges and cuttings of other clothes, but they would work to keep her warm from the biting mountain wind. I sewed a few functional things for myself, since like Perla, I was growing. Not only was I taller, but my chest had begun to swell. I thought it must be the influence of all the daily nursing I witnessed. I felt that somehow the maternal yearning that I now felt toward Perla was causing the budding of my breasts, since I felt strongly that I was still too young to be a woman. My body grew against my consent to prove this otherwise. One day I found blood running down my leg and realized if I had stayed with the Badi, I would be marrying Sasha soon. The dress I had worn when I left now came just to my shins. I sewed a band of discarded gray sackcloth to the bottom to extend its life as I worked on a few warmer items to protect me from the cold.

I never thought about how I looked, since the goats and Perla seemed to never mind, loving me regardless. Yet one day when I saw a horseman approaching the castle, I became instantly self-conscious: I smoothed down my wild curling hair, feeling shame at the patchwork of my dress. I had not thought about how I would explain my presence–unthinkably a girl child alone with an infant–to anyone whom I might encounter. I had strangely forgotten that anyone else existed. The Badi and my first clan were stilled in my mind far away, and the presence of other people seeming remote and abstract. I was alone in the world with Perla and my goats, and I was surprised that anyone else could inhabit the same space. When he approached, I had the irrational thought that we might be invisible, and he might not be able to see us at all.

It was his hunting dog who saw us first, barking and yapping at the heels of my frightened herd. His master rode up and uttered a quiet command to the dog, who returned obediently to the horse's side. As he dismounted, I saw it was the Lord of the estate, Domn Alexandru, the one whom I had encountered many months ago in the sparkling icy wood.

I curtsied best I could while holding Perla, and he looked me up and down, seeming to compare me to the child he had seen the prior winter.

"Where are your people?" He demanded.

"Not here, my lord. I am alone, with . . . my daughter."

"Well, are they returning?"

"Yes," I said. Technically, they would be returning in four more years, so I felt this was not a lie.

"It's unwise for them to leave you here alone. There are bandits and depraved men who would take advantage of a young girl alone."

"I have not seen depraved men, sir. I have only seen you."

I saw the corner of his mouth twitch at a smile, but he remained serious.

"Do you have provisions?"

"Oh, yes! I have a storehouse of food for the goats and myself. And the goats give plenty of milk."

"Yes, well, there are . . . so many of them," he observed, looking around distastefully at my entourage. I agreed that my herd looked substantial at the moment, with my five does and twelve halfway-grown kids. It had occurred to me recently when the little bucks began to get particularly frisky with their sisters that I would eventually have to butcher the boys to make it through the winter. The Lord looked at me again with his sharp steely eyes. I could see that despite what I had professed, he was well aware that I was fully alone in the world. "My household has a need for goat meat," he said. "I'll send someone tomorrow with chickens and dry goods to trade. Would that be acceptable? How many can you spare?"

"Eight, sir. The boys are big and healthy and will be ready to butcher in a few months."

"Fine." Without another word, he jumped onto his horse, clicked his tongue to signal his dog, and left without looking back.

The next day, two of the Lord's household staff appeared. They drove utility horses packed with crates. Their dress was formal, but much less regal than the nobles we had met the prior winter. I could tell they were unhappy with their mission. They looked at me with disdain as they unloaded the crates of chickens and baskets of cheese, sacks of flour, and root vegetables. It was an obscene amount of food, and I protested that it was too much. "The Master insisted," the older one said, not looking directly at me.

I had separated the boys into a small pen. I watched as the men tied their front and hind legs together and secured them over the pack horses. The bucks protested loudly. I felt a twinge of guilt for their impending fate, but also relief. It had become a burden to care for so many, and I had no interest in butchering them myself. As I watched them leave, winding onto the trail back into the woods, I thought how funny it was that the males of most animal species were so disposable. You only needed one herd sire, and the rest had no value except as meat. When babies were born, the females were most desirable. It was the opposite for humans. I knew the Clan had a special place for women and honored the Great Earth Mother and womenfolk much more than the Gentlefolk we encountered, but even among the Rroma, women were expected to submit to their fathers and husbands. The Plague had made women scarce, and therefore more valuable, even pushing elders–like Baba–into roles of leadership out of necessity. With the Pestilence receding into history, the balance was recalibrating, and women were again losing prominence. The fate of a female in the human world was still a risky prospect.

With the departure of the eight rowdy bucklings, things settled down. I hadn't realized how chaotic it had been with so many babies. With only four kids remaining, I was able to relax when we went out to graze. I didn't have to worry about one falling into the lake when I wasn't watching or wandering off to the edge of the woods to be snatched by a predator. It was still a large herd: I was so accustomed to my five goats, and now there were six, and four doelings. I had become very attached to Pebbles' big speckled girl, and the others were two sweet creamy girls and a precious golden doe.

Without as many bellies to feed, I now found I had more milk than I knew what to do with! Perla only drank so much. Although I drank a lot of milk before the Lord had the supplies delivered, now there was so much else to eat. I found I could make stews and even bake some flatbread. After not having anything like that for months, the bread seemed sweeter than anything I had ever tasted. I devoured it like a decadent dessert. With the abundance of milk, I realized I had a storage problem. Fortunately, Domn Alexandru had sent some small casks of wine, so I could add it to hot milk to make fresh cheese as Sasha had taught me. Although I didn't know anything about making hard cheese, I started to set up cheeses to age. Hard cheese was not something traveling tribes could usually afford to buy or store. Now I experimented with finding enough odd receptacles to press the soft cheese into molds and tried to secure a place to store them where the rodents would not get at them. I only hoped that what I stored, with stones on top to press them down and keep the critters away, would magically turn into a harder substance.

I also now had a small flock of poultry. Several hens, a turkey, and even a few ducks. I kept them in a small coop inside the barn next to the goats' enclosure, but after watching them peck around pathetically at the crumbs I scattered in the bare dirt in their cage, I let them loose one day. They were euphoric as they ran about snatching bugs from the air and scratching under the leaves for grubs. After that, I let them out every day. With no cock to protect them, the turkey became the guardian of the others. He made alarm sounds when a hawk flew by or when the girls pecked off too far to the edges of our domain to call them back together. They were an odd family, but I guess we were all an odd family already. I certainly appreciated the delicious eggs the fowl provided, and I knew I could butcher them when I had to without as much remorse as I would have had to sacrifice the baby goats.

The end of the summer seemed to swirl by with long, restful days playing with Perla in the grass and watching my herd, and much work stacking wood, foraging for berries, mushrooms and tubers to eat or dry for the winter. Suddenly, the days became shorter and the light was different, and the inside of the castle required a bigger cooking fire by which to see. The first frost in the morning made me dread the cold to come. I snuggled down in my blankets with Perla, wishing to stay under the covers rather than get up to milk goats and attend to other chores. Perla needed food, and the goats and poultry always needed care. The demands of motherhood and husbandry did not allow for sloth.

When the first big snow fell, our little world got even smaller. The winter came on fast and hard, a brittle cold wind always howling over the mountain. I did my best to bind Perla up in anything I could find to insulate her and hung blankets from rafters to keep any amount of icy air out. It didn't work. The castle was too old and decrepit, and the big stones it was built from probably did not keep the place warm even when it was first built. The cook fires never went out, but I also had to conserve. After the first week or so, it was impossible to traverse the world outside, being layered in thick blankets of snow. I had prepared well, but still had to be modest in doling out wood and supplies to survive. My hands froze when I milked the goats, and I did the bare minimum to care for them in the even colder stables. I melted snow for them to drink from the places in the castle where the roof had collapsed and snow drifted in, without even venturing outside. The goats huddled together and had each other to keep warm. Perla had only me, so I kept her tied close to my chest while I cared for the animals and performed the meager duties that kept us from freezing and starving.

The dark and the cold seemed like it was a permanent state of the world– as if it would always be winter. When I could get our close quarters warm enough, I would sit Perla up, since she could now sit on her own, and play with her with a ragdoll I made, or sing to her. She kept up her spirits, and it was only I who had to pretend sometimes: I put on a smile and sand songs I'd learned from the Badi, or made up tunes with stories woven in. Sometimes this effort seemed as much to entertain me as to keep her occupied. The darkness came in so thoroughly that there was barely light enough to make sure we all were fed and Perla was kept dry and warm. With my animals secured inside the stable and with Perla and I bundled together in our bed, I enjoyed listening to the symphony of the wolves at night. I tried to decipher their howls to determine the messages they sent to one another, across the miles and mountaintops, or perhaps it was more like singing together to pass the long winter nights.

I wondered where my first clan was: maybe hunkered down at the edge of a town in an abandoned barn somewhere, binding rags over feet to keep them from freezing and falling off. It was a harsh life: surviving on the fringes of someone else's world. I knew the Badi tribe had more resources. They often negotiated with locals to let out a whole street of tavern rooms for a few months in an unsavory area of a city, since business was slow for everyone once the snow came.

As always, I thought of Ankah, and wondered where her spirit had gone. She, who had spent so much time listening to the dead, now walking among them. Did she stay and linger, like so many others worried about settling their affairs, to watch that I took care of Perla? Was she here with me now, seeing me eke out a minimal existence alone in the world except for Perla and my animals? Is this what she would have wanted? Or would she have wanted me to stay and marry Sasha and watch over whatever semblance of love could be doled out to Perla in Mama Violca's household? I was sure Mihai would have been a good father, but would Perla have gotten the care, the nurturing she needed with no mother there, even if I had looked in on her? Maybe I would have been able to convince Selene and Iosef to have Perla live with us. Maybe I could have made everyone happy and adopted Perla and still married Sasha? Had I made the wrong decision? These nagging thoughts troubled me late at night.

Despite the suspicion that there could have been an easier way that betrayed fewer of those who had been kind to me, I had the same feeling about that narrowly missed life that I had when the bucklings left: I felt relief. I guiltily acknowledged that as hard as it was to have chosen this risky path, I had barely escaped being buried and smothered in a life that did not belong to me at all. This life, cold and dark, in a pile of stones that barely passed as shelter, this was the life that I deserved. Snuggled with Perla under a pile of blankets, watching the winking red eyes of the banked fire, listening to the wolves sing their haunting melodies–this was the life I now owned.

Chapter Six: Homestead

Just when I thought it would never end, winter finally retreated. I was able to bring the goats out one day, despite pockets of deep snow and melting ice. We walked on narrow strips of dry ground and made our way down to the lake. There, I set Perla down in the bright sun on some dried grasses that had been flattened by the snow. She surprised me by putting her hands in front of her and pushing herself up into a standing position. She wobbled there and looked delighted with herself. She had done some minimal crawling over the winter, but the floor was dirty and cold, so I had only allowed her to crawl on our blankets. I think until that moment I had thought she was going to be a baby forever, but when I saw her there, on unsteady feet with a self-satisfied smile, I realized she was going to grow into an actual girl.

The goats were practically out of milk. In the darkest part of winter, I had stopped milking. It had been too cold to get but a few drops of milk, which froze almost immediately in my pail. Those who still had milk were the four with babies, and the kids were barely nursing. Their mothers had decided it was time to wean them and would side-step to avoid eager noses pushed under their bellies toward their udders. They were all happy to eat the tiny patches of new grass pushing up under the dead leaves and pine needles. I boiled up stews from the new shoots and herbs and the roots I was able to dig up. I fed these to Perla with small bits of the cheese I had stored. Some rounds had been demolished by rats or destroyed by mold, but much of it was preserved and surprisingly good.

Now I had ten goats and no milk. I quickly realized this was a foolish lifestyle, but it gave me so much pleasure to see their lively faces every day and watch the babies growing into awkward juveniles. Feeding and protecting a large herd of animals was a full-time occupation. The store of dried grass was dwindling. Now that the goats had a taste of spring grass, they yelled to go out the second they saw me coming. I had butchered a few of the poultry during the winter, but still had several birds left, including the giant turkey. I let the fowl out with the goats, and when small predators came near, it was the turkey who defended them. I worried about the wolves, though, since as much as I appreciated their songs, I dreaded having to fight them off if they came after my flock. I heard them all the time but rarely saw them. Generations of steering clear of the castle's cookfires and other smells of humans seemed to have made the wolves shy of coming too close.

Still, a day came when a lone adolescent male wandered into the valley by the lake. He was scraggly and looked like he hadn't eaten much over the winter. He was hunting for mice in the tall grass, but soon became interested in the squawks of my birds and fast movements of the goats. I ushered the animals toward the castle, but he followed and hungrily fixated on the big turkey, who was not taking my lead. The foolhardy tom continued to dart toward the wolf to scold him. I held a big staff and Perla on my hip, and decided to sacrifice the turkey, should it come down to it. However, I realized that if the wolf got a taste of free supper, we would never be free from him: he would linger at the edge of the forest, picking us off one by one.

With Perla under one arm, I grabbed the staff and charged at the wolf. Even under-nourished, he was still almost my size, but I was filled with an intense need to defend my small, precious world. He jumped back when I ran at him, swinging the staff and yelling. I came after him, again and again, and he continued to retreat. If he were an older and more experienced creature, I'm sure both Perla and I would have been devoured. This young one lacked confidence, though, so with each lunge, I drove him back. He faltered, hestitating due to my aggressive stance. Each time he circled back to consider me from another angle, he shied from my swipes and battle yells. He was not bold enough to outright attack a human, albeit a small one holding an infant, yet wielding a large stick with a trumpeting turkey at her heels.

His girth of me became larger as he began to accept defeat, but his hunger seemed to keep him there on the periphery, perhaps trying to determine if there was a way to at least grab the baby or the turkey. It was then that I heard barking and a figure on horseback emerged at the ridge along the top of the valley. Before I could recognize it as the Lord, his sleek hunting dog streaked down the incline and went directly for the assailing predator. The wolf may have thought he could pick off one of us, but he had no pretenses about the dog. He shot up the steep side of the valley wall, with the canine a gray streak behind him, barking viciously.

Domn Alexandru approached, and I found myself unable to speak, my heart still coursing from defending against the wolf. "I don't believe I've ever seen a wolf vanquished by a girl and a turkey before," he observed. I looked up to where he was still sitting upon his horse. The light was behind him and his face was as unexpressive as always, but there was an amused sparkle in his eyes.

"My lord," I said, and curtsied, balancing both the stick and Perla. Again, I was dismayed by my dress, which had not improved over the course of the winter, nor had it been enhanced by the brambles it had snared during my recent battle.

"I do not see your people. Did they not come?"

"No, my lord," I admitted. "But I'm sure they will be here soon."

"Hmmph," he said. "This won't do. It's not suitable for a young woman and her child to be left alone for so long."

"Yes, sir, but we have fared well. This is the first time a wolf has come so close."

"Well, it won't be the last time," he replied quickly. "No, it's not suitable at all." His dog reappeared and ran down the ridge, her sleek silver form appearing next to her master, panting heavily. She seemed to be pleased with herself, a giant smile on her face as she looked up at the Lord with her mouth open and her big pink tongue lolling out.

"My bitch has had puppies," he said.

"Congratulations," I said, unsure of the proper response. I noticed for the first time the dog's swollen nipples on her otherwise elegant frame.

"I will send one for you. She is a great hunter, and her pups will be very protective."

"Oh, no sir, I couldn't accept such a generous offer."

"It's not for your benefit," he said sharply. "I'll not have an unprotected female and child come to harm on my estate. My man will be here tomorrow to deliver the pup." With that, he turned his horse and made to depart. He stopped suddenly and turned around to look at me once more. "You're quite sure your family is coming soon?" he asked.

"Yes, sir. I'm sure they just got held up somewhere over the winter. They should be here soon to gather me and the babe."

He harrumphed again. I watched his figure, stiff in his saddle, turn and ride back up the ridge with his sleek dog darting back and forth up the slope. The next day, the same two men who had come the last time appeared and delivered a beautiful light gray puppy in a basket. I had prepared a few rounds of cheese to be taken back as a gift for the Lord. They did not seem to want to touch anything I handed to them. They held the packages, wrapped in the cleanest fabric I could find, away from their bodies, packed them into a riding bag, and went on their way.

I was mesmerized by the puppy, and Perla was delighted with her, too. Although her sharp white teeth sometimes accidentally scratched the baby when her playful antics got too rough, more often she covered her with big wet kisses until Perla giggled so hard she could barely breathe. We called her *Stea,* named after the bright stars that sparkled in the sky in the clear circle of air above the castle. With Stea's arrival, we somehow seemed more of a family. We laughed more, played more, talked more. Perla began to repeat words she heard me saying to Stea, telling her: "No!" or "Out!" when she was getting in the way while I was trying to cook a meal.

Perla also started calling me Mama. I'm not sure how it happened because I don't remember referring to myself in that way. It hurt my heart at first, hearing that word from her when Ankah never got to hear it. I was only a fraud filling in for her real mother, after all. I comforted myself by acknowledging that Ankah was gone and was never coming back, and I would be the only mother Perla would know.

The Lord returned several weeks later, to check on the puppy. Stea romped with her mother while the Lord, always speaking to me from his horse, checked in with me. "No word from your family yet?"

"No, sir."

"That's a shame. The puppy is growing well."

"Yes, sir! Perla is quite enchanted with her. I'm sure she will be a fierce protectress."

"Hmmm . . . That cheese was quite good. You made it yourself?"

"Why, yes sir. There's no one here but me."

"Well, I'd like to buy a bit more. My cheese stores got pillaged by vermin."

"Of course, sir." I ran to gather some more rounds, although my supply was dwindling. I refused the coins he offered me. "I stay here at your pleasure, sir. I can take no coins from you."

"Well, perhaps we'll trade goods for more cheese in the future, then?"

"I'm afraid I'm out of milk, sir."

"Oh, well that's too bad. No milk, but so many goats!" He looked around to survey my herd, covering the hillside.

"Yes, sir. I am rich with goats."

He chuckled. "And yet, you do not have the kind that will make babies and therefore more milk," he observed.

"No, sir. I gave all of the males to you for meat."

"Well, then it is my fault that you have no milk!"

"No, no, sir–of course not!" I insisted, but could see that he was toying with me.

A few days later, his men came leading a beastly golden buck with giant horns on a tether. I insisted that they take three of the four doelings back with them to supplement the Lord's herd. I kept Pebbles' speckled doe, but it was true that I had many more goats than I needed. Still, I could not fathom the idea of parting with my first family–the older does I was raised with on the mountain–and I was too fond of Pebbles and her kid to part with them. Interestingly, the does, who had taught me so much about the instincts of motherhood when their babies were first born, barely mourned for their departed babies. They had not noticed much when their male babies were removed in the fall. Even the ones who had mothered doelings all winter made a few bleats of concern after they left, but then seemed to quickly forget their children ever existed. They were more preoccupied with the next mouthful of fresh grass.

Over the next several months, I had frequent visitors. Every few weeks, the Lord would appear, apparently in the midst of a hunting trip. Sometimes he had other nobles or his vassals with him, but often he came alone. He always asked about my family, and I always assured him that they would surely be coming soon. He would notice some small thing that was lacking, some way that my small homestead needed improvement, and then a few days later some supplies would arrive. I always sent back whatever I had of value: packages of mountain mint, pine nuts I had gathered, baskets I had made from the reeds by the lake. The Lord's household staff always seemed put out to take back my "gifts," but the Lord himself always commented on them the next time he visited, complimenting my craftsmanship or the quality of the goods I sent.

Before I could blink, the summer had passed by and the grasses on the mountainside grew russet and brittle. One morning I woke to shrieks from the stables, and there were babies again, the buck having accomplished his purpose of bringing milk back to my herd. That autumn, I reinforced the stables by patching up the holes to the outside and stuffing the walls with leaves and moss. It would still be cold, but I might be able to milk longer into the winter that way. With this brood of young kids, I sent away all the babies as soon as they were big enough so that I would have enough milk to get us through the winter. The Lord sent me back hides and bladders which made me sad, but I found the leather very useful for making boots for Perla and myself to help keep away the cold from the stone floors of the castle. The bladders were good to use as flasks to store milk for making more cheeses. I only knew the very basics of cheesemaking, and I wasted a lot of milk with my inexperience, but I often would fumble upon a good recipe or method and the results were as fine as any cheese I'd ever tasted.

Perla was walking and talking now–no longer a baby–and I could even give her little tasks to help with. Her helping often made a job harder, but I thought it was important to teach her industry. I had her collect eggs in a basket, pick up and stack pinecones for kindling, and brush out Stea's shiny fur. When I think about my time in the castle, as it became not an old sprawling fortress, but a home for me and Perla, I was probably the happiest I would ever be then. There was a small nagging at the back of mind, reminding me the clans would return to gather there two winters hence, but it seemed so far away. Despite the Lord's frequent visits and questions, he seemed content to allow me to stay in my makeshift house, surrounded by livestock and the unpredictable wilderness.

∞

That winter was as cold and dark as the last, but I was more prepared. Having Stea there, growing into a beautiful large puppy, made me feel much safer than when I was alone with Perla. Stea lay on our feet at night, keeping a little bit of the frigid air at bay. Winter finally receded to spring, then summer, and before I knew it, autumn was upon us again. My body had grown strong, and I was able to lift large stones to fix parts of the castle and build almost anything I needed. I had learned some smithing skills from my first clan, so I could fix almost anything that broke. My work was not refined, but it functioned well enough for basic repairs of tools and cooking items. Most of what had been left at the castle had been in poor shape when it was discarded there, but we made do. I became more than adequate at taking a twisted tool or broken piece of metal and making a serviceable item.

The Lord visited one day in early autumn to thank me for some smoked duck I had sent back to him through his vassals. I had a small flock of ducks now and found that I had no qualms about butchering them, unlike the sensitivity that prevented me from eating my furry beasts. The Lord rarely stayed long, and often would not even get off his horse when he visited, but this time he had gotten down to get a closer look at how I had created a small gate for the poultry pen. I thought he must not be very grand to be impressed by such shoddy workmanship, but he ran a finger over a swirling embellishment that I had added to the gate latch, just for fun.

"You learned smithing from your family?" he asked.

"Yes, sir. My work does not show it, I'm afraid, but my first clan was the finest at metal. There are no better smiths."

"Your . . . first clan?"

"Yes, before . . . I was sent to be married."

"And your married family?"

"I learned cheesemaking from them, sir. And I learned a bit about herbs. But they are mostly performers: the Circ."

"Ah," he nodded. "May I ask you . . . I recall the people you came with a few winters ago, the Ciganyok. You do not look like them."

It had been so long since I had spent time with any clan, my first family or the Badi, that I had almost forgotten that I stood out amongst them. When I lived among the Rroma, I felt my difference only with new people, when they gazed at me sideways or comment on my light complexion or features. Going to new places, I would see the Gentles' eyes stop on me for a moment, before they decided that if I dressed and spoke like a Cigany, I was a Cigany.

"Yes, sir. I was adopted. My . . . mother, she asked the Rroma to take care of me. I was very young then."

"She asked *Ciganyok* to care for her child?"

"She was dying, my lord, and she had no one else—or no one that I'm aware of. We lived on a mountainside, a very tiny house. There was no one else around. It was just the two of us and our goats."

"And your father?"

"I don't remember, sir. I don't think I ever had one, or at least I have no memory of one."

He sighed. "Your mother—what was her name?"

I thought for a moment. She was "Mama" to me and I had never thought of her differently. I had never asked Ankah or Baba. "I'm not sure, sir. I was very young."

"Hmmm. Do you think your family will be coming soon, Jaelle?"

He had asked my name long ago, but he had never spoken it before, so I was surprised that he had even remembered it. "Yes, my lord. I'm sure they will be coming soon."

∞

Perla had been a confident toddler and was now a lively and happy little girl. She had everything she needed in our small isolated world, without any awareness that anything outside of this existed. She loved her dog and her goats and found endless amusements in the summer wildflowers and the autumn leaves. I was busy with mothering and foraging, cooking and feeding our small horde. I worried sometimes about what would become of us, especially when the tribes came back. If I stayed and threw myself on the mercy of the Badi, Perla would be taken and I would likely be banished. I sometimes felt that Perla did not belong to me anyway, so maybe this was the right outcome. I could not reconcile that possible conclusion with the deep attachment that had grown between us. Neither she nor I would be happy with that arrangement, even if it might be right.

As I gathered dried grasses and kindling to prepare for the coming turn of the weather, Perla was occupied building a small house of moss and twigs for her ragdoll. "Mama, I have a question," she said. She was a curious girl, and this was the way she started many conversations, asking me all sorts of things about the world and nature, why the leaves fell, why we eat other animals and they don't eat us.

"Yes?"

"The lady who comes here—where does she live?"

Occasionally a female serf would come with the Lord's entourage and help deliver items, but that was rare. Most of his subjects, at least the ones who made the journey up to the castle, were men. "What lady, my sweet?"

"The one with long black hair. The one with the scar on her face. Where does she live?"

My heart stopped and I could not speak for several moments.

"Mama?"

"Perla–you see a lady with a scar?"

"Not now, but she comes here a lot. You know her! She is always standing and watching us. Why doesn't she ever say anything? And why don't you talk to her? Does she live in the forest?"

"When have you seen her, Perla?"

"Always, Mama. She's always been here. You know that! She comes every day, but she never speaks. Why does she come here if she's not going to talk? Is she your friend?"

I was so dumbstruck that I could hardly find words to reply. Finally, I said: "She must be watching out for us. I'm sure she's very good."

After that, I watched Perla more closely. Sometimes I would see her look up and her eyes would catch on something. She might offer a comment to the air then, like: "This one is the prettiest, you see?" holding up a treasured stone or leaf. She would quickly go back to playing, but I would stare at the empty space long after to try to see my sister there. It made sense that Perla would have the Sight like her mother, but I just wasn't expecting it.

Chapter Seven: Reunion

Another winter passed, just like the two before, except Perla was a more active girl now. In some ways, this made it much easier, because we could sing together, tell stories, and play silly games to pass the time. As Perla's vocabulary grew, I made sure to teach her Rromani and the language of the Country, side by side. She became adept at switching from one to the other, depending upon which language I spoke when I started the conversation. I did not know what direction life would lead us, so I wanted to make sure she was prepared either way. I needn't have worried about her being self-sufficient: she was independent and capable from the beginning. If I needed to go out to the stables or fetch something outside, I could leave her playing by the fire inside and knew she would come to no harm. She was a sensible child, and she always had her loyal dog beside her to keep her safe.

I had always felt alone in my life, even when I was with the clans. I was an outsider when I came to them, and an outsider when I went to marry. I had always had Ankah, whom I loved deeply, but I also felt like an imposter, since I was never sure how much of her love for me depended on her believing I was Gildi's reincarnation. I always had my goats, but I never felt truly, deeply bonded with another human. Perla changed that: we belonged to each other. Even with that deep sense of belonging, I still felt that I had not come by it rightly. I was adopted into the Clan, and she was adopted by me, whether she knew it or not. Honestly, I had stolen her. That contributed to the underlying dis-ease that I did not deserve to be her mother, to have her sweet and devoted love. It did not change my love for her, but it made me feel that my connection to her was tenuous, like I could lose her. Maybe all mothers feel that way: worried for their children, their safety, concerned that they could be snatched away at any moment.

This sense of foreboding permeated my consciousness that spring and summer, as I prepared to leave the castle. I knew we had to depart before the families started arriving in late fall. As the leaves began to turn, I started talking to Perla about going on a journey. She did not seem alarmed by this. Instead, she was excited to venture out. We had never strayed far from the castle, and Perla seemed open to anything. I was wracked with worry. Despite my wanderings with the tribes and my solo journey to the castle, I was still very inexperienced about the world. I did not know for sure, but I suspected the world would not respond favorably to a single woman and child wandering the country on their own. It seemed like a foolish thing to do, exposing Perla to that kind of uncertainty. Still, did I have a choice? It seemed riskier to stay and return her to the Badi. I would lose her then for sure.

One afternoon, sitting together on a bed of fallen pine needles on the slope by the lake, I noticed that look on Perla's face that meant that Ankah was close by. She was making trails in the needles, like a maze, and running an acorn through. I watched her look up and explain to Ankah that the acorn was very smart, and knew not to go down this particular path since there were hungry monsters that way. She often talked to Ankah, explaining what she was doing, or including her in her play.

"Perla," I said, "can you ask the lady what she thinks of our journey? If she thinks we should go away?"

"She never talks, Mama," Perla said without looking up. "You know that."

"Can you ask her anyway? I can't see her the way you can."

She looked at me curiously, apparently this being the first time she had considered that I could not see the lady who visited so often. Then she turned and looked at a place in the filtered sunlight.

"Lady, we are going on a journey soon. We're going to leave our castle. Do you think we should go?"

Perla's eyes widened as she watched the place in the sparkling light. Then she looked at me with a delighted smile. "She talked, Mama! Did you hear her?"

"No, no Perla. I can't hear her. What did she say?" My blood was pounding in my ears.

"She says it's time for us to leave. She says we are going to have an adventure!"

"Can you ask her . . . " There was so much I wanted to know, but I didn't want to upset Perla, so I was trying to think about how to word my question. I stopped when it seemed Perla was listening again. She paused, watching the air, for several seconds, then nodded and went back to running her acorn through the maze.

"What did she say, Perla? I want to ask her . . ." I tried not to let my impatience spill over.

"She's gone, Mama."

"What?"

"She had to go. She said she loves us both. She's going on a journey, too!"

"Where? Where is she going? Did she say anything else? Did she tell us where to go?" Perla didn't even look up from her play. She just shook her head and resumed talking under her breath to the acorn. I sat, my pulse blaring and a deep sense of loss pervading me. Why hadn't I found the words quickly enough? I glanced around, thinking maybe Ankah was still nearby. I wanted to shout to the trees, to tell Ankah I loved her, to tell her I was sorry if I hadn't done what she'd wanted me to do for Perla.

Perla stopped suddenly and looked up. "It's okay, Mama. She was happy to go."

∞

I cleaned up the castle as best I could to remove evidence of us being there, but I had made so many improvements to the structure of our little section and the stables that there was no way to remove it entirely. I chose not to dismantle the pens I had built for the poultry, since they would come in handy for the clans as they arrived with their various livestock. Over the previous months, I had butchered the remaining ducks, chickens, and even the old tom. He had served us well, protecting our flock for so many years, so it was a sad day. I reminded myself that he had a good and useful life as I made jerky from his tough carcass. I stacked the repaired pots and tools neatly. There was no way to hide that someone had been there and I only hoped that no one would guess it was me.

I tied Ankah's wedding blanket and a few essential items to the goats. They were not used to being pack animals, but after complaining a bit, they complied. When it seemed too risky to stay longer, I rallied Stea and Perla, who was bursting out of her small body with excitement. We herded the goats up into the pine forest above the castle. We were just in time, since the first families began to arrive as we were cresting the top of the ridge. I could recognize some of them, but we were far away by then. I thought I saw Baba, with her stooped frame and small stature, and my heart felt a stab of pain and longing. I wanted to rush back down and hug her, to see my cousins and laugh with them and be their little Lyuba again. But all had changed. I was a fugitive, and I had no idea how I would be received. Word traveled fast between tribes, so I did not doubt that news of Ankah's death and my absconding with her newborn baby would have reached my clan.

I took the red thread that Baba had given me from where it always was, in the pocket of my apron. It had gotten frayed and was a sad piece of string at that point. While it had brought me comfort all those years, I felt I no longer deserved it. I had betrayed my clan. My connection to them—and to Baba—had been permanently severed, and it was my fault. I dug a small hole in the pine needles and the dry, dark earth beneath and buried the thread. Perla did not seem to notice. She was curious about the newcomers who were swarming about our home, but even more excited to continue our journey, so we nudged on. I had not thought much about where we would go. I knew so little about the world and nothing about what lay on the other side of the mountain, but I knew this was the direction the Lord always went when he returned to his house. I also knew that the families would be coming from several directions up the other side of the mountain toward the castle, so it seemed we had no other choice. Like many times in my life before, I did what I felt was the only thing I could do, as fate pushed me toward a profound unknown.

I was always leaving, it seemed, whether it was leaving my mountain cabin and my true Mama, leaving my first clan to go live with the Badi, or leaving in haste with grief devastating my soul, carrying a newborn baby that was not mine. Now I was leaving again. It had been hard, sometimes, at the castle, but it was my home; it was the first place that felt altogether mine, where I was not assimilating into someone else's world. I had built a life there for me and Perla and our little herd. As we headed deeper into the woods, following a riding trail that seemed to have been carved by centuries, I felt the deep loss of the life we had built there, even greater than the pain I felt at leaving Baba and my first clan. I felt as if I were leaving myself behind.

∞

It was only a few hours to reach the valley on the other side of the mountain and would have been a fraction of that on horseback. Still, it was impressive that the Lord had come that far each time he had ventured to see me, and that he had sent his servants so far to bring me goods. It must have taken the whole day for them to go there and back, which explained some of their grumpy demeanor. Descending upon the valley, I could see what could only be the Lord's house, although "house" seemed like a diminution of the grandeur of the building. To me, it looked like a compact little castle, made of stone, with soaring turrets and several wings. It stood on the outskirts of a medium-sized town, which had houses so close together that they seemed to be connected, making up the alleys and streets, and with roads and farms sprawling out for many miles in every direction.

The Lord's estate had many buildings connected by a network of roads in a way that made it clear they were part of the same enterprise. There was a magnificent stone barn and what appeared to be an industrious farm, with pastures and vineyards tucked into the side of the mountain. All of the outbuildings and productive land stood at a fair distance from the Lord's primary residence, which stood on its own, surrounded by gardens and orchards. There was no way to pass into town without going through his farm and right past his grand house. Perla was so excited she was practically dancing, forgetting that she had been complaining for the last several miles about how tired she was. She was not used to walking so far the way I had been when I was small.

We walked by the fields and barns, and I saw sheep and goats upon the hillside with a shepherd and dog guarding them. It was strange to think that many of the goats had probably been mine. My caprines had behaved themselves well this far into the journey, with Stea yapping behind them if any began to stray or dawdle. As we drew closer to the town, it seemed to expand in size and became much more foreboding, more like a city than a town. I dreaded walking my herd through the streets. I had no idea how I would be perceived, but I was pretty sure I would draw unwanted attention, regardless. The comprehension of what I had done sank in, and I realized that my vision of traveling unnoticed to find a new home for me and Perla was a fantasy. I could wander over a mountain with goats, but they would ultimately make my ability to blend in or find a place to live or livelihood to support us near impossible.

Accepting what I needed to do, I took a detour off the main road onto a smaller road that led to a smattering of small barns splayed out from the giant stone barn and stables. Several stable hands milled around, carting barrows of straw and carrying tack to be cleaned. Those who noticed us stared as we approached, and I was conscious of our curious appearance as I went up to the one who seemed the oldest and most confident. Despite his apprehension, he spoke to me with civility. "May I be of service, madam?"

"Thank you, sir. I am looking to sell my herd of goats. Your Lordship has traded with me before. I'll take whatever you will give for them."

"That would be . . . quite an acquisition, my lady," his gaze fell over my unruly herd, which had scampered up a great pile of straw and was busily munching away. "I would have to speak to Domn Alexandru. He would not like me to make such a . . . purchase without consulting him."

Before I knew it, the older gentleman was calling over a young stable boy and the boy went dashing off toward the large stone barn.

"Oh no," I said, "I really wouldn't want to disturb him."

"He's close by, it will just take a moment." With that he began walking himself toward the larger barn to meet up with the Lord, who had been summoned by the quick lad and was walking toward us, wiping his hands on a cloth with a puzzled look. I could not hear what they were saying, but his assistant gestured toward me and recognition spread over the Lord's face.

"Jaelle! What a surprise! What is it that brings you this way?"

"Greetings, my lord," I bowed. "I'm afraid it's time for us to move on. I must sell my goats as they are not the most cooperative travel companions," I pointed to the reckless group, who were still invading the straw pile. He chuckled.

"What of your family? Have you heard from them?"

65

"They are descending upon the castle now, sir."

"I see. You have waited for them for so long. Why leave now?"

"There is nothing left for me with my clan, sir," I couldn't meet his eyes.

"What of your . . . husband?"

I shook my head and did not look up.

"I'm so sorry, Jaelle." I realized I had misled him to believe I was widowed but could not correct the error now.

"So, you see why I must move on. I'll find some livelihood to support myself and Perla."

"Yes, I see. Stani, please take these goats to the fields. Give the lady whatever she asks for them." His man uttered some words to a few nearby hands, who rushed to round up the goats and unload the few packages still tied to them. Stea barked and helped to keep them from scattering as the hands placed ropes around the necks of a few and the others followed easily. I tried not to watch as they led most of what was left of my family away. Stani came back with a small pouch of coins. Perla had been stringing a braid of purple flowers and seemed only mildly interested in the goats being paraded away. Stea, sensing my sadness, came to sit by my side.

"She's become a beautiful dog," the Lord observed. "She'll protect you well on your journey. Where will you go?"

"I don't know. I'll pass through this town, perhaps go on to Brașov."

"Why, this is Brașov!" he gestured toward the sprawling city-town.

"Oh!" I laughed. "Well, I'm not sure, then. Clearly, I don't know where I'm going!"

"It's not a good time of year to be traveling, especially when one does not know where she is going. The weather will turn soon. You will need to get settled before the winter comes." I had realized this, but what choice did I have?

"Yes, my lord. Nothing about my situation is ideal." He made a sound of agreement and nodded thoughtfully.

"So, stay here, Jaelle. I have a small cottage, just recently vacated by one of the seamstresses. Her mother has died and she's gone back to her village to care for her father. You and Perla would be welcome to stay there through the winter," he seemed quite pleased with having come up with a solution.

"Oh, no, sir. That is very kind, but I couldn't impose . . ."

"Nonsense! You could earn your keep, perhaps by making some of that wonderful cheese of yours! We have plenty of milk! Plus, you're very handy with a needle, I've noticed." I blushed. I was still embarrassed by our patchwork clothing when I was around him, with his fine clothes. He clapped his hands as if it were settled, and called his man over.

"Stani, please send word to prepare the seamstress's cottage for the madam and her young daughter and have their things brought there. They will be our guests through the winter." And then to me, he said: "You will be most welcome." He turned and walked back to the barn, and once again, my path had been determined for me.

Chapter Eight: The Gift

Perla was delighted by our new surroundings. It was the only place she had been other than the castle, which was the only home of her memory. Having suffered a shortage of conversational partners, she talked to everyone. Each one promptly fell in love with her. Soon, she had people dropping by to bring her old bobbins to play with, delivering biscuits and cakes to her, and coming by just to chat to see how the "young miss" was doing. She learned the names of each person and what they did on the estate, as I was just adjusting to having a roof that did not leak. The cottage was luxurious to me, although I'm sure it was one of the simplest on the compound. It had two rooms with well-sealed smooth walls and strong thatch that did not let in a drop of rain. After the drafty, decrepit castle that was never truly warm, I was thrilled to find that when I made a fire, the small place became toasty within minutes. The seamstress who had resided there had left in haste. Although the place was spotless, there were some boxes of fabric and other articles of her trade that she had abandoned. I set about quickly making new clothes for Perla since we stood out sorely with our patched garments.

Everyone looked so polished! Ankah had made clothes for the Gentles, so I was intimately familiar with how dresses and fine garments were constructed, but even the scullery maids seemed to have clothes that were in good condition, with no visible patches. The clean and simple dress of the Lord's staff impressed me, and I worked quickly to make new outfits so that we would stand out less. We had been dressed like Rroma, which I quickly realized was a handicap. While it seemed we were accepted by the Lord's hospitality, I recognized a few scornful looks.

Perla loved her new dress of pale blue and spun around to see the skirts billow. She would quickly get it stained and torn, being the active child she was, and I would spend much time repairing and cleaning mud from it to keep it in presentable condition. She was so proud of it that it charmed everyone. One day she spied the Lord coming back from touring the estate with his managers and although I tried to deter her, she ran out to intercept him. He had crouched to examine the dress as Perla chattered to him and spun around so he could see how it billowed out. To his credit, he raised his eyebrows and acted as if it were the first time he'd seen a dress do such a thing. "And your mother has a new dress, too, I see," he said as I approached. Mine was plain and rust-colored, but it was the first piece of clothing I had owned that was not stitched from rags or the remains of other garments.

"There was fabric left in the cottage. I hope you don't mind, sir."

"Of course not! Anything I have is at your disposal. If you need anything, let Stani or one of the other stewards know. Is the cottage suitable?"

"It's more than suitable. I can't thank you enough. You must realize my former residence was a pile of rubble?" He laughed. "But even that was at the mercy of your good graces, my lord."

"You and Perla should come for dinner. I'll send someone for you this evening. Yes?"

"Thank you, sir." I was fairly certain I did not have a choice. In truth, I was very curious about his home. We had already imposed so much, though. I felt uncomfortable just being there in the cottage, much less being a dinner guest.

That afternoon, Perla and I walked out to visit the goats in the pastures. They came running as soon as they saw us. After nuzzling us and sniffing and nibbling the edges of our new clothes, they quickly went back to eating the diverse grasses that were still green and abundant on the hillside. The autumn was lingering on, with many splendidly warm days still lulling us into believing that winter was still far off. The goats soon drifted away to feast on the endless grass they'd had so little of on the mountain as if they were making up for lost time.

As we walked back, I realized they had moved on, just as they had when their babies were taken from them. So long as they had fresh pasture, they would be fine. It made me slightly sad to lose my herd, but I was happy they seemed so well-adapted to the life of estate goats. I had not forgotten the Lord's comment about the cheese, though, and I stopped by the milking barns to ask for some sheep's milk to start making some to set up. The kind men there also gave me some molds and presses. I had never seen anything like them, but I acted as if I knew exactly what to do with them as I graciously accepted these tools.

That evening, a young maid came to fetch us. I had scrubbed myself and Perla as clean as I could. Perla was so jittery with excitement she could barely keep still. She chatted with the maid as we walked to the great house and ran up the front steps, despite my urging her to walk slowly. We were greeted by several staff members in formal attire. I felt extremely conspicuous in clothing–though it was the best we'd ever worn–that was still unsuited for entry into a house like this.

My attention was drawn away from my self-conscious reflection as soon as we went through the stone archway of the front door, which was a massive piece of oak taller than our cottage. My eyes bounced from one feature to the next. My breath caught in my throat when I looked up to the vaulted ceilings to see a fresco of a summer sky painted across the whole expanse. It went from dusk at one side to full midnight blue at the other, dazzled with August constellations. A swirling stone staircase looked as if the sky itself had opened and marble had been poured directly from the heavens to form its fluid cascade. The tall stone walls were adorned with tapestries depicting hunting expeditions and noble ladies being brought gifts by fanciful creatures. I had been inside few buildings at all in my short life, and most were barns or humble inns, so it is not an exaggeration to say that I had never seen anything like this home. That the Lord lived there alone was unbelievable to me.

Perla seemed less impressed, as if this were only one of many grand houses that she had visited. She was more excited to see the Lord appear, flowing down the stairs as if he were a living part of the stone, wearing a dark blue evening jacket. She ran up to him, and to my embarrassment, launched directly into his arms. "Perla!" I reprimanded her, but the Lord just laughed and spun her around. He led us to a room with a long table and a giant fireplace built of marble at the far end. The room held the most ornate furniture I'd ever seen. The dark polished wood bubbled and swirled in forms I could not have imagined, turning itself into rams' heads, sprays of wheat, and other whimsical flourishes. One of the many staff pulled a chair out for me and I sat, with Perla across from me. The Lord sat at the end of the table in a chair with a tall back that spired up past his head like a throne. Soon several courses of food arrived. I took only the smallest bites speared awkwardly, taking the lead from the Lord's use of the cutlery, since I was not familiar with such implements. I watched him surreptitiously, matching whatever implement he was employing for the task.

As much as I tried to prompt Perla, she played with the utensils, lining them up and walking them across the dark wood like soldiers, but ate with her hands, as she usually did. The food was foreign and elegant: a smoothly mashed turnip soup that had not a single lump, a glazed pheasant that was so sweet and succulent it melted in my mouth, and a plate of cheeses like I had never seen, with colorful rinds, shot through with blue and green threads. Throughout the dining ordeal, I was torn between being anxious that we would offend by doing something wrong and being tempted to devour the delicacies placed before us. I wished I could do as Perla was doing and just dig in with my hands and suck the juices from my fingers.

I had seen evidence of the intense loyalty of the Lord's staff everywhere I had looked on the estate. This evening, they performed with similarly impressive devotion: though they must have thought we were not worthy of the Lord's company, they behaved as though they were serving nobility. I saw the side of only one mouth curl up when Perla let fly an exalted compliment of a delicious morsel. During this meal, I realized that these were men and women who held the Lord in the highest esteem and would honor any indulgence, even if it involved an unsavory pair of pauper guests.

Finally, we could eat no more. Even with the tiny mouthfuls I had restrained myself to savor, I had eaten more than I had in years. The Lord suggested we retire to the study. I did not know what a study was but followed gratefully. The room was off the great hall and was a strange and intoxicating mix of smells and textures. The overpowering scent of old leather and cedar from the crackling fire filled the space with heat and presence. Busts of large furry animals jutted from the stone mantles: a full stuffed lynx was tucked into a buttress, its teeth in a snarl and haunches taut as if about to pounce. Even Perla was impressed by the creatures along the walls, and she stared up and pointed to new wonders as she discovered them.

We sat on soft leather couches, and I immediately thought I might never get up. We were brought barley tea and tiny cakes and small cordials of sweet wine. The Lord sat across from me, in the dizzying, dancing light of the fire. As I sipped my cordial, I snuck a look directly at him over the glass. As I had imagined when I first encountered him in the woods many years ago, he seemed again sculpted of cool metal, his features smooth and sharp and impermeable. When his eyes went to Perla, though, his face became warm and lively where it had just been molded steel. I marveled at the transformation when he looked at her. Perla had become entranced with a small table of black and white checkered squares with small carved figures. She walked these across the table and began to talk to them and act out great dramas between the dark and light pieces.

"I played the same way with those when I was her age," the Lord remarked wistfully. Then he turned and looked directly at me, studying me. "You know, she bears no resemblance to you."

"She looks like her father," I said, and cast my eyes downward, which the Lord must have interpreted as grief.

"I'm sorry."

I wondered what he could possibly think of me: an orphaned bastard child, a Cigany, now a lone-wandering widow. "You've been very kind to us," I observed. "Not many would be."

"Well, our families are connected." I did not understand at first, then recalled that my Baba and Tata Vornic had known his father and that he remembered them from when he was a child. he continued: "And you remind me of someone."

I waited, but he did not elaborate.

"I lost my own mother very young," he confessed. "My father remarried, but I never became close to his new wife. Then they both died when I was barely a man. The Pestilence took them. I've been alone since. I have an uncle across the mountains, but I have not seen him in many years."

"And no family of your own. You never chose to marry?" I must have been touched by the cordial to be so bold.

"I was engaged. My fiancé was a cousin of my step-mother's. I was not happy about the arrangement so I left for a summer to go stay with my uncle. I thought I could delay the inevitable, and perhaps my uncle could advocate on my behalf. I was summoned back a few months later. The plague had taken them all: my father, his wife, and even my fiancé. I was angry with them and I did not want to marry, but I did not wish for it to end like that. I lost everything. Well, I inherited my father's estate, of course."

"I had an inheritance, too, you know," I said. He looked at me, curiously. "Five goats. Oh, but those are yours now." He burst out laughing.

"Jaelle, you are an odd young lady."

"I must agree with you there, my lord."

"Please, call me Sandor. You are my guest, and no one has called me that in such a long time."

"Sandor?"

"Yes, it's short for Alexandru. I know it's silly: Alexandru Alexandru. My mother always joked that she liked her married name so much that she gave it to me twice! But my family called me Sandor. These days, no one is left who remembers me that way. I became Domn Alexandru when my father died, and no one calls me anything else these days."

"I'm honored, sir." I knew there was no way I could call him by his family nickname, but I was touched.

"Ah! The little treasure has fallen asleep!" he observed. I looked over and saw Perla's head upon the board, her mouth agape and at risk of drooling upon the fine pieces.

"She is not used to such rich food, sir. I'll wake her."

"No!" he stood and with a graceful motion leaned to scoop Perla up. Her head flopped on his shoulder and he looked fondly down at her. "I'll walk you back," he whispered.

His staff fussed and offered to carry Perla back to the cottage, but he shushed them and so they just walked along beside us with a lantern. At the cottage, he lay Perla in our bed of straw and feathers, the softest thing I'd ever had to sleep on, and backed out of the room quietly.

"Thank you, sir."

"Thank you, Jaelle. It was a most enjoyable evening, the nicest I've had in a long time."

∞

Spending time with the Lord became a regular occurrence for me and Perla. He had many duties with the upkeep of the estate. Visitors often came for meals or to meet with Domn Alexandru regarding important financial or security matters. Invaders were coming, and if they arrived there, he and his men might be asked to take up arms. Whenever there was a still evening, however, we were invited to come and dine at the Great House, or sometimes the Lord brought us along to show us a part of the estate that we had not seen yet. Even with more regular contact, I could never bring myself to call him Sandor, and I only called him Domn Alexandru when speaking to others. To me, he was "the Lord" and that's how I referred to him, even in my head.

The estate was like a little village on its own. I had yet to venture into the main town. As it were, I had more than enough of anything I needed right there. Every morning I would wake to a small box of packages on the doorstep of the cottage, filled with food staples like fresh milk and wrapped meat, root vegetables, and cheese. It was more than enough to feed Perla and myself for the day, and people were always stopping by with special treats for Perla. I went to the milking barn to help sometimes, and to collect more milk to make cheese. I soon found there was a hierarchy in the cheese-making process, and when I tried to help with milking or cleaning up, it threw off their whole system.

The man who was in charge was kind, but I soon realized that they were indulging me by letting me help and preferred if I stayed out of the way. They were more than happy to give me milk, however, and I gathered supplies from unused barns and storage sheds to make more presses and molds for the cheese. Only when I came back with some of the first finished cheeses to taste, did Oland, the head of the milk barn and cheese operation, finally seem to notice me as a potential talent. We began to discuss cheesemaking and dairy management regularly, and Oland and I swapped techniques. Any cheese that was finished, I brought to Oland to distribute to the rest of the estate in the seamless functioning of the operation that dazzled me with its efficiency.

Despite my efforts to be useful, people treated us as the guests we were, and no one expected us to work or contribute. I learned a lot about the Lord during this time. As I suspected, every one of the people working the estate held him in the highest esteem. A hard worker himself and expecting the most out of everyone else, Domn Alexandru was always generous and kind to his staff. Many of the older stewards had known him as a little boy and recalled his father having the same temperament: mild and magnanimous. It was rare to have such a kind master. Many of the nobility in the region were fierce and cruel to their serfs. It was not uncommon for a relative of one of the staff to arrive, bloodied and fleeing the vicious tyranny of a count or voivode. Somehow a job was secured for the newcomers, winning their loyalty as well.

There was enough for everyone, and everyone was industrious and mostly cheerful in their duties, as seriously as they took them. Perla and I seemed to get absorbed into the fray of the daily world, with people checking on us and bringing us anything we might need. I might just be thinking I should find some clean sackcloth for cheese when someone would come knocking to deliver me a bundle of freshly folded cloth. I repaired an apron for an elderly neighbor who worked in the laundry. It had gotten caught on a fencepost and tore, but it was simple to stitch up. After that, people sometimes dropped off an item with a ripped seam or popped buttons. With the estate down a seamstress and me living in the seamstress's cottage, it seemed natural to see me as a replacement, especially when I quickly fixed their clothing. I studied the stitches on the items I was given to mend, and my sewing improved to rise to the fastidious standards of the Lord's workforce. Still, they were so gracious in their assignments and lavish in their praise of the completed products that it was clear that they still considered us to be guests of the Lord.

It was about this time that I noticed that Perla, who was different from other children having been raised in relative isolation, was unique in other ways. I'm not sure why I had thought of her sensing Ankah's visitations at the castle a fluke, but somehow I had not considered how this might emerge when we were exposed to others. We had been so busy since arriving at the estate, with such a whirlwind of people, that I had not paid much attention to the names and details that Perla provided me. Shortly, I realized that not only did she know about all of the people on the estate, recalling their names and job duties with exact precision, but she was also recounting the perpectives of the dead. For example, she would inform me that a specific scullery maid's mother was upset with her for not focusing more on finding a man to marry and care for her. Not having been around anyone on the mountain, we also had a shortage of spirits there. In this busy environment, the dead were almost as common as the living.

Once I realized that the intimate facts Perla had gleaned about a person were often coming from their departed relatives, I set out to counsel her about her abilities: "You know it is a family trait, being able to see and speak to the dead. It's called the Sight, Perla."

"But you don't see them?" she asked, not for the first time, still unable to believe that those so present for her were not visible to others.

"No, it's only you who can see them, and others would be upset if they knew."

"But why? It's their family! They have important things to tell them."

"Yes, but others who can't see the dead are scared by people who can see them."

"Well that's silly," she asserted. "If they can't see them and I can, then they should be happy that I can tell them what they're saying."

"I agree, but they will not see it that way. Remember the woman with the dark hair at the castle? She got that awful scar from telling someone what a ghost had told her. It can only bring trouble."

"The lady with the black hair had the Sight, too?"

"Yes, Lyuba, my little light. She had the Sight, but she learned to keep it a secret."

"Who was she, Mama?"

"Ankah. My sister." I choked on the words, not having said her name aloud in years.

"So, you did not get the Sight?"

"No, only Ankah, and now you."

"Can I tell you what they say?"

"Of course, but you must do it in private."

"If there's something really important, can I tell it?"

"No, Perla. It could be dangerous for you to pass on those messages. It is not a talent that people are kind about. They might make us go away if they knew."

She considered this. "What if I find a way to tell them without telling them where it came from?"

"I'm not sure how you could do that, my love, but if you could bring up the concern without letting them know how you know, that might be a way to help the dead feel less anxious and move on. Ankah used to tell me that when the dead stick around, they are very nervous, and very intent on passing on information to their loved ones."

"Oh, yes! They *are* very nervous! They stay close to their family member and chatter in their ear about all their worries."

"That must be hard for you, to see all these people that no one else can. It will be hard not to tell anyone also, but you must do it, to keep us safe here."

"I understand, Mama."

And strangely, she did understand. It must have been a difficult transition for her, going from only having me and the animals as companions in the mountain castle, to being surrounded by people and ghosts. It was overwhelming for me, and I had been around many people before. This was Perla's first exposure to the intricacies of human interaction, and it must have been a lot for a child to deal with. Not to mention having the added complication of deceased people milling around, with rules about who she could talk to about what. Astonishingly, Perla was a master of small talk and social graces. I'm not sure how it happened, after having only me for companionship for her first years, but she was socially flexible, easily striking up friendships with others. Where I was awkward and self-conscious, Perla was confident and smoothly pulled others into warm and comfortable interactions.

To her credit, after our conversation, Perla was cautious but oddly skillful at relaying the messages of the dead. A young baker's assistant, dropping off some rolls to us on his way to bring lunch reinforcements to the barn staff was of particular concern to Perla. "Good morning, Miss Perla."

"Hello, Almos. How are you this fine morning?"

"Quite well, but tired. We are up so early preparing the ovens, and I have not been sleeping well."

"Oh no?"

"No, I just toss and turn, it's terrible."

"I've heard that a good shaking out of the mattress can help," Perla said innocently. "Sometimes the filling gets lumpy and needs a good pounding to get it back into shape."

"Yes, you're probably right. It was my grandmother's bedding. She passed last winter, and no one has probably shaken it out in years."

After he left, Perla leaned over to me and whispered, "It must be hard to sleep with that old woman nagging him all night."

The next day, Almos came by. "Miss Perla! I took your advice! You'll never believe it: there was a bag of coins under the mattress! My grandmother must have hidden it there. My mother was so happy! Now she can pay a dowry for my sister!"

"Oh, my! How wonderful!" Perla said, her delight passing as surprise. When Almos dropped off the rolls the next day and went on his way, she nudged me and said, "Thank goodness! That old woman has finally left him alone. She can rest now, and maybe so can he."

In these little ways, Perla was improving the spiritual welfare of the estate. Not only were there practical matters to attend to, but in some cases, she was able to assist with the grief of both the living and the dead at once. A lovely shepherdess was noticeably despondent in her posture, her slumped shoulders and downcast expression shrouding her youthful beauty. When she came from the fields each day, Perla inquired about the welfare of our goats, who had blended in nicely with the goats and sheep of the Lord's flock. One day, the girl seemed particularly deflated when returning from the fields. "Good afternoon, Miss Beatrix." Perla's cheery voice roused her from her stupor.

"Oh, hello, Miss Perla. Your goats are doing well. They are troublemakers, like all goats, but happy nonetheless."

"Can you stay for a moment, Miss Beatrix? I think my mother has made you something." Perla had prompted me to make a beautiful white collar to replace the one on Beatrix's dress that had become stained and worn. I had spent a long time on the trim that Perla had instructed I should embroider with daisies. When I came from the cottage and handed the young lady the collar, she took it and crumpled, crying piteously.

"There, there," I said and put an arm around her, and Perla wrapped her arms around her on the other side.

When she was able to collect herself, she explained: "My mother loved daisies."

"She passed last year, didn't she?" asked Perla.

"Yes," and the crying erupted again. "She was my whole world."

I ran to get a clean rag to wipe the girl's tears and then stood back.

"She loved you very much, too, I'm sure," Perla said.

"Oh, yes! I was all she had left in the world. All her family died years ago, and my father died when I was too young to remember."

"That is so terrible, to lose the one person you were the closest with," Perla looked at me meaningfully.

"Yes, it's awful. I have nothing left to live for. Sometimes I wish the wolves would come and drag me into the woods." Beatrix seemed startled to hear herself make this confession out loud, but it did not appear to surprise Perla.

"I can see how someone who loses the one person they care most about in the world might want to give up. Sometimes she might even want to walk into the woods and let the wolves take her, just to be together again with the person she's lost." Perla's words struck a chord.

Beatrix nodded and sobbed into her hands again, her tears soaking the new collar.

"I wonder what your mother would say about that? Would she want the wolves to take you so that you two could be together again?" Perla asked, with pensive reflection.

"Oh, no! Mother would not want that for me at all. No, she would be horrified. When she was dying, she told me that I couldn't let her death keep me from enjoying life. She had lost everyone, and she had found joy again in me."

"So, she wouldn't want you to offer yourself to the wolves?"

Beatrix giggled, "No, of course not."

"What do you think she would want for you?"

"She would want me to live: to marry, to have children. There is a young man, but I have not returned his attention." Perla nodded. "I did not want him to get attached when . . . when I was not sure I would still be here."

"Yes, and what would your mother say?"

"That I should allow myself to love him. I should allow him to love me."

"But I wonder, would you feel like you have truly lost her then?" Perla's curious young voice inquired.

"No. No, I guess not. She would want that for me, even if she were alive, and even more so now that she's gone. She would want me to be happy. I'm so sorry. I don't know what's come over me. I seem to have soaked the beautiful new collar your mother made me!" Beatrix stood and held out the new collar, which was still crisp and beautiful despite the tears. She examined the delicate work on the flowers. "You know, one of the last things my mother said to me was that she would always be with me and that I'd know it because the daisies would always bloom. She said every time I saw the daisies I would know she was there and that she would always be with me."

And so, as I sewed and stitched our way into acceptance from our neighbors, Perla provided comfort and counsel. Hardy people as they were, they did not often ask for help. Somehow Perla's unassuming smallness allowed her to get away with delivering messages in a way that people were grateful to hear them. The wise words delivered by this doll-child were palatable. Whereas Ankah had never attempted to use her gift after being struck down so violently, Perla seemed naturally inclined to use her talent for the betterment of others. She had found her calling and was so good at it that it was a little scary. After first being afraid she might reveal her sources, I soon saw that she understood that she couldn't let others know and was careful.

In addition to wanting to comfort the living, I saw that Perla felt a duty to the dead. I often felt it was this concern for the dead–more than the suffering of the living–that drove her to intervene. When Perla was able to resolve the problem that compelled the departed to stick around and they were finally able to leave, this seemed most rewarding to her. Having them mill about and ruminate over their regrets for the living seemed to be the worst kind of torture, and Perla was tortured right along with them. It was like an itch that had to be scratched, and Perla was motivated to find a way to relieve it. She always slept best after helping a lingering ghost finally cross into the unknown. I wondered how Ankah had dealt with it, becoming numb to the grieving of the dead and never doing anything about it: a million itches with no way to scratch them.

Chapter Nine: A Proposal

Winter came on hard. It snuck up on us, lulled as we were by the long, golden autumn afternoons. The weather started to turn, with rain for a solid week, and everything turned to slush. Then it froze overnight and the mud was solid and slippery, with razor-sharp peaks and points. There was an even deeper freeze, and then the snow came, masking everything in sight. I worried about my goats, but like all the other animals on the estate, they were shut up tight in the barns and cared for. The people were no less industrious. After paths were cleared, they went about their daily tasks, albeit a bit slower and more hunched over, bundled in whatever clothing they had, many layers thick to keep out the bitter wind. The Lord made sure we had everything we needed, even delivering fur coats to us. Someone brought us wood for the fire, and the packages of meats and milk and squash were still delivered each morning, though the bundles often stayed frozen for many hours before they were edible. We were invited to dine with the Lord every few days. His spacious house was always cold, though. We ate as quickly as we possibly could in the vast dining hall, which the fireplaces could not seem to defrost, just to get into the study and closer to the fire. I enjoyed his company, but I was always happy to get back to our snug little cottage.

At times, I wondered at the source of his charity for us. He was kind to everyone, so that was not curious, but the lengths he went to ensure our comfort was remarkable. We were so insignificant and lowly compared to him. My view of the world was limited, but I knew enough to understand that we did not fit into the world he lived in. He regularly entertained nobility and planned important defense strategies of the territory with neighboring rulers. We were nothing, and yet he treated us as he would any other fine guest. If his staff found it odd, they hid it well. They may have chalked it up to the Lord's famously generous nature, but perhaps they were drawing other conclusions about his interest in me. I overheard one of the footmen referring to me as the Lord's "lady friend" and something about the ring of it suggested something more romantic.

At first, this seemed unthinkable. I was so far beneath the Lord's station in life, and I had never sensed even the slightest hint of his attention as anything more significant than mere fondness. Still, I knew myself to be inexperienced in this realm, so I had to consider if I might be missing something. After that, I became alert to the Lord's demeanor and the subtle attitudes of his staff. I started to wonder if perhaps even though he could not possibly consider me as a marriage partner, he might want to make me his mistress. Maybe I was the only one who was not alert to this, and even his staff were conspiring to this end. He was an unmarried man, and presumably lonely despite his large estate. I never knew him to have female visitors aside from the wives of his rich guests. No one could blame him if he had the passions of a man.

Once this possibility came into my cognizance, I felt foolish for not having considered it before. It nagged at me, and I distrusted my perception of things. Never having had the sense that the Lord was interested in anything but friendly companionship, I had not considered if it might be improper to be his guest, to dine at his table, or spend nights with him by the fire. Now, I was suspicious of these seemingly innocent activities. What if accepting his hospitality had given him the impression that I was interested in pursuing a romantic relationship? To his mind, I was a young widow, and perhaps more experienced than I truly was. Did he assume I understood his intentions? We were so indebted to him: if he indeed aspired to a physical relationship, how could I refuse him? I lay awake at night wondering how I might deflect his attention if he decided to advance our relationship. I was confident he was not interested in marriage: that would be laughable. However, it seemed more and more likely that a man of his age could only be interested in a woman of mine for one reason. I was upset with myself that it took this long to draw this conclusion, since I may have inadvertently encouraged him.

This new awareness ruined my enjoyment of our time together. I became stiff and formal when we spent evenings together, careful not to make the situation worse by fortifying his intent. Our easy conversations ceased, and I became awkward in our interactions. One evening by the fire, after Perla had played with the carved pieces to her heart's content and fallen asleep with her head on the belly of the Lord's hunting dog, the Lord addressed what had come up between us. "What is it, Jaelle? I have noticed something is different. Do you not enjoy my company any longer?"

"I do, sir. I am very pleased to have your friendship."

"Something is bothering you. I can tell. Please tell me what it is."

"Sir, I don't think I can."

"Come now, your friendship is very important to me. I hope that you can tell me anything."

"I would hate to seem ungrateful, sir."

"Ungrateful?"

"Ungrateful for all you've done for us."

"Well, if I have offended you in some way, please tell me," he said, the look of concern on his face tugged at me, and I felt drawn to reassure him.

"Oh no, my lord. You have not. I just . . . I believe I may have given you the wrong impression."

"Oh?"

"I just would not want you to believe . . . I would not want you to think . . ."

"Go on, Jaelle."

"I am not interested in being your mistress, sir. I am sorry, but I am not. If I have given you this idea, I deeply regret it. We can leave immediately if you wish."

The Lord threw back his head and laughed, startling me. It was not the reaction I had anticipated in any of my nighttime rehearsals of this conversation.

"Yes, yes, I guess that would make sense," he said, almost to himself, continuing to chuckle. I waited, hoping he would explain himself. "You know, Jaelle, I had worried about the same thing myself. I worried if my attentions might be leading you to believe . . . Well, I'm glad we've had this conversation, to put both our minds at ease. I have no interest in drawing you into a clandestine affair."

"Well, that is a relief. Of course, I would never assume you would consider me as a marriage partner. I am sure if you were to marry, your betrothed would be from less humble origins than a shack on the side of a mountain."

His face dropped and he looked suddenly deathly serious, the cold molten iron returning to his features. "If I marry, I will marry who I choose. I learned the hard way that if you spurn your heart in life, you will suffer dearly." He looked at me intensely: "I need to tell you something, Jaelle. I think it will explain many things and reassure you of my intentions. When I saw you the first time many years ago, in the woods by the castle, your resemblance to someone from my past was so uncanny. It was a girl I loved: Alianor." The name rang a bell deeply buried beneath my consciousness. "When I ran away to avoid wedding the woman my father and stepmother intended for me, I journeyed to my Uncle Ulric's to escape. I was young and hotheaded. Staying at my Uncle's, I thought I would hunt and fish and ride throughout the summer, maybe stay through the winter and avoid the inevitable. I even thought that maybe I would never return to Brașov, to my responsibilities. While I was there, I saw Alianor: she was the daughter of one of the keepers of my Uncle's estate who managed the flocks. I loved her the instant I saw her. I pursued her desperately. Eventually, she succumbed to my attentions, but only after I convinced her that I wished to marry her. That was my intention—I want you to know. I had decided that I would marry whom I chose and my parents and the young woman I was engaged to marry could just be damned. It was selfish, but I loved Alianor so completely.

"I had already told my uncle, who did not approve, but he understood something about the mysteries of love. I was preparing to send word back to my parents with my decision when a message arrived. The Pestilence had swept into Brașov. My parents were gone and so was my betrothed, just like that. I was being summoned to return and claim my inheritance, to take over running the estate. I wanted to take Alianor with me, but I wasn't thinking clearly. I was struck with grief. My father had been so kind and so good to me my whole life, especially after we lost my mother. Despite being angry at him for remarrying and his choice of marriage partners for me, I loved him more than anything. I was devastated. My uncle told me he thought it would be disrespectful for me to return with a new fiancé when my parents and dead fiancé were barely buried. I told Alianor I'd send for her in a few months, and Ulric agreed to help when the time came.

"By the time I got established, it was many months later. The financial matters and inheritance were settled quickly, but the estate itself was devastated. We had lost almost half of our staff and overseers. People were still dying, and it was a struggle just to find basic provisions. There were so few of us left. Those who had survived had lost family members, so they were grieving for their dead and afraid of the plague. The estate was running with a small fraction of dedicated people who harvested the overgrown fields and kept the animals from starving. I was pulled into farming, herding, harvesting myself if I wanted to keep it all running. The physical labor was hard, but I could not sit alone in this cold house, so recently departed by my father. Instead, I threw myself into repairing and restoring the fields and buildings. My father had believed in knowing every aspect of running the estate intimately, but as a young man, I had very few responsibilities. After I returned, I had to learn everything without the benefit of his knowledge. Those who were left were my teachers and mentors. Many who worked by my side through that difficult time are still here, working the estate. We developed a bond surviving those desperate times together.

"Alianor inhabited my mind every day, but I was immersed in avoiding the next catastrophe on the estate. I was working so hard to hold it all together that I just kept thinking it was not the right time. Finally, I sent for her, but Ulric told me she had disappeared. She left one day with a small number of her father's goats and no one heard from her again. When I met you, who looked so much like her, when I found you strangely amongst the Ciganyok, I wondered, but it seemed so farfetched. After hearing your story of how you came to live among them, I was sure. Alianor must have been with child when I left. As her condition advanced and I didn't send for her, she must have fled to risk shaming her family. It has hurt me every day since I met you to think of Alianor on the mountain, raising her child—my child—all alone."

I sat waiting, as if there were more to the story, but the Lord was silent. I had been swept up in his struggle, his tale of loss and grief, and the hardship he had endured. My mind was just beginning to put things in order: his servants' inexplicable loyalty, his knowledge of the most mundane aspects of farming and husbandry, his solitary existence. Most importantly, I had begun to understand his intense sadness. I had viewed it first as aloofness, his grave and almost cold expression. However, I had seen that demeanor shift to laughter in a split second and then resume its stone visage just as quickly. Now I understood that this man had known suffering. It was slower to dawn on me how what he was saying related to me. It was *his* story, and he and I were worlds apart. When it finally sank in that I was somehow intricated in his narrative, I felt sure there was some mistake. It was like when Ankah had told me she thought that I was Gildi returned to her.

"So, you believe that I am . . . your daughter?"

"It is the only thing that makes sense to me. If you had seen Alianor, she would be like your mirror image. Of course, when I met you, you were just a little girl, but the resemblance was still undeniable. And there's another thing: it's your eyes."

My Clan had always teased me about my cat eyes. I had little opportunity to see them myself, having only had access to a looking glass on rare occasions, but I had sometimes seen them reflected in water or a cooking pot and agreed the color was like a feline: an unusual greenish gold. They were one more thing that had separated me from my people when I was a child, so I was ashamed of them.

"Come with me," the Lord said, standing and holding out his hand to me. I took it and he led me back out to the Great Hall in the entrance to the manor. There were so many paintings and exotic objects on the walls, I had never been able to take them all in. He brought me to stand in front of a full-length painting of a woman. She was very striking, with gold hair piled on top of her head and an elegant white gown trimmed in gold and green. The embroidery on the dress popped out at me, it was painted with such clarity. I recognized the stitches and knew that Rromani hands had probably made the garment. The woman held a single white rose.

"This was my mother," he said. "Do you see her eyes?" I had been so entranced by her dress I had not noticed, but looking up, I saw that the woman's eyes were a familiar golden hue. "Alianor's eyes were blue," said the Lord. "My mother is the only other person I have known with eyes your color." I stood looking up at this woman, who by the Lord's account was my grandmother. Despite his convincing story, I could not feel any connection to this woman, to him, or to this house, that felt like family. It was a world so foreign that I knew it could not possibly belong to me. We walked back to the warmth and light of the study, with the fire crackling and its fragrant smoke filling the room. When we sat again, I felt as if I was far away, outside of my body. Maybe it was the pungent smoke or the rich food and wine that I was still not used to, but I felt dizzy and removed from myself. "Jaelle, what do you think?" he asked, his expression urgent, imploring me out of my stupor.

"Sir, I . . ." I found it so difficult to find any words. "I am not sure what to think."

"Do you believe you might be my daughter?" I found it hard to respond to this direct question, mostly because I did not. Although the pieces added up, it felt so remote to me that I could not concede this possibility. "Jaelle, I can't see any other explanation. Somehow, Alianor was taken from me, but you have come back to me! I know you are my child, *our* child. You came from love, Jaelle. My love for Alianor." I still could not speak. "This means that you belong here. You belong in this house. It means that Perla is my granddaughter."

This stirred me. It was one thing for the Lord to believe I was his flesh and blood, but another thing entirely that he thought Perla was, too. "No, Sir."

"What?"

"No, she's not your granddaughter."

"But I'm sure. I'm sure you are my child, Jaelle. I've never been so sure of anything in my life."

"That may be true. I may be your daughter. I have a hard time believing it, but I admit the facts are compelling. However, Perla is not your granddaughter. She is not even my child."

The Lord pulled back, sitting up with an alarmed expression. "What do you mean?"

"She belongs to my sister, Ankah. Ankah died in childbirth. I . . ." I began to cry. All of these years, I had never cried. Now I cried for everything: my lost mother, my lost clan, my sister. I had been so alone. I was alone through all of it. Even with Perla–I was on my own to raise her. I had never been able to cry for any of it. The Lord pulled me into his arms and held me. It was the first fully human embrace, other than Perla, that I had known since leaving the Clan. His arms around me unlocked all the emotions I had kept inside through the years of my trials alone, the tears I could not shed because they would have made me too weak to survive. They were tears I felt I did not deserve because I had created my own expulsion. My body convulsed with sobs, and I was overtaken by powerful waves that I could not stop. I cried like that for what seemed like hours, and the Lord just held me, stroking my hair, rocking me against his chest like a child.

Finally, it was all done. I had no more tears and my breathing came in shuddering gasps as I tried to regain control. He disentangled himself to hand me a kerchief and poured a tall glass of wine, which he held out to me. I gulped it down. When I could catch my breath, I looked up at him. His face was serious: "Tell me," he said. I began. It was hard, but I forced the first words to come. I told him about my love for Ankah who had rescued me from death on the mountain. The words began to come easier as I told him how she had raised me, brushed out the knots in my hair, taught me to cook and keep things clean. Then I told him about coming to the castle for the first time, how heartbroken I was that she was to marry and leave me, and how I had agreed to follow her by going with the Badi to wed.

Then I told him about the night Ankah gave birth and her last words to me, instructing me to care for Perla no matter what happened. I described my terror when I found her dead, and my fear for what would become of Perla. Then I told him about my flight, my journey, the wolves, and how I was drawn back to the castle, the only place I could think to hide with her. I came to the time when the Lord came to the castle, his kindness, and how his generosity had helped me through that first winter. He had leaned forward, fully intent and absorbed in my tale as I spoke. When I finished, he sat back and sighed, wiping his forehead. It was drenched in sweat from the heat of the room, which had become stifling. Now he poured himself a glass of wine, leaned back, and sipped it slowly and thoughtfully. It was as if he had forgotten I was there.

Finally, I said, "Sir?"

He looked at me as if remembering I was present. "Jaelle, you have been through so much. No child of mine should have suffered so." He lapsed again into thought, occasionally sipping from his glass and looking up into the dark smoky air.

"Sir, I stole a child. Perla is not mine. She belongs to the Rroma."

"Nobody would ever know that, Jaelle, and from what you have told me, she was better off coming with you. Who knows if she would have even survived if you had not taken her away." This was the one thought that had always reassured me as I questioned my choices throughout the long dark winters in the castle. He had summoned aloud the one possibility that had made me feel as if I had done the right thing. "It makes sense. I thought you were quite young to have a child, but then the Ciganyok marry their children so young. No one would suspect she's not yours. Does she know?" he asked.

"No."

"Good. We will not tell her. She is your daughter. You have earned her." I thought I would have cried so much that I would have no more tears for the rest of my life, but his words stirred more now. Suddenly, he said: "I know what we need to do." I looked at him expectantly. That there could be a solution to any of this seemed impossible, but as always, his confidence was reassuring. "You must marry me." I'm sure my face must have filled with abject disgust at that point, because he laughed again, his big, comforting laugh. "It is the only thing that makes sense.

Listen, Jaelle: no one would recognize you as my daughter, even if I claimed it. It would be suspect, and legally, there is no way it could be verified. You belong here with me, in this house that the Alexandrus have lived in for generations. If we marry, you will have a legal entitlement to live here. No one would ever know, and of course, we would not consummate our marriage. We will need an heir, but we can sort that out later.

"You would live in separate quarters and have full privacy to do anything you wanted. Perla will be well taken care of as my stepdaughter. You need never need to tell her our true relationship. As far as she will know, I will be her mother's husband. No one would dare question my right to marry whomever I wanted. Even if some might wonder at my choice to marry a commoner, no one would or could deny me. One look at your beautiful face and they would believe I was just another victim of love. Actually, I think some of my staff may already think that I had other motives for allowing you and Perla to live here as my guests. They might already reason that I could only be interested in carnal relations with you. It would not entirely surprise anyone if I announced we planned to marry."

I must have been shaking my head, because he stopped and just looked at me for a few moments, clearly expecting a response. When none came, he said, "It may seem strange, this charade, but the whole thing is strange, isn't it? But now that I know for sure you are my child how can I not take care of you? I always suspected, and I cared for you the best I could when you came to live at Vár Buceci, but it is not right for my daughter to have struggled so all these years. It's not right for an Alexandru to live in a little cottage like a servant. It is not fair to you and it is not fair to Alianor's memory. I already failed her so dismally: I will never outlive my shame at not having brought her with me. I'm sure she would still be alive today if I had. I can't make it up to her, but I can make it up to you."

I don't remember the rest of our conversation or leaving to go back to the cottage. The Lord must have carried Perla. He must have said goodnight or told me we'd talk more of things later on, but I don't recall the walk back or anything he said. I fell into bed and the walls came down around me. I slept instantly. Before dawn, I awoke from an awful dream. I was running through a dark forest and carrying Perla. She was a tiny baby again, swaddled in Ankah's star-filled marriage blanket. The wolves were howling. I could not see them, but I knew they were getting closer and closer. I could hear their snarls, feel their breath on the backs of my legs as I ran. I stumbled and fell and covered myself from the teeth I knew were coming. I pulled my cloak above my head for protection, shielding Perla with my own body. Then all was quiet. I pulled the cloak down and looked around, but the wolves were gone. I opened the blanket, but it was empty! Perla was gone! I felt the panic fill my blood as I stood to shake out the cloth. In slowed-down time, out of the blanket's folds floated the knotted red string that Baba had given me. It wafted down, zigging and zagging slowly and silently on the air until it fell upon the dark earth.

∞

The next few days, I avoided the Lord. He invited us to dine through his servants, but I declined, stating I was not feeling well. It was believable, as there was an illness circulating that had many taking to their beds. The winter had taken hold fiercely, and the snow and ice slowed the estate to a near standstill. Even with the whistling wind outside and the dark clouds that made it appear like dusk all day long, the cottage was snug from the fire and cooking pot, as I made stew for Perla that we ate by firelight. While I finished my sewing chores, she played with empty spools, lining the wooden bolts up to converse with each other, or sewing leftover scraps of cloth herself with big, sloppy stitches.

I knew I should respond. I needed to give serious consideration to what the Lord had offered and acknowledge his generosity. He deserved a response. I knew I should be grateful, but terror gripped my heart whenever I thought of marrying him. I had barely absorbed the possibility that my mother was the woman he had loved in his youth, however that seemed to be the truth. Even with no expectation of normal marital relations, marrying the man I had just came to know as my father was overwhelming to dwell on. I pushed it from my mind since it frightened me to panic whenever I reflected upon our conversation or the implications of what he believed and what he had proposed we do about it.

I suppose a different person would have jumped at the opportunity to be brought out of obsolescence, to be provided wealth and security for life, regardless of whether they believed they were entitled to it. I certainly did not feel entitled. The idea of Perla and I moving from our small cottage into the exquisite splendor of the mansion filled me with stifling dread. After many days snowed in and after I had completed every small task I could think of in our tiny home, swept every odd cobweb, and polished every last bowl and pan, I allowed myself to reflect upon my predicament at length while sitting and watching the fire after Perla had fallen asleep one evening. As I sat, I pondered my curious nature: I was not driven to pursue a higher station in life as I knew most young women could only dream. I truly wished I could aspire to be a great lady living in the Lord's home as his wife, if only for Perla's sake. It seemed I was just not made like that, though.

The next day, I prepared to meet with the Lord to tell him that I could not accept his proposal. I determined to tell him that we could stay here on his estate for now, but he would not be burdened with us forever, and would not need to feel indebted to care for us. We would find our own way. If we stayed on the estate for any time, I would work to earn my keep in the cottage. Perhaps it was imprudent to come to this conclusion: I hoped I would not offend him or drive him to ask us to leave for good with my refusal. I sensed that he would want us near, despite not having us as part of his intimate household. What kind of life would that be for him anyway? To be burdened with a wife who is not a wife, preventing him from finding another woman with whom he could truly and honestly share his life and fortune? I told myself that it was in his best interest that I made my decision and hoped to explain it to him in that way.

The afternoon spun by. The gray clouds that had inhabited the sky for days finally parted to allow a whisper of descending sunlight to filter into the cottage windows with fleeting brilliance, teasing us before disappearing completely behind the dark mountain peaks. I waited for the evening knock and invitation from his staff to invite me to dine. I had refused nightly for a week now. Perla was sitting on the floor. She was absorbed in a game of hers that involved a long piece of string tied in a circle. She spun acorns inside the ring, trying to get as many as she could to turn at once.

Suddenly, she looked up and said, "Oh!"

It caught me by surprise, and I turned from the beans I had been shelling for tomorrow's meal. Perla was looking up at something from her place on the floor, but I saw nothing. "Perla?" She turned to me and then turned back to the place in the air. "Is someone here, Lyuba?"

She paused, and then said, "Yes, Mama. She says she's your Baba. She says she's my Baba, too!"

My heart stopped. "Baba! Oh no! My Baba is dead? She's here? Where is she?" Perla pointed and I ran to the spot, holding out my arms, but there was nothing I could feel.

"She says you will upend her if you keep groping her like that!" said Perla.

"Oh Baba, Baba! What happened to you?"

"She says she became weaker and weaker after she heard about what happened to me." She turned to the air: "What do you mean? What did you hear about me?" While she listened, I held my breath, sure the farce of the world I had created was about to unravel.

I almost did not want to ask: "What did she say?"

"She said she heard how you had left with me. You left the Badi—our family—and took me away with you. Did you do that, Mama? I didn't know we had a family! Why did we have to leave them?"

"It was so long ago, Perla. Maybe I made the wrong decision. Did I do the wrong thing? Can you ask her, Perla?" I was almost hysterical: "Please ask Baba if I did the wrong thing! Is she mad at me? Does she forgive me?"

"She says it was the right thing for me but it caused a lot of bad feelings with the Badi. My father . . . my father remarried. He has two boys now. He has moved on. But Sasha . . . who is Sasha? Sasha has not forgiven you. He is still furious at you for leaving." I absorbed this news.

90

Perla told me more with pauses between sentences as she listened to Baba's words: "She needs to warn you . . . it's why she didn't pass on when she died . . . she says they know where you are . . . some of the Lord's men were near the castle hunting . . . they told the Badi that we are living here . . . she says Sasha has organized some of the men to come and punish you . . . to take me! Mama, why would they take me from you?"

I felt icy fear spreading over my whole body. "What should I do, Baba?" I practically shrieked.

"She says you must run. You must go from here where they can't find you."

"Yes, we will go. We will go." I started to look around and think what I needed for our journey. I scrambled to pull a few things we might need together, almost forgetting Perla and Baba all together, my mind whirling with what I had to do to prepare to flee.

"Mama," Perla said, quietly.

"Come, Perla, get your things together. We can't bring much."

"Mama!" she said again, this time with a wail and swallowed sob. She threw herself around my legs and grabbed me so hard I almost fell over.

"Perla, Perla, we must go. What is it? We must get ready. Will Baba travel with us?"

"Baba says I belong with the Badi. She says I am part of their clan."

"What?! No, no it can't be." Even as I protested, awareness dawned on me. It was true. Perla did not belong to me. I had no claim to her.

"Baba is going. She has a long journey. She only came to bring you this message. She is going now to join her husband. She says she has not seen him in a long time. She is going to see him and to be with her other loved ones again."

"No! I need to talk to her! Baba, I need you! I need to talk to you!"

"She is gone, Mama. She was barely here. She just stopped on her way. She said: 'You will know what to do, Lyuba.' She said you always do."

"Perla, my Perla!" I sat and pulled her onto my lap, sobbing. So few tears in so many years, and now I had more than I knew what to do with.

After a bit, she pulled back from me to look at my face. "Mama, what does Baba mean? Why would I belong to them? Is it because of my father? Who is he?"

I told her then. I told her the best that I could about her mother, my beautiful Ankah, and how I had fled with her to fulfill my promise to keep her safe, fearing that she would die if she only had her father's mother to care for her. She listened with wide eyes and asked questions about her family, about the Badi.

"My . . . mother is the one with the scar, isn't she?" she asked. I nodded. "Would the Badi hurt me?" she asked, wondering.

"No, no Perla. They are kind people, good people. Your father, Mihai— he is a very kind man. He was so wonderful to Ankah. . . to . . . your mother. He made her so happy. You were born out of the best kind of love."

"But they will hurt you?"

"I believe so. I betrayed them. I stole you from them."

"Then I will go with them. I will make it right. Then they will not hurt you and I will be with my father and my brothers." She pulled her chest up straight with conviction. "I have brothers, Mama!"

"Yes, yes, I suppose you do."

"This is the way it is supposed to be. You will always be my true Mama. Even though Ankah gave birth to me, she died! I would have had no one. I would have died, too! You needed to take me, to be my Mama. And now I need to go back to my other family."

I recognized that Perla had made up her mind. Despite how it cleaved my heart in two, I knew she was right. The wheel of fate had turned on me again, and my path was chosen. This time, I would be truly alone on the journey.

Part Two

Chapter Ten: The Weavers

The cacophonous racket of the tavern drowned out any thought or memory. It was a nightly ritual that made the dwelling on unpleasant feelings almost impossible. For that, it was a blessing. Most nights, since I had come to Alba Jula, I fell, exhausted, into instant slumber, drained completely from the grueling work. I had came upon the tavern, with its amber glow pulling me off the frigid streets and had found kindness in the husband and wife who owned it. Flora was a large, doughy woman with a radiant smile. When I explained to her that I had run from a marriage to a man I could not love, she understood. She had been a young woman herself, not too long ago.

Flora and Wilk had been running the tavern since they married and took it over from Wilk's father, a frail old man who sat in the kitchen most days, roasting and eating chestnuts. Sometimes they could get him to do small chores, like peeling potatoes, but mostly he sat and picked small particles of nut meat from the shells that littered the floor beneath the stool upon which he sat most of the day. There was another young woman who prepared food in the kitchen while Flora served the rowdy clientele. Until I came, the girl had also had to wash dishes and scrub pots, so she was eager to have my help. My hands quickly became red and chapped from the work, but I barely registered the discomfort. The toil in my heart, a deep pervading sadness, would not budge despite my body's complaints from standing all day and leaning over the never-empty sink.

The young woman's name was Vania, and she had been with Flora and Wilk since she was barely more than a girl. She was orphaned young. She would have been destitute if Flora had not taken pity on her, taught her to cook and bake. Vania was a few years older than I was, I guessed, with skin pale and pickled from the lack of sunlight and unforgiving climate of the steamy kitchen. She was a serious girl, who rolled out bedding and slept in the pantry at night, rising in the morning to start the baking for the day before most were opening their eyes. Wilk and Flora lived in a small apartment above the tavern, and Wilk's father slept in a room off the kitchen in the back since he could no longer navigate the steep stairs. It was in the father's room where I slept upon some blankets in the corner. Everyone called the man *Tati,* even the customers, and I never knew his true name. He was a sweet, childlike entity, who barely spoke, but smiled constantly. I took over care of Tati, keeping him clean and dry and waking in the night to help him find the soiling pot, relieving Flora of the burden of her father-in-law's daily needs.

Alba Jula was a busy metropolis, compared to many of the places I had been. It was said to have been built upon an ancient Roman settlement, and crumbling white walls ran through the city from that time. Many who frequented the tavern worked the surrounding estates during the day and toiled in a life cruel and unforgiving. For a few hours, they came to abandon their cares with others, to cling to some simple merriment that made the long days of labor easier to bear. The effort of running the tavern kept us all busy and working the end-to-end expanse of each short day with few moments of reprieve, but it was not altogether unpleasant. Our responsibilities kept us suspended in motion, with barely a moment to rest. This suited me fine, and it seemed to suit Vania, too. Even in the slower evenings with few customers when we had time to sit and sip a cup of broth, we did so in companionable silence, each of us thinking our own thoughts and rarely conversing. We worked well together and did not need to talk much to accomplish our tasks. I was relieved that after my first introduction and remarks about my unusual accent, no one showed any curiosity about who I was or where I had come from.

I had little time to sit and dwell upon the past or what I had lost, but my grief snuck up and punched me right in the gut when I least expected it. I would see a bowl of acorns and think of Perla's spinning tops on the floor of our cottage. A whiff of flour would remind me of the scent of her hair when I stood over her, helping her knead out bread. I tried not to think where she was: if she liked being a big sister, if the Badi were treating her well. I suspected Violca would put Perla to work as a fortune teller as soon as she realized she had the Sight. I hoped our lessons about prudence in revealing too much of what she knew would help temper the demands of the Circ.

I also tried not to think of the Lord. Now that I was far away from him, I could finally think of him as Sandor. I pushed away the memory of how he had looked the night I had told him I was running. I could not explain how I knew about the Badi coming, since he was not aware of Perla's gift to see the dead. I told him the intelligence had come from a runner from the Clan who came to warn me of the plan to bring a mob to the estate. Although I had finally given Sandor a name, I could still not think of him as my father. He held my hands and told me he would protect me from the Ciganyok, that I need not fear if I wanted to stay there. He even said he would not let them steal Perla from me, and that his men would take up arms to make sure they would not kidnap her or harm me. He even said he would evict them from the old castle and make them move on if they raised a hand against us. To think of those families jettisoned into the cold winter due to little more than my selfishness was too much to bear: I begged him to leave them be and let them continue to stay in the castle every fifth winter as they had for generations.

I know he did not understand. My decision to run to avoid a skirmish and Perla appearing resolved to return to them encouraged him to accept our choice, although he did not agree with it. He had kept Perla with him in the great house until the Badi came, with instructions to hand her over peacefully when they arrived. He gave me a thick fur coat that had been his mother's and some gold coins for my journey before packing me into a carriage to deliver me several towns away to get a head start. He said I could return at any time, and he would still honor his proposal. Sandor insisted he still wanted to acknowledge me as his family and this was the only way he could see for the law to allow it to be so. I told him that he should not wait for me but should marry his heart's choice. Tearfully, Sandor told me that his heart's choice had died with Alianor, and there would be no other to replace her.

Our dog, Stea, who had guarded Perla since she was a baby, would go with her to the Badi. I implored Sandor to make it clear that if they were to take her, the dog would have to go along. In Alba Jula, it gave me some small comfort to think of Stea curled at Perla's feet at night when I could not be there to hold her as I had every night since she was born. I barely recalled my parting with Perla, since it had been so excruciating for me that I had partially blacked out. I only recall us clinging to each other before parting and handing her a knotted red string to hold until we could be together again. I think I knew as the carriage left the manor gates that I was unlikely to see her again: I was losing her forever.

As I sat, chopping onions in the kitchen of the tavern, I recalled the journey of many days that brought me to Alba Jula. Sandor's carriage had dropped me in the next largest city, and there I connected with a caravan of Rroma heading to Sebeș. While they looked sideways at my rich fur and Gentle appearance, my fluent use of their tongue and strategic name dropping bought me passage and safety for a time. We parted at Sebeș, and I continued north on foot until, cold and depleted, I had come upon the white walls of Alba Jula and refuge in the tavern. The whole journey was a numb blur as I reflected upon it seated in the tavern kitchen, punctuated by a deep empty feeling like hunger in my gut. As I peeled and sliced the onions, I did not use the Rromani trick of holding a stale piece of bread in my mouth while cutting the glistening white orbs, and so no one questioned the tears running down my face.

∞

I passed the winter in the tavern, still in a daze of grief. When the thaw of spring came upon the city, with trees unfurling phosphorescent green leaves, I felt as if my own blood had thawed. Having heard of Deva as a center for trade, I had always wanted to see it and the magnificent castle there. With veins of gold shooting through the mountains, mining was a large enterprise, and Deva was known to be a rich and lively city. I saw it as a place I could get lost. Overhearing the fortune-seekers dreaming over ale in the tavern, I came to understand the easiest way to get there was by boat on the Mureş River. A local sheep merchant told me he had commissioned a barge to transport bundles of wool to sell in Deva the following week. No one seemed surprised when I told them I was moving on. Flora pulled me to her ample bosom, wishing me well, and Vania nodded her farewell with the same nonchalance that she had welcomed my arrival at the tavern, my departure only calculated in the extra work that would be required of her.

The sheep merchant was courteous and gave me suitable privacy on the barge. He did not charge me fare, although I offered. When we arrived, he busily began arguing with the handlers at the port about how to unload his bales of wool and brushed off my gratitude, wishing me a safe journey. The sights and smells of Deva hit me as soon as I stepped off the barge. Vegetable markets, brimming with the first shoots and bounty of spring wafted green decadence, mixing with the aroma of spices from the herb sellers, engaged in brewing teas for every ailment. I immediately saw the need for the merchant's bales of wool: the most colorful carpets and fabrics I had ever seen were draped over stalls and on the arms of young sellers who asked passersby to feel the silky sheen of the woven threads. Intricately painted pottery was stacked in tall rows and gold jewelry stalls were guarded by large intimidating men. Elaborately decorated jewel-toned eggs were on display, with young women engaged in the art of applying dazzling patterns and swirls. And, of course, the Rroma were there, selling ironwork or embroidered goods, or clustered around a cape laid out with gold and silver trinkets.

Despite not knowing anyone or even having a place to stay, I at once felt more comfortable than I had felt in months. The overlapping scents and dizzying merchandise, combined with my anonymity, filled me with an unexpected sense of wellness. I wandered through the stalls, looking at items and watching the busy transactions. You could barely tell where the market ended, since the alleyways spidering out from its fringes were laden with crafts and colorful shops, selling a great variety of items and services. I stopped in front of a tavern, briefly considering going in to seek work. Recalling the grueling heat of the kitchen, and feeling my hands still chapped and irritated from the work, I continued on my way. I bought a roll from a baker, then a small wedge of sweet sheep's milk cheese from a young man selling perfect rounds, glistening in the morning sun.

One could easily get lost in the branching and winding streets. With no frame of reference and little ability to judge where I might be heading, I made my way, soaking in the sights of everyday life in Deva. Everywhere I looked there was something new. Potters sat at their wheels, spinning with hands skillfully forming fluid shapes while assistants stacked dried products to be fired in open kilns. An open courtyard revealed what appeared to be women practicing a dance routine, dressed in colorful embroidered gowns while a drummer sat and tapped out a rhythm on a taut hide stretched over a clay drum. I watched a skinny dog steal a sausage from a butcher's cart, and the butcher, red faced, chasing it.

I had traveled through many cities, but always as a part of a Rromani caravan. Our arrival had frequently drawn scorn and even aggression. It had been stressful arriving in a new place, unsure of the reception we would receive. For the first time, I felt invisible. I could be a passive observer and not have all my attention going to keeping myself safe. It was a liberating feeling, to travel through a world that did not immediately judge me as different and dangerous. At the edge of my enjoyment of this new experience was a twinge of guilt that felt like betrayal. My people, those who had raised me, did not have the luxury of going unnoticed. Once again, I felt the deep, sad truth that I did not really belong anywhere.

Finally, I came to what appeared to be the edges of the commercial district of the city and my view was not blocked by buildings. Out of the expansive flat landscape, a single mountain peak with an imposing stone fortress at the top rose glistening in the sun. I knew this must be the grand palace at Deva, since this one monolithic mound was the only feature to the area. It looked surprisingly stark and foreboding, though, rather than splendid as I had imagined. Farms and estates skirted the bottom of the mount, sprawling out in all directions in subjugation to the fortress's dominance. The farmland came right up to the edge of the complex maze of busy streets and shops that I had just left. After the convoluted mountains I had navigated my whole life, this dramatic scenery felt so foreign. Yet in stark contrast to the displaced feelings I had only moments before, the perspective of standing and looking out over the green patchwork to see this grand monument felt exactly right to me. Absorbing the impact of the view, I felt as if I had come home.

I began to walk in the general direction of the mountain, on small rambling paths between tiny homesteads, all visually dwarfed by the single massive hill in the distance. Chickens and unkempt dogs ran underfoot, and dirty children played and shrieked with laughter. Harried women ran to check on a crying baby before returning to whatever tasks absorbed her. Old men sat smoking pipes and looking up at the sky, speculating about the weather. At the perimeter of all the activity were emerald geometric segments of farms, creating a verdant mosaic of interjoining angles already flush with new green abundance.

I approached one small farm, which had a muddy paddock absent of livestock. Most likely the animals had been led out somewhere to graze for the day. There were some fruit trees and a vegetable garden, but no place for grazing. What drew me in to this particular homestead was the quick movements of a young woman working a loom under an open patio off the side of a small tidy shack. A baby sat at her feet and played with empty spools on an old worn carpet as the woman chose different colored threads off a rack to feed into her machine. Her darting hands moved a small shuttle between the threads. Finished wares were folded or hung on racks in colorful layers. I had never learned to use a loom, and I was impressed by her efficient labors. The cloth she was producing was a very fine quality, a contrast of smooth refinement against the humble surroundings of the simple house.

"Greetings, madam," I said as I approached, and she looked from her work as if startled from a dream.

"Greetings."

"I have never learned to work a loom. Your talent is extraordinary!" The woman looked down, embarrassed, and mumbled thanks for the compliment, clearly unused to being recognized in her daily work. "I am new to this region, and I wonder if you might have room and board?"

She looked surprised at my request. "We have nothing here," she said. "It is just my husband and our children, and the sheep."

"I do not require much. I can sleep outside—over there on the porch. I can help with the children and the housework. I wish to learn to use the loom as you do, so I will do whatever is needed if you might be willing to teach me."

The woman looked slightly suspicious, but I could see a brief flicker of hope cross her eyes at the prospect of assistance with her daily chores. "I would have to ask my husband. He has gone to market, but he will return this evening."

"Shall I return then?"

"Yes. Yes, but I can't make promises."

"Of course. And what is your name, madam?"

"Liana," she said, "and this little miss is Havaska. We call her Vaski, right Vaski?" she spoke down to her daughter, lilting her voice up and smiling down at her to catch the little girl's attention. Vaski smiled up at her mother and waved her little fists, clasped around some bunches of tangled thread.

"She's delightful," I said, truly meaning it despite the sting in my heart.

"And you are?" Liana asked.

"I am Alianor," I said, barely thinking. "Alianor Alexandru."

∞

I walked around on the small dirt paths between farms and small cottages. I saw many homesteads similar to the one I had just visited. All had meager gardens and some animals, children scattered and either playing or completing chores depending upon their age. Most homes seemed to be engaged in some craft or food production. Many were weavers like Liana, and had looms filled with carpets and fabric, each artist seeming to adopt a slightly different style of interpreting patterns and color variations. Even seeing so many different weavers at work and comparing their wares, I knew I had made the right choice. Even the best of them paled in comparison to Liana's exceptional product.

After walking a while, I stopped to greet an old woman picking peas who reminded me of my Baba. She walked me through her herb garden, pointing out the plants and telling me different ailments they could be used for. I liked her and helped gather eggs from her ducks. I cooked them up for her in an omelet seasoned with fresh chives and the bright green peas. The woman, whose name was Johanna, said no one had cooked for her in years. I told her I would visit her another day. When I left, she kissed my cheeks and told me I reminded her of her daughter who had moved away to join her husband and start a family many years ago. She had not heard from her since the Pestilence had swept through, now well over a decade ago. She feared she had died, or surely she would have visited or sent news. My heart was heavy as I walked away, waving back at Johanna as she stood at her gate, watching me depart. I wondered how many families were ripped apart by the disease, and how many generations it would take to heal.

Everyone I encountered seemed caught up in the demands of their daily lives. Although I was a stranger, all seemed open and friendly to me. Again, I was struck by the difference of traveling alone as someone who appeared to be a Gentle woman, as opposed to the anger and suspicion leveraged at my tribe when we traveled together in unknown territory. Although I had a few people comment on my unusual accent, no one seemed particularly concerned that I could be a threat. When I had wandered most of the day, I started to see the shepherds coming back. They were returning from the far mountain ranges that made up the low shallow basin surrounding the palace mount, which rose in the center overlooking it all. Mostly older boys led herds of animals back to their farms. There were some mules, oxen, and cows, but mostly sheep. I saw few goats. Even with the bountiful local production of wool, it was still not enough to provide for the diversity of textiles I had seen. This further explained the need for someone like the sheep farmer I had caught the barge with from Alba Jula to ferry in supplements of wool.

I followed an older boy, maybe 12 or 13, herding a few dozen sheep back along the footpaths. I realized he must be Liana's son when he turned the sheep in and led them into the gate that held a small enclosure attached to their larger paddock. I followed behind and introduced myself as an acquaintance of his mother's and asked if I could help. The boy, whose name was Damir, led the sheep one by one into a narrow channel between the smaller and larger pen. As each one went in, there was a board that slid down to lock her into place while Damir sat behind on a little stool and milked her out. When one was done, he pulled up the board and put it down again for the next sheep to file in. It was a very efficient system, and I was impressed with not only the mechanics of the design, but Damir's studied handling of the milking process. I offered to take a turn. Surprised, Damir handed me his stool and laughed when I filled the bucket with speed. There were only about two dozen sheep, so the whole process did not take long, but produced four large buckets of milk.

Damir complimented my milking and was even more astonished when I easily hoisted two of the heavy buckets and walked with him toward the house. Liana, noticing us coming up with our buckets, ran to grab the ones I carried. Thanking me, she immediately began to pour some into a large pot on the outdoor brick hearth. Another smaller pot was simmering with some broth and vegetables, and she had been in the middle of chopping new onions and parsley to add to the steaming froth. Just as she returned to her chopping, little Vaski started howling and pulling at her skirts. Damir stepped in and lifted Vaski up, nuzzling her belly and making her laugh, but moments later the baby was howling again.

"She always gets cranky this time of day," Liana explained, taking the baby from her son and sitting down on a bench against the house to nurse her. I took up where Liana had left off with the chopping and saw relief upon her face. As she sat nursing her babe, her shoulders dropped and released the tension that had been there. After a few minutes, the girl had fallen asleep, her mouth wide open around her mother's breast, but no longer suckling. "I'll just put her down so I can finish," she said, and began to tuck away her breast to prepare to stand up.

"No, it's fine, I can take care of it, Liana. Allow me."

Liana sat back, still cradling her sleeping child, and watched as I stirred the warming milk and the soup. I noticed she had a dough for flat bread prepared, so I rolled and flattened some between my hands and fried these up on a cast iron pan atop the stove with a little ghee and some herbs and garlic thrown in. Liana watched me with her head tilted back, resting against the outer wall of the little cottage. As the sun began to slip down the sky and behind the far mountain range, it lit up the palace, pouring pink and amber light over the cold gray stone. Damir had run to fetch his younger brother, Liana's middle child Filep, from a nearby yard where he had been playing with friends.

By the time Liana's husband, Janek, came walking up the path to his home, dinner was prepared and ready. Vaski had awoken from her nap and was sitting on my lap sucking on a chicken bone, and Liana was ladling out the soup for her husband and the rest of us. She introduced me briefly, telling him that I was new to Deva and had helped her and Damir with the work that evening. After the meal, we all sipped some of the warm milk and listened to Janek tell of his day at market, of the few remnants he'd sold, and the rich merchants who came to buy the wares and re-sell them for much higher prices in other cities. He told a hilarious tale about a stodgy old merchant who tried to talk him down to a quarter his original price, and how Janek had tricked him into paying double by the end. We were all laughing heartily by the conclusion of the tale. It had been so long since I had laughed.

I helped Liana clean up and set up the rest of the milk for cheese. Without discussing anything further, Liana pulled out some carpets and blankets and laid them out on the far end of the outdoor patio for me. As far as I knew, there was no conversation with Janek or formal decision made about my being able to stay. Somehow, I was pulled into the midst of their family as if I had been a visiting relative, and no more was said about it.

Chapter Eleven: Abundance

I had not realized I had been asleep, but being around lively children and the smells of animals and things growing roused me from my stupor. The past winter at the tavern seemed like a dream, and my departure from Domn Alexadru's estate seemed an eternity ago. Now I sat in this expansive bowl of budding garden and family, with the Grand Palace of Deva always hovering in the backdrop with its subdued tones. The fortress was like an entity, I discovered, and I sometimes had the sense that it was a person, watching out over the landscape. Some said that one of the stone masons who had built the castle a hundred years before had sacrificed his wife and mixed her remains in with the mortar to destroy a curse and keep the stone from collapsing. Perhaps it was she who watched over the plains, a silent sentinel built into the stone.

I knew little of the voivode who lived in the castle and ruled over the territory. The last Duke, a prince of Hungary, had died young, leaving behind a wife and two small children. Since he had been governing for just a year and his brother only a brief time before him, it seemed no one felt connected to the ruling class. A new ruler of the region was appointed, and little was known about this one, except that he was a fierce military leader who had successfully fended off several Mongol invasions, and so was viewed favorably by the populace. I would hear gossip sometimes, about the aristocrats and nobility who were involved in the running of the city—which one had a son who was a drunk, whose wife was philandering with a neighboring count—but it interested me little. I was aware of the fine houses dotting the slope of Cetatii, the peak atop which the castle lay, but it seemed like another world. The village where Janek and Liana's house sat, was referred to by all as "the Commons." Some of the people had jobs with the rich families and vague royalty who lived surrounding the citadel. It was considered very fortunate to work in a fine home instead of laboring in the fields or markets or toiling away over a loom.

For me, toiling at a loom seemed a luxury. Liana was pleased with how quickly I caught on, and shortly Janek built a second loom for me to work side-by-side with his wife. I learned the subtle techniques that made Liana's fabrics shimmer and rise to a level above the pretty utilitarian cloth that was omnipresent, however varied. Liana's attention to detail and careful weaving led to a remarkably smooth surface that sparkled in the light. I soon learned that she used a thick oily substance derived from her sheeps' wool to keep her calloused fingers from catching on the strands and which gave the fabric a glossy sheen. Liana was proud when I was able to recreate the effect, and even more surprised when I created variations that improved upon on her designs. These began to bring in more than Liana's own cloth, and soon there were even commissioned requests for my designs. Whatever finances came in, I declined, no matter how often Janek offered to give me more than a fair share. I assured him that the food and companionship was payment enough, and that the skills his wife were imparting upon me were priceless.

I had family in many forms before, but I don't think I had ever had a friend. There was Isa, whom I had loved, but she quickly became a sister to me, and that relationship subsumed our friendship. Liana was different. I enjoyed her company tremendously. She was quite a bit older than me, but I felt we were similar in so many ways. She was hardworking and thrifty, making do with the stingy allowance life had doled her. She wondered at my comfort with Vaski, and I explained that I had cared for my niece for many years from the time she was a baby. Together, we cared for the children and traded off responsibilities, sometimes fetching Filep to watch his sister so we both could work. Liana did not like to rely on Filep, since she felt it was not a boy's role to care for babies, but she was a pragmatist. She confided in me that she had lost a child, a stillborn girl, in between having Filep and Vaski. She grieved for this girl, who would have been the natural caretaker for Vaski, had she lived. It was a hole that could not be filled, so she made do and sought help from Filep when it was required to complete her tasks. In her loss, I also felt our alliance, though I would not speak of my particular flavor of mourning.

The muddy footpaths and bare shrubs sprang forth with grasses and blossoms, and the Commons dripped with pollen from the fruit trees and gardens. What had seemed minimalist when I had first arrived now seemed lush and abundant. Although I had worried about explaining myself to others in the community, Deva was where I found that people overall are not very curious about anyone except themselves. A sentence or two, and most people will accept your story at face value and seek only to tell their own. I realized I could be anyone I wanted. I had always been a truthful person, so fabricating a past was not comfortable to me. Instead, I found a flowery snippet from my past could be spun into a quick tale, and no one was the wiser. I could say, "When I saw the Circ perform . . ." or "When I was a seamstress on a grand estate . . ." and present a few details that created the illusion of a normal life, and people just filled in the rest in their minds.

While I was simply focused on learning a trade with which to support myself, it seemed I had attracted attention just by being in the community. Unfortunately, it was not just my talent at the loom that was drawing mothers of marriageable young men to stop by to chat with me and Liana about the weather and what new things were in season at the markets. After a matriarch had ambled away, Liana would raise her eyebrows at me and tell me the backstory: "Her son is the one with the big nose who smells like manure."

I realized I was of an age that people would expect me to be seeking a husband, but truly that was the last thing on my mind. I had escaped two prospective marriages of convenience, and I did not wish to pursue another one. Not that marriage to any of the young men in the Commons would be convenient. I saw being tied to a husband, especially here, as a burden more than anything that would bring me comfort in life. Also, after raising and losing Perla, I had no interest in having children, despite the joy I found in Liana's. When I was not weaving, I was perfectly happy to walk around with Vaski on my hip, pointing out pretty flowers to her, or helping Filep learn to spin a top, or milking the sheep or sheering wool with Damir. I loved the little family life I had stumbled upon, but I had no desire to carve out my own place in the world with a man and children of my own.

Even so, the mothers stopped by and chatted with us, and sometimes paraded their sons by to casually introduce them. Most of them *did* have big noses or smelled like manure, so I found none of their charms particularly appealing. I was still young enough that no one thought it odd that I was not intensely pursuing marriage, and most seemed to find my lack of interest to be rooted in modesty. If anything, I was swept up in the art of the loom; learning how to turn threads into shimmering fabric was what filled me with passion. I acknowledged my good fortune at choosing the most gifted weaver to teach me her craft. The fact that she was also a lovely person and becoming a dear friend made the discovery even sweeter.

As spring gave way into steamy summer, our habits shifted to accommodate the hotter weather. We woke early, as Damir herded the sheep out of the crooked gate up to the hills in the morning mist. After working all morning, we would rest in the shade for part of the afternoon before resuming our weaving until our evening meal. At least once a week I would visit the old woman, Johanna, and cook her a meal while she spoke to me about her life and losses. It felt the smallest thing I could do for her. Helping my hosts also felt like the least I could do for their hospitality, and I assisted in any way I could find to make their lives a little easier. With the extra money brought in by doubling the family's production, Janek was able to purchase some necessities for the home, upgrade and repair some items that were failing, and even buy an occasional treat for the children or his wife. I continued to refuse any payment or gifts, but I did use some of my newly woven cloth to sew myself a light green dress that had pale yellow and saffron threads blended in like a sunrise. Liana admired it so much, that I made her a dress, too, to replace her standard dun-colored garment that had lived through many repairs and too many seasons.

The dress I made for Liana was a deep midnight blue, and I used some of the embroidery skills I recalled from watching Ankah for so many years to sew a border of stars and swirls reminiscent of the marriage blanket Baba made that I still carried with me. When Liana tried the dress on completed for the first time, her eyes filled with tears. Even Janek, who was returning from the market, was impressed by his wife in her new dress. He picked her up and twirled her around, telling her he'd marry her all over again. It made me proud to see evidence of how my contributions enhanced the little world they had made for themselves. It quieted the gnawing ache that always lingered, just behind my belly and near my heart.

∞

Word came that the wool that we had sent to be processed in the early spring was ready to be picked up. There was a family at the foot of the mountains that Janek and Liana had relied on for many years for all their spinning and dying. It did not account for all the thread Liana needed for the year to make her wares, but it was a sizeable amount. Janek decided that we should all go together to pick it up, since we were so far ahead in the production. He borrowed a pair of horses and a cart for the journey from a wealthier neighbor, so we packed some supplies and headed out. Filep, Liana, the baby, and I piled in upon some blankets and carpets in the back. Filep was very jealous of Damir, who sat up front next to his father to learn to drive. I tousled Filep's hair and distracted him until the sour look on his face was replaced with one of excitement for the journey.

It was only a few hours' drive, but we set out at daybreak and stopped mid-morning for a picnic along a branch of the Mureș. It was a glorious day, and my heart swelled as we sat and watched the boys run and the baby toddle about after them in the tall wildflowers. While there was much love in this family, there was not much time for taking holidays. We were all exhilarated with the novelty of being free from daily chores and enjoying the brilliant June day and each other's company. I watched the light play on Liana's face, which was more relaxed than I'd ever seen it, and saw what her husband must have seen in her to want to marry her years ago. She caught my eye and smiled and pulled me next to her in in a warm embrace. Together, we watched the children tumble about, until Janek told us we'd better get on our way.

When we arrived in the shaded hills at the foot of the mountain, the air chilled and a slight breeze cooled the sweat on the horses' necks. The road wound through a thick deciduous

108

woodland dotted with majestic evergreens. We came upon the family's settlement, which was the size of a small village, with houses, outbuildings, and sheds covering the forested mountainside. The patriarch came to greet Janek, and his wife, a weathered but hearty woman, kissed Liana's cheeks and mine when I was introduced. There were dozens of family members, some introduced to me and many just milling about, and many children who immediately seized upon Damir and Filep and drew them away to play. Since I had never been there before, we were given a tour of the operation for my benefit, which was impressive in its magnitude. There were barns to store the bales and balls and skeins of wool, and whole buildings devoted to spinning and dyeing, filled with spinning wheels and barrels in all shapes and sizes.

The process spilled outdoors to basins and racks set up for washing and drying, and thread in all stages of development. The wife described the process and how all the machinery worked. She pointed out vats, explaining how some of the creamy white product was dyed before spinning, some dyed after spinning, all depending upon some involved formula that I had trouble following. She elaborated upon the raw materials that made up each color. I was astounded to hear how some of the pigments came from so far away, while many, like the nut husks used to make some of the darker threads, were harvested right there on the mountain. The crowning glory of the tour was the barn where the finished product was stored. Outside I had noticed some young men chopping wood and carving out cones and bobbins that were stacked in giant pyramids. Inside, the carded and spooled threads in rainbows of colors were piled to the rafters.

While at first it appeared that there was no organization to the teeming towers of threads, it soon became clear that they were arranged by customer, separated into sections depending upon who had commissioned the finished merchandise. Janek's order was placed aside, and the husband knew precisely where it was stored. We moved the cart to right outside the barn, and family members began helping hand-over-hand to send out the spools. I had observed Liana's dwindling supply of thread stored in an enclosed room off the back of their house, sealed to keep out the rodents and other critters. Now as they packed everything into the cart, I wondered how it would all fit in that small room, and also how we would fit back in for the return trip. Apparently, they had encountered that particular challenge before, because when it all was complete, they had left a little room carved out in the back with the tall spools stacked against the sides, enough for a few people to fit snugly.

Janek worked out the final financial details with the husband while we said our goodbyes to the wife. She sent a son to fetch a big jug of mead and several jars of honey from their own hives as parting gifts. It took some time to gather up the boys, who were dismayed to leave their friends' company, but soon we were ready to depart. Filep was ecstatic to be smooshed up in front between his father and Damir, and Liana and the baby and I piled in the little chamber in back and we were on our way.

We waved goodbye to the family, who all came out of their houses and away from their work to wave, children lined up and jumping and hollering their farewells. We could not even see the menfolk in the front, the yarn was stacked so high. We slowly ambled onto the narrow lane, the load a significantly increased burden for the horses. In the back, Liana and I adjusted ourselves in with Vaski, who had grown fussy and wanted to nurse. We lay back upon the folded blankets and the uneven melody of the rocking and jarring cart becoming a soothing accompaniment to the underlying steady rhythm of clomping hooves. We soon fell asleep with our heads together and the baby nestled between us.

Chapter Twelve: Along the River

Summer eased peacefully into autumn, and our abundance continued. It was not long before the nights became cool. It was chilly in the mornings as I awakened on the floor of the porch. Liana began to speak of when we would move the looms indoors, since in the winter months it was not possible to work in the open air. I had rarely been inside Janek and Liana's house–I had no purpose to go in, and felt it invaded their privacy. One cold morning, Liana brought me inside and showed me where she thought we could set up the second loom. Janek was on his way to the market, and nodded, saying that we would need to bring my bedding inside soon, too, and that I could set up next to the children. In the dim light of the cabin, something contracted inside of me at this generous suggestion. I asked Liana if she minded if I took the day off from work and told Janek I would accompany him to the market, as I had some things to buy. They seemed puzzled, but agreed. Janek and I soon walked the meandering streets to the edge of the city, and then through the narrow alleys filled with shops toward the main market and the docks.

I had not been back to the city since the first day I had arrived in Deva. It was less lively this time of the day. The streets were empty except for some early shopkeepers starting to sweep off their steps, or peddlers navigating carts over the uneven cobbles to take their wares to set up in the market. Since I was coming along anyway, I had offered to carry extra rolls of cloth for Janek to sell, telling him I would come back in the evening to help bring them back. When we got to the edge of the market, we set up in a small wooden stall and I helped Janek roll out reams of cloth and lay them over the table and hang them against the back of the stall. I realized I must have walked right by him on the day I arrived, mesmerized as I had been by all the colors and patterns that were so familiar to me now. After we were done, I told him I would come back at the end of the day.

"Be careful, Alianor," said Janek. "Deva is mostly safe, but there are some pickpockets and Ciganyok that will try to swindle you. If you have trouble, come back here right away."

He asked me if I needed money, and I told him I had my own, still having most of the gold coins that Sandor had given me. I walked along the river, where houses were built very close together, only opening upon the winding streets that seemed to crisscross at odd angles, spreading out every which way. Soon I came to a place where the houses did not seem so stacked practically on top of one another, and the rows of houses turned to small cottages with a tree or two and sometimes a small garden in a fenced yard. There were fishermen leaving in their boats for the day, as the river teamed with fish. Therefore, it did not surprise me to hear shouts and voices from some boats I came upon. I was admiring the herbs laid out in one small cottage garden, when I recognized the language as Rromani. I stopped in my tracks and turned toward the boats that I had paid little attention to before and saw several small boats and one large boat with many levels and people all over it. They were shouting to people on the smaller boats and all were dressed as only the Rroma could be.

I walked toward them swiftly and stood watching the men upon the shore, tossing ropes and shouting directions to the smaller boats. I had heard of tribes who lived completely on the water but had never encountered any. After one young man finished what he was doing, he turned to head toward the plank of the main boat but stopped when he saw me standing there.

"Good day," I said. He looked taken aback to hear me speak his language. "May the river bless you today with many fish," I continued.

A big smile came across his face.

"May you be blessed as well, madam," he responded. The throngs upon the boat had stopped and were watching us now.

"What do you call yourselves?" I asked. He hesitated, wondering probably whether to give their true clan name.

"Iordanescu," he said, "And you?"

"I am Fieraru," I said, using Baba's family name. "From the other side of Erdély."

He laughed and I heard laughter on the boat. A few curious youngsters came off the boat and then a few adults as well. They swarmed around me and began asking questions. We swapped family names and discussed families we may know in common. Before I knew it, I was swept on to the boat, and being fed sweetbreads and rosewater tea. It had been a long time since I had spoken so freely. I had found the Gentle tongue easy to master, perhaps because I learned it from my mother as a babe, but there are nuances and a poetry in the Rromani language that are unequaled. I had taught Perla to speak both and she could easily switch from one to the other, but she had been my only Rromani conversational partner in five years. I had spoken little when I caught the ride with the Rromani caravan after leaving Sandor's on my way to Alba Jula. Now I was able to use phrases and converse with unrestrained joy, not realizing how much I had missed it.

I was nervous that there might be some warning about me or message that had spread this far: the People are renowned for communicating information over large networks. However, since I was not aware of any Iordanescu relatives or connections from my prior families, I knew I was probably safe. Still, I quickly invented a cover story for why I knew the language so well and why I did not still travel with my tribe. The story was mostly true: I explained that my mother asked a Fieraru family to care for me when she was on her deathbed, and so I traveled with them for many years until I was reunited with my natural father. My father then cared for me over the past several years, but when he pressured me to get married, I could not see myself marrying a Gentle, so I had run away. At this they nodded, understanding exactly. While they would find the insubordination of a daughter refusing to marry unacceptable under normal circumstances, they found it perfectly reasonable to refuse to marry a Gentle man. Although I myself had Gentle blood, it made sense to them that, having been raised in the traditional way, I had absorbed the Rromani ethic that it was generally taboo to "mix" with non-Rroma.

"If it's a Rromani husband you seek, then we can help you!" a sharp featured old woman declared, and then she and another older lady began talking among themselves and listing all of the local eligible bachelors they knew from local families, debating the merits or drawbacks of each.

"No, no, Pepira, that sloth would not make a good husband! I would not wish that on my own daughter, so why on this bright little thing?"

"But it's a *good* family!"

"Yes, but even a good family won't save her from a life tied to that lazy slug. No, we can do better than that for her."

I tried to explain that I was not actually in the market for a husband at all, but they seemed not to really take that to heart. I was swept from one topic to the next by the rowdy bunch, In the space of a few hours, I heard of all the tribes in the whole territory, including the gossip of who to stay away from and whom I could trust. I learned of the Gentle businesses and families who were friendly to the Rroma and those that could only lead to trouble. From the Iordanescu clan, I was informed about the several branches of tribes who were "boat people." They lived upon the water, making their livelihood primarily from fishing among other things. They traded and socialized, but did not usually intermarry, with the families of the craftspeople and wanderers who lived upon the land.

After sharing stories and warnings and feeding me sweet sticky treats the likes which I had never tasted before, they patted me and embraced me, and sent me on my way. They pulled up the ramp to their boat and went out to open water to continue on along. The Iordanescu explained that there were about a hundred miles of river that they traversed every year and they tried not to stay long in any one place, since that was the best way to avoid trouble. I waved at the rambunctious family as they floated off and felt a sense of sadness and longing for the people of my heart.

I turned back to the path to continue along the way I had started hours before, but I stopped almost immediately when I saw a dilapidated house covered in vines with an overgrown garden. It looked as though it had seen several seasons without someone caring for it, but it called to me, and I could see how it would look, scrubbed down and repaired with vines cleared away and garden planted. "Excuse me sir," I said to the man who was in the next lot, trimming the limbs of a fruit tree. "Can you tell me who owns this house?"

"That would be Stephan Turay," he said, and put down his tools. "He owns the Owl's Nest, the tavern by the market at the docks. You know the one?" I shook my head. "No, of course not. No respectable lady would. The house was his mother's. She passed two winters ago. I wish he would sell it so that I could have a decent neighbor again. I trimmed the trees in the spring, but I have my own lot to worry about. What business is it to you?"

"I'm looking for a place to set up a shop. I'm a weaver and I have been apprenticing, but I'm ready to go out on my own."

"Not a great place for a shop, unless you have a product people will walk for. You know how people are, they'll buy the first thing they see in the market rather than walk two blocks down to buy one that's twice as good at half the price!"

I thanked him and headed back to the market. The Owl's Nest was easy to find, and the man was not joking that it was not the kind of place a young lady would feel comfortable. Having spent the past winter in a similar tavern, though, I walked right in and ignored the stares and comments and went straight to the man who was clearly the tavern owner.

"What can I do for you, miss?"

"I was just over along the river and saw a house that I was told belonged to your mother. So sorry for your loss, sir."

He ignored the niceties, "Yes, what of it?"

"I'd like to buy it."

Despite his surprise that anyone would be interested in a house that he considered worthless, and despite his personal opinion—that he was liberal in sharing—that women should not be allowed to own property, we negotiated a price and I paid him with a good portion of the gold that Sandor had given me. I then spent a great deal of time finding out where to purchase the best bulk yarn and went and secured a large selection that I asked to have delivered to my new address the following day. After my trip to the mountains to meet the yarn-making family and the monumental effort that went into producing the product, I wondered at how cheaply I was able to buy a vast quantity of the finished material. Still, I realized that the price I paid was still above what Janek could secure in a year, and that he and Liana were only able to afford their yarn because they contributed the bulk of the raw wool.

That evening, after returning from market, I broke the news to Janek and Liana that I would be leaving them the next day. While they were astonished that I could afford to buy a house to set up shop when I had come to them as a pauper sleeping outdoors, they accepted the coins I paid them for the second loom that Janek had built, and agreed that Liana would send a bit of her cloth for me to sell in my store as I got started. The next day, Janek borrowed a horse and cart, and the whole family accompanied me to bring the loom over to my new property. We could barely get to the door, the place was so overgrown, but Janek and the boys helped clear away much of the vegetation while Liana and I went inside to assess the damage. The building had a large porch in the front and was only one large room inside with a stove and some worn furnishings. I had bought the contents, as the tavern owner wanted nothing to do with anything left from his mother, considering it all worthless. Fortunately for me, while most of the objects within were old and needing repairs, there were enough basic cooking utensils and furniture, once given a thorough washing, to meet my basic needs. Having made do with much less before, the place seemed brimming with abundance to me.

When the family had given me as much time as they could afford and Janek had set up the loom on my freshly scrubbed porch, I sent them away, telling them to come and visit me soon. I embraced Liana, whose cheeks were fresh with tears, and kissed the boys and the baby. Liana's parting gift to me was a small tub of her special lanolin, the thick oil from the sheep that made her fabric glisten. That night I slept in my own home for the first time, and although it felt like much more than I could ever need, I was proud that I could finally have something that was all my own. Lying in bed that night, I thought of Sandor—my father—and that this was the inheritance that he had been able to give me, though I had declined so much more.

∞

The next few months as winter approached, I spent the mornings weaving, then broke in the afternoon and worked on cleaning and setting up house. There was a lot to do, as the property had been neglected terribly. The previous inhabitant had been elderly and unable to do much in her declining years. The neighbor, Bartolan, and his wife, Gaeta, were pleasant and welcoming, relieved that someone was caring for the place. Bartolan was a carpenter who could build almost anything, and Gaeta worked in a fancy home on the flanks of Cetatii. From what I understood, she worked in the greenhouse caring for their plants. It seemed an odd occupation, but she left before sunrise and came home early in the day, bringing cuttings for Bartolan to grow in their own garden. Their two daughters had grown and moved to other parts of the city to marry, so they also seemed happy to have some companionship, and someone young on whom to impart advice and to share homemaking tips.

Gaeta was full of energy, even after returning from her workday, and enjoyed bringing over samples of new recipes she had learned from the cooks at her fancy job for me to try. She brought me stuffed cabbages, in sauces thick with paprika, and spongey sweet cake with cream. It was clear I was not going to starve in my new neighborhood. Since my house faced the river, I saw boating activity at all hours of the day. I had the first choice of the carp and other river fish the men brought in. I had not eaten much fish before, but it became a favorite of mine. The fish was so fresh and the fishermen were so accommodating, willing to skin and filet for me right on the spot. I might roast up a filet, just brought in from the river, and eat some for breakfast and then have the remainder for my evening meal with some root vegetables. Gaeta taught me about spices. I had always cooked with herbs, but she introduced me to a smoky red paprika that seemed to make everything come alive.

Again, I found that people asked me few questions about my past. It almost didn't matter what I told them about where I had come from or why I was alone in the world. Everyone had their own hardship, and once they knew you had come from yours, they were apt not to pry. My neighbors on the other side were almost never there. It was a father and son who also worked near Cetatii. Bartolan, who knew the history of the whole area and was familiar with every family's story, told me that the wife had been killed a few years before in an accident at her work in a mill. The husband and son also worked the mill, and mostly kept to themselves, private in their grief.

A few doors down, past Bartolan and Gaeta, was a seamstress named Borbola and her husband, who worked on one of the many larger plantations that helped to feed the Cetatii populace. Borbala was a rambunctious round lady, whose voice carried out over the water when she yelled at her several children throughout most days. It sounded quite ferocious when I first heard her shouting for her little ones, but after I got used to it, I realized it was just the way she talked to them. Perhaps she needed to yell, since she had so many children. I was unable to track them at first, but finally counted six, including three that were very small, including one lodged mostly on her hip, two older children, and a young teenage daughter, who worked as a maid on a nearby street. I'm not sure how she had time to do any sewing, but her porch was full of wares, bolts of cloth and small sewn goods and blankets. Her main livelihood was taking commissions for clothing. Borbala barely had to eye a person up and down and spin them around once to be able to create a custom garment that fit perfectly. Customers came to pick up finished items they had ordered. Between the traffic to her home and all the children, it was an active house.

She took an interest in my fabric, seeing the lovely sheen that I had perfected when learning from Liana, and started to send customers over to my house to pick out patterns or colors of cloth if she did not have what was required. I began to take orders for the fabric from some of her wealthier clients, and soon it was more than I could handle on my own. Little Filep, Liana's boy who had long been idle and had no serious responsibilities yet, began to be the runner between our houses, taking orders and returning with fabric in a little cart that I had Bartolan build for the purpose. Filep took pride in his new job and was especially happy when I paid him some small coins for his trouble. When Liana was not too busy, she and the baby came along with Filep, and I was always happy to see her and little Vaski. She was still a little amazed that I had somehow had a small fortune in my sack as I slept on her floor outside and milked her sheep. Now she understood why I never accepted payment for my labors. I told her that in my opinion, I had benefited the most from the arrangement, since it was her aptitude that had forged my own.

I knew Liana's technique was something special, but now having more access to the public than when I had been sequestered in the Commons, I could see the interest her distinctive fabric sparked in clients. If they walked past my house to get to the seamstress, they stopped and sometimes came up onto my porch to touch and wonder at the shiny cloth. Then, when they went to Borbala's they had in mind a special garment made from mine and Liana's fabric instead of the standard bolts that Borbala invested in. Borbala did not mind, since she made money either way, buying fabric from one of the big producers across town or buying more expensive fabric from me and Liana, she just factored in the cost to her price and we all made out handsomely.

Soon, winter made it impossible to do outdoor business, so I moved the loom inside. There was no shortage of customers. They continued to come, even trudging through snow to place or pick up orders at Borbola's. I gave her samples and usually she just did all the business herself and then told me what was needed. Without the merchandise on the porch, my house did not attract attention unless someone knew to come looking or if Borbola sent someone over to discuss a custom order. A knock on my door startled me one day, and I opened it to find two Rromani ladies, dressed decadently as some of the wealthier tribes tended to do. They spoke to me in Hungarian, with thick accents as they struggled over the words, asking to buy some superior cloth for the wedding dress of the adolescent girl. I responded in Rromani, and their eyes lit up at my flawless delivery. "What kind of fabric would you like, my sisters?" I asked.

"My dear, you speak Rromani!" said the older woman.

"Why yes, I am Fieraru," I said.

"Really? How is that possible? You are a Gentle!"

"I was raised Fieraru."

"Well then, where are your People?"

"It's quite a long story, which I am sure would bore you until the candles burned down, but I am now here in Deva on my own." They nodded, accepting this vague explanation.

"How marvelous that you are here! I have never heard a Gentle speak Rromani before! It's quite a surprise," she confessed.

"Of course. I am so rusty at it, though, I'm surprised you could understand me. It's been many years since I left my Tribe."

"Well, you can't be much older than my Mala here," she said, gesturing to her barely blossoming girl.

"Yes, well, I left when I was very young."

"Ah, well, you still speak Rromani like a true daughter."

"What kind of fabric would you like for your dress?" I asked the girl.

"I was thinking purple, of course," cut in the mother. "She is marrying a very wealthy man, so she will need the color of royalty." Pride seeped in as the woman explained the good fortune of her daughter marrying a Zamfir prince. The Zamfir tribe was famous for their jewels. None could compare with the skill of their smiths. They created the most remarkable cut gems that sparkled with inner fire through secret techniques they passed down father-to-son through generations. Their stones were valued above any others and Gentles everywhere drooled over Zamfir treasures. Among the Rroma, the Zamfir were well-known to have descended from royal blood. Many families claimed a noble title and dripped with gold jewelry that dazzled with fire-filled stones.

"How lucky she is," I agreed, smiling at the girl who looked down shyly. I showed them some samples and spools of yarn with colors I thought might complement the young bride's glowing skin. We settled on a deep maroon shade that faded to a peachy pink at the edges. "This will show her worth without bragging," I said, and the mother agreed.

We talked of local families, of which I knew little, except what I had already heard from the Iordanescu boat clan. The lady was happy to fill me in on all the juicy details. She herself was of the Volpe tribe, but there were several other clans that populated the area. My ears perked up when I heard there were Bihari, a circus clan that was a friendly rival of the Badi. The Bihari claimed to be the oldest Circ, generally understood to have performers unlike those seen anywhere else in the world. The older woman told me where they performed in the warmer months and described some of the daring performance she had seen. "Those people are barely human!" she delighted to tell me. "No humans can bend the way they do–it's unnatural. Clearly the spirits possess them. I had some offers of marriage for Mala from the Bihari, but I can't see my treasure going to live with bears and fire-eaters!"

I agreed that Mala deserved the very best.

"And you do, too, little one!" cried Mala's mother. "You are still so young. You could marry easily. Shall I try to find a nice Zamfir man for you? Perhaps a widower, someone rich who will spoil you?" I told her that I doubted a Zamfir prince would stoop to marry a Gentle, even if she were raised Rroma. She nodded, agreeing that it was quite a disadvantage to be of Gentle blood. "Well, maybe you can try the Machvaya? You know they winter in the inn a few blocks that way," she pointed behind my house, gesturing several streets away.

"No, I was not aware."

"They are not so picky. And if you can pretend to have the Sight, you may find a husband in a minute!" she laughed a big hearty laugh, and we finished our business. I thanked her profusely and we parted with traditional blessings. They would return in several weeks to pick up the finished fabric.

∞

Borbala continued to buy my fabric to make clothing, mostly for her more discriminating clients. It kept Liana and me busy throughout the cold winter when we could do little else but weave and eat and sleep. I realized while alone in my new cottage that being around Liana's family had insulated me. Surrounded by people, it had numbed the pain inside me, distracted me with the frenetic business of family life, children, and animals. Alone again, I felt the despair of losing Perla deeply. Sometimes I even felt like I was walking around with a knife physically protruding from my chest. The pain was salient as I watched the long shadows move across my floor over the short days. The weaving helped, since my hands now knew the work and I could slip into an almost meditative trance. I slowed my breathing to match the movements of the shuttle. Sometimes I would look up and be amazed that I had created a few inches of fabric while I was barely conscious.

I coped with the longing for Perla by indulging in fantasies of what she would be doing if she were there with me. What would she like about the house, what would she be playing with? She would have loved weaving. I could have built her a small loom to practice on. These were the hardest daydreams to entertain and caused me such anguish that I determined to shut them out. Instead, I tried to think of her playing with the Badi children, caring for her half-brothers. I imagined Mihai, smiling down at his daughter with delight at her wonderful stories and loving spirit. Shifting to seeing her in this way, as fulfilling the life that I had stolen her from, made the wrenching loss of her more bearable than when I pretended that she could still be with me. Still, when I listened to my heart at night, it insisted that she belonged to me.

The traffic on the river slowed in the winter. With passage difficult, barges and travelers went by only occasionally. It gave the illusion that the whole world was sleeping, with the trees on the rim of the river turned white and the ice creeping along the edges against the frozen washed-out sky. I could hear evidence of wakeful life, though, in the streets behind the one that faced the river. My small property backed against a large building that had a storefront and a family living above it, so I would hear the pots being clanked at dinnertime, and the shuffling footfalls and squabbles of children, punctuated by jubilant laughter or a sustained cry. I could also hear the merry sounds of evening revelers in the streets behind mine, with some occasional drunken singing or a fight.

Word must have spread among the Rroma families because soon I had a few customers a week, coming specifically to buy fabric from the Gentle woman who spoke Rromani. If I had been a true Rroma, I doubt they would have questioned me more for living on my own, since no Rroma was ever alone. However, looking like the other Gentles, they nodded knowingly, as if they acknowledged that I could never truly belong to a tribe. They still enjoyed the novelty of being able to converse and bargain in their native language and could then describe exactly the pattern and colors of the cloth they desired for some blessed occasion. Liana and my fabric, it seemed, lent itself to marking key moments in life rather than being used for mundane everyday wear.

In addition to the Rromani callers, I started to attract attention from the elite Cetatii, who sent their tailors to purchase fabric. Smetimes they even made the journey themselves. An older Cetatii noblewoman got out of a carriage one day, assisted by several attendants and the driver. She picked her way across the snow-covered lawn as her entourage tried to encourage her to go around to the side path that was already swept clean. Clearly, she was not used to being encouraged to do anything, as she snapped at them for chiding her, smacking away arms offered to stabilize her. "What? Do you think I'm an old woman?" She came to the porch where I had already opened the door to greet her. "Are you *the* Alexandru? The one who is the weaver?" she demanded.

"Why yes, madam."

"Well, you're nothing but a child! How can that be?"

"I assure you, madam, I am a weaver. Would you like to come in and see for yourself?"

She looked skeptical and studied the doorframe, as if she thought it could collapse on her, before poking her head in slowly to make sure it was not a trap. Her party tried to follow her, and my house being small as it was, she shooed them back out the door to wait outside. I had apples roasting on the stove with their fragrance perfuming the toasty air. I could see her shoulders relax when she ascertained that this was a normal abode and not a dangerous hovel. "I am in need of fabric for a gown. It will be my son's wedding in April. I have only one son. The daughters . . . worthless! They have been nothing but a hassle to marry off. Do you know how hard it is to find good families to take your daughters? Almost impossible. I had to send one off to Budapest, just to find a good bloodline!"

I nodded, as if I sympathized with this unfortunate plight.

"My son, though, he is my delight! Just like his father was–rest his soul. Of course, it all falls on me, since I am alone in the world!"

"What type of fabric are you seeking, madam?" I prompted.

She started, as if recalling her mission, and began looking around, poking through layers of folded cloth and racks hanging finished goods. "Yes, yes, I hear you are the best, and of course I need the best. Hmmm . . . this is very nice, very nice. Yes, my neighbor had a dress made for the Winter Ball from some of your golden cloth. Oh, it was very nice, very nice. Too nice, really, for a lady like her. She did not do it justice, I'm afraid. I loved that gold color, but I won't imitate my neighbor, that would be unseemly. Although, wouldn't it be fun just to show her who really deserves to wear gold? No, no, it needs to be something different, something spectacular!"

"Madam, may I suggest something?"

She looked at me alarmed, as if unsure if she should take suggestions from someone in my position, but she nodded slightly.

"A woman of your standing should have a dress that truly dignifies her. It should speak to her experience, her prosperity, and her position in life. Not to mention, it should be faithful to the occasion. You are about to give away your beloved and cherished son into marriage. Perhaps you need a fabric that sparkles like the stars at night, but is still dignified and enduring, as you are."

I took a small band of folded cloth from a pile of fabrics that I had been experimenting with. I had been testing out color combinations, and this was one I was particularly pleased with. It was a silver-gray, shot through with lavender and white so that it seemed to come alive. I held it out to her, showing her how it changed as the light fell on it. She was speechless as she fingered the fabric, tilting it to see how it seemed to shift and alter, reflecting the red glow from the fire even as it maintained its starlight appearance.

"My dear, you are truly talented," she said, the words pried from her mouth as if admitting this was a huge concession.

The order was quite large, and the Duchess Arany, as I found she was titled, ended up ordering several more lengths of cloth for other dresses for summer parties she was already planning, in colors I suggested to compliment those occasions and her esteemed person. She paid a large retainer, and I knew that Liana and I would be kept busy for the rest of the winter.

Chapter Thirteen: The Oracle of Deva

More wealthy women like the Duchess came. When they visited, they seeming to want not just a fabric, but reassurance. I found I had a gift for intuiting exactly what kind of vestment they should wear before they even opened their mouth. Additionally, because I was getting the inside gossip on what parties were coming up and who was wearing what, I could influence an aristocratic lady to select a different hue than what she originally had in mind so that she would stand out. This way, she would not be embarrassed by a dress that was too similar in shade to a rival. I found the nobles were particularly insecure. I never knew a common woman to be so preoccupied by what others thought of her. Being so vulnerable left these ladies open to suggestion. When I told them what the color would do for them, how it would complement their physicality, announce their social bearing, and reinforce the way they wanted to be viewed, they believed it. Because of that, they felt powerful wearing the garments made from my cloth.

While there were some men who commissioned fabric, most was custom made for women, especially when word caught fire and it became fashionable to have fabric woven by "the Alexandrus." The demand kept us weaving at all hours. Liana's fabric had always been spectacular, but now there was a pipeline to the people who would pay the most for it and who seemed always thirsty for more. I began increasing the cost when demand became so competitive that I was taking orders for two seasons ahead. As the river began to thaw and great sheets of ice escaped their birthing place with thunderous noise, we were in such high demand that Janek built a separate weaving shed for Liana: she took on two young apprentices to help with the work. By spring, we were a bonified operation. Little Filep was finally old enough and had proven himself worthy to take over his brother's prior role with the sheep. Damir began to run the transport of goods between our houses and helped his father expand and man his stall at the market. We tried to direct the traffic there to manage the ordering, but people still showed up at my cottage to consult with me and give their commissions directly. It was part of the experience for the elite, who could tell the story of how they visited *the Alexandru* in her humble shack.

Although our prices were now inflated, I still gave the best deals to the Rroma families who came to purchase fabric for special occasions. Through them, I kept informed about the underground community that lived on the dark fringes of the glittering world of the Cetatii that I was starting to glimpse. In the morning, I might be visited by a Cetatii countess seeking to dress her two competitive daughters in gowns that highlighted each one's best features without overshadowing the other. But then later in the day, I might have a rowdy Rroma family, who had saved every penny just to have a wedding gown made for a cherished child going to her new family. They would tell me of their problems and the difficulties of their hard lives. It was so much more compelling than the petty jealousies of the noblewomen I served. I could let my guard down with my People, the ones who still felt like my true clan, despite the fact that I belonged to no tribe.

My neighbors were not pleased with my Cigany visitors and asked why I tolerated their business when I had so many rich carriages stopping by to place orders. "They're just families, same as the others," I responded.

Borbala watched her children closely when the Rroma came around, afraid of losing one to the Circ, not realizing all Rromani weren't affiliated with the circus. "You know their women wear almost nothing!" Borbala whispered to me with wide eyes. "I saw them last year at the arena. Those women! They are harlots, all of them! Did you know they live with bears? They are like animals themselves. Who could live like that?"

I did not argue, since I knew she would not believe that Rromani women were more chaste than the stories I heard about the noblewomen of Cetatii, who seemed to delight in laying with each other's husbands just for sport. In fact, the dramas that I became privy to were so complex, I began to understand the deep insecurities that plagued the women. Securing a husband in the vicious inner circle was hard enough, but then to keep one away from the prying hands of a rival who might sap the lifeblood of the family seemed near impossible. I heard of multitudes of bastard offspring among the house servants, as well as children raised with royal titles whose parentage was questionable. I did not enjoy the pain behind the stories, but they were intriguing, and gave me insight into the plight of the fragile women. They seemed worried away by the sheer dilemma of keeping and maintaining a husband, if only in the public eye. It saddened me, especially when I knew of so many good, hardworking husbands who would never stray from their plain, unremarkable wives.

Somehow the fabric I wove kept the illusion going, I found. The Cetatii women truly believed if they could just wear the right dress, their lives would pull together in neat seams: they could draw in that desirable marriage partner and keep those they already possessed perfectly stitched to their sides. A gown could not do that, I knew, but they believed in it so fiercely. The dresses developed into a commanding mythology in their own and others' minds, as if it were the fabric itself upon which their social and marital success would depend. Therefore, when they came to me, it was not just with the request for cloth, it was a request to build upon a shared fantasy, to believe with them that the dress would indeed make them irresistible and successful in love. For women who were truly doomed if they failed to create a favorable marital alliance, it was more than a dream for a comfortable life: it was survival.

I never worried about the Rromani girls, going to a husband's family where they would be absorbed, becoming an integral part of the fabric of their new clan. They would be loved and cherished, I felt certain. The Cetatii girls, young women with peachy complexions and sparkling eyes, those were the ones I worried about. I saw into the future that they would become the older women, painfully trying to keep their husbands faithful while desperately maneuvering to secure advantageous partnerships for their own children. It was heart-wrenching to watch the drama unfold and know nothing could interfere. Meanwhile, in another world, whole families survived on mountainsides, marrying whom they loved and living out their years together while their clothes became threadbare and hands calloused. The suffering was tragic because it seemed so avoidable. Yet these women, raised on myths of perfect cloth, had no idea there might be any other style of life.

∞

By summer we were so busy that I moved Janek and Damir from the little stall in the market into a shop on the street behind my house. They protested, since they felt they could not afford the lease, but I paid the owner of the building for the year ahead and told the men we would worry about next year later. I felt that having a proper shop would direct some of the traffic there, for those who sent their servants to purchase cloth and for those who knew what they wanted already or wanted to see the full range of merchandise. It was a place to display finished goods and give a full selection of the spectrum of colors and patterns we were perfecting and expanding upon all the time. Because everyone had adopted the misnomer of the *Alexandrus*, and asked for the fabric by this name, this was what Janek had a woodworker inscribe on a plaque above the storefront. He was not a reader, nor was I for that matter, but he had asked a bookkeeper to write down the letters to give to the carver. When I found out what was written there, I shook my head. "It is really Liana's fabric. We should call it *Liana's*."

"Alianor, we can't change what people ask for. They already want the cloth made by the Alexandrus. What is Liana's name, or our humble family name, anyway? Pék? It came from my grandfather's father who was a baker. We are not bakers. Our shop would not sound any better as the *Péks*. The *Alexandrus* has a ring to it, and people know it."

"I just think she should get credit," I complained.

"She is getting credit. She's getting credit every day in payment for her cloth like she's never gotten before. She has basically a whole school set up to teach weaving to two young apostles who hang on her every word. She's quite happy. She likes the name."

I could not argue, and I knew Liana would not be comfortable with her name above the store, anyway. It just seemed like another layer of the story I had falsely woven for myself. Despite all the evidence that I was, in fact, Sandor's daughter, it still felt like a farce: I did not feel any ownership for his surname. Still, it was appropriate to have a business that was founded on others' fantasies to have a name that was also only tenuously true. So, I gave in and accepted that we would be known this way. Among the Rroma, I was known as the Fieraru weaver, although that felt no more true to me, even thought it was Baba and Ankah's heritage and the tribe in which I was raised. Occasionally, I worried that I had given away too much by exposing myself as linked to that clan, in case anyone was looking for me. It was not a logical fear: Deva was far away from the Badi tribes. Even so, a blonde Gentle woman who spoke Rromani was unusual. It would be noteworthy to anyone who was familiar with the story of an adopted Gentle girl who ran away with a Badi newborn, a baby who was only recovered after five years.

Now that the Badi had Perla back, I hoped they had no further need to seek vengeance upon me. I had heard of killings by honor, but it was my own guilt that told me that there could still be those who wanted to harm me for taking a child from them. I also thought of Baba, of all she had done for me, and wondered if she was resting well, knowing Perla had been returned to the tribe. It hurt me to reflect on her final message to me: that I did not belong, but that Perla did. I knew Baba had loved me, but ultimately, I was not her child. Ankah was her daughter and Perla her granddaughter, and I had taken her granddaughter away from the clan. I also felt guilt for contributing to Baba's death, since I understood that when she had found out about Ankah's death and about what I had done, she grew weak and eventually perished from heartache.

All the prosperity I was now experiencing felt badly won. I did not think I deserved to be happy and successful. I was an immoral person: I had stolen a child. I know Perla had seen me as her mother and I had done my best to raise her well in the short time I had with her, but our relationship was founded on a lie. She would grow to despise me for what I did, I was sure of it. Perhaps she would be the one to finally come looking for me. When she was older, maybe she would lead the Badi to me and make me to suffer for taking her from her father. That someone might try to hurt me paled in comparison to the possibility that the person I loved most in the world might grow to loathe me. Not only had I hurt her and the Badi, I had also hurt Sandor. I know he supported my decision to leave–he had little choice–but I had deprived him of the healing he was seeking, his attempt to rectify his mistakes. I often wondered what life would be like if I had stayed and married Sandor, setting up a sham of a marriage to my father in order to gain a dubious inheritance. I would be no better than the Cetatii women, angling for an advantageous situation for life.

Even now, I shuddered to think of living that lie: I determined that the lies I lived now were preferable. Regardless of the path of deception I chose, I could not help to think of myself as a truly flawed woman. These were the thoughts that kept me up at night, as the fire burned low and night birds sang brief refrains or shouted an occasional alarm. During daylight hours, I tried to pay for my indiscretions in small ways, being kind to the Rroma families, being generous with my attendance to the noblewomen who looked for comfort in the thought of a new dress, but I never really got rid of the feeling underneath it all that I was corrupt at heart. At night, the doubt crept in, and despite the things going right in my life, I felt I was unworthy of it all.

One morning, after a night of irregular sleep and waking when it was still dark to dwell upon my errant decisions, I heard a light tap on the door. The sky was still mostly black, with dark blue-grey clouds sprawling over the sky atop the river, the edges laced with just the palest amber glow of morning. I thought I might have imagined it, but then I heard the tap again. I went to the door and stood in front of it, a moment of concern and my lingering nightly fears halting me from opening it at this hour. I heard the tap once again, light, but authoritative. I opened the door a crack and saw a Rroma woman standing there alone. She was very young, close to my age, barely in the bloom of womanhood. She was wrapped in a dark shawl against the chill in the receding night air. "Yes, my good sister?"

"Fieraru? May I come in?"

"Yes, yes, please," I said, opening the door fully and stepping aside. "Call me Alianor." I gestured for her to sit on one of the chairs that Bartolan had repaired for me. I put a kettle of water to the stove and turned back to face her. "What is it, Friend? Can I make you some cloth?"

"No, thank you. I am not here for cloth," she replied. She looked at her hands.

"Well?"

"I am Zhulyi," she looked up, as if that might mean something to me. I waited. "I was Machvaya, but now I am married Bihari. I am visiting my mother. She is staying at an inn a few streets away."

"Yes? I've heard the Machvaya stay nearby. I do not know them. Zhulyi, it is? May I help you? Is there something I can do for you? It's quite early, and I was still in bed."

"Yes, I'm so sorry. I had a dream and it woke me. I had heard of you before. My cousin came to you for cloth for her wedding. It was beautiful; blue like a shimmering lake."

"Thank you."

"I'm sorry to wake you. I know you are Rrom. Have you known anyone with the Sight?"

"Yes, I've known several. My sister was gifted, and her daughter."

Zhulyi sighed, seeming relieved. "Then perhaps you will not think me crazy: I dreamed exactly where your house is, and I saw you in your bed. But you were not sleeping. You were wide awake. When I awoke, the Spirits told me to go to you."

"What do you think they could have wanted?" I wondered which spirits might still have business with me.

"They said you . . . needed me."

"I see."

"I don't know what they could mean. I have nothing to offer. I am just a regular woman except for the Sight. It's the only thing that makes me special. It's why the Bihari wanted me–why my husband married me."

The water began to boil. I poured it over some crushed rose petals and mint. I said, "Your vision was right–I was not sleeping."

"Ah," she said, not sounding very surprised.

"I do not sleep much. I wake and think of all the choices I've made. I wonder if I've made the right ones. Do you do that?"

"I don't think I've had many choices."

"Really?"

"No, most of my life has been decided for me."

"What about going to the Bihari to be married? Did you worry about it or think you made the wrong decision?"

"I had no choice in that. They wanted me. Our parents arranged it. I did not decide."

"Hmmm. Did you ever think that it was a mistake?" I asked.

"Probably. But what good is it to worry about things you cannot change?"

"So true, and yet I do," I confessed. I turned and poured some tea and offered her some, sitting in a chair at an angle from her. I tried not to stare, but I could watch her a bit from the corner of my eye as I sipped the tea. She was quite lovely.

"Well, you and I must be very different," she said. "My whole life has been determined by others. Even if I wanted to regret any of it, what good would it do? Even coming here this morning, I was just following the advice of the Spirits. I suppose I could have ignored the instructions, but they would not have left me alone until I heeded the words."

"My sister saw the dead. She learned to ignore them, they wanted her to meddle in the lives of the living and she felt it brought only trouble."

"Oh, I don't see the dead," explained Zhulyi. "Not the human dead anyway. The spirits who speak to me are part of the fabric of the Universe. They do not belong to any human entity, or no more than they belong to the trees and grass and stars, anyway."

"Ah, yes. Ankah–my sister–she told me about the voice of the Mother."

"Yes, yes, that's it. It's more than one person, it's like all the sounds of the universe combined into one, all the spirits wound into a single voice: a mother's voice."

"I don't think my sister had anyone to guide her, to help her understand the voices or what to do with them. She learned to follow their advice, but she had to learn to ignore the dead on her own."

"Yes," Zhulyi agreed. "It is hard for those who don't have someone to teach them. My mother does not have the Sight, but my Bibi is gifted. She has taught me a great deal. I had a cousin who saw the dead. It drove her mad."

"Yes, I can see how it could."

Zhulyi was silent, sipping her tea. I watched her honey-colored eyes drop down to the surface of the steaming liquid as she blew on it to cool it.

"You know, my sister found me? The Spirits told her to go to the mountain, and she found my mother dying there. My mother told her to take me. I would have died with no one to care for me if she hadn't listened to the voices."

Zhulyi looked up, intrigued. "I wondered . . . it is not often to see a Gentle adopted by a Rroma clan, speaking Rromani so fluently."

"Yes, but I have no clan now." I felt my energy dropping away as I shared this. I was not sure why I trusted Zhulyi so. I had never been so candid with anyone, except Sandor, who knew my whole story.

"If you are Rrom you will always be Rrom. We are all your clan."

"Yes," I agreed. "I have felt that way toward the Rroma. I just don't always feel like it's mutual. I left the family of the young man I was supposed to marry." Her eyebrows raised. "I had no one left to guide me, but the funny thing is, his mother helped me to run away."

"Really? Why? Did she want you to leave? Was she unkind to you?"

"No, the opposite. She was kind. She treated me like a daughter, although we had barely gotten a chance to know one another." I had pondered many times why Selene had helped me escape, why she had not sounded the alarm. When I blamed myself for running away with Perla, I sometimes reflected on why Selene had packed a bag for me. What did she know and why did she help me run?

"She had the Sight, you know," I said. "The woman who would have been my Mother-in-Law."

"She must have known what the Spirits intended for you, then."

Or for Perla, I thought. I flashed through the years Perla and I spent together in the castle, our closeness, caring for her like a mother. If she had stayed with the Badi, she would have had no one to do that for her. I knew that in those years, I gave her all that Ankah would have given her if she had lived.

"Maybe," I concurred. "Maybe it was the right thing."

"If your Mother-in-Law had the Sight and she helped you to leave, then it was probably the right thing."

"Yes, it may be true."

"It sounds to me like maybe you didn't have a choice at all."

"Really, how so?"

"I think it's different for us: we who are born Rrom. Please do not take offense. We are trained from the time we are born to listen to our elders and take their advice. I would never consider doing anything to slight my parents." Zhulyi paused and sipped her tea. "The Gentles are different. They are more independent, they do not have the fierce family loyalty that we have," she continued. "They might take a parent's advice on who to marry, or they might not." I thought of Sandor. "You were born a Gentle," she continued. "Even though you were adopted by the Clan, you can't change your heritage, you can't change how you were made. Plus, it sounds like you had some help in making the decision to leave."

I had often wondered, if Selene had not been there, had not handed me the bag, would I have really left? Maybe I would have gotten to the edge of the forest and turned back. I was in an altered state of devastation from finding Ankah dead. Maybe I would have gone a short way carrying Perla and then snapped out of it and returned. I might have gone back to wake everyone to tell them about Ankah. Selene being there and sending me on my way made it impossible to turn back. I saw that now.

"Yes, she did help me make the decision."

"And you are who you are. Ultimately, maybe you would have found a way not to marry her son anyway. She may have known that."

I had to agree with that. Although I was always fond of Sasha, the idea of marrying him had terrified me. Being his wife and being taken to his marriage bed was something I was not sure I could have done, when it came time. I had only come along to be close to Ankah. Even if Ankah had lived, would I have run away at some point to avoid that fate anyway?

"Yes, I think you may be right," I said. "You know, that was not the only time I've run from marriage. I came to Deva to escape a marriage." It was not the whole story, but it was more than I had told anyone else. For the first time I acknowledged to myself that even if the Badi had not come for Perla and had been intending to harm me, I probably would have run away from Sandor and all he was offering me anyway. I remember wishing I were made differently so that I could accept all that he was ready to give me. "I may have just been born like that," I agreed.

"I sometimes have thought that none of us really have a choice in anything. We do what we do because we are who we are, and I'm not sure that's really the same as making choices. If we listen to others, or don't, it's because of how we're made. Honestly, if I were born differently, if I had a choice. I never would have agreed to marry my husband."

"Really?"

"Yes. He's an awful man."

"I'm sorry."

"I come to see my mother as often as I can. Of course, I love her, but it's really to get time away from him."

I didn't know what to say. She finished her tea, and then began to gather herself to leave.

"Well, Fieraru–Alianor, I must go. I'm still not sure why I was supposed to come, but maybe just to meet you and have this little talk. I was feeling dispirited about my life, but for some reason, talking to you has made me feel better."

"Zhulyi–thank you. I don't know why, but I feel better, too. You have brought me great comfort."

"Perhaps I will come visit you again? Maybe at a more reasonable hour?" she laughed.

"Yes, please. I would enjoy that."

"Goodbye, Alianor." She kissed me on my cheek and like a flash, she opened and closed the door and her graceful form disappeared through it.

I lay back down upon my bed, my cheek feeling strangely as if Zhulyi's lips were still upon them. With the sky now pale blue across the horizon, I stared into the air above my bed and soon was asleep before I even realized it. I did not wake until many hours later, when Damir arrived to discuss some business, after I had already missed a whole morning of weaving.

∞

I saw Zhulyi sporadically after that. For a week after she came that first time, I really thought I might have dreamed her visit. It was so unreal, and we had talked so openly without even knowing one another. It did not seem it could have happened. Then she appeared again, one afternoon while I was outside weeding my new vegetable garden. I had done a lot to shape the small property back into fruition, and it was starting to look like any other house on my street, the plot cared for and productive. Zhulyi appeared from the back of the property, having come through the tiny side alley from the street behind.

"Greetings, Fieraru."

"Zhulyi!" I clasped her hands and she kissed my cheeks. "How wonderful to see you. Will you come in to visit? I baked some raisin bread this morning."

"Yes, that would be nice." We went inside and I laid out some slices of the spicy sweet bread on a plate while I warmed some milk with honey. Liana kept me supplied with sheep's milk, which I savored. "I brought you something." Zhulyi handed me a pouch and when I opened it, it had several packets of herbs inside. "Some teas to help you sleep better," she explained. "From my mother."

"She is so kind. Please thank her for me," I said. "I actually have been sleeping much better since your visit. I do not have many people to talk to."

"I find that so funny. You are so popular. Your cloth is known so well, and I know your shop is doing well."

"You know of my shop?"

"Yes, of course! My mother stays on that street, so she keeps up with all the news."

"Yes, well, most of the people who come to buy cloth want to tell me their own story. No one seems to want to know mine. I guess you're the first person who has wanted to find out about me."

"Well, although the Spirits brought me to you, I admit I am here of my own volition today," she laughed. She nibbled the end of a piece of bread and I watched her push a strand of dark hair back into the cloth that wound around her head.

"I'm so glad you came," I said. "How long will you stay at your mother's?"

"Just today. I return to my husband tomorrow. I need to be there for the performances."

"Do you perform in the Circ?"

"Oh, no. I tell fortunes. Not real ones of course, but . . ."

"Yes, I understand. My sister did the same."

"Really?"

"Yes, she was married Badi. She hated it. She called it telling "pretty lies" to the Gentles."

"Precisely. Yes, I hate it, too. But it's the reason his family chose me to marry him. I am useful to the Bihari. It is my duty to them and to my husband."

"I have not seen the Bihari Circ yet. They say it is spectacular."

"Oh, it's like nothing else. Truly, it's an honor to be associated with them." She paused and I could tell she wanted to say more.

"But it's hard on you to be married to a man who does not treat you well."

She looked at me. "Yes," she said simply.

"And what of your mother? Does she have any advice for you?"

"I share little of my troubles with my mother. She has her own misery to deal with."

"Oh?"

"She is not well. It's why she stays back with her sister's family in the city here. She does not travel anymore. Her legs do not work well, and she shakes all the time. She is like an old woman, yet she is not that old."

"How awful."

"The healers give her teas and charms—they do help—but she still suffers."

"So, your own troubles are . . ."

" . . . kept to myself," she finished. She sipped the warm milk I had given her and ate a few more crumbs of the bread. "But it gives me a reason to visit her often. My husband at least does not deprive me of that. He probably prefers me to be away anyway. It gives him time with his . . . lovers."

"Oh, Zhulyi. I'm sorry."

"Yes, well, I don't even mind that he has them. It keeps him from bothering me. He's just so cruel. I've never met anyone so unkind."

"Does he hit you?"

"No, but I would almost prefer that. He berates me, tells me I'm worthless. He says he regrets marrying me just about every day. He criticizes everything I do. Believe me, I am grateful he does not hurt me. I've heard of that happening to other wives. He has never beaten me. He is just so . . . hard. Perhaps it's my own fault."

"Your fault?"

"Well, when I first married him, I prayed to the Spirits not to have children. I saw quickly how horrible he was, and I knew what kind of father he would be. It worked. I have never conceived. It's given him another reason to hate me, but I'm sure he'd find fault with me no matter what." I looked at my hands, unsure of how to comfort her. "You'd think he'd be satisfied—he has bastard children. He has a boy with the trapeze artist that is his favorite: She's talented, very beautiful." I could not imagine anyone being more beautiful than Zhulyi. "Her husband died right before she had her boy, so nobody gives her any grief about it, but he looks just like Aamon, my husband. I have to pretend that I don't know, but everyone knows. I am shamed in my husband's family. I am just a barren woman, despite being able to bring them money for my skills."

"Zhulyi, that is terrible. I'm sorry you have suffered so."

"It is not so bad. I have some freedom. My mother-in-law passed a few years ago, so I can run my household how I wish. My father-in-law is mostly kind, although he ignores how his son treats me. No one really speaks to me, except my husband when he is accusing me of some new thing I failed to do or calling me names. He has stopped laying with me, though, so I am grateful for that. And since I have no one to talk to, I just listen more to the Spirits. They brought me to you, so I am happy to have their counsel." She looked up then and smiled, which was so incongruous with her sad tale.

"I'm happy for that, too, but it seems wrong that you must be treated that way."

"Perhaps you had the right idea: running from marriage. I wish I had the courage to do that."

"I'm not sure it was courage. It may have been the opposite: Fear. Fear and cowardice. I have never been good at making myself do something that seems distasteful to me, but so much of life requires that of us. I would be a better family member—I might even have a family—if I were better at forcing myself to do what is expected of me."

"Yes, but it comes with a price, too," she said. I could not argue with her, since she clearly knew the cost. She stood to go, and I had the sense she was leaving too soon.

"Thank you for coming to see me, Zhulyi. Please come again when you can."

"Or you can come to see me," she said. "You should come to see the Circ. It's worth the trip to Arad."

"Is it true that there are bears?" I asked.

"Oh yes, we have bears," she said.

∞

As it turned out, Liana had always wanted to see the Circ and convinced Janek that we should all go. Now that she had more help with her weaving, taking time away was not such an issue and they could afford the leisure. It was not a long journey, but we set out in the early afternoon, since the performances generally started right after dusk. The baby was getting big now, but we handed her off between us, and Janek and Damir put her on their shoulders for longer stretches. When we entered Arad, a steady flow of people and the occasional carriage helped to identify the direction to go toward where the action would take place. The Circ was set up in a giant amphitheater unlike anything I had ever seen. The Badi would have been envious of the formality and glory of the setting. Zhulyi later told me how the Bihari negotiated with the local authorities to pay a high rent and exorbitant tax for the use of the stadium and to keep their summer quarters there. Despite the general suspicion of the People, nobody seemed to mind taking gold from them. In the winter, the Bihari retreated to the mountains and spent the time practicing routines and planning the next season.

Liana and Janek were aware of our Rromani clientele, although most of them came to see me directly. They had inquired about it, and I had responded much like I had told Borbola: They are families like any other and they want cloth for special occasions. However, they were quite surprised when we arrived and I conversed briefly in Rromani with a few people I encountered whom I had met before in the commission of fabric.

"Customers," I explained, as we walked away, but the looks shared between them showed that there would be questions later. It was the same look they had after realizing that despite sleeping on their floor for several months, I had enough gold stashed away to purchase a house and launch a business.

Outside the arena were hawkers of all sorts, selling candies, food, and trinkets. Tiny Rromani girls sold strands of necklaces made from river pearls. Most of the sellers were Rromani, but there were Gentle peddlers there also, taking advantage of the influx to sell whatever they had available: winter apples dipped in honey on sticks, small punched tin boxes, and ribbons woven with flowers. I bought fried sweet bread for the little ones and a necklace for Liana. She protested, but I insisted she should have something so she could always remember her trip to the Circ. We stood on a queue to purchase wooden coins stamped with a star that would serve as our ticket to be collected when we went through the gates to the auditorium. In the frenetic crowd, I had forgotten to look for Zhulyi, but I felt a tug on my skirt by a small boy.

"Would you like your fortune read, miss?" He pointed to a tent, painted in gold with celestial symbols on the outside of the dark canvas and draped with garlands of evergreen and flowers. As I turned to walk toward it, Liana grabbed my arm.

"That is witchcraft, Alianor," she said. "Best not go in there."

"Oh no," I assured her. "It's just a friend. I will go to greet her and be right back."

I ignored the concerned looks exchanged between the couple as I went through the tent flap. Before I could say anything to Zhulyi, whose face lit up as soon as she recognized me entering the tent, a startlingly attractive young man pushed in. He smiled at me and said in Hungarian: "Greetings, fine miss. Pardon my intrusion." Switching to Rromani, he said: "The money, wench." Zhulyi wordlessly handed him a packet of coins. Confident his wife's Gentle client would not understand, he said: "Is this all of it? What have you been doing in here? You have *one* job. Can't you just do it right? Worthless!" He turned and flashed his white teeth at me in another ingratiating smile and, effortlessly switching languages, said: "Enjoy your reading, my wife is the best fortune teller around—very gifted!"

He left and I could see Zhulyi deflated. She sat down on her stool and put her hands in front of her on a table laid with candles, a small silver bowl of water, and a deck of what looked like very weathered playing cards. She sighed, and after a moment, she looked up at me. "I'm sorry," she said.

"What are you sorry about?"

"I'm sorry you had to see that."

"Zhulyi–I'm glad I saw it. Now I can appreciate what you are handling. You're right. He's awful."

She looked up, gratefully, and smiled. "It's such a joy to see you."

"I can't stay long. My business partners are outside."

"Yes, of course. My husband's bastard showed you in, I suppose? I apologize for my language. It's not his fault; he's just a child. It's just more insult to me, every day. I'm sure Aamon will train him to speak to me in the same way. I'll have to answer to him as a master, as well." She gestured at the silver bowl and cards, "That's what my future spells out for me." She chuckled and looked up at me, and despite the seriousness of the situation, I had to giggle, too. "Let me pull a card for you," she said, "before you go."

She shuffled the stack of cards, and I could see dark images and complicated patterns on the reverse of the stained and slightly tattered deck. She spread the cards in an arc before her and told me to choose. My hand went over the cards until I noticed one with a slightly bent edge and a small tear. As I reached for that card, I heard Zhulyi's intake of breath. I slid it from the array and flipped it over. I leaned in to see, as it was quite dark and smoky in the tent. The image was a tower that reminded me of the fortress at Deva. This tower had flames coming from the base and stones falling down all around.

Zhulyi looked at me, alarmed: "Change is coming, Alianor."

I really don't know what came over me, but as I stood to leave, I reached down and put my hand over hers, possessively. She looked startled and raised her face to me. "Perhaps it is coming for you, too, Zhulyi."

∞

The performance was as grand as we had been told. To start, there were women who rode bareback on two white mares around the great circle of the arena, even standing upon them with arms outstretched, as if they were extensions of the animals. A man who reminded me of Nandu, but with a pointy beard and a giant whip stood in the middle, snapping the whip and announcing the evening's events. There were even musicians in an orchestral clump providing an echoing and eerie cascade of forcefully moving music. Acrobats and fire-eaters, more daring than any I had seen with the Badi came out, one after the other, in synchronized routines that seemed impossibly coordinated. A small army of contortionists piled dangerously upon each other.

And then there were the bears: they looked to be a mama and two babies. A young woman led them around and had them do tricks as they growled and roared, even placing her head in the mama bear's mouth. After that came a man with a trained wolf, and an owl that flew circles above the audience members' heads before diving to receive a small brass ring from her master. She flew circles again, and then dropped the ring for the wolf to catch in his fierce jaws. Just when it seemed that the spectacle could get no more astounding, the air dancers began.

The Badi had a tightrope act that had always enthralled me, but this was in another category altogether. The Bihari had a tightrope, too, but piled people two and three high while walking across it. Then the trapeze artists began their daring flights. Agile men climbed with inhuman speed to the top of four tiny ladders, placed square to each other across the ring, barely visible against the night sky. Scantily dressed women ascended after them. They sat upon tiny swings, and the men began pushing them toward one another, at some invisible time frame aligned with the still pounding crescendo of the music. They flew though the air, barely missing one another as they stood on the swings, their bodies moving dramatically with the music, or hung upside down. The four of them swung in a crisscross pattern, perfectly timed so as not to collide. The orchestra swelled, and the strong male helpers pushed them even harder each time the swing returned.

Then suddenly it was a jumble, as a performer on one side somehow flipped, and ended up standing on the swing of her partner across from her. The mirror image was happening on the swings of those going in the alternate direction crossing them. The men grabbed empty swings and threw them back and the women reappeared upon their original seats after being flipped from the arms of her counterpart. It was a thrilling and confusing design pulsating through the air, and the audience was enraptured. Just then, the men captured the swings upon their return and held them tight. From above, descending from wires on scaffolding higher still than the swinging women, a single feminine form descended standing upon a bar that was sturdier and wider than the others, barely dressed in dazzling white. The intake of breath around the theater was audible.

The music shifted to a slow, reverent melody as she danced and swung against the stars, weaving around one side of the swing and then the other in rapturous liquid movements. She began to rotate her body along with the music, compelling the swing to move just from her own motions, leaning back as she held on to both sides of the descending strings. As she got the swing into full motion, all at once she let go of the sides of the swing and dropped in the air, grasping the bar with her hands, and then flipping over it several times in a dizzying circle, each revolution punctuated by gasps from the crowd.

Everyone in the audience was swept up—countless viewers overtaken by longing. I looked over and saw that even Janek's mouth was slightly opened as he gazed upon the beauty in the air as she took ownership of the entire night sky. The music wound down and the woman's swing eventually was lifted back into the darkness above. As she disappeared into the scaffolding, I was abruptly made aware of six men on the ground, three on each side of the ring, who were pulling with all they had to raise and lower the swing, one tying the ropes to secure them to great nails protruding from the ground while the other two leaned back and held fast to keep the ropes from slipping. I assumed this woman was the same one that had won Zhulyi's husband's affection. It occurred to me then that this woman was holding the whole amphitheater in a spell. All were captured, right down to the burly assistants working to keep her afloat in the air without harm. Rather than being resentful of this, even if just for the sake of my friend, I was impressed. For a woman to hold that much power over so many was truly remarkable. It was a different kind of power than the one that comes from money and status—like the Cetatii women I had become familiar with—but it was power, nonetheless.

∞

As we walked back along the streets in darkness, only lit by the moon, we talked little. Janek and the boys walked in front. Janek held a sleeping Vaski, and Liana and I trailed behind. We dropped back a little, as I could tell Liana wanted to speak to me. "Alianor, how did you come to speak the Ciganyok tongue so well?"

"I lived among them for a time. They were very kind to me when I was an orphaned child."

"Truly? How astonishing. You never spoke of this before."

"No," I said.

"I know you ran from a marriage. Was it to one of *them*?" I could not see her face, but I almost felt her shudder beside me.

"Yes, the young man I was supposed to marry was Rromani."

"Well, I can see why you ran then." My heart closed a little bit then to the woman toward whom I had so much fondness. I did not respond, and we just walked along quietly behind the men. "It does explain a lot, though," she said after a time.

"What's that?"

"You do have a way about you. People respond to you. I don't know if you see it, but it's like a little bit of magic that follows you around and makes things happen."

"I have never seen it that way. If anything, I feel followed by a curse."

"Well, that's the Ciganyok way, isn't it? Their magic is sinful. It's dangerous even when it appears to be good."

I imagined the trapeze artist then, and felt certain Liana was thinking of her, too. "I have never seen that among them. I have seen only generosity and good will," I assured her.

"It's witchcraft all the same." We did not speak the rest of the journey. Janek had insisted upon routing by my cottage to see me safely home. When I kissed Liana goodbye, I felt her stiffen a little as I embraced her. "Good night, sleep well," she said formally. I spoke briefly to Janek and Damir to discuss some business for the following day, and then they departed. I stood on my steps watching them walk away and was not surprised when I saw Liana remove the pearl necklace and put it in her pocket.

Chapter Fourteen: The Shadow

Our business still flourished for the rest of that summer, but I saw little of Liana. Janek's attitude toward me did not seem to change. We still conversed and planned for our expansion, as orders continued to pile up for several seasons ahead. By fall, Janek had help from a neighborhood crew to build Liana's weaving shed into an all-season building where the work could continue into winter, and they had taken on two more seasoned weavers to assist with the orders and learn Liana's unique techniques. I took on one of Borbala's older daughters to assist with my weaving. She was quite young and was mostly useful for organizing and cleaning up the house and greeting visitors.

I still had my Rromani customers, who chose to come straight to me instead of going to the shop, but I directed most others to the store when I could. A few noblewomen insisted on coming to me exclusively, always claiming that I had a gift for helping them choose exactly the right hue to complement both them and the event they were planning or attending. Zhulyi visited sporadically, and it was always a treat to see her, though I worried for her. She seemed more despondent each time, and I could see the toll her marriage was taking on her. I told her about a "marital prison" that I had heard of. The bishop in a local city would banish troubled couples to a small room for six weeks, where they would be forced to share one blanket and a tiny table and work out their differences.

Zhulyi cringed when I told her this. "If I had to live in a room with Aamon for six weeks, I would surely take my own life." We laughed over this, but I knew the humor shielded a darker pain that was undeniable. When the Bihari Circ began to plan their migration to the mountains in Cozia for the winter, I could see her begin to crumble. She dreaded the long winter where she would be likely to have little opportunity to travel to Deva. We said our goodbyes and when she left for what we imagined would be the last time we would see each other before the spring, Zhulyi held me by the shoulders and looked into my eyes. "I will visit you in my dreams, Jaelle." I had told her my Rroma name, since I knew she would hold it secret, and she only spoke it when we were alone.

I was surprised, then, one night to hear her distinctive tap on my door. I had gone to bed as the first snow was falling, damping the fire low and feeling lonely and sorry for myself as I sometimes still did. I opened the door to see Zhulyi, bundled with her head covering sparkling with a layer of snowflakes. She looked like an ice fairy. "Come in! Zhulyi! I'm so happy to see you! Is something wrong?"

"My mother," she said. "She is not well." Her face looked drained.

"I'm sorry," I said.

"Some good has come of it, though," she smiled weakly. "Aamon has agreed to let me stay with her for the winter. He will have the whole winter to carouse with his sweetheart, so I'm sure he's thrilled, but I will be able to stay with my mother to nurse her."

My heart lost heaviness I was not even aware it was holding, and I hugged her excitedly. My arms were immediately saturated by the cold flakes covering her, and we laughed as I came away quickly, shivering as my skin touched icy fabric. I helped her remove her outer layer and drape it near the fire. I had already prepared the house for sleep, but I perked up the fire, lit a few candle boxes, and put water on to boil. The room began to warm, and soon Zhulyi was able to unwind her damp hair covering. I gave her a brush, and she smoothed out her tresses as they fell across her shoulders, reflecting the firelight. I had never seen her hair unwrapped before and was entranced by the dark locks reaching all the way down her back.

"What is it?" she asked me, when she felt me staring at her.

"You're just so . . . beautiful," I said, unable to verbalize more. The snow was falling now in great sheets, thick and determined. "How will you even dig your way back to your mother's?" I asked.

"She will not expect me. She knows I am safe with the *Alexandru*," she laughed and surprised me by pulling me into her arms on the bench before the stove. We sat, entwined.

As we sat and watched the flames, I had the strangest sensation that the fire flickering before us was entering our skin, inhabiting our bodies. I felt the tendrils pulsing through my veins, visiting all my organs, and spiraling through my head, leaving sparks in its wake. It was as if we had become the fire, and there was no division between us, just as there were no individual flames. We merged and became one, a surging and powerful elemental connection, as if we were part of all fire that had ever been or ever would be. As her skin touched mine, I lost track of what was mine and what was hers, and the concept of us as separate beings lost all meaning.

We may have sat for hours, as time also lost meaning, and we existed only between one crack or snap of flame dancing before us and another. Perhaps we even dozed, as the candles had long since burned down and sputtered out. I felt us move to my bedding in a trance, but it was as if we were moving through water in a dream. We must have been sleeping even before we touched the bed, since I have no memory of anything after, only the sensation of her form pressed against me and the deep understanding between our bodies that we were one entity, no longer two separate beings.

∞

That winter was the happiest I had been since losing Perla. Zhulyi visited me most nights, coming after dark and often leaving well before morning. It was remarkable to me, since I no longer felt alone. Her entry into my world was a salve to everything that pained me. I experienced no more nightly fears or regret for past decisions. All made sense in the larger journey of my life now that she was in it. For her, I felt my presence dissolved the concern she felt for her mother and the distress she had experienced in her six years of marriage to Aamon. Our bond was so strong that while we talked about many things, often we would not talk at all. We would lay together and feel the peace that overtook us when the walls between us fell away. To call it magic would be to trivialize it, since it was as if a basic truth of the universe was revealed whenever skin touched skin and we became one.

In the daylight hours, when working at my loom, my hands flew through the motions and I would suddenly have another piece completed. I was more productive than I had ever been, though the days seemed ridiculously short. The long nights were when I did my true living, within the solace of Zhulyi's arms as our souls blended and merged. I asked her once why she thought it was like that. It was curious to me, having never had any connection to another living being like the one I had with her, disregarding my attachment to Ankah and the maternal bond I had developed with Perla, which were similar, yet not the same.

"We are sisters," she explained, "like all women."

"I have not felt like this with other women."

She laughed. "No, I admit I have not either. But it's the great connection between us all that comes about when we are together. It's bigger than us. Remember that the Rromani race was created when the sun chased his sister, the moon, across the sky to lay with her. We are no different, although some might feel it unnatural."

"That union caused a shadow over the sun," I recalled from the tales of my childhood.

"The shadow is always there, Jaelle," Zhulyi said seriously. "Our love does not make it emerge. It just reveals what already exists." I had never heard her use the word "love" in reference to us before, so I ignored the dark message she had implied and pulled her to me. With her hair in my face, the fragrance of woodsmoke and rose in its tresses, I cared little for the shadows of the world. I remember feeling as if we were living in an extended dream. Nothing before or after mattered–nor existed for that matter–and I lived only for the moments in her arms.

Still, when Zhulyi's mother began to worsen, she had to forego her nightly visits. I went with Zhulyi to visit the woman, to show my respect for her and bring her a gift of a silver shawl I had woven for her. It glistened with pearly radiance, and her sunken face lit up when she pulled it around her. I could see what Zhulyi had described in her shaking body, which could no longer rise from her bedroll. She often forgot where she was, or even Zhulyi's face, becoming confused and angry, swiping at her with a curled claw and insisting she had had stolen her daughter. One morning Zhulyi came to my door, and without words I knew her mother had passed. I held her as she cried. Later, I made the arrangements for her mother's body, wrapped in the shawl I had woven for her, to be burned upon a simple raft upon the river, along with a few of her treasured objects: her cooking pot and a long, carved staff of beechwood.

My neighbors were unhappy with the ritual and with the small cluster of relatives who lined the shore to honor the elder's passing. They had already become colder to me, somehow prescient of the nocturnal visits and my connection to the Rromani families who came for cloth. Borbala had stopped sending her little daughter to help me, claiming she needed to begin training her in her own work as a seamstress. The father and son who lived on the other side of me, who had never been friendly, began to scowl whenever I encountered them and did not reciprocate my greetings. As much as I wanted to deny it, things were shifting. The universe that had expanded around us, protecting us, was dissolving. I felt the Shadow encroaching.

I fixed upon the solution one day when pondering how I could hold on to Zhulyi. She was preparing to leave in a week to go back to her husband's tribe. He had sent for her after hearing about her mother's death, and Zhulyi was making final arrangements–getting ready to return to the life she despised. After dark, she arrived, and we sat sipping juniper tea. "I wish it could stay like this," Zhulyi said wistfully.

"Perhaps it can."

"You know it can't. I must return to the Circ. Soon it will be the season again, and they will want me there."

"What would happen if you didn't return?"

"Aamon would come looking for me. He may not truly want me, but it would hurt his pride if his wife did not come back to him. Besides, you know I cannot stay here. Your neighbors are already unhappy with clanfolk about. They would not tolerate it."

"We don't need to stay here." I had thought through many scenarios of how to keep Zhulyi close to me on the nights she had spent with her grieving family after her mother's death.

"Then where would we go? Who would accept us? And what of your business?"

"My business will do fine without me. I think it's time I turn it back over to Liana and Janek anyway. It was theirs to start."

I told her of the plan that I had been concocting. It was quite simple. We would return to Brașov: I would marry Sandor as he had asked of me before. Zhulyi could be employed as my maid so that I could keep her close to me in the house. I was certain Sandor would agree to it. Having never mentioned Sandor before, though, the whole thing took some explaining. I found that when I began, I could not justify his entry into my life without also explaining Perla, so I had to spool the story back even more and start from the beginning, to when I had left the Badi with Perla in my arms. As I told my tale to Zhulyi, who had known some small snippets from our conversations, her eyes grew wide and at some points brimmed with tears.

"Jaelle, why did you never tell me this before?"

"I have held it so close to myself. I'm ashamed of what I did."

"You were just a child. I don't know how you survived all those years by yourself, but you did, and you kept Perla alive."

"I'm afraid she hates me now."

"I doubt it. You are the only mother she's known. If anything, she must miss you terribly."

I cried then, thinking of Perla not despising me as I'd imagined, but missing me as her Mama. Zhulyi held me, and when the tears stopped, I told her the rest of the story, how Sandor had taken us in and revealed what he believed to be our connection. She was as surprised as I had been when she heard his solution, to marry his own daughter in order to guarantee my inheritance. When I told her that I thought he would still honor this proposal, and that he would certainly allow me to have my own "maid" come with me, she blanched a bit.

"I am basically a servant now," she said. "It would not be much different."

"Of course, you would not be expected to serve me, Zhulyi," I played with a tendril of her hair. "But it would provide us a way to stay close–to stay together."

She took my face in her hands: "I want to serve you, Jaelle. I want us to serve one another, always."

Despite the soundness of the plan, she was wary of being accepted into the house of a grand lord, or any house at all for that matter, as one who had stayed in permanent structures only for short periods while caring for her bedridden mother or during winter months. Still, I had her try to imagine what life would be like for two women wandering together, one Rrom, one Gentle, and how we would be received. There were not many places we would be welcomed. Her other option, returning to the Circ and Aamon, did not bode well for her. She said when she thought of her prospects in returning to him, she felt like she was suffocating. I knew that feeling well. She consulted with the Spirits, since she felt conflicted about leaving her duties as a wife and her obligation to the Circ. She was not one who shirked her commitments. They were silent except to echo the prophecy suggested when she had read cards for me many months before: Change is coming.

We planned to leave within the week, and I began to take stock of what I needed to do. There was very little, as I intended to turn over the business completely to Janek on the final day. I did not choose to say goodbye to Liana, since she had grown uncomfortable in my presence. While I regretted missing the opportunity to see the children again, it seemed best to just pass my good wishes for them through their father. The house was much improved from when I had purchased it, and I was not sure how to leave it. It had been so good to me. I cleaned it top to bottom, scrubbing everything to honor its kindness to me. I decided to give the papers of ownership to Damir, since he was almost of an age to begin considering marriage and would need a place to start his own family.

Although I had amassed some wealth from my business, I found it poignant to use the last of the gold coins Sandor had given me to book passage for two on a coach returning to Brașov. The day prior to our departure, I went to visit Janek and told him I would be leaving. I explained that the business would belong exclusively to them and gave him the papers to the house for Damir. Although he seemed genuinely saddened, he did not ask for an explanation. I could sense his relief. Despite having brought his family a good deal of fortune, I knew that my association with the Rromani was problematic for them, and their lives would be simpler without me in it.

"Alianor, you have been a blessing to our family," he said, kissing my cheeks.

"Thank you, Janek. Your family showed me hospitality as a total stranger. Please send my good wishes to them, and especially Liana. Tell her I will treasure her friendship and always appreciate her excellent tutelage. She is a remarkable weaver and she deserves to be acknowledged for her skill."

Janek thanked me for the papers to the house, telling me Damir would be delighted, as he had recently been speaking of marriage to the daughter of the man who ran the bakery nearby the shop. Having both ownership in a business and a home to offer her would make Damir a viable husband, when the time came. Janek did not inquire where I would go.

I waited that night for Zhulyi to arrive, knowing that she would be coming as soon as she could complete her preparations to slip away. When daylight came and she had still not arrived, I went around through the back alley to the street where her mother's family was keeping their apartments. The door was open and there was scurrying inside. A cousin greeted me, and when I asked for Zhulyi, she said: "Her husband came for her last night. The Circ is moving to new territory in Oradea. He came to get her as they are leaving straight away. She told us to tell you she was sorry when you came looking for her."

My heart dropped and blood pounded in my ears. I could barely hear as the cousin continued: "We are moving on, too. We've been in one place too long and the winter is leaving. It's time for us to go also." I gave her my thanks and walked in a stupor back to my house. I had just a small bag packed. I walked to where the coach would be leaving shortly. The driver asked where my travel companion was, but I just shook my head and climbed inside. For several days I rode toward Brașov. Through the fog of my grief I was aware of the irony that I had gotten nowhere in my life. If anything, I was going backwards. It was as if I were tied to a flexible string: I had run until I could not run any longer, until the tautness of what bound me snapped me back to return and face my destiny. I did not reflect on what awaited me. I had gone completely numb inside. All I could see were Zhulyi's dark eyes; I could only smell the scent of her hair in my nostrils. I was barely aware when we stopped for breaks along the way. I drank little and ate nothing.

When we stopped finally in the city of Brașov a few mornings later, I got out and looked around, disoriented. I had only been through the city once, when fleeing from the Badi and Sandor, but it looked different than I remembered. A church had been erected in my absence, confusing my sense of orientation. Still turned about in my bearings by the unfamiliar layout of new streets surrounding the church, I finally looked to the horizon. This allowed me to decipher the direction of the mountain and Sandor's estate. Despite the jumble of the city, I found my way to its edge and to the road that led to the Alexandru property. My body ached from being cramped in the coach and I was unused to walking. Not having consumed anything for days, I was lightheaded. I began to float, my awareness hovering above my body as it drew near the house.

The mansion was as grand as ever. Trees were beginning to bud, and I noted a few improvements. I walked past the great house's curving stone entrance gates and continued down the road that led to the complex of barns, cottages, and outbuildings. I was struck again how the compound was like a small self-contained town keeping the estate running. As I passed, I pulled my hood up around my head, but the few people I saw busily engaged in work were unfamiliar to me, paying me little mind. I kept going until I saw the expanse of fields and pastures, with sheep and a few goats grazing. None seemed to be my goats, but a few looked as though they could be their daughters, round with kids or nursing new babies who jumped and played nearby. I kept walking.

At the beginning of the mountain trail, when the trees became dense, and light was filtered by the morning sun, I came back into my body. My feet felt the stones beneath my shoes, and I felt the cool watery shadows of trees upon my face. I suddenly felt that I could breathe, although I had not been aware of holding my breath. The clean mountain air filled my lungs: I was suddenly ravenous. I began picking new leaves and edible shoots as I walked, making sure to thank them before popping them into my mouth. I had not had to forage in a long time, but the habit returned to me easily: the plants old friends I had not seen in many years.

The climb was arduous. Unused to such labors, I stopped by a stream to rest and chewed some bitter wild rose buds to get back my strength before continuing. By mid-day, I could see the crest of the mountain. I knew the castle and the lake lay just on the other side of the ridge. Coming over the pine barricade at the crest, I could see my old home, where I had spent so many years raising Perla and caring for our animals. It was empty, but it still called to me, reminding me of all the time we had spent there, sheltered from the world and creating our own family and tribe made up of two humans and many creatures.

As I walked down the ridge and toward the ruins, I recognized some of the structures toward the outside that I had reinforced to hold livestock and poultry. I could almost see them brimming with critters, as they appeared when quietly shut in for the night to protect them from predators. A movement caught my eye, and I saw a gray flash. A wolf appeared, coming from inside one of the old pens, tempted by residual smells of prey. He slinked out, seeming as surprised to see me as I was to see him. He stood with yellow eyes trained on me, frozen for many moments, then flashed up the ridge.

I lay down my bag, and then walked toward the building, placing my hand flat on a giant stone that had fallen from its place in the foundation. It hummed and told me something, but I could barely hear it. I walked around the whole perimeter of the castle, listening and observing. I walked around it three times before picking up my bag and entering the old doorway leading in from the stables. I found my old quarters, inhabited since by another family who had left some broken items and a few tatters of fabric. It was dirtied by mouse nests and droppings, but still familiar. I swept and cleaned it and went to get fresh bedding of pine needles and soft dried grasses. I found an old pot, made a fire, and began to boil water.

Walking down to the lake, I pulled some reeds to salvage the tender parts inside and began to make a soup. On my way back in, I recalled the tale that Ankah had told me long ago about how Selene had made soup with stones to heal her children during the Pestilence. I felt more in need of healing than I ever had, so when my eye caught a deep gray stone poking from the moss, rounded and circled with a white band, I picked it up. I brushed it off and dropped it in my pot. That night, as I sipped my stone broth, flavored with lake tubers and herbs still half asleep that I found unearthed from layers of dead leaves, I could feel the nourishment returning to my limbs. I had come home.

Chapter Fifteen: The Secrets of Stones

It did not take long for Sandor's people to learn of my presence in the old castle. I knew he would quickly be alerted when I saw a few men on horseback out hunting the ridge. I raised my hand to them in greeting, but they did not approach. The next day, Sandor arrived on the same strong stallion I had first seen him riding in the icy woods when I was still a child, though the horse was much more sedate and seasoned in his maturity. Though only two years had passed since I last saw him, Sandor, too, had aged. His face, which had always reminded me of metal, looked brittle, and his eyes sadder. He jumped down from his saddle and embraced me.

"Jaelle—I did not know if I would ever see you again!"

"Nor I you, Sandor."

He pulled back slightly, surprised to hear me call him the name I had only said in my head the last few years. He smiled.

"So, we are finally on more familiar terms?" he enquired, some of the old sparkle returning to his eyes.

"Well, forgive me if I still am not ready to call you 'Father,'" I said, and we laughed.

"I have worried so much for you. You will have to tell me all your adventures."

"First tell me of Perla. How went it when the Badi came?"

Sandor described the gang of men that had arrived to demand her return. They wanted me, too—to be turned over to them for punishment. The leader of the group could only be Sasha, the way Sandor described him: a flashy and ardent young man. The group seemed suspicious that Sandor was keeping me sheltered in the great house and demanded entry to investigate. Sandor had armed reinforcements there in case things got tense. Perla came out to speak to the gang, and they calmed and talked peacefully.

"Perla was magnificent," Sandor recalled. "She greeted her 'cousins' and said she was eager to return to meet her family, and especially her father and brothers. They seemed surprised that she knew of them. Then she spoke to them in the Ciganyok tongue, so I'm not sure what else she said, but they were clearly smitten with her. She insisted upon bringing the dog, Stea, with her, and they agreed with no issues. I hope you won't mind, but I paid them a great deal for their trouble and told them that you had gone far away and that none of us were likely to hear from you ever again. I checked on her again here at the castle a few times before they left in the spring. She was living with her father and his wife and seemed to be very bonded already with the two little boys—her brothers."

I choked back tears, and realized it was all I wished for, for Perla to be reunited with her family and accepted. "Thank you, Sandor," was all I could say.

"And you, Jaelle? How have you been? Tell me what the last few years have brought you. I see you are wearing some very fine fabric. I hope that means you have fared well?"

I looked down at my dress and smiled at the compliment to my weaving. I could find few words to tell my story. I just shook my head. "It's been a long two years, Sandor."

"For us both, it would seem," he replied.

He gave me some updated news of the estate: who had gone and come; new buildings and developments. He said there were new goats, and that all my original goats had disappeared when the Ciganyok left, but not their young kids. The babies remained with the herd and still roamed with the large flock of sheep. I was not bothered by this news, knowing that my sweet friends were getting quite old, and the Badi would treat them well in their declining years. Despite Sasha's rage at me, he was always kind to "our" goats. It was all in balance, for them to return to him; after all, when I'd left—in addition to taking Perla—I had taken his beloved Pebbles and her kid. This was justice.

"And why are you here in the castle again? You must know you can stay on the estate. You can stay in my home, or in one of the cottages if that would make you more comfortable."

"I needed to come back here," I said, unable to explain how I yearned to be where I had spent years raising my little girl.

"Well, you can come with me now, if you wish."

"No, thank you. This place suits me better," I gestured to the crumbling walls.

"I have thought about it many times, Jaelle. I realized I may have put pressure on you by proposing for you to marry me. I only wanted to be able to claim you, for you to be entitled to what is due you. I hope you realize that you could have stayed with me even if you chose not to marry me. I care not what anyone thinks: I still would have claimed you as my daughter, even if it would not have meant anything legally."

"I'm sure you would have, but it was a good time to leave, with the Badi coming. It would have caused you a great deal more trouble if I had been there."

"That may be true, but you are my daughter, and I would defend you. I would defend you now."

"This way was better: Perla left peacefully and there was no need for bloodshed."

"Yes, but I can see that despite your fine clothes, you have suffered hardship."

"It is all of my own making, Sandor. I have no one to blame but myself."

He regarded me, and looked as if he wanted to say more, even opened his mouth, then closed it again. "Do you have supplies?" he finally asked.

"The forest is brimming with supplies," I replied. "It's spring. Soon the summer will bring its abundance and I will feast and prepare for fall and winter."

"You intend to stay on here, in the castle alone?"

"I stayed here with a newborn and survived. I'm sure I'll be fine on my own as well."

He couldn't disagree. "I will check on you, then. You can come to me for anything, you know?"

"Yes, thank you," I said.

∞

As devastated as I was, the forest renewed me. I had spent years without the company of trees: the small orchards and young trees in Deva were but singular presences. Surrounded again by the magnificent old stands, I felt embraced by friends. The quiet filled my ears and head and heart, and I was awash with peace. At night, I heard the melodies of the wolves, and remembered their songs. One night, I heard a rustling: I sat up in the nest of the bed I had made on the floor. The fire was burning low, and around the stone corner I saw a wolf. It was the same one who had been here when I arrived, I was sure. He stood in the doorway, looking at me as I sat frozen, looking directly at him. I was not afraid, since I sensed that he was just curious about who had taken over his refuge.

I spoke to him and sang him a Rromani lullaby about a wolf who steals away a little girl to marry. Perla had loved that song. He sat listening. When the song was over, he backed out, glancing back at me a few times before disappearing. I smiled to myself and went to sleep quickly, with no fear in my heart. In addition to the wolf, who became a frequent visitor, I also had other creatures who began to come from the forest to investigate the castle's new resident. I had a badger who would come by at dusk to see if there was anything good to eat that I might have dropped on the ground, and several young deer who grazed close by, seeming to feel protected by me. Also many squirrels and foxes scouted the perimeter, and chipmunks dived in and out of the stone. The birds came, too, and I watched the sparrows nesting in all the open places in the badly deteriorated rooftops and eaves. There was more sky than roof in most parts of the old fortress, so at night the bats and owls came through and I heard all manner of nightly winged visitors.

I did not remember so much activity in the years I had been raising Perla, but then, I had been overcome with the tasks of caring for her and the animals. Perhaps the smells and sounds of livestock and humans had kept the wild animals at bay, or perhaps I just had been too swept up in my responsibilities to notice. Now, there were no barriers between me and the forest creatures, and they drew close around me and the castle, living in the ruins about me as if I were just another one of them. Having no animals of my own and never having learned to hunt, I ate no meat except a lake fish here or there. The fields and undergrowth of the woods provided an abundant buffet of grazing, and I ate stews of berries and barks, wild onions and tubers, and never felt hungry. I dried and stored what I could to prepare for the winter. I felt I had everything I needed, as I needed very little.

Alone in the crumbling stones, I began to hear the wind in ways I had never heard it before. The trees spoke a language I had not bothered to pay attention to, whispering together as they rubbed branches above and entwined roots below. Now I began to listen deeply. I heard every scuffle on the stone by the small nails of tiny rodents and understood the yelping barks of the foxes at night as they called each other to mate. Even the clouds breaking up the dark sky at night seemed to tell me the stories of when they were other clouds, over other mountains, underneath different arrangements of stars. I was listening now to the earth and sky with my whole being, as I never had before. My whole life I had been surrounded by people and animals and noises and thoughts in my head, as I planned, and worried, and pondered. Now I was truly alone in the world, and the silence that came with that allowed me to finally hear all the voices– that had been there all along– but had been drowned out by my distracted mind.

I was sad at times, yearning for Zhulyi. All I had lost filled the dark sky at night, and I felt very small in the vastness of the dark. I came to understand from the voices that spoke to me through the forest sounds that it was a wonder that Zhulyi and my soul had crossed paths at all. We had located each other somehow across the incalculable expanse of time. Out of all the humans that had ever lived and would ever live, we had found one another now, in this lifetime: had seen and recognized each other. That we could connect and be together–our hearts converging for any amount of time–was nothing short of a miracle. I recalled that it was the Spirits who had told Zhulyi to seek me out. They must have known what they were doing. Perhaps they told her to leave again and maybe they would bring us together again someday. If not, I had been enriched by loving her. I worried for her, and her fate with Aamon, but it was beyond my control. There was a freedom in having the choice taken out of my hands, made by forces that I could not understand. Maybe Zhulyi was right: maybe we never decide anything.

The summer passed, and I grew more connected to the small stones under my feet and the giant stones that made up the castle walls. I felt there was a lot I could learn from them; when I placed my hands upon them, I felt their low, quiet, endless presence speak to me. I took off the shoes I had made and walked barefoot most of the time. The needles of the pines felt decadent, and by the end of the summer, the weakness in my feet from years of being protected by leather soles had left. There were no more barriers between me and the earth. I moved carefully through the woods and harvested fern fronds and found great communities of mushrooms. I was familiar with many that were edible, but there were so many more: of all colors and every shape imaginable, that I had never seen before. They mostly grew from the trees that had fallen, as if the forest herself gave birth in her demise. I realized every entity was in deep communication with all around them. It may sound strange, but the trees told me which mushrooms were safe to eat.

The fall came and I dried and stored supplies. Winter passed like one long night to me. I slept and woke in the dark, melted snow or got fresh water from the spring that fed into the lake, and made my daily tea and stew. I sipped my broth in the barest dawn: I sewed some; stitched and cleaned some; and the day would pass into night again before I knew it. Another spring and then summer came, as wondrous as it only can be on top of a mountain. I spent the days end-to-end in reverence of the glory around me.

Sandor visited me often, but I had little to say to him. He brought me some candles and dried meat, which I added to my stews, but other than that, I lived off the abundant vegetation around me. He wondered at my ability to live and survive on my own, as he had when he had first come upon me raising Perla by myself. "Are you not lonely?" he asked me once, on one of his brief visits.

"I have been lonely my whole life," I responded.

Another winter passed. Before I knew it, the snow was melting and in barely the blink of the eye, luxurious spring was giving way to verdant summer. Another blink, and then the tips of leaves began to color and crisp with the first cool nights. I realized the clans would be returning to the castle soon: this would be the fifth winter since I had parted ways with Perla and had headed out to Alba Jula and then Deva.

"You can come back to the estate," said Sandor, who knew I wanted to leave before the tribes converged upon the mountain. "You can even have your own cottage back. We've lost another seamstress–pleurisy."

"Thank you, Sandor. I am not fit for human company anymore."

"Nonsense! You are a delight as you've always been, although it's true the mountain has made you rougher." He glanced down at my feet.

"I will be leaving soon, but perhaps I'll come back in the spring," I said.

"But where will you go?"

"I don't know," I said honestly. I had lived now for so long on the graces of the earth and her mysteries that I suppose I just expected her to tell me where to go next: She had been mute on the subject. "Perhaps I will return to my mother's home. I don't know that I could find it, but I could try." Sandor's face filled with pain. "I don't know that it would mean anything," I continued, "but maybe it would help things make sense to me to see the mountainside again."

"You will stay with my uncle," Sandor said, suddenly filled with an authority he rarely used with me: "I have not seen him in many years, but I will send you with a letter to recommend you. He may be able to connect you to Alianor's—to your mother's—family. I wish I could accompany you, but the Voivode has informed us of another invasion coming. I must prepare my men in case we need to fight for the crown."

A few days later Sandor returned with an extra horse, suited up for travel, and a package filled with a new dress and shoes, as well as some other small provisions. He gave me a letter for his uncle and told me the basics of how to find his estate, many days' travel over the mountains. "I feel that I should send you with reinforcements, a chaperone of some kind, but I'm sure you would reject that."

"He will be my chaperone," I said, stroking the neck of the bay gelding he had brought me to ride. "What is his name?"

"He is Sorrow: his mother died giving birth to him. The milk maids raised him in the barn with the sheep, so he is one of the most compliant fellows around."

I looked into the horse's dark eyes and saw a kindred soul.

Chapter Sixteen: Roots

Sorrow and I headed out across the mountains at a leisurely pace. I was not used to riding, and I found the saddle uncomfortable. I considered removing it and leaving it on the side of the trail. Sorrow seemed used to it, though, so I persevered. I enjoyed the last moments of my solitude, knowing that more would be expected of me when I arrived at Count Alexandru's estate. Sandor had told me a little of his uncle, who had been a friend and confidante to him when he was younger, but I felt uncertain if I would be palatable to him. Even if he believed I was Sandor's child, as Sandor did, that did not guarantee me an excellent reception.

I slept close to the trails, eating dried rations and making small fires at night just to warn away predators. Sandor had indicated landmarks I should watch for along the way. I encountered no person in the earlier part of the mountainous trail. The journey was unremarkable, except for enjoying the scenery and Sorrow's company. I took my time, seeing no reason to rush. It was still early autumn, and though I had no idea where I would stay through the winter months, I had plenty of time to figure that out. I may have also been delaying my entry into Curtea de Argeş, the city closest to where Sandor's uncle resided. I began to pass through some smaller towns and larger cities, but did not stop, despite being fascinated by the unusual weaving techniques I saw displayed in some of the markets. My modest dress and fine mount endorsed me enough to be mostly left alone by people I encountered. In one town, though, I was harassed by a group of men who demanded to know why a woman was traveling without an escort. When I mentioned the name of the Count Alexandru and showed them the seal on the letter from his nephew, they left me unmolested, even escorting me to the edge of the town.

Following Sandor's directions, it was easy to find the city of Curtea de Argeş, then follow the Argeş River to Albestii de Argeş and the Count's estate. As impressed as I had been with the small community that Sandor governed, the Count's properties were more extensive and even grander. It was almost a city by itself, with giant stone gates marking the entry to the mountain complex, and neat roads made from powdered marble. The manor itself sat high and sprawling, with spires and peaks shooting up at irregular intervals, upon a great circular drive overlooking the massive enterprise. In the distance were stables and a mill, and several workshops with carts filled with goods coming and going, all in the frenetic business of the estate. Not feeling comfortable going up to the great house, I went to the stables first.

A vassal there looked at the seal of the letter I carried and immediately took Sorrow's reins and led him to be fed and cleaned. The stable hand pulled a serious-looking older man in livery to the side and speaking quietly, pointed toward me, and the man came over to greet me. "Madam, I am told you come bringing word from the Count's nephew? How is the Lord Alexandru? Is all well with him?"

"Yes, Sir. He's quite well. I have a letter with a private message for the Count that I am to deliver to him personally."

"Of course, my lady. I will see to it immediately. The Count is away for the day on business, but we will have rooms prepared for you to wait for him. You have no other bags?" He eyed the travel-worn sack I carried.

"No, Sir. I have journeyed light, expressly to see the Count."

"Well, we'll see you're made comfortable until he returns."

Although it was easily walkable back to the manor, he insisted on having a small carriage equipped to bring me there, and the driver delivered me to the door, where other uniformed staff, who must have somehow been informed of my arrival, stood waiting to greet me.

I was ushered inside by the stewards, and barely got to see the vast grand hall before being brought into a narrow passageway off the side to a suite of rooms. Servants began coming with pitchers of boiling water to fill a great tub. A large tray of fruits, cold meats, and cheese was brought, along with wine. "From the Count's vineyards," the vassal explained. After the flurry of activity, the lady in charge—a steely woman who carefully avoided looking at my dust-stained dress—asked me if there would be anything else that I needed.

"No, thank you."

"The Count should return this evening. Please feel free to use the house as if it were yours. We have not seen the Count's nephew in many years. The Count will be most grateful for any message you bring."

When alone, I took out the one other item of clothing I owned: the previous winter I had sewn a dress in preparation to travel from the castle but had never worn it, wearing the one Sandor had given me instead. I hung the dress I had made over a chair to air out. The furniture in the room was elaborately carved, and there was a silk dressing screen with delicately embroidered white birds flying through clouds. I looked closely at the screen to see the small, almost invisible stitches making up the design. Except for Sandor's house, I had never seen painted walls before, and these were tinted a sky blue. I looked up to see a painting of angels holding a golden banner between them and flying through clouds across the vast concave ceiling.

I had bathed regularly in the mountain lake but was embarrassed to see the water in the tub turn quickly brown as I scrubbed clean first my hair, then my body in the giant vessel they had prepared. The water was incredibly warm, with steam rising into the air, reminding me of the hot springs we had stayed by when I was a child, when Ankah and I had stayed in to bathe so long Baba had scolded us. It felt magnificent to wash away years of grime in ways cold mountain water is unable. I scrubbed my feet, but they improved little, having developed a hard drum exterior and permanent darkening from walking on pine for two years, being only protected by foot coverings in the coldest months.

It felt odd to be within walls that did not breathe with gusting mountain wind. I already felt out of my element being in an enclosed space; it took me a while to realize that the underlying unease I felt was due to the complete lack of noise. The thick stone walls and sealed interior made everything silent. I was used to living among birdsong and rustling leaves, never a moment without the sounds of the trees and creatures around me. Now, even my footsteps disappeared on lush carpeting after I exited the bath and used large drying cloths to remove all the moisture from my limbs and hair. I found a brush and several small tools I could not identify on a small table. There was a small looking glass there, too, and I picked it up and saw a face I didn't recognize. My reflection revealed remarkably sad eyes, but a bright complexion and overall attractive youthful features. Somehow, I had expected to see an older, darker Rromani face when I looked at myself. What I saw instead was a Gentle woman who did not match at all with the way I felt inside. If I did not know better, I would pass as any other of the common folk of the land; I only looked foreign to myself.

I ate some of the food that had been left and drank a glass of wine. I had intended to venture out of the quarters, since I'd been invited to see the rest of the house. I sat down for a moment to test the mattress on the narrow, intricately carved bed. It was stuffed with goose down! I lay back, feeling as though I was lying upon the same clouds painted on the ceiling above and gazed up at the angels suspended there. Before I knew it, I had dozed off. I didn't wake until I heard a half knock and maids coming in with oil lamps to light the fire in the grate and clean up. The severe lady had returned and announced in her harsh, Slavic accent: "The Count has returned. He is eager to see you. You will join him for dinner."

A few minutes later, she returned to escort me to the dining hall. A large man was sitting at the head of the long banquet table, which reminded me of Sandor's great hall. He stood and came toward me, then stopped in his tracks. "Why, you look–" he said, and stopped, faltered, and then seemed to recover: "My dear, welcome to my estate! I hear you bring word from my beloved nephew."

He came close and kissed my cheeks, still seeming to observe me closely. As his beard brushed my face, I had a sharp memory of a beard like that. It was dark in the dining hall, even with all the torchlight and candles, but I could see the reddish cast to his beard and hair, streaked with gray. It stirred a memory of a large man like him. I had so few memories of the shack where I was born. Only one stood out, plucked from the obscure remnants of the warm embrace of my Mama and the smells of wildflowers on the hillside with my goats: I remembered a large, finely dressed man coming and giving my mother a small sack of coins. She was standing then, so it must have been before she got sick and took to the bed. I recalled it–just that one moment of him handing her the coins–as if it were a painting, with no recollection of moments before or after.

Now I was the one who faltered and lost my words, but uttered greetings as I introduced myself. I had brought the letter from Sandor from my rooms with me, and I handed it to him now.

"Please, sit and eat," he said, and a steward helped me into the heavy wooden chair and began to pour water and wine for me, heaping more food than I could possibly eat upon my plate. The Count brought the letter back to his place and gestured to his manservant to bring him a small knife to break the seal. He opened it and brought a candle closer to read its words. I had been around few learned men and found the phenomenon of reading mysterious. The act of capturing and interpreting words seemed more like witchcraft to me than anything of which the Rromani were accused. How had Sandor captured the essence of such a complicated message for his uncle?

The Count put the letter down, took a big draught from his glass, which his servant refilled immediately, then picked the letter back up. His eyes flew back and forth over it again. He did this one more time, glancing up at me while sipping from his crystal glass. I looked at my food and tried to remember how to use the metal utensils to stab a small piece of savory meat from a tiny pie that had been placed before me. "So, you are Sabine," he said finally.

"Sir?"

"I realize you have a different name now, but I remember you as Sabine. It's what your mother called you."

I felt a twist in my heart at the words: *your mother.*

"Unfortunately, I don't remember that. I barely remember her," I admitted.

"I never knew what became of you. I sent someone to check on Alianor, and they found her deceased–you were nowhere to be found." He looked at me, examining me across the long table. "You look just like her, you know."

"So I've been told–by the Lord Alexandru. It's how he determined who I was upon meeting me."

"Is it true you were raised by Ciganyok? It's quite remarkable."

I nodded.

"And for you to cross paths again, in your father's woods, no less," he wondered. "Staying at Vár Buceci."

"I did not believe it myself when he first told me his suspicion of who I was."

"The resemblance is striking: you are quite the twin of your mother. I can see how he recognized you. And he's right that you have your grandmother's eyes. Sabine was a beauty, too." He saw my mystefied look. "Ah. Sabine was also the name of Sandor's mother, your grandmother. I admit, I found it presumptuous when Alianor named you after Sandor's mother, but she insisted. She knew how Sandor loved her. Sandor never knew, though." I still must have had a baffled look on my face because he seemed to understand that more explanation was necessary: "You may think me cruel, but I did what I thought was best for the family. I believed Sandor would move on after his infatuation. I assumed he'd find a noblewoman among his new associates after taking over the estate. He certainly had offers. There were families across Europe vying to have their daughters marry him. He never wavered, though. He insisted that Alianor was the only woman for him, even after I made sure she disappeared."

I started, alarmed to hear this confession. "At first, I just wanted to conceal her pregnancy. I thought it was kindest, both to preserve her reputation and his. I arranged to have her leave in the night, not even telling her father. Of course, she insisted on taking some of her goats with her, but that made sense–she was a shepherd's daughter. I bought a remote plot of land for her and saw to money and provisions.

"I told her that I'd send word to Sandor that she was expecting, so he could come to marry her and make things right–I never did. Instead, I told her he had changed his mind and was going to marry a local warlord's daughter. She was heartbroken, of course. I continued to bring her goods and made sure there was a midwife there when she gave birth. By then, Sandor had sent a letter to have her brought to Brașov, but I told him she had left and given no word to anyone. I was the only one who knew where she was, and I kept it secret. I felt terrible, especially when he refused to marry after that, and seeing how it broke Alianor's heart. I always felt it was in the best interest for all. I sent a stipend to her regularly and checked on both of you myself a few times a year. I felt it was my penance, to suffer myself by seeing what I had done: it seems I caused suffering all around." He looked at me, and I dropped my eyes to my food. "You must despise me," he finally said.

I pushed a piece of carrot around in some gravy. "No," I said finally.

"It would have been unseemly, but he could have married her. I see that now. He would have been no worse off, being that he's been alone all these years anyway. And he would have had her. You would have been raised with him in Brașov, with every need met. Instead, your poor mother died, and you had to be raised in such . . . low circumstances, by *those* people."

"I don't really see it that way. I don't see it in any way except the way it was," I tried to explain: "They were good to me."

"Sandor said you ended up by yourself, still a child, living alone in the old fortress."

"Yes, but that was my own fault. It had nothing to do with . . . the family who adopted me."

"I'm not sure how that's possible."

"I left them on my own. I ran away."

"I can't say I blame you. I only wish I had helped your parents to be together instead of designing for them to be apart. I have often wished that I could return and do it again. I'd bring Alianor to Sandor myself. I was only trying to protect him. I did not realize at the time: there are many things in life worse than falling in love with someone society does not think is suitable." I nodded. "How can I make it right?" he asked. "Sandor asked me to help you. He does not know what I've just revealed to you, but I will tell him. What else can I do to put things right, Sabine?"

It felt odd to be called by a different name, but I was used to the sensation, having had some practice with it. "Sir, I regret the suffering, too. I've seen how Sandor has lived with the pain of losing my mother. But I don't think there's a way to change anything. My mother is gone, so he can never be reunited with her. It may seem strange to you, but I don't really remember her, so I don't miss her– although I've often wondered about her. The family who cared for me was kind and treated me well. There is nothing that can be any different than it was."

"Yes, but if I had made other choices–"

"–But you couldn't. Not really." I said, surprising myself by interrupting him. "A friend of mine believes we can only make the decisions we are built and shaped to make. Given the situation, you did what you thought was best in the moment based on who you were. Maybe you're different now, but at the time, you could do nothing else." He looked at me intently. I continued: "You did what you thought was required of the situation. I have done the same. If our choices were wrong, how can we know, other than through the filter of time in retrospect, when it is too late to change anything?"

He sighed. "That is very generous of you, Sabine. I'm sorry—should I call you by your other name?" He glanced at the letter. "Jaelle?"

"No, it's fine for me to be Sabine now."

"I see the point you have made, and of course I am unable to change the past. Still, I will never stop regretting that you could be with your mother now, living a happy and indulged life together with your parents in Brașov. You'd probably be married now to some fine lord. You are certainly old enough. You must be . . . twenty this year?"

"I was not sure how old I am."

"And you did not find someone to marry? Sandor mentions you've traveled quite a bit."

"I have traveled, but I have not found a suitable marriage partner."

"Perhaps that's how I can help you. You are past an ideal age, but I know many fine men I can commend you to—a widower perhaps—someone who will not mind that you are so . . . mature."

"That's really not necessary."

"You still look so young, and it's not too late for you to have children."

"Sir, please—do not take offense, but marriage is not to my interest."

"Well, I understand that, too. I have not been much interested in marriage either."

"Really?"

"Oh, I've had plenty of opportunity, and I was engaged once. There are still many women who vie for my hand, hard as that might be to believe," he chuckled.

"I imagine you are quite the catch," I said, glancing around at the expanse of a room with all it's fine furnishings.

He laughed, a hearty laugh with a tenor that reminded me of Sandor: "Oh yes, well, that's perhaps the problem. I never wanted to be 'caught.' I never really wanted to share any of this with anyone. I saw all the strategic unions—and trust me, I could have used some strategic unions at times—but it seemed so artificial. I envied Sandor, when he fell so deeply in love with your mother. Of course, I thought it was youthful infatuation and expected he'd get over it. Yet I have never felt that toward a woman. Yes, yes—I do understand marriage is a concession—a business arrangement very little to do with love. I suppose I just never found an arrangement so appealing I could settle for it."

"But you were engaged once, you said?"

"Yes, it was a well before you were born. I was a very young man. Our parents wanted me to marry a cousin of ours. It was a very advantageous partnership, keeping some desirable property in the family, so my parents were quite in favor of it."

"What happened?"

"Turned out she preferred my little brother–Sandor's father–and he was smitten with her. When he confessed his love, I was more than happy to gracefully bow out. That would have been your grandmother, Sabine."

"Oh!"

"Yes, and to be honest I was relieved. She was a lovely girl, but it was not my desire at the time to be saddled with a family. My parents were just as happy; it was all the same to them and they kept the entitlements they were interested in. They did not mind which son made the partnership. I had political aspirations of my own, and soon after, they came to fruition: I was appointed my current title and moved here. I'm sure many thought it was my injured feelings that made me move so far away, but truly I was most pleased with the way things turned out."

"And you are satisfied now–alone?"

"I am hardly alone. I have many friends with whom I spend time. I am busy with society and political engagements–the obligations of my title are demanding. It can be uncomfortable at times, going to parties and weddings for my friends' children, growing old without a family of my own. Some may think it odd, I'm sure."

"But you prefer it?"

"Well, it is most convenient for the style of life I have chosen," he said, and raised his drink to me.

∞

It seemed the Count did have quite the busy social life, after all; he went to parties almost every night, and often stayed away a few days at a time. There had been no real discussion of how long I would stay, but it was soon assumed I would be making myself at home in the manor. I was fitted for dresses and slippers and given more invasive pampering. Several servants were sent to scrub my feet of all remnants of the mountain once the head mistress became aware of their unfortunate condition. Mrs. Moravek was the wife of the main steward, the Seneschal of the household. Despite there being no great lady of the estate for her to serve, she was in charge of the female staff, and took her duties very seriously. When two of the maids were overheard in the hallway gossiping that perhaps the Count would prefer a *woman* for once, they were seriously reprimanded.

If anyone found it unusual that I should be kept and well-attended, they were careful not to show it. Mrs. Moravek saw to that. I was treated as any guest and let to wander the estate at my leisure, only pushed upon to inquire what and when I would like to eat and what color would I like the next dress. There were a few eyebrows raised–Mrs. Moravek's included–when I requested to go meet the weavers responsible for making cloth for my new wardrobe.

Nevertheless, I was taken well across the compound in a small carriage to some clusters of houses tucked into the forest edge.

The Kadlec family was a humble group, who seemed alarmed to be visited–perhaps worried that they had displeased someone. I reassured them that I was just interested in the process and amazed them when I understood the terminology and mechanics of the weaving. I asked where the nearest sheep were kept, and if there might be lanolin for treating the fabric. We discussed the merits of using the rich oils. One daughter had a small pot for soothing cuts and waterproofing footwear, so I showed them the trick I had learned from Liana for how to make the weaving possess that shiny, luminescent quality that had made our fabric famous. They seemed skeptical, but when I wove a few rows myself and showed them the technique, they were speechless. I tried it on some cotton they had on another loom, and that worked well, too.

The servants who had accompanied me exchanged looks. I was sure there would be conversations in private between the staff with reports back to Mrs. Moravek, but I was not concerned. The Kadlecs seemed surprised when I kissed them goodbye like family, but they assured me they would try out the new technique. When the new dresses came, I could see that they had perfected the method. I sent back my compliments. In new dresses and with all remnants of the mountain removed, my exterior was like a new person: my inner life was as pained as ever, though. I had cleansed much of my grief during my solitary reprieve, in two years of breathing fresh air and living among the stones and trees and creatures. I still felt a hollow core inside me, especially now as I again pretended to be someone who did not feel genuine.

The Count, who insisted I call him Ulric, had told me that he would bring me to meet my grandfather when he returned from his next trip, and would also bring me to see the place where my mother had lived. He was finishing up some business that took him away for several days. When he returned, he slept most of the next day–or so I was told by one of his attendants. I did not see him until the evening meal. We arranged to leave early the following morning, since it took a bit of a journey to get over the mountain to the far edges of the estate where the livestock were grazed. I wore some new boots that Mrs. Moravek told me were suitable for the trip, and we set off in a small carriage with only the driver and an armed assistant deemed necessary by the Marshall of the estate to carry out our protection. From what, I could not imagine.

The Count's property expanded in every direction, it seemed, and we were taken on winding traces of roads over a mountain to where the foraging was best for the sheep and cattle. On the way, the Count became pensive and seemed to be lost in his head: "I was only taking Sandor with me to show him the duties of a master," he said. "We were having some trouble with an illness affecting some of the livestock, and I brought him, thinking it would be a good opportunity to see firsthand what the responsibilities of running an estate could entail. He was still a spoiled boy, and I thought it would do him good to see what lay ahead of him in marriage. You knew he was engaged to be married?"

I nodded, "Yes, he had told me he had run here to escape that fate."

Ulric chuckled. "Oh yes, he thought his bachelor Uncle Ulric would help talk his parents out of the union. Anyway, I made him come along to show him how all things affect all other things when you are overseeing a property. I was losing a fortune on the sick livestock, and I needed to see for myself what was going on. When he saw Alianor, it was all over. He could not keep his eyes on the problems we were there to inspect. He was talking to her and flirting. I had to practically drag him away. He learned nothing of the business that day—that probably goes without saying. Over the next few weeks, he went out hunting almost every day. I suspected he was coming here to see her, but what could I do? He was his own man already, not a child. I thought it was harmless and might help him to get it out of his system before he settled down to take over his duties."

He sighed and shook his head. "Maybe I should have interfered more from the beginning. I realize that would mean you would not be here, my dear, but it really was a disaster from the start. Perhaps I could have stopped it when I saw it happening, but young men will be young men, no matter how you try to curb them. Finally, one day he sat me down and told me that he loved her. I had never known her name before, but he told me he was in love with Alianor and planned to marry her. He asked me to send a message and give his parents the news and break the engagement to the young woman he was supposed to marry. He finally talked me into sending a message to his parents. I was not in favor of it, but I could see he was not going to be dissuaded. Just as I was preparing to give in and help the poor lovestruck fool, word came from your father's estate that my brother and his wife—and Sandor's fiancé—had died. The young woman had been staying with them in preparation for the wedding, and the Pestilence just swept through and knocked them all out. The sickness decimated half of their staff, too, but they managed to send word.

"I made Sandor wait two weeks before setting off. Nobody was traveling much in those days, since the plague was taking hold all over, but I thought it best to give it time to run its course before he went to take over there. He was in a stupor and blamed himself. He felt he had caused his parents' death by defying them, and that he should have been there with them. He never went back to see Alianor while he was waiting to head home. He wanted to take her with him then, but I discouraged him. It would have been disrespectful to his parents and the memory of his betrothed to come to their gravesides with his new fiancé. I convinced him that it would undermine his new authority as head of the household, and finally he agreed that he would send for her in a few months. By then it was clear she was with child, and you know the rest."

We had crested the largest part of the mountain and were descending into a cool valley of pastures and grassy hills, dotted with livestock. Despite the recent turn in the weather, it was still filled with wildflowers. A young man who was out repairing a fence saw us coming and ran to greet us. "Your Excellency, so gracious of you to come visit us!"

"I've come to see the elder Sedlak. Is he still alive?"

"Yes sir, my grandfather still lives, though he is not what he once was, my lord."

"Fine, we'd like to see him nonetheless."

We were led to a small, modest house and led inside where the young lad introduced his mother, who was assisting a shell of an old man by the fire. When we walked in, the man looked up and, seeing me, stood quickly, weaving and unsteady so that the woman and young man ran to catch him. "Alianor!" he called holding his arms out with wide eyes.

"I'm so sorry, my Lady, my father-in-law thinks you are his daughter. She disappeared long ago. He's not well. He's been quite demented these last several years."

I walked to him and held out my hand, which he took. "Alianor, I knew you were still alive!" he said earnestly. I looked into the wrinkled face with cool blue eyes cloudy with age, now brimming with tears. I held onto his hand, and the two holding him up helped him back into his seat.

"You are very kind, my lady. You see he's quite confused," the woman explained.

"No, it's alright," I said.

"Shall I send for my husband, my lord?" she asked the Count, who looked at me.

"I would like to meet him," I said, calculating that this would be my mother's brother. The young man went off to fetch his father from the fields, and I sat next to the old man, who continued to hold my hand and cry.

"Alianor, Alianor! Where have you been, my child? I have missed you so!" I patted his hand and uttered a few comforting words. I had hoped to reveal my identity to him but could see it would just confound him further. The woman offered us oat straw tea and fresh biscuits. My uncle refused but I accepted gratefully.

"I am so sorry, madam. He has not been himself," she kept apologizing, but I reassured her that I was fine with the old man grasping my hand and crying against my shoulder. When her husband arrived, he came in and greeted the Count, bowing low and uttering reverent acknowledgements for his visit to their humble farm. When he stood, he glanced toward me, then stopped and stared with his mouth slightly agape.

"Why, you look–I'm so sorry, my lady, but you look just like my sister!"

"Yes, your father seems to think that's exactly who she is," his wife said, shaking her head in embarrassment.

"Well, it seems there is a reason for that," I said.

∞

We were back on the mountain road, heading to the small shack that was my birthplace. Ulric was quiet, reflecting on the reunion, no doubt. It was for the best, since my own head was filled with the conversation we had with my mother's brother, Gustav. Having had no idea what had happened to his sister, he and his father had mourned for her over the years in a shroud of ambiguity. She left one night along with several goats—five, to be exact—and was never heard from again. The young lord had been coming around to visit her, so they suspected it had something to do with him. When she disappeared, they could hardly make accusations: it might have been handled harshly, and they feared expulsion from the property. When they heard the young man had returned to Brașov, they concluded she had gone with him.

It was a deep injury to the brother to hear that she had lived about an hour away in a little mountain shack with a child out of wedlock. He wept and said he'd wished to believe all this time that she had gone with the young lord and he had married her. Alianor had confided in her brother that's what Sandor had promised her, but Gustav found it strange that she never came back or sent word. It also finally made sense to him why the Count had been so generous to their family over the years; even in times that were lean for everyone else, the Count had always made sure their house had resources for repairs and they always had enough of everything.

I had not gotten much into the details of what happened to me after my mother had died. I only mentioned that I was raised by a family who adopted me and only recently became reunited with my father's family. The Count was prepared to accept blame for the tragic outcome, explaining that my father had intended to marry Alianor, but that he had intercepted and ruined their intentions. Ulric offered his heartfelt apology for his interference, saying he realized now that Sandor's love for Alianor was not the disaster he thought it was: "I realize now there are much worse things in life than falling in love with someone the world does not approve of," he concluded.

My grandfather did not seem to understand any of what was being explained, but at that point, he stood up and, in a moment of astute clarity, said to Ulric: "The past cannot be repaired, my good man. Quiet your heart! My daughter was a gentle and forgiving soul, and she would not wish you to suffer for your past mistakes." His lucidity was short-lived, as upon our parting, he was back to calling me "Alianor" and begging that his daughter come to visit him again soon.

Gustav and his wife hugged me close, and even their son—my cousin—who seemed intimidated by the whole situation, kissed my cheeks and said he wished I'd return. I told them I would visit if I could, but that I was unsure of where I would end up. "I know you may be used to grand houses like the Count's, but you are always welcome in our home," Gustav's wife assured me.

As we went on our way, I thought how surprised they'd be to learn that I had been raised with much less than what they had, despite my fine clothes. Now, back on our journey, I reflected on the scene. It unlocked a piece of the puzzle, and I wondered what life would have been like if my mother had stayed with her family along with her bastard child. I imagined that as much as they grieved the loss of a daughter and sister, in some ways it was a kindness that they had not had to live through the shame and ostracism that would have come of that. Still, knowing Sandor now the way I did, I felt confident that he would have come to claim both Alianor and me at any point, if he only knew.

It was hard to sit next to the man that caused such an injustice, knowing that it was he who had constructed such an unfortunate outcome. I did not hate him, but I saw him suddenly as selfish and indulgent. He was free to live his life in whatever manner he wished, choosing no partner at all above being tied to one he found distasteful. Sandor never had the option to make his own choice. I thought about Zhulyi's worldview that I had adopted: Ulric was only able to make decisions based upon who he was. In this case, though, this one man's choice affected so many other lives: not only mine, Sandor's, and my mother's, but also the family my mother left behind. At the same time, could I really say that what he had done was worse than what I had done, taking a child who did not belong to me away from her tribe and raising her as my own? In some ways, Ulric was not at fault for how he was designed: he was raised to make him feel he had an entitlement to interfere, even convincing him he was doing the right thing. Still, I could not help feeling any fondness I had developed for him dissolving.

We stopped upon a grassy hillside tucked into the winding trail off the far side of the mountain. The driver helped me down to stand next to Ulric, who looked out over the vista of valleys and trees, glowing like a firestorm in the afternoon light. The trees were starting to turn colors and the tall grasses arranged themselves into peaks and waves of red and golden hues. "It's just this way," he directed, and began to lead me toward the beginning of the incline. None of it seemed familiar to me, but when we looked over the edge of the hill down into the steep valley, I saw a pile of deteriorated boards in the footprint of a small cottage. It struck a chord deep within me that resonated and ricocheted around, making all my limbs tingle as we descended through the tall dried weeds and brambles. Mrs. Moravek had been right that I needed boots for this sojourn.

"The goats actually helped with this," Ulric remarked, smiling, and I had a faint memory again of him as a much younger man, but still large and impressive. I could suddenly see the big silver buttons on his coat in my child's mind, amplified and huge in my vision when he came and spoke to me with a friendly smile and gave my mother coins. We stopped before the pile of rotted wood and rubble, grown through with weeds. There was nothing left of the shack, but I recalled now the shape it had been. I remembered how dark it had been inside when I went to bring my mother apples to eat, since she could no longer cook. I turned and looked at a cluster of trees a distance away on the hillside. "Her grave is over there, if you'd like to see it," said Ulric.

"Thank you," I said. "I'll go myself. You can return to the carriage. I'll just be a few minutes."

"Of course, my dear. Take all the time you need." He began to hoist his heavy frame back up the hillside, where his armed guard had been standing at attention to watch us descend. I made my way toward the trees, stepping on fallen apples that had rolled and rotted. I remembered now the exact taste of the somewhat sour fruit, sitting under those trees with my goats in the hot sun, while my mother declined inside the dusty cabin in the dark.

When I got to the trees, I saw a small gravesite and a little unmarked headstone at the top. I had hoped to feel some remnant of understanding, some connection to my lost childhood or to the woman who gave birth to me. Instead, standing and looking down at the grave, I felt nothing. I looked up to the ridge and saw that the Count and his guard had disappeared, probably to give me privacy. I knelt by the grave and wished Zhulyi were here to see if there were spirits about to give me a sense of something that was outside of my reach.

When nothing moved inside me to give me any direction, when I felt no stirring of emotion or even loss, I stood. Taking one more look up to the empty ridge, I began to climb down the hillside. I walked through tangles of overgrown weeds all the way down the hill and into the dark woods that began as the grass gave way to needles and moss. The trees closed in around me, embracing me with the tenderness I had grown to recognize. I kept walking until the shack and my mother's gravesite were far behind me and I was utterly and completely lost in the woods.

Chapter Seventeen: The Oracle of the Forest

"Cunrad, please bring me that golden spool–that one, right by your elbow."

The young boy looked around, and finding what I was gesturing at, handed me a bobbin of yellow thread. He was an easy-going boy, which was why I had hired him to help me in the shop. His father was part of the Woodworkers' Guild, and he would soon leave my service to enter training. In the interim, he was a useful presence in my small studio. It was hard to find a niche in Sibiu that was not dominated by the guilds. One could only be born or marry into the Weavers' Guild, and all fabric in the region was manufactured and traded in strict accordance with guild standards. In Deva, any person could set up a shop and weave to their heart's content. Not so in Sibiu, where one could weave, but would not be able to sell in any market except the Saturday free market where prices were kept low. To restrict sales to one measly day a week was not much of a livelihood.

Instead, I had found a way to survive by completing embroidery on commission and setting up a shop of herbs and small cutlery items that were not overseen by the Metalworkers' Guild. It was not hard to be invisible in Sibiu, an even larger city than Deva with much more civic organization. The guilds were the center of everything, coordinating all aspects of trade in and out of the city and even overseeing the armed security of the red brick walls that ran the perimeter, built in response to an invasion of the previous century. My favorite part of Sibiu was the Strada Cetatii, a magnificent street with an arching fortress and impressive stone tower that was centrally located in the heart of the city. The craft guilds ran all business on that street, but it was a sight to see the grand construction of this fortified neighborhood. The markets were lively and diverse, and free to all so long as they did not conflict with the regulations of the guild or compete with their products. One could make a nice living with their skills, if they kept a respectful distance of the territory controlled by these legally-protected associations.

My own shop was on a street perpendicular to the Strada Cetatii, far enough away to not threaten any guild business and obscure enough in content to escape scrutiny. The rising classes in Sibiu were always looking for new ways to entertain or seeking wedding gifts for the elaborate celebrations that transpired when daughters of one guild were strategically married off to sons of another. I was often called upon to emblazon a guild symbol onto a banner to adorn such an event. It was not creative work, and I much preferred when I was asked to decorate the hem of a gown for a special gathering in scrolling vegetation and flora. My favorite had been a dress for a beauty from the Pottery Guild who was being wed to an aristocrat from the Chefs' Guild. I was asked to embroider a pattern of small crossed knives among tangles of vegetables in subtle hues on the train of her wedding gown to acknowledge her acceptance by marriage into this esteemed occupation.

It was a competitive climate, with gossip and intrigue that could destroy a person's guild membership overnight for those who were careless. If one kept her head down and did not trample upon any of the existing alliances, though, it was possible for an outsider to carve a small, quiet life amidst the activity and clamor for celebrity. The trade masters were like kings in the city, with all social life revolving around their whims. All was decided in brutal negotiations between the guilds, and then drank over at fancy taverns into which one who was not a member could not set foot. The work life was intense, and the party life glamorous for those who were intricately involved in the inner sanctum of the city's civic world.

Cunrad's family was on the periphery, his father still a minor journeyman, not yet having achieved the status of a master. Cunrad would be trained and employed by a master soon, and the hope of his family was that he would rise among the ranks of fame himself, where his father had not yet succeeded. Despite the aspirations for him, he was a mild youth, who had no objection to taking direction from a woman. He was compliant and helpful and completed tasks without complaint. I had only been in the city for about three years, but I had built up a small following of customers who relied upon me for their embellishments.

I also had an even more flourishing business as an herbalist. I had stumbled upon this when I had done a kindness for a Rromani woman I met in the market and bought out her sheaths of chamomile, mint, and lavender. I sewed small, colorful bags decorated with symbols, which were like magnets for the women who came into my shop. I did not even have to say much, since they interpreted their meanings from the obtuse symbols. An eye became a protective eye, a moon seemed to soothe reproductive worries, a flower represented purity. Soon, I was purchasing large glass containers–bought from a Journeyman from the Glassmakers'

Guild, of course—to store dried herbs. A customer would come in with a concern that she would whisper to me with large eyes. Confidently, I would stride to a specific urn and take it down from the shelf. She would select one of the jewel-tone bags, and I would scoop some of the herb into it with a silver scoop made by a member of the Metalsmiths' Guild.

The key, I found, was simply to look straight into a person's eyes and say: "This will help," and then explain how to brew the tea. I never made promises, but I was careful to give very precise directions about the time of day, how often to prepare it, and how long to steep the herbs. People yearned for reassurance: fortune tellers everywhere had long satisfied a desperate need for concrete guidance. As independent as a person was, I had found, they still craved to be told what to do when feeling insecure. I did not feel guilty about this ruse, since I never misled anyone. After all, I had never known any situation that a good pot of tea did not improve.

Having so few possessions my whole life, I was suddenly greatly fulfilled to be in my shop surrounded by the glass urns of rose petals and green ferny things. It was like bringing the forest—my favorite place—indoors. Minding my shop was a full-time occupation, but I spent Saturday mornings at the market, and did not open my shop until noon so that I could replenish my supplies. On the edges of the market, like any market, dwelled the Rroma. Quickly, they learned to seek me out, and several went foraging for herbs just for me. I had learned better than to have them visit me at my place of business, so I went to them instead. I enriched them and they enriched me. It was always refreshing to speak Rromani in hushed tones and to ask after their families.

"Mrs. Sedlak, may I leave a bit early today?" Cunrad's earnest face looked at me. "The Journeymen's Ball is this evening. My father will present me to my new master."

"Of course, Cunrad. How exciting!" I still was not used to being called by the name I had assumed. I felt close to it, though, being that it was the name belonging to my mother's sweet family. After leaving the Count, I had even considered going back there and living among my mother's people. The woods had pulled me in, though, and the further I went into the forest, the more I felt at home among the trees. I felt more connected to them than I ever felt toward humans, even those sharing some relation to me. Even so, I had assumed the Sedlaks' name as my own. When I finally arrived in Sibiu after wandering weeks in the mountains, it made for a good story to explain that my husband had died and I was searching for a way to support myself on my own. I had convinced the owner of this building to allow me to set up shop, and he had agreed that I could pay at the end of the month.

It was a bit of a dance in the beginning, convincing people to give me supplies on credit and scrambling to pay them back with the first paltry sales and commissions. Within a few months, I was solvent enough to pay for my lodging up front. There was a small courtyard behind the building and a small room at the back where I set up house for myself, using the yard to cook and hang laundry. As before, I found people remarkably unconcerned with the details of my past. They were easily satisfied to know that I had been married to a farmer who had died the year before.

As a widow, I had some freedom and credibility that I was never privy to before. It was as if being formerly wed bought me a place in society that I had never experienced as a young single woman. Being on my own had always brought some element of discomfort to others, as if it was somehow indecent for me to be living by myself. Being a widow somehow resolved this for others. They were suddenly able to see me as matronly and established, despite being similarly bereft of any visible attachments. I wished I had thought to become a widow sooner.

Cunrad was sweeping up, hurriedly finishing his tasks. "It's fine, Cunrad. You can leave now—no need to stay any longer. Come by tomorrow to tell me all about the Ball." He looked at me gratefully and put the broom away. "Give my regards to your mother." He nodded and scooted out the door. He had been helping me in the shop for the past year. I would miss his seriousness, his quiet acquiescence and the way small chores satisfied him when they were completed well. He was a good, hardworking boy. I had no doubt he would make his new master very happy.

"Good afternoon, Mrs. Sedlak." It was a regular customer, the wife of a prominent master, coming in with two of her serfs in tow carrying baskets of her purchases from the market. She spurned the herbs and pretty things in my shop and came only to give me assignments. When they were complete, she would send someone to pick them up, but she liked to give me the specifics of her commissions herself.

"Good afternoon, Mrs. Krempel. How is your husband, and your beloved son?"

"They are fools, both! Spending money like it grows from the earth. I swear if they did not have me to manage it all they would be paupers, begging in the market!"

"Yes, they do rely upon you," I agreed.

"And, of course I am put in charge of managing the Metalsmiths' Ball, as if none of the other wives could do it. Well, that is my burden, I suppose." She heaved out her massive bosom and looked to the rafters.

"It is hard being the one who holds it all together—but you do it so well, Mrs. Krempel! You can hardly fault them for asking you."

"Yes, yes," she said, looking at me as if she just finally noticed me. "It's true. Who else could do it?"

"What are you looking to do for the ball. Perhaps a giant banner like last year, or something else?"

"Oh no, it can't be like last year. That was marvelous, of course. You were brilliant– the way you stitched the scrolls and guild marks. They are still complimenting me on it, so many months later! But this must be something different. I need to make a statement: a *bold* statement."

"What is the statement you'd like to make?" I inquired. It seemed Mrs. Krempel was always making bold statements.

"Why, that the Metalsmiths' Guild is the best! All these other guilds, they are so petty, so cheap. Metal is the most important one, binding it all together. Where would this city be? How would it be defended without metal?"

"Hmmm . . . Then whatever we make to decorate the ball, it should have metal to support it." I recalled a thought I had when lying in bed the night before and reached for a scrap of parchment and a piece of charcoal. I drew long arching shapes like tall curving spears, and then drew flaps of fabric spooling from them. "These could be positioned all the way down the Strada Cetatii on the way to the main square, and then installed around the square. They should be shaped like large lances, with a spade at the end, like this," I said drawing, "but tall enough to make a bridge between them so that one will have to walk underneath like an arched passageway. Each one will be emblazoned with a different tool or metal implement, and in the center of the square will be a . . . a free-standing portico shaped structure–metal of course–like this . . ." I kept drawing, ". . . with a space to walk inside and a banner around it with the Metalsmiths' Guild symbol. Isn't there a competition that goes along with this ball?"

Mrs. Krempel nodded, dumbstruck, as she looked down at my drawing.

"So the winning entries could be positioned all around the square on stands between the lances, and then the first place winner's entry could be hidden inside the portico–but you would only know what it was once you visited inside, since it would have a wide banner going around the outside to block your view until you entered. It would keep the grand prize winner a surprise until the last final moment." I stopped, a little embarrassed at my enthusiasm. "Just a few ideas," I said, beginning to pull the paper away.

"No, no, this is perfect! It's dramatic, it shows our status–it's just what we need."

"How far away is the ball?"

"Only four months!"

"Do you think your husband and son's shops would be able to make the lances and the portico in time?"

"Oh yes, they will. They will have to."

"And the Weavers' Guild: will you be able to secure the fabric for the banners?"

"I'll have it sent to you right away."

"Well then, I can certainly create the banners in time."

"This is wonderful," she put a hand over her impressive chest, swooning, and sighed deeply. "They are going to be singing my praises again for another year! I am quite the genius,"

"Yes, you truly are."

∞

Life was fine for me in Sibiu. I had a comfortable living and a shop of my own. Although I was well-known for my crafts, I was virtually anonymous in the hubbub of the city's active life. I could almost imagine that I had always lived there, among the red stone walls surrounding the city and the magnificent buildings, new ones always being constructed. I was a small innocuous flower in a field of flowers, blending in and accepted as commonplace, leaving attention to be drawn to the flashier blossoms. Even so, when someone remarked upon my accent, or I saw a child that reminded me of Perla invoking the old familiar stab to the heart, I was reminded that I did not really belong here. It was like an injury that had healed over: unexpectedly, the phantom pain re-emerged as if the wound was still fresh and bleeding.

At times, I thought of Zhulyi, too; I wondered where she was and if Aamon had improved his treatment of her. I hoped so. On nights I could not sleep, I tried to imagine her making him a meal and him nodding approval and even giving her a smile. I hoped that she had made the right choice. Other times I wondered: should I have gone after her? I sometimes indulged in fantasies where I followed her to Oradea and convinced her to flee with me. Should I have put up more of a fight? I had to remind myself that she was the one who left me. Maybe she felt like she had no choice with Aamon arriving to collect her, but couldn't she have slipped away if she had tried? She must have felt that going with him was the right thing. Perhaps the life I had offered her, living as my handmaid on Sandor's great estate was worse than being an under-appreciated wife. Maybe she had not wanted to go with me at all, and Aamon arriving allowed her an escape. These were the thoughts I tortured myself with.

Then one day, I saw her! She was right in the market in Sibiu. I ran across the crowded square and touched her shoulder. She turned toward me and I saw I had made a mistake. The young Rromani woman who turned toward me looked nothing like Zhulyi up close, although she was very pretty in her own way. She looked alarmed to have a Gentle woman touching her, since that was generally unheard of—unless one was in danger. The general sentiment was that Ciganyok were untouchable.

"I'm so sorry," I said in Rromani. "I thought you were someone else."

She smiled: "You speak our tongue," she said delighted. "You must be the Sedlak."

"Yes," I replied.

"My grandmother asked for you. It's why I'm here today."

174

"Your grandmother? She asked for *me*?"

"Yes, she heard of you from my cousins who have been selling her herbs to you. She is a medicine woman, and the herbs you have been buying–most have been picked by her hands."

"I did not know," I said.

"No, I'm sure you didn't." She smiled again, and I felt a twang of connection to her. "I am Simza," she said.

"I am Jaelle," I said, the name slipping out. I had not had an occasion to use a first name in Sibiu, since all knew me only as Mrs. Sedlak.

"Well, you have saved me the trouble of having to find you, Jaelle! When can you come to meet my grandmother? She lives in the forest. It's about an hour's walk, I'm afraid."

I suppose I could have asked more questions about why her grandmother wanted to meet me. Something about Simza's calm, pleasant demeanor and confident attitude made me want to do what she asked of me without question. We arranged to meet the next Saturday morning in the market so that she could show me the way. Until then, all I could think of was Simza's smile: the flash of white teeth and her sparkling eyes. She was only a little older than I, but old enough to be already married with many children, yet she had come to the market alone. Although I knew it was unlikely, I could imagine her unattached and unfettered, able to whisk off and disappear with me into the wide world. It was silly–but just like that all my pain washed away, and all I could think of was Simza as I lay awake in bed. I imagined us holding hands and walking down a road toward a sunset, or perhaps back at the crumbling castle, cooking together and laughing over an open fire under that stars. It was foolish, but somehow it made me feel better.

It seemed to take forever for Saturday to arrive. Finally it came, and I put on my old walking boots from Mrs. Moravek. I had discarded them for slippers and simple hard-bottom shoes for walking the uneven streets in Sibiu. Today, they felt appropriate. I wore a dress the Kadlec weavers had made for me at the Count's estate, which was the one I had been wearing the day I met the Sedlaks and saw my mother's grave. It was dark gray, and good for traveling. I had repaired the damage from being snared on brambles and tangles those weeks I wandered in the woods, insetting several vertical panels of dark brown fabric in evenly placed stripes on the skirt in order to disguise the places where the dress had torn through.

It was barely daylight by the time I got to the market: the pale, transparent glow of morning still creating deeply bruised shadows. There were not many people setting up that early, but a few busy folks rushed this way and that to arrange their wares and several carts were being driven into the square. Simza was there already, casually watching a young peasant woman setting up tomatoes in a large pyramid from atop one of the outer walls. She sat with her leg hanging down and swinging slightly, seeming more the carefree gesture of a girl than a woman.

175

"Simza," I said to get her attention. She saw me and smiled, jumping down and landing solidly on both feet.

"Jaelle! You are here. I worried you would not come," she smiled, a little shyly.

"Of course I would come," I said, and returned her smile.

We set off, and she led the way through the winding streets to the edge of the town and took a side path that cut around a field in an unobtrusive manner. We walked through more fields until the land became less managed and wilder. We passed a fence that marked an outer barrier of grazing land and entered some shrubby low trees and bushes. The wild roses were blooming and perfumed the air, and Simza stopped and picked some berries and offered some to me. She walked ahead of me, as if she had come this way many times before. She wandered in a meandering manner forward, winding left and then right, and then back left again, but when I looked close, I was able to see the light footpaths that she was following.

Soon we were encased within the tall steeple of pines in the shadowed forest. I felt instantly at home in the church of my heart. I had not been back in the woods since I came to Sibiu; I had not realized how badly my body had yearned for it. I felt I could breathe again. Everything came into sharp focus, and it was as if I could see for the first time in ages. The spilling ferns and deep texture of the bark all stood out in crisp dimension. I looked at Simza through the underwater light, and she smiled at me. We slowed, and she fell back to walk next to me.

"They know you," she said.

"Who?"

"The trees."

We walked on, and I let the peaceful quiet wash over me, cleansing me of the loneliness of the last years; I remembered who I was. "Excuse me," I said, and stopped, sitting on a log to remove my boots. My feet remembered the softness of pine needles and earth and fallen twigs. Tears began to stream from my eyes. Simza looked at me and took my hand. "Let's sit for a while," she said. We sat in silence and she held my hand.

"I apologize," I finally said. "I don't know what came over me."

"No need to apologize. Tears are the way we wash away sorrow. How can it leave your body otherwise?" I laughed. It was such a Rromani thing to say, and so refreshing to my ears. "The trees will help you heal. They are generous in that way."

"I have been alone for a long time, but I have never felt alone in a forest."

"Yes, they are our true community. You can never be alone with trees surrounding you."

"I have not seen you in the market before last week," I remarked.

"No, I bring Baba's herbs to the edge of town to meet my cousins. They sell them for us. The city is no place for forest people."

"Do you live with your Baba?"

"I do now. I have for some time. I lived with my husband's family but he was killed about eight years ago–by some Gentles. I don't know what their argument was, but they murdered him over it."

"Simza, I'm so sorry." She looked at her lap. "Do you have children?"

She brightened. "Two," she said, smiling. "My son is married now. They live with my husband's family. My daughter just went to join the family of the man she will marry soon. With my son married and my daughter gone to her new tribe, they do not need me as much. So, I came to help my Baba for a time."

"I see. Do you miss them–your children?"

"Every day. Especially my daughter. It is the burden of mothers that their daughters must go to their new families." I nodded my agreement. She continued: "My son is very independent, and he has his new family now. They have a child, a little boy. Do you have children?"

"No, I don't."

"Oh, well that's strange."

"Yes, I suppose it is."

"No–I mean it's strange because my Baba said she had a message for you about your daughter."

"A message?" my heart raced.

"Yes, my Baba, she is with the spirits mostly," Simza explained.

"Oh, well. I do not have a birth daughter, but I have a . . ." I could not figure out how to explain Perla. ". . . a daughter I adopted."

"Yes, that must be the one."

"Is she unwell? She is not dead, is she?" My stomach dropped out away from me, fearing that something had happened to Perla.

"No, I do not believe so. It's a message about her, though. I'm sorry, but I don't know the details. Let's be on our way so Baba can speak to you about it."

We gathered ourselves and continued on, hurrying now, as the anxiety pulled at the edges of my mind. Simza must have sensed it, since she said no more and picked up her pace. After some time, we came upon a clearing and a meadow with a stream and a little shack. A black and white dog came barking toward us, and greeted Simza with kisses, sniffing my feet and the hem of my dress. There was a fenced garden there, brimming with flowers and herbs, much of it spilling out the sides and crawling along stone pathways.

"Many of my grandmother's roots and herbs are found deep in the woods," said Simza, "but there are many that she grows right here." A woman came from the shack, hearing the dog barking. She was not as old as I expected–or at least did not seem so very old–but her clothing was threadbare, and her bare feet were gnarled and dark.

"Baba Tsura, this is the Sedlak," said Simza.

"Please call me Jaelle," I said, and reached to kiss the woman's hand. I noticed spots of age and a soft papery texture to her skin, which smelled of lavender. "Forgive me, but I am quite alarmed that you have word of . . . my daughter."

"She is in good health," Baba Tsura said and turned away. "First, we will have tea. Sit. The water's boiling," she said and bent to grab a handful of mint before going inside. Simza gestured to a large stump with several smaller sections of logs surrounding it. We sat on these, and a few minutes later the older woman re-emerged with a pot of tea and some wooden cups stacked in a column. Simza helped to arrange the cups, and poured the steaming tea, setting a cup in front of me. The strong smell of the mint wafted up and entered my nostrils, somehow relieving the nagging fear inside me. I sighed and breathed in the steam.

"So, now, where were we? Yes, your daughter," and she said a name. It wasn't 'Perla' though: it was Perla's True Name, the one Ankah had whispered to me when she was born. Baba Tsura must have realized it was Perla's secret name, because she made a gesture and a wave to keep any evil spirits from recognizing it as she spoke it aloud. "Your daughter is well. She is with child, actually– her second."

I did some calculations in my head. Despite knowing Perla had grown into a young woman, I still thought of her as a tiny girl. It was not logical, but I felt she should still be a child. She would be about fifteen. It made perfect sense that she would have children by now.

"Madam . . ." I had so many questions, but I was cut off before I began.

"Call me Baba Tsura–please, no formalities here," she shook her head. "I admit, you do not look it–but you are one of us, and we are all family."

"Baba Tsura," I started again, "How have you come to know of her? Please tell me where this communication comes from?"

"From your sister, Ankah–of course," she said.

Upon hearing her name aloud, as I had not in so many years, I gasped: "You have spoken to her?"

"Oh yes, Ankah is known to me."

"But how? Has she not passed over?"

"Oh, she has passed," she said smiling. "Yes, she has passed over. She is no longer a ghost, although she was for many years as she watched over you: you and Perla." This time she spoke the familiar name.

"But you have spoken with her?"

178

"Yes, she is true Spirit now, but she still checks in on you, on you both. I know that Perla is not your birth daughter–Ankah told me how you came by her." I looked down at my tea, afraid to meet her eyes. "But you are her true mother. Ankah's mortal flesh betrayed her: she could not be there for Perla, but you stepped in, just as she had asked of you."

"She asked me . . .?"

"Yes, she asked you. She knew she was dying, so she told you to take care of Perla, no matter what . . . and you did."

"I never knew for sure. I thought . . ."

"She knew. That's why she said what she did. Whether you understood fully or not, you did as she wished."

"Selene must have known. . ."

"Yes! Selene . . . Selene is an ally. She is known to us, too. She may have helped steer you in the right direction." Baba Tsura had the storytelling voice of one sharing a legend, or of a juicy piece of gossip: "Selene knew that to become the woman she needed to be, Perla needed to be raised with you as her mother, away from the tribe. Selene knew that you were not the right woman to carry on her family line. She loved you, but she knew it was Perla that should be the one to carry her gift." I was flustered by this, not understanding her meaning. She continued: "When Perla returned to the tribe, Sasha married her!" Baba Tsura explained. I felt a shock of pain in my chest. "Now their child has Selene's gift! She will carry on the family line."

"Sasha married Perla?" It seemed so unexpected, though it probably shouldn't have.

"Yes, it took him a while, though. He was hurt and angry at you for many years and refused to marry. When Perla was returned to the family, after she grew into such an honorable young woman, and with Selene's prompting, he became willing to marry his little cousin. He was the one who had gone to fetch her, after all, wasn't he?" I nodded. It gave me a sense of unreality that she was so familiar with our story. "Perla is gifted already, and Selene knew that their child would carry the gift as well."

"Have you ever . . . have you ever spoken to Perla?"

"Oh no, child! Perla only speaks to ghosts. She is not in touch with the spirit world once they pass over–at least not yet. You do know that not all gifts are the same, yes? Selene is helping to train her, but her sight is limited. The child, though, the child is quite magnificent, though still barely more than a babe!" I sat back and sipped my tea. It was still hot and burned my mouth. Baba Tsura carried on: "I have been speaking with Selene for many years now. She asked me to keep a lookout for you. When I heard of the Gentle woman in Sibiu who speaks fluent Rromani buying up all of my herbs, I knew it must be you. Then Ankah visited to tell me the rest of the story so that I would know what to tell you. She knows you have been alone this whole time, even when it seemed you had found companions."

I had a flash of Zhulyi and wondered if Ankah had checked in on me when I was with her and knew about my love for her. I felt a stab of shame. "Ankah wanted you to know that Perla is well," Baba Tsura continued, "and she knew you needed to hear that you did the right thing. She is proud of the way you mothered Perla. She says she knows now why she needed to come find you on the mountain–because you would be the one to raise her child."

It was all too much already, but I had to ask: "Baba Tsura–Ankah had told me once that she thought I was her sister reincarnated. Her sister Gildi had died during the Pestilence years before she found me. Do you think that's true?"

"It may be true. This mortal world is like washing a tub of laundry, you push a piece down into the Otherworld and another piece floats up. When it's wet, it all looks the same. Hard to tell what's what."

That was not the answer I was looking for.

"Jaelle, we are all part of the same soup. When you put a carrot in the stew, it bleeds its flavor into the porridge: the meat and herbs and all the juices of everything you've thrown in there blend together. When you eat that carrot, it's got some of the meat, some of the herbs, and some of the water in it, but it's also got the fire from below the pot in it, too, and the wheat from the bread dipped in, and probably some moonlight and starlight, too. None of us are really any one thing, not here and not in the worlds above and below either. So, do you have some Gildi in you? Most definitely. We tend to get stirred together, life after life, with the same ingredients: with the ones close to us that we were tossed into the soup with from the beginning." Though still not as clear as I would have wished, this was a more satisfying answer. "The really lucky spirits, they get dissolved away completely: they become the broth that infuses all else. If you still cling to your design as a carrot, you are not yet done with the journey."

"Thank you, Baba Tsura. I have so much to learn."

"Yes, well, you have traveled far, and much of it has been alone. When we travel together, we learn together, with all our minds helping one another. None of us were meant to wander alone."

"I have not found my tribe yet."

"You made a sacrifice. When you chose to raise Perla, you left your tribe. You gave them a gift by raising her, but you can never return to them. Still, you are one of us, Jaelle. You will always be one of us, regardless of the body you inhabit now. You are just a Romani carrot grown in a Gentle garden!" This made her laugh, a little chuckle at first, and then more and more. It was contagious to see her, with tears beginning to run from the sides of her eyes, and Simza and I began laughing, too. Soon we were all gasping for air.

After a while, we all sighed and sipped our tea as we tried to catch our breath, still erupting in small giggles spilling out here and there. "Well, I have wasted away a perfectly good morning," said Baba Tsura rising and brushing out her rumpled dress. "Oh, Jaelle, I have a bundle of herbs for you. It will save a trip for Simza to give them to you now." She went and fetched a large bundle wrapped in sack cloth that was in a basket by the garden. I had only a few coins in my apron, but Baba Tsura brushed them away. "You will come back at the end of the summer and train with me. The herbs know you well, but honestly, child—you have no idea what you're doing!"

"Thank you. Yes, I would love to learn more." I stood to go and then a thought occurred to me, "Baba Tsura- I'm sorry, I have one more question. My Baba—I always called her Baba, but she was Ankah's mother, the one who raised me—Have you spoken with her?"

"Oh no, child. Your Baba—she is now the broth."

∞

Simza and I walked slowly back through the woodland between Baba Tsura's house and the edge of the city. I still dangled my boots in one hand and held the package of herbs like a baby in the crook of my other arm. We did not talk for a good time, moving in comfortable silence through the trees. Finally, it occurred to me to ask her: "Simza, do you see things like your Baba?"

"Oh no," she said. "I am not gifted like that. I mean, I talk to trees and rocks just like any normal person, but I do not speak to ghosts or spirits from beyond the veils. No, thankfully I do not have that talent."

I felt a sense of relief that she was like me, not a conduit to the dead. "Thankfully?"

"Yes. I have to say, I have not observed it to be such a gift. If anything, it's a curse. Such a burden to have the trials of this world to manage and then to also have to mediate the demands of the Otherworlds, too? No, thank you! I'm happy to have just this one world to manage. It's plenty!" She smiled at me from out of the corners of her eyes.

"I agree. It certainly is plenty just to manage this world."

I did not see Simza again for many weeks, only her cousins in the market. Then she came one day bringing me a large packet of herbs and holding a separate small one. I was happy to see her, and I asked after her Baba. "Baba is well, thank you. She's as prickly as a meadow thistle, but I enjoy her company. She sent this for you," she said, holding out the smaller packet. "These mushrooms are special healing medicine. They are called *Umbrela*. She only gathers them once a year. She spent a whole day going to get them specifically for you. She said to make a tea, but only on a night when you will not see anyone else and you have nothing to do the next day. They are very powerful."

"Please tell her thank you." I could not help myself from blurting out: "It's so good to see you, Simza!"

She smiled, and passed me the packet with both hands, cupping my hands above and below and pressing the packet to my palm. She held her hands over mine and said, "May these serve you well, Jaelle. They helped me a great deal after my husband died." She turned and I watched her retreat, weaving through the crowded market and away from me, back to the forest.

The next several weeks were busy finishing up the banners for the ball for the Metalsmiths' Guild. I had spoken confidently, but the truth was it was an enormous amount of work. I hired a young daughter of the Weavers' Guild to help with the sewing, since it was over a hundred pennants to complete, and I needed to focus on the embroidery. Each time I had spoken to Mrs. Krempel, the number of banners had increased and the size of the lances to hold them grew. We had finally settled on a size and number. The girl was feverishly working away to sew the pennants with the ties to hold them to their poles while I embroidered symbols onto the ones already completed late into the night every night. My hands were cramped and aching, and I saw the patterns of the guild whenever I closed my eyes.

Finally, the week of the ball arrived. Fortunately, I was not responsible for the installation. This would be handled by those who were charged with setting up for the grand ball. Mrs. Krempel sent serfs each day to pick up those banners that were already completed. I got the final measurements on the portico, and my assistant and I made some adjustments to the banner that would go around the outside of that structure before I began the final embellishments for that design. I neglected all my other customers that week, since I had too much to do, but everyone in the city was focused on the ball as well and understood my priorities. There was nothing that could not be put off to the following week.

The morning of the ball, Mrs. Krempel herself came with her servants to pick up the final band to adorn the central structure in the main square that would hold the prizewinning submission. "Very nice work, Mrs. Sedlak," she said in a rare compliment to me as she ran her fingers over the embroidered banner, handing over a purse with the final payment. "You must come later to see the finished effect. I must say, I have really outdone myself this year! It's true, I had to crack the whip on those oafs in the shops to finish all of the poles, but a good manager gets the best out of people, even if she has to work harder than they just to get it done."

"I can't wait to see it, Mrs. Krempel. I'm sure the ball will be a tremendous success due to your efforts."

I had been up most of the night, and assumed I'd be able to rest after the project was completed. After Mrs. Krempel left, though, I found I was too wound up to sleep. I puttered around the shop cleaning up the devastation left after weeks of focusing on the work for the big event. Occasionally, the bells on the shop door would ring, and someone would come in looking for a tea to calm pre-ball jitters, or a balm so that their unrequited love interest would notice them. The streets were busy with preparations, but the interruptions in my shop were few and far between.

As evening neared, I heard the bells ring and found Cunrad, dressed in finer clothes than I'd ever seen him, accompanied by his mother. His mother greeted me, and I kissed her cheeks and put a hand on Cunrad's shoulder. When had he gotten so tall? "Look how stately you look! Your new master must be so impressed."

Cunrad squirmed in the stuffy velvet and pulled at the lace collar. His mother slapped his hand and said, "We just came by to thank you for everything, Mrs. Sedlak. Cunrad's new assignment is working out beautifully. He's already gaining praise from the Master."

"Why of course he is. Anyone would be impressed with such a hardworking and talented young man."

"He's going to be moving to his master's house soon so that he can begin his training in earnest."

"How wonderful! Well, no one deserves it more. I have missed you in the shop, Cunrad, but of course you are destined for better things than sweeping up after an old lady."

"You are hardly old," Cunrad objected, smiling.

"And you are ever the gentleman." I embraced him, and they went on their way to join the excitement of the evening.

I made myself a meal of stale biscuits and cheese as the music picked up and well-dressed party goers rushed by the shop. I could see just the end of the Strada Cetatii, where my banners were flying elegantly in a steepled arch made by the curved poles at the entrance to the street. I regretted that I had not gone earlier to see the full effect of the installation. This late, the event was now restricted to anyone not affiliated with the guilds. I could go in daylight to see it before it was dismantled.

I was exhausted, but unable to still my racing thoughts and my chittering pulse, which was accelerated from the weeks of activity leading up to this night. It was as if the whole city was buzzing and alive. Despite having no more to do, I could not seem to relax. Instead, I walked around and around, putting things right and cleaning up my work area. I went out to the courtyard in the back to put some water on to boil, thinking some tea might help me wind down. Coming back inside, I noticed the small packet from Baba Tsura that Simza had brought me tucked into a corner of my worktable. I had thought little of it, having been so preoccupied with my duties. Recalling the instructions, I realized I had no responsibilities left and nowhere to go the next day. The city would undoubtedly be late to rise the following day, and shops, including mine, were expected to be closed.

Bringing the light package outdoors and opening it, I saw it contained only three small shriveled dark mushrooms. As unimpressive as they were, I poured these into a small pot and filled it with boiling water. I sat outside and sipped the hot liquid as the music and sounds of shouts and laughter rose across the rooftops. The flavor reminded me of the stews I made in the years I spent alone in the castle, with only the forest accompanying me. It was a comforting taste, bringing me a sense of peace as I sat, once again alone despite the revelry about me. Soon I began to yawn uncontrollably, and so I shut up the shop and retired to my small quarters at the back of the property where I slept. I collapsed onto my blankets without undressing, falling asleep as soon as I lay my head down.

I awoke in full darkness but blinking because there were swirls of light and movement, such as when you become snow blind or have looked toward the sun too long. I rose unsteadily, and the upward lifting movement gave me the odd sensation that I was a great mountain coming alive. All my muscles and bones expanded and creaked and I stood next to my bedding and stretched out my arms toward the ceiling. Suddenly lightheaded, I almost fell and caught myself on the doorjamb. I opened the door and some light spilled in, but something about the movement turned my stomach inside out, and I found myself retching outside the door.

I must have been asleep for hours, because the city was mostly quiet. There were only sounds of the kinds of distant late parties that occur after other events have ended, and taverns that still had not shut their doors. A cat yowled in a nearby street, making me jump, and I heard something crash over. The night was still radiating the heat of the day, and I found I was desperately thirsty. I scooped a cup of water from the rain barrel. It tasted delicious! It was fragrant and fruity and seemed to spin alive down my throat, filling every pore of my being with moist, glorious fulfillment. Just as soon as it went down, though, it came back up again, and I was once again vomiting at the side of the courtyard. Rather than standing back up, I lay down flat on the dirt, to calm my spinning head. I looked up at the stars, which seemed to be vibrating, and watched as they pulsed and grew, larger and smaller. One grew so close it seemed to come and dance right before my eyes before snapping back, as if pulled by a string, to its rightful place in the sky.

The cool bare earth felt wonderfully refreshing against the heat of the summer night. As I ran my fingers and palms over the smooth packed clay of yard, my body began to sense that I was lying on a delicate crust, just a thin firm layer of earth. Underneath, I became prescient that there was a vast space that mirrored the sky I was looking at above. Glowing earthworms and beetles swam through an ocean of red and gold sparkling waves of dirt that was somehow also vast and empty as the air above. Feeling the pressure of my weight upon the earth, I grew startlingly aware that at any moment, I was going to break through the thin barrier and fall endlessly into the Underworld. I tried not to move at all, since any vibration might perforate the delicate shell. I lay there for what seemed like hours, petrified that any movement would tear the surface apart and I would go tumbling through.

While I lay, I could feel my pulse resonating and could hear my heart beating in time with the currents below and the glistening diamonds spiraling above. I was sandwiched, I realized, between the great expanding blackness of the night sky and the turbulent red waves below, both exerting equal pressure in opposite directions. At any moment, I could collapse through to the glowing sea below, or could just as easily fall out into the expanse of swirling darkness above. Both were equally terrifying. After being trapped between these two worlds for what felt like an eternity, I realized that the only thing I could safely do would be to align with the fragile earth itself. Once again, I became the mountain, my flesh merging with the ground below me and turning to rock and humus and root. The sheer cliffs of my body grew and changed over eons as I erupted from my diminished position to tower above the boiling waters below. I reached the branches of my body into the night air and stretched upward to hold back the great sky.

I stood with arms outstretched, fully suspended between these two massive powers, becoming a power in my own right with the resiliency of stone. I stood, my grand form emanating its own strength that was unshakable. The two great powers succumbed. Sensing their defeat, each released its pressure at the same time. My body crumpled and became flesh once again, and I fell, slumped over my knees, catching my breath. All the blood began to flow normally through human-sized limbs that had transformed back from granite, and I took deep gulps of air. Now I went to the rain barrel and drank and drank, filling the thirst of the ages I'd spent holding the place between the worlds. Finally satiated, I looked around. All was back to its normal size, and the ground below had once again become a solid entity. However, everything that normally seemed still was pulsing with energy. My teacup was brimming with a life of its own, and the wooden stool by the stove radiated a ring of light around it like a halo. The embers of the fire were alive with a quiet but persistent snapping of gossiping crackles and sparks. Even the small wisps of smoke were turning and dancing and shapeshifting into almost recognizable forms.

I opened the door to my shop and went through the sleeping interior to the empty street outside. Torchlight still burned, casting deep, otherworldly shadows that moved across the uneven cobbles. My feet were bare, and I could feel every irregular stone as if I were feeling them with my hands. My legs began to reacclimate to the motions of walking, as I assembled them to the task of moving forward. It took great concentration to make all my limbs move at once, but soon I was able to coordinate all the movements so that my body went forward of its own accord, as if I were walking on air. I drew near the entrance of the Strada Cetatii. Standing before the tunnel of banners, I saw how truly large they were: three times as tall as a person, with the rippling fabric undulating down in triangular sheaths.

The fabric was tinted in all the colors of metal, from deep black of iron to steel grays, to copper, and the golds and silvers of the softer metals. I had known this, of course, having made the pennants myself, but seeing them all perfectly aligned, in the full spectrum of the craft, waving in perfectly matched banners down the corridor of the alleyway was breathtaking. I walked below them, looking up and marveling at the architectural magnitude of it all and the symbols emblazoned upon the gently undulating sheets. Although all were familiar to me, being that I had labored over each stitch, the final product was alien and strange.

The many torches had burned down in their sconces upon the walls, but in between the banners had also been strung round tin lanterns with candles that still burned bright. The globes were perforated with designs and the slight breeze made dots of candlelight from the lanterns spin and speckle the alleyway in gyrating patterns. As I came to the part of the street that opened into the market, I saw the magnificent portico set in the center, with the surrounding banner undulating like the breathing of a living being at the heart of the square. Then my eyes were drawn to notice glistening objects around the perimeter. There were painted black boxes placed in regular intervals, upon which shiny creatures seemed to sit. Each one seemed to be moving, like animals crouched and breathing.

I went toward the first, but as I stepped in that direction, movement above drew my attention. A black figure stood atop the wall, watching me. At first, I mistook it for one of the gargoyles that had been built into some of the fortress walls, created by the Stonemasons' Guild. However, the slight movement of the whites of watching eyes betrayed the form as something living. The rest of him was flat and dark as a shadow. The clouds unfurled from in front of the full moon for a moment, allowing me to see the glint of a weapon in the figure's hand. I stood paralyzed, like prey caught in the gaze of a predator, as his eyes bore into mine. We stood with eyes locked, frozen in time. Then, he nodded at me, and as if my head were tied upon an invisible string connecting us, I nodded back. His form relaxed and he turned his gaze across the rest of the courtyard and abruptly walked to guard another spot. Just like that, I recognized him as one of the endless sentries who typically defended the wall at night. In addition to the regular duties of patrolling the city, he and many others would be employed tonight to safeguard the treasures in the exhibit.

I continued my way toward the first box and saw a wonder sitting upon it. It was spinning, so I had trouble focusing on the moving parts to interpret what it could be. A brass stand held a large circle while smaller circles inside of it tilted and shifted. On these bands were small glass orbs that rolled and yet somehow did not escape their gilded paths. As one shifted up, another shifted down in a slow, hypnotic rhythm that moved methodically, but did not cease. I watched this elaborate design, surprised each time the inner bands rose and spun and came back about for the balls to circle again eternally, of their own volition. I could not comprehend the mechanics of this seemingly magical machine. I finally determined it must be imbued with a charm, since there was no logical explanation of how it could move on its own, its parts completely synchronized with each other, sparkling balls rotating in their ever-balanced journeys. It was clear why this entry had won a prize.

I visited each of the entries in the exhibit, all displayed upon similar black boxes along the perimeter of the square. Each one was dazzling and delightful in a different way. I had always thought of the Metalsmiths' Guild as a practical establishment: charged with the mundane tasks of creating the cooking pots and weaponry of the masses. I now saw the artful life of the guild that I had somehow missed. There were some utilitarian objects, but even these were elevated to the finest level of craftsmanship: a copper cauldron with gemstones inset in its handle like eyes that seemed to make the pot appear as if it were truly alive, and a sword that had such intricate patterns carved into its hilt that it must have taken years to complete. The blade of the weapon was made from two colors of metal that were somehow blended together, like a marble, in dotted and folded waves. Baba had always told me that when the Tribe made tools and weapons, a spirit was born into each one: that spirit then needed to be honored, tended, and conversed with during their use. This was why we spoke to the knife when cutting the onion, to implore it to help drive away the tears.

Whether the makers of these items realized it or not, they had also given birth to spirits that were plainly living within the metal confines of their forms. As I traveled the arc of the exhibition, I easily found the spirits dwelling within each creation. I began to speak to them, in low whispers: "You are truly magnificent. I've never seen such a remarkable sword," for instance. In reply, the item would glow and puff up, as if heartened by my praise, and sometimes the wind would pick up and I could almost hear words in the whistle of air circling by my head. In this way, I had deeper conversations than I'd had for years. Not since Zhulyi had I felt so connected and heard, as if within a few moments the entity and I would have such communion that nothing else existed. I had to almost tear myself away from each one. I could usually tell when the conversation was over, though, as the flaring excitement I would sense under their metallic surfaces would retreat to a calm and steady pulse, and it was time to move on to the next.

By the time I got back around to where I had started, I was exhausted with the effort of so many interactions. It was as if I had attended a party and had been immersed in the thrall of exchange the whole night. It was now time to go home: but I had forgotten to visit the portico. I realized it as it billowed out its curtained walls that I had so painstakingly adorned. The entrance was at the far side of the square, so that it could not be seen from the alley leading into the expansive court. The First Place winner of the competition would be sequestered, as I had envisioned, to be discovered only upon entry. As I approached the small openwork building, I had the sense that I was encroaching on the home of a larger-than-life presence. The fabric on the outer walls was silken light gold, with a sheen that had practically made me drool when Mrs. Krempel first had it delivered to me. Now, the silver thread that I had woven into the skin of the cloth danced in marvelous designs, turning from the familiar symbols that I had intended into intricate and complicated pictorial messages that were foreign and indecipherable.

I gave the enclosed shrine a wide birth as I moved around the back to the entrance, wary of what living thing might be inside. The scrolling metalwork making up its skeleton came to a point at the top, like a steeple pointing to the heavens, and a lantern hung in its interior cast flickering ruby light that pulsed like a heart. As I stood in front of the small temple, with flaps hanging in folds where they had previously been tied open, I was suddenly transported to the front of the tent where I had found Ankah dead. I was gripped with a mortal terror, certain that when I went inside I would find her there again, drained of all life. Despite my paralyzing fear, I watched my hands move of their own volition, reaching to pull apart the curtains to gain entry. I looked first to the floor, expecting to see blood pooled at my feet, but the light from the moon outside spilled only on stone. I made myself fully enter, feeling the soft folds of fabric brushing my back as they fell closed behind me.

What I saw completely baffled me: I had thought the moon was in the sky above, but I must have been mistaken, because here was the moon, floating inside the chamber. The soft face of her hovered in mid-air, a diffused ivory glow. Green and white stars encircled her, dancing about her head, teasing her, the sparkling dervishes flashing playful pinholes of colored light that appeared and disappeared. I watched the movement, trying to make sense of what I was seeing, since none of it could be linked to anything of this world.

"Can you believe that pearl?" I jumped at the voice behind me. Having become accustomed to the whispered voices of the metal, this one seemed brash and loud to my ears. I turned quickly and recognized the black form of the soldier from the wall, but this time up close, holding open the curtain of the enclosure.

"Wh . . . What?" I could barely find my own voice and it sounded harsh as it creaked out into the air.

"The pearl . . . it's amazing, isn't it?" the guard said. "I've never seen one so large. Can you imagine the oyster that spit up that thing?" He cracked a smile to show a mouth with many missing teeth. I had trouble drawing my eyes away from the black spaces in his grin but looked back and saw that of course the moon was a pearl, the largest I had ever seen. It was an ocean pearl, and perfectly round, not the irregular river pearls that I was accustomed to.

"You need to step up on the box to see it best," he said, pointing to the floor. I had not noticed, but there was indeed a small black box there. Since I seemed uncertain, he took my arm and steadied me as I stepped up and precariously tried to balance myself, a feat with my tremendously swimming head. He held my elbow until I stopped swaying, then graciously backed away. I looked down upon a black velvet covered table with a magnificent silver necklace. The work was so delicate that you could barely see the structure of it; it held the pearl in a cloud of fine wires, scaffolding a whole universe of diamonds and emeralds in its midst. "I'll leave you alone so you can admire it. You'll forgive me if I check to make sure it's still here when you leave," he said, chuckling as he left, letting the curtains fall in his wake.

I stood looking down. I could see it now in its intended form, as a piece of jewelry. And yet, it was more than that. I felt the air vibrating around me and tried to track its source. It bubbled up through my feet and into the rest of my body. My sternum jostled with the power of it, and I worked to keep my balance upon the narrow step. I watched as the silver coils began to snake and weave, each tendril seeming to have a mouth and a voice hissing and whispering. "Fieraru," I heard the word as a chorus of voices, deep and yet female, maternal and resonant. I looked around, but the curtains remained closed. The voice had come from within. The pearl itself was speaking, it seemed. I listened, and just heard the whooshing and flap of the fabric as it filled with air and deflated, the lantern above sputtering.

"Fieraru," I heard again, this time clearer and closer, and as one woman's voice, although it had the intonation of hundreds and thousands of combined voices. It was recognizing me, I realized, and it saw me as part of the metalsmiths' tribe. All was suddenly in clear focus: I stood in the middle of a shrine to the goddess of metal, built by those who worshipped at her temples. My own tribe, the Fieraru, and the Metalsmiths' Guild of Sibiu, were all part of the same clan, despite having no awareness that they shared allegiance. They all honored and placated the spirits of the elements that give birth to and inhabit metal works. That she had been dominated and owned by men was only a temporary condition, I saw, since her true nature was female and would always be as a mother and protector. She let men forge and create with her, implanting their marks on her body, but the metal that cuts, that cooks, that adorns, was all her work, despite the hands that made them.

The pearl within the sparkling scaffoldry shifted and changed then, and I saw in her my own daughter's face: my little Perla. "Mama!" she said.

"Perla!" I croaked out, my voice abrading the air.

"Mama, it's me." I saw her, and I knew it truly was her, not another hallucination brought on by the tea.

"Mama listen: I have something to tell you," her eyes flashed in earnest and I recognized the sweet face as the one I had loved and held and cherished, only more mature now, still childish and round, but much older than the child I'd left: "Mama, I want you to know that I love you more than anything. I have missed you so much. I know I needed to come back to my tribe. It was the right thing to do. I am with my family. Others are still mad at you for what you did, but I know you did what was right. You are my true mother, and I needed to be with you for those years to become who I am now." I was crying, with the tears streaming down my face in what felt like sheets of water. "Never doubt that I love you and I will see you again. Even if we can't be together again in this life, our spirits are always connected. We will always be together, even if we are apart. You are a part of me, and I am a part of you . . . always."

I gasped and tried to respond, but the words came out sputtering, having no meaning. Perla's voice continued: "I love you, Mama," she said, and then her face faded and flickered. The pearl glowed, as if inhabited by Perla's memory, then darkened out and became the smooth sheen of its natural body once again. The pearl that had scried my daughter was once again, just a pearl, though truly a beauty.

I felt myself falling, but strong arms caught me as I tripped backwards. It was the guard again, my faithful gargoyle. "I'm sorry, madam," he said, helping me to stand. "I thought I heard voices in here. Just wanted to make sure you were safe. Forgive my grasping you like that. You seemed to be fainting."

"No . . . thank you. Thank you. You're very kind. I would have fallen," I said. "I need to go home." I felt the urgency of returning to my safe little abode and my comfortable bedding. I needed sleep and to calm my spinning head.

"I'll escort you, madam. I don't think you're in any shape to walk alone. Even with the guard about, it's not safe for a lady to be out this time of morning by herself."

He helped me out of the portico and yelled to another sentry on the wall: "Andors! I'm escorting this lady home. Take care of the perimeter!" He held my elbow most of the way, since I stumbled often, and my walking was awkward and problematic. At my door, I said: "I'm so sorry. Thank you for helping me home."

"It's no problem. Just doing my civic duty. We've all had too much ale to drink at one point or another."

I fell upon my bed as soon as I could find my way by touch through the dark shop, across the outer courtyard, and into the small cubicle where I slept. It was not really sleep that overtook me–that was a long way off. I lay with colors swirling and lights flashing, whether my eyes were opened or closed, and dreams came in and out until the reprieve of blackness finally overtook me.

Chapter Eighteen: A Mother's Voice

I was walking behind Simza again, holding my boots in one hand, and a small bag with some belongings slung over my other arm. The forest unfolded before us and we were silent, having spoken a little upon meeting up at the market and then expending our conversation as we entered the wood. I thought of nothing but following her feet. Since the night of the Metalsmiths' Ball, I had a sense of well-being and calm, and nothing had bothered me. I had been destroyed for a few days, barely able to function for the swirling lights and bending vision that still lingered. After a while these resolved, although I still saw a trail behind moving objects and shadows transforming in the corner of my eyes sometimes. I slept soundly at night, and some of the thoughts I had tortured myself with regularly for years had vanished.

Word was sent through Simza's cousins of when Baba Tsura would be expecting me, so I finished lingering projects. I had already paid off my rent for the upcoming two seasons with the windfall I had made from the ball, and I let my customers and neighbors know I would be away visiting family for several weeks before locking up my shop. On the day it was time to leave, I went to the market and there was Simza, once again ready to escort me. It was a good thing, too, since I don't think I could have found my way on my own. I would not be likely to be able to find my way back by myself, either. This time, like the last, I focused entirely on Simza, and paid little attention to the landmarks that might guide my way there or back.

Baba Tsura was in the garden, sitting upon a stump and pulling weeds, talking to them the whole while. "Ah, Jaelle. You're here. Good. I need some help with these weeds." She put me to work right away so she could finish a stew that was cooking over an open fire in a compact round iron cauldron. She showed me what and how to pull, and how to thank the unwanted plants for nourishing the ground and breaking the way for the earthworms. "You must always speak to them, honor them, and let them know that they are valued. Tell them they will live again as nice humus and go back into the garden when they break apart."

I began my tasks and then noticed that Simza seemed to be gathering her things for a journey. "Are you going somewhere?" I asked, alarmed.

"Yes, I must go see to my daughter's wedding. And then I will stay with my son and husband's family for a time to help with the baby."

I was devastated, but tried to hide my disappointment. "Will you be back soon?"

"Not until the spring, most likely. Now that you are here to see to Baba, I am free to tend to my own business. Thank you, Jaelle. I know it will benefit you to learn from Baba, but it will help me, too."

I had no intention of staying through to the spring, but I did not say so. Soon, we sat together over a quick meal, and she embraced us to head on her journey while there was still light. I watched her walk into the woods in another direction and disappear into the ferns and shadows. That evening, feeling the loss of Simza's departure, I sat outside with Baba Tsura sipping tea. My head had followed Simza, but Baba Tsura wanted to discuss my education: "I will show you the entire cycle of the spirits of the plants," she was saying. "It's important for you to see it all. One might think you would start in spring with new life, but that's only the middle of the story. The beginning comes with Death. In the autumn, the trees drop their leaves, making blankets for their roots and for the seeds that will sleep below the cover. Many plants die after their spawn are spread, and then the trees embrace them through the winter. I know you can not hear the spirits yet, but you will learn to hear them, Jaelle." If she was aware that I was distracted, she did not reveal it. She went on: "They are in everything. You will learn the voice of a leaf decomposing, preparing another spirit for birth. This is an exciting time, because it is the decay of life that gives birth to new life. We must honor the decay, as we honor the decay of our own bodies!

"Look at me!" I jumped at her loud exclamation. "I'm not the trim and sassy lass I used to be. My body is done making babies and my breasts no longer make milk to feed little ones, and yet I am now in the height of my power! I can see the earth for all it has to offer and share that with others. My purpose now is to feed others with knowledge, which is why it was important for you to come here. You will carry on with all I have gathered: like the decaying leaf, I will send all of my nourishment into you, blanket you, and give you everything you need to learn and grow. And from that, your wisdom will sprout and grow shoots that will turn to roots and strong branches. This is very important work, Jaelle."

"I am grateful that you would share your knowledge with me, Baba Tsura, but what of Simza? Or one of your other relatives. You have so many. Why not teach them?" I had lost my enthusiasm for being there. For the past week, I had fantasized of working side by side with Simza, our arms touching, laughing together as we lived, ate, and slept close together.

"I have given them all they need to know. Some people learn a little and some learn a lot. I have had many students over the years, but now it's your turn. I knew you were right for this work when I first started talking to Ankah. She told me how you took your daughter and raised her away from everyone, surviving by your own skill, as barely more than a child yourself."

"Well, I had help," I admitted, recalling Sandor's generosity in the early years, as I raised Perla alone in the ruined castle.

"We all have help," she said.

"I have to tell you, Baba Tsura, I'm not sure how long I will be staying. I have a business to attend to back to in Sibiu."

She laughed: "Jaelle, you only have now, this moment with me. Tomorrow is not guaranteed."

"Yes, I am here now, and we will see about tomorrow when that comes, but I do not want to mislead you. I am not intending to stay more than a few weeks."

"We'll see," she said, dismissing my words with a wave. "Now tell me, how did the Umbrela serve you?"

"Very well, I think." I told her of my strange journey, being pulled apart by the sky and Underworld, and becoming the mountain. I described the exhibition and how I had communed with each thing and spoken to the spirits of Metal. "They recognized me as Fieraru," I said, still wondering at that revelation.

"I told you: you are one of us. It does not matter who gave birth to you or what you look like. Anyone can tell that you are Rrom." I laughed, relieved that she felt that way. It was a high compliment. I then went on to explain how I had approached the small pavilion, fearing that I would find Ankah dead inside all over again, and how I had found the pearl instead. "The spirits of the Umbrela are very powerful," Baba Tsura explained. "They help you to revisit the most difficult parts of your life and put them in order." When I told her about my visit from Perla, Baba Tsura nodded. "It seemed as if she were really there," I recalled. "It did not feel like something created by the magic of the Umbrela."

"Yes, I'm sure she was there. Perla is quite capable of scrying you. She's gotten more skillful with her craft over the years."

I withheld the entire message, for some reason not wanting to share that private experience, but Baba Tsura did not pry. I felt she knew anyway.

"Well, it's as I hoped, Jaelle. You had many negative spirits surrounding you, pulling at you all the time. It's why I recommended the Umbrela. Once again, you can see how Death is the beginning. The Umbrela recognizes things in you that need to die, pass away and decay, which is only right because it is a mushroom. Mushrooms sprout up on dead things, but they are not parasites. Oh, no–they give out even more than they take. They are all connected to one another. Did you know if something happens on one side of the forest, the mushrooms speak along the roots of trees all the way to send messages to the trees and plants at the other side of the forest? It's true. They are the great communicators. Our People have always known this, which is why we honor the mushroom as much as the mightiest tree."

"It did seem to set some things right for me," I acknowledged.

"Yes. So now, every time you see a mushroom, I don't want you to see a plant for you to eat. You will see a teacher. A mushroom is someone to talk to who may have important messages for you."

"When I was at the castle, I used to harvest mushrooms. I don't know how I knew which ones were poison. It seemed the trees told me."

"See! The forest was speaking to you even then."

"Yes, but I've never heard any voices. Do you actually hear words?"

"There are voices, definitely. Not so much words, although they are capable of speaking any language we can. No, we learn to interpret the way a tree bends and then you hear in the wind that rustles the intention of the tree."

"Ankah used to tell me that she could hear the voice of the Mother of Everything in the way a leaf grew."

"Yes, yes exactly. You will be able to do that. But first, we will speak to all that is dying within the wood. This forest has certain spirits who live here, and you will come to know them, too. First, you will learn to speak to them, and then you will hear them speak to you. But even sooner than that, we will sleep!" She laughed, and the lines around her eyes folded into their natural shape, clearly born from years of good merriment.

We retreated into the cabin, and Baba Tsura showed me the place Simza had been sleeping. As I nestled into the warm blankets covering a nest of dried grasses and moss, I could feel the indentation of Simza that she formed by sleeping there, night after night. Resting in the imprint of her flesh, I felt close to her, but still jilted. I had imagined that she was looking forward to my visit, but I realized now that it had all been in my head. She had her own life and priorities, and I was not included in them. Lying in the dark, it made my face flush with embarrassment that I had let my hopes make me so foolish. My thoughts turned back to Zhulyi, knowing that at least my feelings for her had been real and returned. I was overcome with the deep comprehension that no one would ever love me like that again. I fell asleep pining for Zhulyi, lying in the impression of Simza's body.

∞

As Baba Tsura predicted, I did not return to Sibiu in a few weeks, nor a few months. At first the idea of my shop closed up tight, with customers awaiting to place orders bothered me. After a while, it seemed inconsequential. I had not left anything of true value. Eventually, the landlord would conclude that I had abandoned our agreement and would dispose of its contents to make room for the next tenant. I had grown comfortable there, but aside from Cunrad and his family, I had made virtually no real connections. Soon, it seemed more of a blessing than a loss to be relieved of the responsibility to return.

Baba Tsura was a demanding teacher and expected my full participation in everything. If I seemed to be wandering away inside my head, which I did often, she would snap her fingers in front of my face and say: "Jaelle! The task right in front of you needs your attention!" She was incredibly fit, I found. When we walked for miles so she could show me where to find an herb in a swampy area that didn't grow anywhere else, I had trouble keeping up. I had gotten the impression that she needed caring for from Simza, but I soon saw that Baba Tsura was extremely capable of taking care of herself and me as well. I would hardly realize I was thirsty and there she would be, with a cup of water with crushed mint. I thought I had done well at the castle on my own, but now I realized that the spare broths I had survived on were barely edible fare. She showed me how to speak to a giant mushroom, growing in fruity layers from the base of a tree. I learned to ask my knife not to hurt the spirit within, and gently cut a hunk off without killing it. The boiled down stews were so thick and hearty, one would think only meat could taste like that.

In addition to the culinary mastery I was developing, Baba Tsura taught me something new every day about the healing energies that resided within the plants. Even the spindliest weeds had potent medicinal properties, but one had to be careful to speak in certain ways to all that was harvested in order to fully benefit. Baba Tsura taught me this language. "You need to speak to them first before they will speak to you, Jaelle," she would chide me when I grew impatient for not hearing the voices that she asserted were all around us, guiding us. I had always assumed that people were either gifted with having the ability to hear such messages or not. Baba Tsura assured me that even those who heard spirits naturally had to develop the talent for understanding the words of trees and plants. Being able to hear the voice of the Earth Mother was a *skill*, she insisted, that anyone could learn. I had just not learned it yet.

Throughout the long winter in the wood, Baba Tsura and I spent hours around the cooking fire. She told me stories, like Rromani fairytales, that seemed too fantastical to be true, but which Baba Tsura relayed with authority as historical fact. In between these legends, she instructed me in detail about the vegetation we had painstakingly harvested and dried in the preceding months. As she explained many of the uses for the herbs we had stored, I realized that often when I had recommended a certain tea for an ailment in my shop back in Sibiu, I had been right! When I mentioned this to Baba Tsura, she just laughed at me. "You have great instincts, Jaelle, but you were like a child, grabbing at any shiny thing. Your instincts will keep you alive, but they will not make you successful at your craft. You need to be better than just guessing right sometimes." I was suitably admonished and vowed to study harder.

As Baba Tsura had promised, in the spring we watched the snow recede and the green shoots, so carefully tucked in for their long sleep before germination, begin to unfurl and reach for the sun. After the long days and nights of my education, I was now able to see how each plant looked from the very beginning, as it started its new life, born from Death. We ran about the forest, from one clump of growing things to another, as Baba Tsura enthusiastically described how to talk to these seedlings from the very beginning: "You have to encourage them," she said. "They are just babies starting out. It's all new and they are unsteady on their fragile stems. Let them know you will check on them." We watched all season as tiny shoots turned to massive flowers and seed heads, growing top heavy and full of life. "This is the love life of the flowers," she explained when blossoms heaved out perfume and bees and butterflies crawled upon their sticky embellishments.

I had always loved the forest, but now I felt I was beginning to understand it. Baba Tsura had me sit for hours watching small yellow curlicues arise from a field of star-like moss covering a fallen and decomposing tree. If you sat very, very still, you could see the vibrations, synchronized between all the tiny antennas. Were they hundreds of small beings, or one large connected entity? It was hard to tell, or maybe it didn't matter. When the wind picked up and a stand of trees would rustle together, Baba Tsura would say: "The spirits are afoot!" She told me when the wind blew like that, just in one place, you knew there were presences near. She also told me there were tiny people who lived in the forest, the Bitty Folk of the wood. I found this whimsical, but she became insulted when I suggested it was a silly myth. "Just because you have not seen it does not mean it's not true, Jaelle! You would not have believed a pearl could speak to you either, if you had not seen so yourself."

In time, I agreed with her that there were things at work that I just did not understand. I tried to keep my mind open to the possibility that there were things that I just could not perceive yet. After all, how could a tiny shoot carry the energy and knowledge within it to become a mighty seed stalk? It reminded me of when I was a child watching the baby goats, amazed that the newborn kids could stand and know how to find the teat minutes after emerging from their mother's womb. Life was full of mysteries, so how would spirits or Bitty Folk be any more miraculous than an acorn turning into a massive oak? It was all magical, and I understood little of it. I began to honor it—even worshipping the mystery.

At night we watched the stars and Baba Tsura told me they were living in the past and we were watching ancient light that had traveled through time. This proved, she said, that time was folded in places. You could step into a place by accident that had existed long before the human race, or long after we expired. If you did not know, you might not even realize it. If you watched very carefully, you could see the wrinkles in the fabric of time across eons: "This is one reason we can talk to the Dead," explained Baba Tsura. "Once you recognize that all is happening *now*, within one moment, it becomes easy to speak to people who are no longer here. They are as real and alive as we are, if you can just find the doublings in the curtains of the universe to bring them closer." Baba Tsura spent a lot of time speaking to her own ancestors: those who came before her, who she said gave her knowledge about things they had learned.

"Your mother is your closest ancestor," Baba Tsura told me, when I explained what little I knew about my roots. "You should speak to her." I told her how when I had visited her grave, I felt nothing. "Yes, of course!" she said. "What did you expect? For her to stick around a place that caused her so much pain and suffering? Where she lost her love and her daughter? Who would stay in a place like that?"

One day she sent me on a mission to speak to my mother. She sent me to a glade several miles away, along a route I had not taken before. She guided me by telling me to follow obscure directions: follow the stream until I saw the roots of a tree that looked like a big black hand reaching over it; then follow the deer paths to the left until I come to a clump of mountain laurel. Amazingly, it worked. I found myself in the small wooded valley that she had described, with sharp cliffs of dark shale on either side. Baba Tsura had prepared me that I would not be likely to hear my mother's voice, like I might if I were gifted with the Sight. However, I could still communicate with her if I concentrated and listened carefully.

I chose a carpet of starry moss to make myself comfortable. The whole valley was covered in ferns, lush and lacy with overlapping shadows. When I sat, I was at eye level with them. Then I just stayed quiet and listened. At first, I was distracted by the small sounds: a crow flying from tree to tree and cawing; bees buzzing about. Then I felt the overwhelming urge to lie back, so I lay flat on the earth, looking up at the pieces of sky between the pines that shot through the small valley. The ferns framed my vision, a blur of green circling me like a halo. I felt the true magnitude of the earth below me, solid and comforting. As much as I tried to stay alert to all that was going on, I soon fell into a trancelike sleep. I awoke to soft, sweet chirps of birds. A gentle rain misted down, twinkling through the rays of light. All was glistening around me. I prepared to stand when something moved, just slightly, in the corner of my eye. I turned to see a beautiful orange fawn curled up—not even a full body's length away from where I had lain for hours. The dark gold of her coat camouflaged with the rust needles and leaf litter that lay under the ferns, her white spots mimicking the specks of sunlight that filtered through. Her solemn dark eyes watched me, yet she was still as a statue.

"Hello, sweet baby," I said quietly. "Are you all alone here?" She was under a spray of ferns, protected from the gentle pattering of rain. All became hazy and steamy in the undergrowth, as the warmth of the ground met the cool droplets. I saw her nose twitch as a tiny drop hit it, then a small bluish tongue reached up to lick the drop away. I found myself smiling at the brilliance of it all: her perfect disguise; her small, still existence. "Where is your mother?" I asked her. My heart ached for her, here all alone in the wood. I realized that if the mother deer was indeed nearby, she would not come back while I was there, so I gathered myself up. "Goodbye, sweet little one."

I picked my way backwards through the dripping, mist-filled valley, back along the stream to the cottage. Baba Tsura's dog, Django, came running out to greet me, with sharp, quick barks punctuating the air. Someone came out of the doorway, but it did not match the small frame of Baba Tsura. We had few visitors over the fall. The whole winter had gone by, and we had no company but each other. In early spring, Baba Tsura's grandchildren, who I had come to think of as "the cousins," sporadically came to call, punctuating long spans of time with only each other to speak to. They dropped in occasionally to check on Baba Tsura and to collect bundles of herbs for the market. As I got closer, I saw that our visitor was Simza. "Jaelle!" She exclaimed, coming toward me with a radiant smile. She embraced me and held me for many moments. "It's so good to see you! Baba Tsura has been telling me all about your lessons." Baba Tsura came out of the house, carrying a bowl. She greeted me and ladled out a cup of cool water filled with floating petals, which she handed to me.

"How are your children?" I asked Simza. I was surprised to find I truly did care to know, having had a long winter to nurse my hurt feelings.

"Wonderful! My daughter is married now! And my son's baby is growing well. He can say 'Baba Simza' now! It warms my heart! Baba—I did not tell you yet—they're expecting another child!"

Baba Tsura nodded and smiled. "The family is growing," she observed. "Now sit, Jaelle. Tell us about your day. Did you find your mother?"

We sat at the table and I relayed my experience in the valley of ferns and finding the baby deer in the mist. "I did not hear any messages—no voices or anything—but it was a lovely day."

"Have you no eyes, child?" Baba Tsura seemed annoyed. "You could not have gotten a clearer message if it had hit you over the head!" I was stunned by the reprimand, and sat, trying to figure out what I had missed.

"Baba," Simza chided, "she's still not used to your lessons. A good teacher is a patient teacher," she said, and reached over to tuck a curl of Baba Tsura's white hair back under her black headscarf. She turned to me. "Tell us what you were thinking when you found the baby deer."

I thought for a moment. "I wondered where its mother was. It was so quiet and still. I had been there for hours and it had not made a sound. I almost missed it."

"It was there all along, but you did not know you had company," Simza repeated.

"Exactly. It was so perfectly disguised!"

"It was there and not there."

"In a sense, yes. I was worried that I had kept its mother from returning."

"So, you thought you might have kept the mother away."

"Maybe."

"Maybe?"

"Or maybe it was all alone in the world. Maybe it had no mother at all. It may have been orphaned for all I know."

"Like you?"

"Well–yes, but I had people to take care of me."

"Not your mother, though. Were any of those who adopted you like a mother to you?"

"Yes, but I had to fit in first. I was out of place. I had to figure out how to make myself fit into their world. It was all foreign. I even had to learn to speak another language, learn how to behave."

"You had to blend in."

"Yes." It dawned on me then. "I had to blend in. I had to camouflage."

Baba Tsura beamed at Simza. "Such a good girl. So smart, like her Baba."

"Jaelle," Simza continued, "you went to the glade to get a message from your mother. If you knew for a fact that seeing the baby deer was a message from her, what would you suppose she was telling you?"

"I'm not sure . . . that she knows that I was left all alone; that she is with me sometimes, even if I don't know she's there; that she knows what it's like to be all alone. I think about that sometimes–she was all by herself, raising me, with no one. You know, I think she may have died of a broken heart? I don't think she meant to leave me, but I don't think she had the strength to continue. Maybe she was saying she's sorry she had to leave me all alone."

"Hmmm," said Baba. "But was the little deer safe?"

"Oh yes. She was safe under the ferns. She blended into her surroundings. She was not even really getting wet when it started to rain. She was . . . protected."

"Yes, she was safe."

"Do you think ghosts can protect us?"

"Ghosts, no. Ghosts can only pester and fuss about. But the Ancestors… the Ancestors can protect us."

"Do you know what my mother was trying to tell me? I'm sorry, Baba Tsura. I'm not good at this. Can you tell me what her message was?"

"It's not always in words, Jaelle. It's in the feeling, in the experience. You said you had a lovely day. You said you were worried for this baby, but that she was safe and dry and taken care of, and maybe just waiting for her mother to return. Have you been waiting for your mother to return?"

"Of course not. I hate to say this, but I don't really feel connected to my mother at all. I have almost no memory of her. What I remember is that she was very sick and couldn't care for me. I had to fend for myself. She was barely a mother to me. My goats were more mothers to me than she was."

"You sound bitter."

"No, it wasn't her fault."

"That doesn't mean you're not bitter."

"The Clan took me in. I had almost no life before they came along. I was barely surviving. They are the whole reason I survived. They kept me safe."

"How did that come to pass?"

"Ankah found me. Ankah heard the voice of the Mother of Everything—she told me—who told her where to go. She didn't know what she would find, but when they arrived, my mother begged them to take me."

"How do you suppose that happened?"

"Ankah listened to the voices."

"No, Jaelle. How do you think it happened that the voices were calling to her?"

I sat, feeling more bemused than ever. "I have no idea," I admitted.

"Could it have been your mother?"

"What do you mean?"

"Could your mother have called out for help?"

"Who would she have called?"

"Perhaps her own ancestors. Isn't it possible she called upon her own ancestors and these are the ones who found an ear in Ankah—someone who was capable of hearing their message and lead her to where your mother and you were?"

"I always found it an odd story. Who led Ankah to me? I have wondered that. Why would the universe care about a child who was about to be orphaned. Orphans are made every day. Especially then–the Pestilence was barely over."

"I know this is not how you have been taught to think. Those who have the gift of Sight are trained to understand these things. Those who don't have the gift have to learn it in a different way, like my Simza here. Clearly, she understands Otherworldly matters, but she has had to learn over time, right my Precious?" Baba Tsura pulled Simza toward her and Simza nestled against her, resting her head on Baba Tsura's shoulder like a child. It was comical, as she was bigger than her tiny grandmother. I was struck then, by a recollection. Sitting on the floor by my mother's bed and resting my head upon her lap.

"I remember she would talk to herself toward the end–my mother," the memories came flooding back. "She talked to the air, as if someone were there. She was very ill."

"Was she really talking to the air?" Baba Tsura asked.

"Do you think she could have been talking to the Ancestors? She was a dying woman. She was not in her right mind."

"No, but those who do not have the Sight are sometimes given the gift when they are very ill or when they take special medicine, like the Umbrela. Just because their minds are altered by the sickness or the medicine does not mean it's not real. They can sometimes see things as they really are. They may even be able to reach through the folds of time or across the veils to speak to the Dead."

"My mother called them." The realization hit me: "She called them, and they summoned Ankah. It's the only thing that makes sense."

"What do you think your mother was trying to tell you today, Jaelle?" Baba Tsura asked, her eyes intent upon me.

"That she's sorry she had to leave me, but that she put me someplace safe. She put me where I would be protected."

∞

Simza only stayed a few days and then was gone again. We resumed what Baba Tsura called my "training" in earnest. I learned now, not just the practical techniques of harvesting the healing barks, leaves, berries, roots, and flowers, but to recognize and appreciate the world of the unseen. It was too subtle for me to pick it up easily at first, and Baba Tsura often had to lead me through interpreting the advice that was being shared so generously with me by the spirits of the forest. I saw no clear messages in an owl swooping down in front of me to catch a mouse at dusk, but Baba Tsura did, and she patiently–or sometimes not so patiently–helped me to understand. When a tree that was near the cabin creaked ominously one day for several minutes in odd gusts of wind, Baba Tsura worked with me a whole afternoon to help me understand what it had told me.

When I began to see these things myself, without her assistance, she was very proud of me. "You're growing into the Craft, Jaelle. Soon you may even be ready to work on your own."

When Simza came back a few months later, she was impressed with how much I had changed: "You are really becoming a healer now, like Baba! This is wonderful progress, Jaelle."

I came upon the two of them with their heads close together one evening a few days after Simza had arrived. Baba Tsura was shaking her head vehemently.

"Well, we should ask her. It's only right. At least to give her the option," Simza was saying.

They stopped when they saw me. "What is it?" I asked. "Is something wrong?"

Simza looked at her grandmother, then said to me, "We were discussing your prospects."

"My . . . prospects?"

"Yes, well, Jaelle–you know that your body will not make babies forever. If you are going to marry and have a family of your own, it will have to happen soon. My husband's cousin was widowed some time back. He's a wonderful man. He and his wife had three children, but they are grown and married. He's expressed the wish to marry again."

"And?"

"Would you consider it?"

"I don't even know this person!"

"No, but . . . your options are limited, at your age. Don't you want children?"

"No! No–I don't want children. I had a child. I had Perla. I can't ever replace her."

"No one is asking you to replace her, but at some point, you need to move on with your life. This cousin . . . Tamiro, he is very kind, and a very attractive man for his age."

"Then why don't you marry him!" I snapped. Simza look down, injured. "I'm sorry, Simza. I do not feel I'm the marrying type."

"That's what I told her," Baba Tsura agreed.

"I have never been inclined that way. The idea is quite distasteful to me."

"You may not get another chance. I am just looking out for you," Simza said, sounding hurt.

"I thank you for your concern. I am better off alone."

The evening that Simza left, Baba Tsura and I sat by the fire. "I know why you did not want to consider Simza's proposal to marry the cousin," she said. I waited. "I know you love another." It was dark and I could not see her face well in the firelight, and she bent it over her tea as she spoke. "She's fine, by the way."

"What?"

204

"Zhulyi: she's well."

"You know of Zhulyi?"

"Zhulyi is a Seer, and she can easily scry you. She knows you are with me–we have talked often."

"What!? Why did you not tell me this before? I've been here for three seasons! You never thought to mention this?"

"You never asked."

"What did she say? Is she being treated well? Is Aamon still terrible?"

"They have a little boy now."

I felt a stab in my gut, as if I had been impaled.

"Aamon is treating her better, now that they have a child together."

The thought of Zhulyi in the act of making a baby with Aamon turned my stomach with jealousy and repulsion. I looked at Baba Tsura then with curiosity.

"You knew of my love, but never said anything. Do you think I'm abnormal?"

"We're all a little abnormal, especially those of us drawn to be healers. It is never wrong to love another, Jaelle, although it certainly can complicate things. For you, I'm afraid it will be at your peril."

"I feel as though she's my soul's mate. I ache for her," I began to weep with the feelings I had tried to submerge, shoved down over the past five years as I had lived without Zhulyi.

"Yes, she very well may be." I was surprised to hear Baba Tsura agree.

"What should I do? I have tried to move on, but she haunts me."

"Jaelle, what you had with Zhulyi was a miracle. When one soul recognizes another, no matter how brief, it is an occurrence to celebrate. If you never see her again, you will still have the treasure of your connection. You may find her in another life, at another time more suitable to your affection. She is a married woman with a life she has fought for. You are best to honor what you had and resign yourself to see her at another fold of the cloth."

"And I will be alone this whole life?"

"You may be. We all come in and go out alone, Jaelle. And yet we are never alone. If your studies have taught you anything, I hope they have taught you that we are all One: with the earth, the Mother, and with each other. We are alone, yet not alone–always. When you dissolve back into the veils, you will be united with all you've lost, and then you will see that you have only been temporarily separated from all you love and from your true form, as part of one endless entity that is infinitely large and yet could fit inside an apple seed. Do not be impatient, since you still have much to learn on your own as an individual before you can join with the all that exists and with all that has ever existed."

"It is torture to be alone and to think I may be alone to the end of my days."

"When my husband died, so many years ago, I felt the same. Even with all I knew, I resented that he had left me to ride out the rest of my years on earth alone. Yet I have found such peace here on my own. I look forward to seeing him again, but I am content to enjoy the solace and focus on other relationships, like my relationship to the forest and to my grandchildren—and to you, Jaelle." She smiled at me, then, and I felt the warmth from her that sometimes eluded me.

"Thank you, Baba Tsura. I don't know if I've said thank you. I've been a most ungrateful student."

"You have your moments."

After that, I tried to be a more devoted pupil. I had felt this whole time that Baba Tsura's knowledge was being inflicted on me, as something that I had to do. Something shifted after this conversation, and I began to seek out the lessons more actively, to participate more fully. Knowing that Baba Tsura was the only other living person who knew about Zhulyi—and accepted me—deepened my affection for her. I began to see her as an ally and became thirsty for not just the information she was sharing, but for her approval. My learning accelerated then, and things started to fall into place in my mind. What was effortful before came more naturally to me, and I saw the things Baba Tsura had been laboring for me to understand without even trying. When the time came that marked when I had been with her for a full year, we celebrated.

"You have seen the full cycle of the seasons now, Jaelle. I have taught you everything I know that can be taught. Everything else will have to come from your own investigation. You still have much to learn, but you will learn it on your own, with practice. It's why we say we are *practicing* the Craft, because we are always working to learn more."

I did not realize at the time that she was graduating me. When Simza arrived shortly after with a young girl in tow, however, I became aware that I was being dismissed into the rest of my life. The girl was only eight or nine, ready to go to her future husband's family, but was said to have the Sight. Baba Tsura would train her for the next year so that she could be of better use to her new family. Her dark eyes were wide and still, reminding me of the fawn I had seen in the woods, and she spoke as little. Simza had brought a package for Baba Tsura, which she unwrapped carefully. It was a small, perfectly round black cauldron. Baba Tsura then presented it to me, saying she had it made by the finest smith she knew. It touched my heart as soon as I saw it. She named it and told me to speak to it by its name. It would serve me well, she said.

"Come with me to meet my family," implored Simza. "We are settling in at our winter quarters. You can meet my son and my husband's family." Having no better options and feeling that—although it had not been explicitly stated—I was being evicted, I agreed to travel with Simza for a while. When I embraced Baba Tsura, she would not say goodbye. "I will see you again, Jaelle. I will be right here in the forest when you need me."

It was a few days' walk, and Simza and I talked little on our way. She told me about a few of the relations I would meet, and mentioned again the cousin, Tamiro. "I know you have no interest in marriage, but it will not hurt to meet him."

"No, I suppose it would not hurt," I agreed.

When we arrived in Rupea, I was reminded of Deva by a giant stone fortress–Castrom Kuholm–rising on a mount above. This one was said to hold blood in its stones also, from a Dacian king who had committed suicide there. We got some strange looks coming into the city. At first, I thought we were getting the normal scornful looks reserved for the Ciganyok. I realized that, once again, I had forgotten what I looked like. How strange it must be to see a Rromani and Gentle woman strolling along the streets together–like Zhulyi and I would have looked, I realized–drawing unwanted curiosity anywhere we went. Perhaps Baba Tsura was right that Zhulyi and I might have to wait until a more ideal lifetime to safely enjoy each other's company.

Simza's husband's family wintered over in a run-down building attached to the back of a tavern on the edge of the city. The tavern owners tolerated them since they repaired all the broken kitchen equipment throughout the winter as part of their rent. At other times of the year, the family traveled in a familiar circuit from town to town, finding work repairing metal weaponry. This region experienced frequent invasions from the Ottomans, and most cities spent every resource building up armies and arms to defend against the incursions. There might be a peaceful year or two, but always another influx of marauders could come at any time, so all able-bodied people, serfs and slaves, were commandeered to fight when needed. Even farmers were soldiers when the raids came.

Simza's parents-in-law were gregarious people, reminding me of my Uncle Milosh and Aunt Lala. They clearly adored Simza and her son–their grandson–Fane, and his lovely wife, Crina. Fane and Crina's son was a rambunctious child of two, and much loved by everyone, including his Baba Simza. Crina was relieved to see Simza return, since she was exhausted by carrying their second child and was grateful for the help with the boy. The family was gracious to me, although I got the typical questions about my appearance and how I had come to speak Rromani as I often did when encountering new Rroma for the first time. Simza's married family were metalsmiths loosely related to the Fieraru Clan. I had known this but did not expect to feel so comfortable suddenly surrounded by the clinks and clanks of smithing repairs and whoosh of billows from the fire in the courtyard. I found myself lulled by endless conversation about the strengths and characters of metal, along with the perennial arguments debating how to best repair a carriage wheel–about which all metalsmiths had strong opinions.

I fell in to helping with the baby and cooking and doing some small sewing repairs. There were so many extended relatives I could hardly keep track, and children I was never sure to whom they belonged. While they did not travel together much of the year, in the winter the family enjoyed residing together in the expansive quarters of the old building: catching up and enjoying each other's company through the darkest part of the year. In a few days' time, the family treated me as if I'd always been there, discussing the plights of relatives as if I knew them all intimately, along with their foibles and adventures.

"That Cousin Baltu—you know how he is always getting in trouble with the soldiers. He has a temper like a viper! It will be the death of him!"

"Well, you know he has not had much to live for since his brother died. They were as close as if they were twins."

Run-ins with the soldiers were common, and I recalled that it was such a misfortune that had befallen Simza's husband. Technically, all Rromani fell under the "property" of a local voivode and could be called to duty at any time. However, except in the direst of circumstances, most warlords found the Ciganyok too undisciplined for battle and agreed that their status as pilgrims allowed them leniency with picking up arms. Most of the local generals preferred to use the Rromani talents where they were most reliable: in the repair of swords, shields, and lances, which they were required to repair with no charge, in service to their liege. This arrangement usually led to a cordial, if disdainful relationship. However, when young men and drinking were involved, things sometimes became violent for no good reason. I learned that it was here in Rupea that Simza's husband had been killed. I asked her if it bothered her to be there, so close to where he had perished, possibly with his murderers still about in the city—maybe even passing them on the street. She replied: "It will bother me no matter where I am."

It still embarrassed me that I had developed such an affection for Simza when we had first met and I hoped she did not suspect. While that had long since simmered, I still found her very beautiful, and enjoyed working next to her and laughing together as we made meals or played with her grandbaby. After I had been there about a week, I heard shouts of greetings and children running to hug and hang on the legs of the new arrival.

"Ah, it's Tamiro!" Simza said, wiping her hands on her apron and running to greet him.

The man she hugged was solid like a tree with a generous smile. As she had noted, he was quite attractive for a man his age, likely at least a good decade older than I. "You must be Jaelle," he said reaching to kiss my hand, which made me blush with the formality of it. "I have heard so much about you. I understand you have been keeping Baba Tsura out of trouble this past year. The family thanks you!"

"Well, it is more likely Baba Tsura has kept me out of trouble—but you are welcome."

"It's good you are here. I need to consult with a healer. I understand you are gifted."

"I hope not to disappoint you, but I am still learning. I'm barely more than a novice."

"Nonsense!" Simza jumped in. She leaned over conspiratorially to whisper to Tamiro: "Baba Tsura says Jaelle is the most talented student she has had in decades."

"Well, good. I need your services, I'm afraid."

"You can handle this, Jaelle? I need to take the baby from Crina so she can lie down. She's feeling the sickness again."

"Of course."

I followed Tamiro to the kitchen that opened out into the back yard where much of the smithing occurred. He sat and removed his boots. As he leaned over, I studied him unobtrusively, and saw skin–smooth and leathered from the sun–and a body, lean and muscled from being accustomed to hard work. "I should never have let it get to this point," he said. "It started out as a metal splinter. My daughter-in-law was able to remove it, at least I think it's all out, but it began to fester anyway." He unwrapped some cotton from around his foot and put it up on a stool. The skin had a bluish cast, with yellow and white oozing from a dark menacing spot on the ball of his foot.

"How could you even walk on this?" I asked, alarmed.

"Barely. It's why I was so relieved to see that you were here. I am in quite bad shape."

I began to boil water in a big pot and ran to get my cauldron. It was the size of a small pumpkin, and I still marveled at its perfectly round design, and how it fit my hands perfectly. Before I had left Baba Tsaura's, we had hand-selected and carefully wrapped herbs that should be in any healer's kit. It was a final lesson to me and a first lesson for Baba Tsura's new student, who watched as we discussed the properties and qualities of each plant and root. I had packed them all within the perfect black interior of my new vessel.

"I see you're making good use of it," said Tamiro, gesturing to the pot as I poked through the cloth packets within. I looked up, questioning. "The cauldron," he explained. "It's one of mine. Baba Tsura asked me to make the smallest, roundest, blackest vessel I have ever made. Did she name it?"

"Yes. I'm sorry, I did not realize you were the one who had crafted it. It's beautiful. I cherish it."

"I'm so glad!" he said. "It makes the effort worthwhile, then."

I began to crush herbs in a small bowl to make a poultice, but first had him soak his foot in boiled water in a shallow bowl that was specifically used for washing feet at a corner of the kitchen by the door. I felt him watching me as I turned the dried leaves into a paste. I looked up to see a smile and eyes that sparkled with amusement. "How can you smile when your foot looks like that? I'd say it's a serious affair."

"Oh yes–the pain is extraordinary."

"Then what amuses you?"

"They told me that you were able to speak Rromani fluently, but I did not expect you to have no accent whatsoever. It's odd to hear."

"Yes, the Fieraru adopted me when I was very young."

"You know they conspire for us to marry," he said.

I startled at his frankness: "I had gathered as much."

"I understand you are not in favor of the idea."

"I'm not the marrying type."

"I see. Well, let's agree to be friends then. One needs friends in life."

I looked up and saw only sincerity upon his face. "Yes, let's." I said. I had him rest his foot upon a stool. It had drained somewhat but was still swollen with pus. "We will need to draw out the rest of this festering stuff, and I suspect more metal shard hides within."

"One of my cousins died of a wound such as this. Started as an ingrown toenail and spread. It was a miserable death."

"You will not die," I said. I painted a thick paste upon the wound, whispering to the metal shard that I could sense, sleeping tucked away deep down, urging it to come out. I wrapped Tamiro's foot in clean strips of cloth and began boiling some roots for tea. "You need to heal from within and without. You must drink this tea for many days."

"Oh yes. I recall the smell. Baba Tsura has made me drink that when I've had other ailments. It's terribly bitter."

"So is amputating a foot."

He laughed then, a big hearty laugh that resonated through the room. "She was right, then." I looked perplexed. "Simza said I would like you. You are a funny person, Jaelle. If you were not saving my foot right now, I'd like you anyway!" Now I laughed, too.

Having Tamiro arrive into the mix of the boisterous family somehow made them all more dear to me. I had felt–as usual–on the edge of things, but once I began nursing Tamiro's injury and spending much of the day in the kitchen, changing bandages and making endless poultices and teas, I felt as if I had found my place. He was never far and pulled me in to every conversation. "Ask Jaelle about that. I'm sure she knows about such things," he would say, and look at me–not to flatter, I saw–but as an expert to be consulted with. I had never had the experience of my opinion mattering, but suddenly others were coming to me for illness, pain, and for emotional concerns, too. The kitchen became my informal hospital. Tamiro's confidence in me had boosted my standing as a healer in others' eyes.

"Ah, no sleep again, cousin? Jaelle can make you a tea for that, I'm sure. It's the worry keeping you up–no? Jaelle will know what to do."

A few days after I began assisting Tamiro, I unwrapped his bandages and saw a pointed bubble below the bruised surface. "It is ready to come out," I concluded. I sat Tamiro with his foot upon the stool and prepared him for some acute pain. I held his foot in both of my hands and got down to eye level. I saw it, below the surface, a dark looming presence. I could feel it, resentful of being disturbed and happy in its comfortable bed. I must appeal to it, I realized. It was not going to come out willingly. I reached out with my mind to the shard. It was metal, and I needed to appeal to it as metal. "Fieraru!" I hissed at it and pushed on both sides of Tamiro's foot. He gasped in pain, but when I looked, a small round circle of black had appeared in the middle of the wound. I picked up some small pliers nearby and grasped the end. The expunged sliver was so small that Tamiro laughed out loud.

"That little thing has caused all this trouble?"

"It seems so," I observed. I cleaned his wound again and wrapped it up, a little saddened that now I might have no reason to sit with him in the kitchen. I needn't have worried, because even as he was completely recovered, he still sat nearby, talking to me and drawing me into conversations with others. He retold the story of how I had saved his foot to anyone who would listen, the splinter bigger and fouler with each retelling, until it became a joke of legendary proportions.

"How big was that splinter, Cousin Tamiro?"

"Why it was as large as a carriage, I swear to it!"

"That must have been very painful!"

"Yes, but Jaelle called it out of me! She confronted the monster, pulled it out by the head and wrestled it, squirming and massive, from my body. You should have seen it! She had to pound it with a mace to kill it!"

"That's astounding! I've never heard of a splinter so big or so fierce!"

"Nor had I. But Jaelle showed no fear of it, nor no mercy. It was truly heroic. I owe my life to her."

All would laugh and make merry of the situation. The grave state of his foot–which very well might have killed him–was celebrated as a victory, and I was humorously honored for having saved his life.

At night I slept with Simza in a pile of children and unmarried female relatives, often with her little grandbaby tucked between us. In day, I held court in the kitchen, where I was quickly promoted from chopping onions for the communal meals to brewing teas for every variety of ailments. A few of the children began calling me "Mama Jaelle," though I had no children, and it stuck, and all began referring to me this way. I was seen as a matriarch, being of a certain age and involved in the intimate details of the family's health. With such active business, I soon depleted my stores of herbs.

"Simza, I am running low on supplies. Do you know where we can buy more herbs?"

She looked up from scrubbing a mound of turnips, "Yes, there's a market nearby. I can take you."

"Oh, no!" Tamiro broke in. "Simza, the city gets more dangerous every day. I will escort Jaelle."

We walked through the dirty streets toward the market. There was a buzz of hostility in the air, the peasants agitated. The soldiers seemed rowdier than the ones I'd seen in other cities, who typically took their station seriously, their behavior seen as a reflection of the ruling nobility. These men were slovenly, half-drunk, and uncouth. We had not gone far, when a group of four or five accosted us.

"What's this here? What are you doing with this Cigany, lady? Has he kidnapped you?"

"Yes, is he harming you? We can pound him to a pulp for you if he's laying a hand on you."

I quickly looked around and adopted a confused expression. I began chattering quickly in Rromani to Tamiro, looking back and forth between the soldiers and him. "I'm sorry, Gentlemen," Tamiro said, with a pronounced and fumbling accent. "My wife does not speak the language of the Country, and I speak very little. We are only pilgrims here, waiting to worship at your fine church, once it's finished being built. We are indebted to you for protecting the streets so well so that religious people like us can come to pay our respects."

They seemed confounded but mumbled a few more things and then held their weapons up, as if suddenly on duty, letting us pass. Around the corner, Tamiro and I let out relieved breaths, and smiled at one another. It was clear that what Tamiro had said about the city had been true, and even with quick wits and good improvisational skills, one could fall prey to violence easily in this place. There was a conflict brewing, and all were on edge. It seemed the whole city was tainted by a history of violence: the commoners and soldiers at one point in the city's past had taken up arms against the nobility, even barricading themselves within the citadel for months to defend against the oppressive rulers. Whether the invader was from within or without, the city seemed born to fight. If there were no visible intruder, then the soldiers were determined to find one on the streets.

"Why does the family come back here?" I asked Tamiro. "There are many other less bloodthirsty cities, with more civilized defense forces."

"Yes, but it's not easy to find a place to quarter a family our size. We are safe at the tavern, and it's a tradition to spend winters here. Coordinating a change when we come from so many different places to over-winter would be hard."

"I suppose so," I agreed. We walked, blood still pumping somewhat on high alert and on the lookout for further trouble. At the market, I was able to buy what I needed quickly, and we returned without further incident, passing the same group of unruly soldiers but waving to them politely and bowing our heads.

"You must not go out on your own, Jaelle," Tamiro cautioned. "There is no saying what a group like that might do to a young woman alone."

I was relieved to get back to the noisy interior of our shelter, which seemed like more of a sanctuary after having seen the rest of the city. I prepared my herbs in the kitchen and sent children to find family members for whom I had bought specific treatments. Tamiro worked out in the courtyard on some repairs, poking his head in occasionally to chat with me or one of my patients. When he took a break, I poured him tea and he took off his boot so I could check the healing of his wound. It was covering nicely, new skin growing over the hole and no swelling or discoloration. I expressed my satisfaction with his healing.

"It's still a little tender," he said, "but I believe we've avoided amputation!"

Tamiro did not ask me about my past, or any specifics about my life; I inquired little into his own history. It seemed we knew one another without this. Our temperaments were compatible, and we had a comfort that had spontaneously developed between us. We were never far apart during waking hours. If I did not see him for a few minutes, it was unusual. Just when I would notice his absence, he would reappear, and I would feel relief wash over me. I felt safe with him, I realized. I was unsettled when I was away from him, and it began to seem unnatural to separate from him in the evenings to retire to sleep. I would seek him out first thing in the morning, usually in the kitchen at first light, where he was preparing his tools for work for the day. He was an even earlier riser than I was, and he would greet me with a smile, as if he were waiting for me to appear.

There was a wedding to occur. Arrangements had been made for a cousin to have his new bride delivered to him from a distant city and she and her family converged upon the house. It was only about a dozen more people, but it made the atmosphere even more crowded and rambunctious than usual. There would be a ceremony in a few days, and then her family would leave and she would become part of her husband's family. She looked so young and terrified. I took her aside into the kitchen and made her a tea from valerian and lemon balm to calm her nerves. She gratefully sipped the tea and I made small talk with her.

"You've come from very far, I understand."

"Yes, Mama Jaelle. It took us many weeks to get here."

"It must be a desirable partnership for your family to travel so far."

"So I am told."

"Yet you are distressed by it?"

"Only that my family will be so distant."

"And still, you will have a new family."

"That's what they say."

"It does not feel that way to you?"

"No, I am among strangers. When my family leaves, I will have no one."

"I have not known your betrothed long. They say that Ravniko is an excellent smith."

"Yes, I have heard."

"He seems very kind."

"Yes, I have no objection to him."

"And he's not terrible to look at either, is he?" I nudged her and she giggled a little.

"No, not terrible."

"It will not take the pain away of losing your family, though."

"No. I will miss my mother and my little sisters," she said and gulped back a sob. "I can't stand to think I might never see them again. And being so far away, how likely will it be that I will ever see them?" I had noticed the two little girls that had come along with the party, friendly and spirited children who had blended in quickly to play with the already existing horde. "You know," I said, "once you are a married woman, you will have some influence in your husband's family. Perhaps you might even be able to suggest a partnership with one of your own sisters when the time comes. It's not unheard of for sisters to marry into the same family, you know."

She perked to alertness. "Yes! Yes—Misha will be next. She's not too far behind me. They are already discussing her prospects." Her face, still round and childish, began to take on a determined look. After that, I noticed her scouting purposefully around at her new family members, assessing her options.

"Your tea must have worked," Tamiro commented, noticing the change in the girl's demeanor.

"I admit, it was not the tea," I said.

"Oh? Have you other magic to rely on?"

"It's not magic. Most people just want to be told that all is not lost. They need hope."

"So, hope is the magic tincture?" he teased me.

"I suppose so. The remedies work–of course–but they are made more potent by hope."

He surprised me then, by reaching over and gently taking my hand. He looked into my eyes: "I can attest that it was hope rather than your poultices and teas that healed my own wound."

I looked down at my lap, but I did not pull my hand away.

∞

The evening of the wedding came, and all the food had been prepared in advance. The family crowded into the courtyard, although the air was cold. The cord was fasted: it was wound, crossed, and tied around the hands of the young pair, joining them together for life. The bride's sister held one end of the broom, while a younger sibling of the groom held the other, and the couple walked over it and into marriage. Cheers went up and then the merrymaking began, with music and dancing into the night. Tamiro–who was cheerful even when in pain or working hard at a task–seemed pensive and subdued. I sat by him, since it felt the normal thing to do by this point. "What troubles you, my friend?" I asked him.

He sighed. "I can't help thinking of my own wedding. It seems so long ago that I was young and filled with expectation of a happy married life."

"Things don't always work out the way we expect," I said.

"No, it seems they never do, in fact," he agreed.

I had never asked about his wife and hesitated to do so now. "You had a good life together?"

He looked at me. "Yes. I have no complaints. Life was hard–as it always is. We struggled, but no more so than anyone else. We were happy together. Our children were healthy. We were blessed."

"It must be difficult to get used to life without her."

"I don't know that I ever will, honestly. It's like you've lost an arm, but not the dominant one that you use all the time. The one that is just there, taken for granted, holding the nail steady as you strike it. One day it's there, and the next it's not. You can still find a way to work and function, but a piece of your body is missing."

"I'm sorry, Tamiro."

"We all have our sorrows. We are not guaranteed safe passage through life without ills."

"That does not make yours any less painful."

"You have had your own share of sadness, Jaelle. Simza has told me a little and the rest I can just tell. You wear your grief almost as a garment. Maybe that's why I felt so comfortable with you from the moment I met you. I recognized you as a fellow mourner." We laughed a little

215

then, and he reached over to take my hand. "It's not so bad, is it? To sit together and share the burden a little?"

"No, it's not bad at all. In fact, it's a great comfort," I said, realizing it was true.

"You know, when Simza first mentioned you to me, I told her I was not interested. The family has been trying to get me to remarry for years, since my wife died. I have not been interested in starting over, and I had my own ideas about someone who was not Rrom. I admit, I was prejudiced. When we met, it was as though I recognized you, though. It did not matter what you looked like or the specifics of your past. I saw *you*."

I looked at him then, and the sincerity in his face overwhelmed me. At that moment, I could not imagine not having him right there next to me, every day for the rest of my life. Without any proposal or discussion, from then on, it was understood that we would marry. Our hands would come together whenever we sat next to each other, and the family's knowing glances became less surprised to see us openly express our affection. Soon after, one of Tamiro's sons arrived with his family, and then a second son. Both sons had plump and pleasant wives and rowdy grandchildren to hang all over their Dedu Tamiro. They kissed me and greeted me as if I were already their stepmother. The sons, Oleksandr and Viktor, were like their father, hardworking and cheerful. They were tender toward their wives and playful with their children. Tamiro had a daughter, too, I learned, who lived with her husband's family on the other side of the Carpathians.

It seemed perfectly natural and yet completely alien to be immersed so fully and so quickly into a family. I walked around with a sense of unreality half the time, with wives who came to me to consult on care of a child and grown men calling me "Mama." It seemed ironic that I, who had been alone with no family for so long, was abruptly at the heart of a thriving network of relations. Yet I did not feel as if I were playing a part, as I had when I sometimes had taken on a persona or story in a new city. This felt genuine to me, as if it had been my life all along. It was disorienting, and still profoundly reassuring to be enmeshed in this new continent of warmth and connection. And it was all because of Tamiro. He had drawn me in, invited me to participate in his rich universe with barely a blink of his eye. It was as unremarkable as if he had just flicked away a piece of ash from my hair that my previous existence fell away: my life became his life and his world.

I had not known where Tamiro had slept, exactly, but I found that he had staked away a corner of the apartments for his family who would be arriving. They all moved into these quarters. Like a tide, I was carried with them. I no longer slept with Simza and the children, but instead slept among the throngs of Tamiro's unwieldy brood. Sheets of cloth and blankets were hung to roughly divide the space and give some small semblance of privacy, but it was a mass of our extended family in that part of the building. Because Tamiro and I were still unmarried, I retired among the children for decency's sake. Often, though, I would wake to Tamiro piled in among us, reaching a hand across a sleeping child to touch my shoulder.

No wedding arrangements had been discussed, since it was almost as if we were already married. Eventually, Simza came to me and asked what our plans were. "It seems that you and Tamiro have become inseparable," she remarked.

"Yes, we're quite attached. You were right, it seems, to suggest we would be a good match."

"Have you discussed a date to wed?"

"No, actually it has not come up."

"Hmmm. May I ask what you are waiting for?"

"I do not really see the hurry. Things are very pleasant as they are."

"Jaelle," she said, and I could sense a note of a lecture coming through her voice, "you realize you do not have much time left to bear a child?"

"I have no interest in having children and I doubt Tamiro does, either. His own children are grown, and he has grandchildren now. That part of his life is passed."

"You might be surprised."

"I don't think so. I can't imagine him wanting to start over with a new family. A bride, perhaps, but we are not young dreamers to think we can start a new brood of youngsters at our ages."

"You should talk to him," she urged.

Although I enjoyed the simplicity of our unspoken arrangement, I saw Simza was right: it was not going to work forever to simply not discuss the future. One morning, when Tamiro was working out in the courtyard on some spears that had been requested for the city's infantry, I joined him. It was cold, but sunny, so it made it feel like a milder day. The steam came from his lips as he worked, but he paused when I came out, to smile at me in that way that always seemed as though we were sharing an amusing secret.

"Do you need help with something?" he asked, since I did not usually interrupt his work.

"No, thank you. I just . . . Simza thought we should talk . . . about our plans."

"And what does Jaelle think?" he teased me.

"I think she may be right. I just don't want any misunderstandings."

"Oh?" A flash of worry crossed his brow.

"Tamiro, I was wondering if you expect to have more children."

"Of course! You are still young, and I am still above ground!"

"I see. I must confess that comes as a surprise to me."

"What's the matter, Jaelle? Don't you want children?" He had stopped his work fully and stood up straight to look intently at me.

"No, actually, I don't. I did not realize you might expect that from me."

"Well, you are not so young. It might be your last chance."

"My last chance? But not yours? So, if I should die, you could still go on fertilizing the earth?"

"That's not what I meant. I just thought you might want your own children."

"What of your children, and your grandchildren? If we marry, would they not all be ours?"

"Yes, of course, but most women want their own babies."

"I am not most women, Tamiro."

"I am aware of that." He put down his tools and took my hands. "Jaelle, it is not so important to me. I assumed you would want children—but if you do not, it will not sadden me. Besides, the Earth Mother has a way of providing blessings even when you are not expecting them. You may find that we become blessed, even if we do not intend to be."

I had always wondered how women kept from having babies every year. Studying with Baba Tsura, I now understood the many measures available to women who did not want to conceive, or who became pregnant when they did not wish to be. "I will not be having any babies, Tamiro. I want to make that clear."

"If those are your feelings, I will respect them," he assured me. I breathed a sigh of relief to have the discomfort of the conversation over with, but there was more to come. "Now," he said, "perhaps we should discuss when we plan to marry? The children are asking if they should make preparations for us soon." He pulled me into his arms, and I leaned against his chest, hearing the steady melody of his heartbeat. He whispered into my ear, "I must admit, I'm becoming eager to make you properly my wife."

I shivered and nestled into his arms. "Soon," I replied.

"Is there any reason to delay?" he asked. He kissed my forehead and ran a finger down the side of my face, looking at me intensely.

"No, except . . ."

"Except?" he pulled back to examine me.

"We should get the blessing of my father."

Chapter Nineteen: Pearls Along the Path

We traveled to Brașov during the first break in the weather in February. It did not seem wise to travel with just the two of us, since it seemed to evoke too much curiosity and hostility for a Rromani man to be seen alone with a Gentle woman. Viktor and his wife left their children with Oleksandr and his wife so that they could accompany us, and Simza decided to join us as well. With the five of us and my hair wrapped and head down, I blended in more and we attracted less attention. It was always safer for our kind to travel in bands: most violence came to those caught alone. The roads were still icy with snow still covering the land, but the air was not frigid.

It was only two days' walk, and we stopped the first night near Rotbav. We sheltered in a solid old fortress with the Rromani tribes wintering there. They were loose family relations and welcomed us in. It was odd to see a similar arrangement to what I had experienced in the old castle during my childhood played out with strangers. The music and dancing went on most of the night, and we got little sleep, but were fed well enough to keep on our journey the next morning. By afternoon, we reached Sandor's estate, and the familiar stone gates that announced the compound. I saw the place through my companions' eyes as we approached and felt them grow silent and serious as we entered the property. Perhaps I had not given them proper warning of what to expect, having only told them that my father owned some property and ran a sizeable enterprise. For those who were unused to typical housing at all, sleeping much of the year under the stars, the massive house and sprawling array of snow-covered orchards, barns, and outbuildings was intimidating.

The large circular driveway was cleared of snow, and the stone steps devoid of any ice. As we approached the giant wooden door, it opened to reveal a flurry of maids and several well-liveried men who came out to greet us, hands on swords. "We are here to see the Master, Domn Alexandru," I explained, not recognizing the young faces of the guards.

"What business have you with our lord?" one inquired.

"Please tell him that Jaelle is here to see him. He will be eager to greet me, I assure you." They looked skeptical, but one went back inside to deliver the message while the others stood at attention in front of the doors, looking down their noses at the dress of our troop. My company shifted their feet and tried not to stare at the grandeur of the creamy stone façade. Tamiro kept a hand clasped firmly at my elbow. After a few minutes, Sandor came to the door in a rush, glanced at the faces of the others, then swept me into his arms in a warm embrace.

"Jaelle! It is so heartening to see you!" Then to his guards, "Why have you kept our guests out in the cold? Come in, come in!" and we were all ushered into the great hall, with the men-at-arms exchanging nervous looks, but heeding their master's direction. My companions looked stunned to find themselves in the vaulting palace of the house's interior, with painted ceilings like they may only have seen before in a church. They huddled together and seemed unsure where to look first.

The Steward arrived, summoned from his own quarters, and recognizing me, bowed deeply. "Madame, it is an honor to see you again. And you have brought . . . friends, I see." I made brief introductions, and Sandor directed his staff to take our coats and prepare rooms for us, to their dismayed looks. We were then ushered to the study to await as a meal was arranged. Seated upon the leather couches, servants rushed to fill cups with hot mulled wine. The Rromani guests looked stiff and uncomfortable as they surveyed the room and sat with cups in hand.

"I can't tell you how I've worried, Jaelle. I'm sorry to say, I thought you might be dead. When Uncle Ulric sent word that you had disappeared from his care, I feared the worst. It has been five years: you could have at least sent word you were all right!" He said this last bit with a gently chiding tone.

"I'm sorry. It was thoughtless of me." In fact, it had not even occurred to me in all this time that Sandor would have known I had left his uncle's estate and might be concerned. Now, I felt selfish for not having this small consideration cross my mind.

"And what brings you here now, in the middle of winter? Of course, I am most happy to see you–but you might have come at an easier time for travel. Is all well? Is there something you need?"

"Thank you. I am well. We only came to ask for your blessing: Tamiro and I . . ." I reached for Tamiro's hand so Sandor would be clear who I meant: ". . . we plan to marry."

"I see! Well, that is . . . that is quite a surprise." He looked at Tamiro's face intently, as if seeing him for the first time. He stood suddenly and seemed agitated, moving restlessly toward the door. "Let me see if your rooms are ready and then we will have a meal. We can discuss it more over supper?" He summoned a chamberlain, who confirmed that we could retire to our lodgings now, and we were led to a series of rooms on the second floor. I had never even ventured to that part of the house, having had my many prior visits limited to the public areas. There was a bit of confusion at first, since the staff had assumed that Simza and Tamiro were a married couple who would share a room, but soon we sorted out that Viktor and his wife, Jana, would take one room, Tamiro the second, and Simza and I could share the third that had been readied. As unsettled as I was by Sandor's abrupt change in demeanor, I was happy to not be left alone in the large room that reminded me of a crypt, still cold with some small warmth yet spreading from the freshly lit fire. I worried for Tamiro, who must be even more distressed than I, having the experience of such a place entirely foreign to him.

As soon as we were alone, Simza looked at me and with an awed tone said, "Jaelle—I had no idea this is what you came from."

"Well, you must know I have not come from this at all! I have only ever visited this house: I've never lived in it or any like it. I am not accustomed to this style of living."

"Still, your father is wealthy. You should never want for anything."

"I have not wanted for anything, even when I've had nothing. I do not consider myself entitled to any of what belongs to my father."

"Well, perhaps you should," Simza said. She lay back on the soft feather bed, which was enormous by our standards. "I think I should want to be entitled to it."

After the lack of sleep from the previous night visiting at the fortress and the mulled wine, Simza fell quickly asleep. Having not been much apart from Tamiro, I felt the absence of him, and opened the door to the hall. I was alarmed to find the Marshall in the hallway, on guard with a few other men. "Good evening, sirs." They nodded at me. I walked down the hall to the room Tamiro had been given. "I must see to my acquaintance," I explained.

"Madam, we will be right here. Please alert us if you need anything."

I knocked lightly and Tamiro opened the door quickly, seeming relieved to see me there. I went in and closed the door, realizing that it might seem improper to the guards to be alone with him, but not quite caring. He embraced me and seemed dazed as he looked down at me.

"Jaelle, this is not a world I'm comfortable in." The confident air that I had so admired in him, his finesse in the most difficult situations, had seemed to evaporate. I did not recognize the insecure quality of his grasps on my arms.

"I am not comfortable with it either. I never have been."

"I was under the impression that you had grown up like we did, with the tribe and living off the land and our wits."

"I did! I only discovered that Domn Alexandru was my father ten years ago. I did not seek this type of lifestyle then–or since–when he has offered it. I am still not willing to accept it."

"I wonder how you can want the humble life I can offer you when all of this is available to you." He sat in a nearby chair and put his head in his hands. I kneeled in front of him and took his hands away from his face to make him look at me.

"Tamiro–listen to me. I have no claim to this. I never have. I am not a legitimate heir and even if I were, this is not a life I aspire to. If it were, I never would have left it once I found it."

He looked at me and shook his head, not seeming to be able to believe I could forsake the luxury that surrounded us. "It seems foolhardy, Jaelle. Most women would be happy to settle down to such an easy life with a rich patron–even one who could not legally claim to be one's father."

"Yes, I'm aware. I have often wished I were the type of woman who merely wanted wealth. It would have made things simpler."

"So, if not fortune, what is it that you want from life then?" he asked.

Reflecting on his question, all that came to mind was Perla. I did not want anything except to see my daughter. It was not a discussion I'd had with Tamiro–our easy understanding had not afforded us this type of conversation. I realized then that as much as I enjoyed our togetherness, I had not entrusted him with the most basic facts of my life. Our relationship had required so little in the way of accounting for ourselves that it had been a welcomed reprieve. There had been no pressure to explain anything. He had been given some basic background about me from Simza, but it was undoubtedly sparse.

Before I could venture to determine that this was the time to detail my history, a rap on the door drew me to my feet. "Come in!" I called.

The Marshall moved his large frame well into the doorway, as if to confirm my safety before saying, "Pardon me, madam. I am told that dinner will be served now."

"Thank you, we'll be down straight away." I said. The Marshall paused then, as if waiting for me to move, but I just met his eyes until he dropped his gaze.

"Very well," he said and began to back out. "Shall I . . . ." he started to say.

"I will inform the other guests," I said. He nodded and retreated the rest of the way out the door.

Dinner was a tense affair. My friends were full of compliments for the wide array of dishes presented to us, but had little else to converse about, concentrating on trying to eat in a way that was suitable to the environment. They fumbled–like I had at first–with the silverware, and tried to hide their astonishment at the unfettered feast laid before us. Since wine glasses were refilled whenever they were even slightly emptied, all drank more than they probably would have otherwise. Domn Alexandru was formal and polite, but more reserved than I had ever seen him. When the meal was over, he asked if any would like to have cordials in the study. The others declined: they apologized for being weary from travel and went off to bed.

I followed Sandor into the study, and sat as I had so many times, across from him on the leather cushions. After a serf brought some small glasses of cordials and we were left alone, I looked at him and wondered what he could be thinking. His face had retreated to cold iron, having lost all the warmth I knew he possessed. "I am sure I have displeased you," I said. "I am sorry if I have imposed. I only hoped to have your blessing. It is clear you do not approve of my intentions so I will inconvenience you no more. We can leave first thing in the morning."

Something gave in his expression, and the steel melted, revealing a man growing weary in his middle age alone. "It's just not what I wanted for you, Jaelle. I understand if you could not accept the offer to marry me to have access to my legacy. I even understand why you would wander the world alone, spurning company. But why you would demean yourself to marry such a lowly man, a . . . *Cigany*," he almost spat the word, "who can offer you nothing in the way of security or fortune?"

"He is a good man," I said slowly, in an even tone, masking my indignation.

"He may be, but he is of the lowest caliber of social status. You would be like a slave–untouchable–should you stoop to marry him." I tried to stifle the rage that I felt building inside me, but he continued: "I have an alternate proposal. I offered to marry you before and I will offer it again. If you desire to keep this man's acquaintance, that is fine with me. It may even resolve the problem of an heir if you are to have his child after we are married–one would just hope the child would inherit your complexion. Your man can live here and work on the estate. I'm sure we can find a position for him. He would be treated well. We would just need to be discrete in your relations with him."

"You would have me little better than a whore!" I exclaimed.

He looked shocked by my outburst. "Jaelle–I'm only thinking of you. This is not for my benefit."

"I'm sorry, it's just such a preposterous arrangement. I am not able to even consider such a mockery!"

"Then let me arrange for you to marry someone else–a nobleman! I have a few in mind who I believe would agree, especially if I explained you are my daughter and I am unable to rightfully claim you. There are some widowers–some who would not be alarmed by your lack of traceable heredity, or your . . . advanced age."

"Sandor, please! Do you know me so little? Do you not recall I am the same woman who lived for years on little more than lichen soup in a pile of stones on a mountain by herself? What would make you think I would settle down with some rich old widower just to have some measley comfort?"

"No—no, I suppose you would not," he conceded.

"I only wanted to inform you of my decision and I thought you would be happy for me. Is not being married to a man I care for—even one who you believe to be of such low status—better than being alone in this world?"

"I am unable to say, Jaelle. I have been alone for so long and have been unable to find it in my nature to settle—not at any time. I have had so many who have tried to push their daughters on me over the years—even ladies of royal breeding—matches that would have been of tremendous political advantage for me. I've had local farmers, millers—even my very own stewards—try to push their pretty young daughters into my arms, hoping for a leg up in the world. I have not compromised, even to stave off loneliness, even when it would have benefitted me enormously or improved my fortune or social position."

"Then you know why I refuse. Did you not yourself hope to wed my mother—forsaking all of society's conventions? How could you deny me the same?"

"Others might have scorned my choice, but I would not have sacrificed much by marrying your mother, other than disappointing my family. I am afraid this decision of yours will bring you into harm's way, Jaelle. It is a dangerous thing for one of our kind to marry a Cigany. It can bring only strife and hazard, to both you and him."

"And yet when you thought I had married a *Cigany* and that Perla was my daughter, you never once scorned me."

"I already had an inkling you were my daughter, and I felt responsible for whatever had befallen you. I can't say I would have been so accepting otherwise."

I took a sip of the cordial, and its sweetness burned my throat. I looked toward the crackling fire, unsure of how to bridge the gap that had occurred between us.

"Have you seen her?" he asked abruptly. I looked at him, befuddled. "Perla. You didn't know she's at the castle with her family? I thought you'd have remembered that it's the fifth year?"

I speechlessly shook my head.

"She is well. I was up there with a hunting party a month ago, on the winter solstice. She has a daughter. She seems very content. Stea is still with her! She's getting to be an old dog now, but she is still Perla's faithful guardian."

I stood, overcome with emotion from Sandor's disappointing response and hearing of Perla's presence, so close to us. I said: "I thank you so much for your hospitality, sir," and turned and left him there. I went upstairs to the hall where the guards still stood on duty outside the doors, more in service to preserving the Master's house than protecting the guests within. Simza was asleep in the wide bed, and only briefly roused to greet me before falling back into slumber. Soon, I too was asleep, having exhausted myself in the effort of travel, the drain of an upsetting reunion, and confronting the deep haunting absence that still dwelled within my heart where my little girl should be.

In my dreams, I was swimming through a mighty ocean during a terrible storm. The waves were as high as houses, and crashed all around me, tossing me every which way. Tamiro was on a boat and looking out for me–yelling to me. I knew that if he caught sight of me, he would jump overboard to try to save me and then we both would be lost. Realizing the only way to keep him from throwing himself into the waves was to conceal myself from his sight, I went under the surface of the water, hiding myself so that he might survive the roiling storm. I was under the dark and endless ocean, sinking down into the blackness. Feeling panic overtake me and doubting my conviction, I struggled to breech the surface again, but I was too far down. I was disoriented and could not tell which way was up. Thrashing, I awoke to Simza's groans and a thick quilt wrapped over my face. I sat up, gasping the cool air in the room. The fire had burned low and was almost extinguished in the dim light of morning.

I got up and splashed some water on my face from the basin that had been laid out and went into the hallway. The guard had switched sometime during the night, and the new faces there were young and alert, hiding curiosity behind stern professionalism. I greeted them and went to Tamiro's room. I knocked lightly and again he opened it almost instantly. I wondered if he had slept at all or had just risen early as he usually did. I went in, closing the door behind me. "If we are to marry, I must tell you some things," I said.

∞

The trek to the old castle was harder in the winter, with trails barely trampled down and partially filled in by subsequent snowfall. Sandor had insisted on lending us horses for the journey, which I had tried to refuse. Now, I was grateful we had accepted, as the incline became steep and the trail more occluded. What would take a few hours in fair weather took us to mid-afternoon even with the relative ease of horseback. I had prepared Tamiro in detail of what might be expected, and the others had been filled in to understand that our reception might not be the warmest. I dreaded having to head back down the trail at night if we were turned away.

At the ridge above the castle, we looked down upon smoke rising from different parts of the sprawling building, which seemed to have tumbled even further into ruin. A cluster of men lingered around the stables, and a few women and children were hauling water from the freshwater stream that emptied into the lake. I did not recognize anyone. As we approached, they looked from face to face, recognizing the Rroma among us, but clearly disoriented by me among their ranks. Tamiro went out ahead, calling greetings and introducing himself, and engaged in a back and forth with them, sharing family names and finding connections in their distantly overlapping lineage. When they got around to inquiring what we might be doing on the mountaintop, he said: "We are here to see a member of the Badi clan: Perla. Do you know her?"

"Of course. Everyone knows Mama Perla," we were told, and a nearby youth was sent to fetch her. Several men offered to lead the horses to drink and be given feed, and we thanked them and went into the darkened stone passageways. The sounds of cooking and communal life echoed through the halls and off the thick stones.

I heard her before I saw her: "Mama!" She ran at me and threw her arms around me, not a girl any longer, but a full-grown woman, sobbing and holding me tightly. I held her, so alarmingly big! Her chin rested atop my shoulder as she clung to me and cried. I wanted to cry with her, but I was so anxious to be disarmed that I could not allow myself that release. I feared I would die on the spot with all the emotion that would surely spill out. "Oh, Mama, Mama," she said over and over, as she cried, and I held her tightly. Finally, she disentangled and I saw a girl a few steps away, watching us with widened eyes. She was the twin of the girl Perla had been at three, with enormous dark eyes and an alert, inquisitive little moon of a face.

"Mama, this is my daughter!" She said and reached for the girl and pulled her into our embrace, as she had still not let go of me with one of her slender arms wrapped about my shoulder. "This is Ankari. We call her 'Kari.'" Kari looked up at me, assessing me in a way that made me feel she could see right through me, but saying nothing. A flash of gray came shooting up to us, and there was Stea, barking and wagging her tail. She had gotten very old, but still had the enthusiasm of a pup as she greeted me with excited nips and kisses.

"You are not welcome here!" The voice coming from behind us was familiar. I saw it was Sasha, now in the full peak of manhood, arms and chest strong and rippling with intense energy. "You are a thief and a coward. You get away from here or you will come to harm!"

Tamiro stepped forward. "Friend," he said, putting his hand on Sasha's arm, "we mean you and your family no harm. My betrothed has had many years to dwell upon her mistakes and seeks only to make peace with you and yours."

"Your betrothed?" Sasha asked, looking at me.

"Yes," I said. "This is Tamiro. He will be my husband soon."

"You know that she has no honor," Sasha said to Tamiro. "She was to wed me and ran off to steal my baby cousin instead. She is a traitor."

"I have heard the story. To be fair, you are in your right to hold a grudge. On the other hand, Jaelle was all but ten years old and had just lost her sister," Tamiro chided. "Perhaps you may never forgive her for that—as is your right—but must your wife suffer because of that old

226

injury? Clearly, she has missed the woman who was the only mother she knew. They have been separated ten years now." Sasha looked back and forth between me and Perla, who still clung to me. "Perhaps all may be seen as part of the grand design?" Tamiro continued. "Life would not have bended to deliver you this radiant wife and child had Jaelle behaved as she was expected to, yes?"

Perla looked at Tamiro with admiration. I regretted that he had only come so lately to the knowledge of all that had transpired. I felt my affection for him deepen then, and was grateful for the words he spoke so eloquently. Sasha shifted from foot to foot, a physical manifestation of what seemed to be going on within him as he weighed what Tamiro had said. "You're right," he said. "I will never forgive. But it's true that I ended up with the right wife and child after all of the suffering. You may stay, but only because I know my wife's heart hurts for missing you."

Perla looked at her husband with gratitude. Little Kari looked up at her father and reached a small hand to him. Sasha knelt and scooped her up. "Don't get any ideas," he said, looking directly at me. "This one is not for the taking." He laughed then, a silly laugh. It was such a contrast to the seriousness of his demeanor a moment before that it took us all off guard. Soon, we were all laughing, too, and although Sasha would not meet my eyes after that, he let us pass and go forth into the castle, where I was reunited with many of my relatives. Quite a few had passed on to the Otherworld in the years that had expired since I had seen them last, but there were still members of my original clan. Cousin Milosh had become Clan Chief after Baba had passed into the void. He and Lala were getting older, but were still in cheerful good health. "Our little Lyuba!" they exclaimed, pinching my cheeks as if I were still a child. "To think we thought we would never see you again!" They were delighted to meet Tamiro and surprised that I was yet unmarried.

All knew about how I had absconded with Perla, but they were aware that she had long since been returned unharmed to her rightful place with her people. Perla brought me to see her father. Mihai's hair and beard was streaked with gray. I feared he would be hateful toward me, but instead, he thanked me for taking care of Perla. Always a man of few words, he surprised me by telling me that Perla had spoken highly of the excellent care she had received from me, and believed she would have died without me providing a mother's love. Mihai's wife was timid, and the two boys–Perla's brothers–were quiet like Mihai. I could see how Perla had been well-nurtured, returning to this gentle family unit. Mama Violca had died before Perla had even returned to the clan–choked on a bone, I was told. It seemed that in the absence of a grandmother, Selene had stepped in to counsel Perla in her blossom into adulthood and in the management of her Gift.

While the others went to see about a meal and settle in, Perla led me through the honeycomb passages to get to a room on the far side of the castle to see Selene. Tata Iosef had died in an accident many years before, she regretted to tell me. On the way to see Selene, she updated me on others from the Badi clan: "Isa lives with her husband's family in Moldova. She married into the Ursari clan and has five–no, by now I think six–children! We saw her just last summer."

"Six children! Does she still perform?" I recalled Isa's great skill on the sky rope.

"Oh no, but she's trained some of her children. Some have married away already. She takes care of the bears now. She is amazing at it. She speaks to them like they are her children, and they listen!"

"How remarkable! I saw a bear with the Bihari Circ near Deva."

"Deva? Oh, Mama! It has been too long. I must hear everything. Mama–I must warn you: Selene is not well. She spends more and more time with the Spirits. Sometimes she does not even recognize us. We do our best to care for her, but she is not as she once was. We keep her away from the activity so that she does not become agitated."

I was completely disoriented as to where we were in the castle now. Even living many years there, the place felt different and was as if it were not my home any longer. I had thought I knew every part of it, but this section felt unfamiliar. We went down a long narrow hall with an arched ceiling and into a darkened room. There was a fire banked low, and a few small oil lanterns, making long shadows across the stone ceiling that rose like a tent roof, converging in a point in the middle high above. I was sure I had not seen this room before.

"Mama Selene–someone is here to see you," Perla went over and placed her hand on the arm of a shrunken form lying back upon the bedding. She had the high cheekbones of the woman I remembered but was much diminished. Selene's long black hair had turned completely white and her face was sunken, her long arms little more than skin over bones. She looked at me, dark caverns around her watery eyes that glistened but did not seem to focus well.

"My daughter . . ." the words were spoken with effort, forced from parched lips.

Perla knelt and helped Selene to sit up more, then gave her some sips of cold tea from a nearby cup. Selene smacked her lips and then refocused on me.

"Mama Selene," I said, "It is I–Jaelle. I would have been your daughter-in-law, but I went away with Perla. Do you remember?"

"You took the baby," she said.

"Yes! I took Perla away after Ankah died. Do you remember Ankah?"

"I was just speaking to Ankah a moment ago."

Perla turned to me. "She speaks to Ankah often. Sometimes I have sensed her here, but other times . . . I'm no longer sure what's real for Selene and what is a product of her demented state."

"I am not demented!" Selene spoke up in a wavering voice and tried to sit up, becoming upset.

"Of course you're not," I said, and urged Perla to move over so I could sit on the floor by Selene's side. I held her hand and began to tell her all I had learned about herbs and teas studying with Baba Tsura, things I thought might calm her to hear.

"Tsura is a wonderful healer! I know her well!" Selene exclaimed.

"Yes, she said you were acquainted. How is it, Mama Selene, that you can converse with a woman who lives so far away, knowing her as if you are old friends?"

She smiled and gestured for me to come closer, as if revealing a secret: "It's the trees!"

"The trees?"

"Yes! The trees carry our messages. It's just like this," she squeezed my hand. "Did you feel anything?"

"I felt you press my hand," I said.

"And just as fast as that, the trees all the way between here and Tsura are aware and relay the message, from me to her and back again, as fast as speaking. Once you link up with the trees, you can receive messages from far away in no time at all." She was speaking slowly, but intently: "The trees fold time and eliminate the distance between us, so you may talk to those who are quite far away, even beyond the veils of this world. It's one of the great secrets of the Universe."

"Baba Tsura mentioned folding time to speak to the Dead before, but she must have skipped the lesson on linking up with the trees. I'll admit, though, I was not always the most vigilant student."

"Some find it easier than others. Others barely need try at all. It comes naturally to them, like breathing. Some need to practice."

"I suppose I might need practice. I have had little experience with such things."

"It might come in handy. You could speak to Baba Tsura just to say good morning, as if her cottage in the woods of Sibiu were right outside your window. You could even speak to those as far away as Oradea."

My spine prickled and I became alert.

"Oh yes," Selene continued, "one could speak to someone all the way in Oradea if she were so inclined." She was looking right at me now, and the glassy look had left her eyes. She was smiling. Then a grimace crossed her face and her head dropped back against the bedding that had been placed behind her to prop her up. She closed her eyes.

Perla nudged me, saying: "We should let her rest. She has not spoken so much in weeks. She has her moments, but they wear her out."

I kissed Selene's hand, and when I did, she grunted a satisfied acknowledgement.

I held Perla's hand as she led me back along the passageways until features of the castle seemed familiar again: this was where I had dried and stored cheeses; this was the place the roof caved in one winter during a huge snowstorm. It still felt like a different place than the home I had made with Perla for so many years and where I had come back to live alone. "What was it like to come back here, the first time after you went to live with the Badi, I mean?" I asked her.

"Oh, that was a very hard year. It had already been decided I would marry Sasha. He was so much older than me, such a fine young man and the reason I was back with the Badi. I knew he had been promised to you before and still held so much anger toward you. I was terrified. When we came here that winter, I missed you terribly. I was here, but homesick at the same time, if that makes sense. I was homesick for you—for my Mama! I swear I felt you here, as if you had just been here."

"I had. I returned to Vár Buceci and left right before the clans returned for their next winter gathering."

"So, I just missed you? How terrible. Oh!" She stopped and reached into her apron pocket. She pulled out a worn piece of red thread. Much of the color was gone and it was frayed from being worried over, but it still had its knots. "I've held this every day. I missed you so much, Mama!"

"Perla, I have suffered without you. I've missed you every single day!"

"Oh Mama!" She wrapped her arms around my neck. Now with the present danger gone, we both stood and cried, holding each other in the dark passageway.

∞

We all slept little that night. My friends were relieved to be among their own people in a more relaxed environment. Once the crisis of the arrival had been resolved, they settled in to meet people, eat, and drink. I was so elated to be in Perla's company again, it was as if I were drunk. I was giddy and did not want to leave her side for an instant. Tamiro joined us, and we relayed our time living together in the old fortress to him. I had never talked about my stay to anyone, so it was good to share these memories out loud. It made them real, as if I had been carrying them around as fairy tales but hearing them from Perla's lips made them things that had truly happened. Tamiro laughed when I recalled the time I had fought off the wolf with only a staff and a turkey to protect me. "That's my Lady!" he said. I had told the story to Perla many times once she could talk, since she was just a babe when it happened and didn't remember it firsthand. As she had as a tiny girl, she still enjoyed the retelling.

The evening went on like this, recalling both shared memories and pieces we had missed. When I told Perla about my time in Deva, how I had learned to weave, and become famous for it for a brief time, Tamiro's eyes got wide. "My dear, how did I not know that I was wedding such a renowned woman?" he joked. At some point, he begged our forgiveness and said he must retire, saying that such an old man could not keep up with young ladies for long, especially ones so fierce they could fend off wolves. After he left, our conversation became more serious. We shared our successes and troubles from the time we had been apart.

I told Perla about my experience with the sacred mushrooms and how I had seen her in the pearl in Sibiu. "Yes, Mama. Selene finally taught me to scry. It is a more advanced skill, or I would have done it much sooner. I scried you as soon as I learned to do so." Strangely, the timing of when she said she gained the knowledge to contact me did not match up. She told me that she had learned to use a bowl of water to see places far away five years before, when they had last spent the winter at the fortress. She had used it to contact me while alone in a back room of the castle, testing out her new skill without Selene's knowledge. The festival of the Metalsmiths' Guild in Sibiu had only been two summers before. I mentioned this inconsistency to her. "We mostly scry in real time. If we are scrying someone who is aware we are doing so–who has the Sight–we can see one another and speak right now, as if we're having a conversation. When I scried you, I could see you on a hillside, by a gravesite under some trees. You ran into the woods. I spoke to you, but I did not think you heard me."

"I heard you, but it was years later, when my mind was altered by medicine."

"That makes sense. Selene's thinking may not be clear as it used to be, but she was right in what she told you: time bends. It appears as though we start in one place and travel in a straight line to the end when we die, but it's just not like that at all. Time is much more malleable than people realize. When I scried you, I was not fully aware of this. Since you do not have the Sight, my scrying you did not reach you while I was doing it. It waited until there was an opening in your consciousness for the message to come through. The Umbrela is sacred medicine, so it can do that for people. It may open a portal from one point in time to another in order to help one heal."

"You are so wise, Perla! How did you become so learned? Was it all Selene?"

"Mostly, yes. I've had many conversations with Ankah, too. I still do not view her as my mother, but she has been an important teacher to me. I've consulted with her often."

"I can't imagine what it must be like to speak to the Dead, or to converse across miles to others as Selene mentioned. Is that true? Can you really do that? Would you be able to speak to someone who is far away if they also had the Sight?"

"I am not so skilled with that as Selene, but it can be done. Tell me about Tamiro, Mama!" she said, changing the subject, although I would have liked to converse more on that topic. "He seems so kind. Do you love him?"

"I am very fond of him. It's true that he is very kind, and I believe he loves me."

"Do you hesitate to marry him?"

"I hesitate to marry anyone. I have long felt I was not intended to marry."

"I don't mean this to be cruel, Mama, but you may not have many other options in the future."

"I'm aware of my 'advanced age,' if that's what you are suggesting."

"Well, that, and also, not many Rromani men would marry someone who is not Rrom."

"Do you know, Perla, it still surprises me when someone points out that I'm not Rrom?"

"I'm sorry, Mama, but you must know that's how the world sees you," she said tenderly.

"When I am around other Gentles, I do not feel like I belong, despite being accepted and blending in. Around the Rroma, I feel like I am with my true people, but they see me as different and that makes me feel separated, even from the ones to whom I feel closest. It seems I can never fit in anywhere."

"It is a hard life you were born into."

Perla had not been aware that Sandor was my father. I had learned of this only right before she and I were separated, and she was such a small child that she would not have picked up on it. I told her then of what I had learned and of Sandor's proposal before I fled Brașov the first time. I relayed the story of when I had returned and come back to live at Vár Buceci on my own, and how I had left before the clans returned. I described my trip to meet Sandor's Uncle Ulric and my mother's family, and of going to the place where I was born and where my mother had died. She was touched to know that I was standing by my mother's gravesite when she had scried me. Perla was most surprised when I told her of Sandor's reaction when I had come back to ask for his blessing to marry Tamiro.

"How could he? Doesn't he realize this could be your one chance at happiness?" she said.

"I think he just wants to make things right. He wants me to have an inheritance or to be set up for life with a wealthy man. He is a good man, but he is prejudiced against the Rroma, like most Gentles. He sees marrying Tamiro as throwing my life away."

"That is infuriating! Tamiro will take care of you. I can tell he loves you. He may not have a title or a fat piece of property, but that does not mean he will be a poor husband!"

"Domn Alexandru sees things differently. Our people have always had nothing but each other, with little more than what we carry from place to place. Our inheritance is each other. I wouldn't expect a Gentle to understand that."

"No, but you certainly do. Despite how you appear, you must marry one who understands this also," my sage little woman-child said.

The next several days were a joyous time. Perla and I were rarely separated. I got to know her daughter, Kari, who was most often at her mother's side. Perla encouraged her daughter's closeness, and I couldn't help but feel that she had been so harmed by our separation that she never wanted her own daughter to have the experience of distance, even for a moment. Perla told me in confidence that she was expecting another child. She had not told Sasha yet, since she wanted to make sure the baby was healthy first. It was still early, and she had miscarried the prior year, so did not want to get his hopes up until she was certain. The baby was a boy, Perla told me. She could tell.

I went to sit with Selene several times, but she was never as articulate as she had been when we were first reunited. She mostly slept, and when she was roused, she was thirsty and complained of nebulous pain and phantom things that no one else could see. There were evil spirits under the bedcovers, poking her, she said. Another time she fearfully told me there were people in the corner watching her and talking about her. "Tell them I didn't do it! I didn't take the baby!" she yelled. I had hoped to have a conversation with her about the night Ankah had died, but it seemed each time I visited she was either asleep or in an aggravated state. Mostly she did not even recognize me, and once she told me that I couldn't have my money back, even if I was unhappy with the fortune she had read for me. "It's *your* future. I'm sorry if you're not pleased, but it's not my fault that your life will turn out badly," she said, and turned away toward the wall.

I avoided Sasha, and when I encountered him, I looked down and tried not to meet his eyes. After I had been there a few days, he came by where I was sitting with Perla and Kari. "Come with me, Jaelle." I got up and followed him, exchanging a look with Perla, who seemed a bit worried by his request. He led me out to the cold stables and brought me to a pen. Inside were a brood of round and placid goats, lounging with pregnant bellies bulging out while they chewed their cud. They jumped up and ran to the stall door when they saw Sasha. A large speckled buck with giant horns stood in the corner. He told me that while all our original goats had passed on, this buck was the son of Pebbles' pretty baby that I had loved so much. He admitted that he had taken back my goats, including Pebbles and her baby, when he came to fetch Perla. I told him I did not blame him, and that I was sure the Lord had no misgivings about it either.

"I would have taken good care of you, Jaelle," he said, sadness and a touch of anger entering his eyes.

"I know," I said.

"I meant it when I said that I ended up with the right wife, though. Perla is the best thing that has ever happened to me."

"She is the best thing that has ever happened to me, too."

"I was so mad at you for so long. It is hard to think differently about it, but it's true what your fiancé said: If you had not left with her, I would have married the wrong woman."

"I agree. You were very kind to me, Sasha, but I would not have done you justice."

"You know, Jaelle, before my mother became so impaired, she told me that she had helped you to leave. Is that true?"

"Yes, she packed a bag for me."

"She said that she knew that Perla was the one for me, but that she would only become the right woman by leaving with you–if you raised her. She said Perla would not have survived otherwise."

"I always felt that might be true. It's why I took her. I thought she might perish without the love of a mother. I tried to raise her with all the love I had to give."

"You did a good job. She is the most splendid woman. And Kari is the perfect daughter."

"I'm sorry I hurt you, Sasha. You did not deserve that. I would not have been the wife to you that Perla has been, but it was wrong to leave you after all the kindness you showed me."

"I am tired of being mad about it. It has taken a lot of energy. All has turned out as it should," he said. He held out his hand and I took it in a gesture of peace between us.

When several days had passed, Simza took me aside to let me know that she and the others felt it was time to return to their family in Rupea. She said, "I understand if you can't come with us, but we must leave tomorrow."

Tamiro concurred. He told me that it was time to head back. "Jaelle, I know how much this has meant to you. I want more than anything to have you come with me, but I know you may be torn. If you feel you must stay, I understand."

"No," I said, "I will leave with you. I would love to stay with Perla until the end of my days, but this is her life now and her family. Even if I would be welcomed to stay, she needs to have her own story."

Perla had conflicting feelings, but generally agreed that it was important for me to go. "Mama, we have only just begun to catch up. I truly wish you could stay longer, but Tamiro needs to return to his family and you must go with him. There is nothing for you here except for me. It would be selfish for me to keep you here, when you can have a full life with Tamiro. Maybe you can still have children and then I could have more little siblings!"

I did not correct her.

We agreed that if nothing else, we would meet here again in five years. I went to say goodbye to Selene, who was sleeping. I placed a kiss on her forehead and somehow knew it would be the last time I would see her. Before we left, I asked to see the string I had given Perla so long ago. I tied another knot in it, so that the two knots that had been at each end overlapped and were now connected and tied into one. "My beautiful Perla! You are always in my heart. See if you can scry me again! Maybe I'll get better at it and be able to see you!"

She agreed. I kissed little Kari, who was still shy of me. All the others had come out to wave us off. Milosh and Lala both sobbed and laughed as they hugged me goodbye, and even Sasha kissed my cheeks. Sasha said to Tamiro, "Take care of my mother-in-law. She is a good woman, despite having made some complicated choices."

As we rode away on our loaned horses, I distracted myself from the pain of separating from Perla once again by conversing with Tamiro. I explained Zhulyi's perspective that one can only make the choices one is designed to make: "Perhaps we can only do what we are made to do. There may be no true decisions, only the path that opens before us based upon who we are."

"If that is the case," Tamiro said with a sparkle in his eye, "I am made precisely to love you, since that seems not to be within my will to change." I smiled with the warmth of his affection. I appreciated him indulging me in this, as he had indulged so many of my sojourns over the past weeks.

It was a faster descent off the mountain than it had been going up. At Domn Alexandru's estate, we headed to the stables and found the hands there who could take the horses to wipe them down and feed them. Someone sent for the Lord and he arrived, looking frazzled. "I did not know when you would return," he said, and I felt the implication that he was not sure I would return at all.

"We stayed longer than expected. My apologies."

"How did you find Perla? Is she well?"

"Yes, very well. Thank you, my lord," I had subconsciously slipped back into more formal address. "Her husband is no longer at war with me. All has been forgiven."

"What a relief!"

"Yes, it was such a hardship to have that barrier between us." I looked him in the eyes as I said this, aware of the great gulf that had spawned between the two of us. It was as if one seam of my life had been stitched closed only to tear open elsewhere.

Sandor took me aside. "Jaelle, I want you to have this." He handed me a sack that I assumed held coins from its weight.

"Thank you, but I can't accept it."

"Nonsense. It is the least I can do."

"I do not want your money. I never have."

"I know, but you will not accept anything else. Please take it, Jaelle. Can't a father at least pay for his daughter's wedding?" I saw he was sincere, and so I accepted the bag he held out to me. Walking back to the others, Sandor grasped Tamiro's hand and forearm. "I give you my blessings. You will find no finer woman."

"Thank you, my lord," Tamiro bowed his head. "I am aware she is a treasure."

The trip back was uneventful. We stopped to sleep at the castle we had visited on the way, and the families there were happy to have us back for the night. Learning our lesson, we abstained from the drinking and revelry and went to sleep early with the sounds of music and cheerful shouting all around us. As we walked back to Rupea, I noticed Tamiro limping. I did not say anything at first, but when we arrived back to the apartments and I saw him wince as the children jumped up on him to greet their Dedu Tamiro, I pulled him aside. "What is it? Are you hurt?"

"It's that darn splinter. I must have gotten something in the wound again."

Upon removing his boots, I smelled a sour odor and saw that there was green pus that had broken through the healed skin. It was festering and red all around. "This did not just happen! How long has it been like this?" I demanded.

"It started hurting when we got to Braşov," he confessed. You were so devastated by the Lord's reaction that I did not wish to trouble you more. When we got to Vár Buceci things were so busy. I thought it would heal up on its own."

I scolded him for not telling me sooner and forced him to soak his foot in diluted vinegar. I started a regimen of root teas to try to purify his blood against the infection. As he sat with his foot elevated and bandaged in the kitchen, his children came in to discuss plans for the wedding. Jana said, "It is only a few weeks to the Spring Equinox. That would be the perfect time."

Tamiro agreed, "The sooner the better."

"You will not have a leg to step over the broom unless we can get this foot healed," I admonished him.

The plans for the celebration moved forward. Although I did not wish to make a big fuss, I began to sew a new dress so that I could at least look presentable at my wedding. It was not the nicest material; I had been cautioned that the streets of Rupea were worse than ever and we shouldn't venture out more than needed. We had to purchase fabric from a shop on the corner that sold lesser quality than the selection that would have been available in the market. It was still a nice dress when it was finished, a cream-colored cotton, but I did not have enough material for the bottom. I had to sew a band of green as a hem from a borrowed remnant left over from someone else's dress. I was reminded of when I had sewn sack cloth to the bottom of the dress I had outgrown after the first winter Perla and I had stayed in Vár Buceci. I was still in the same position, I realized, piecing together the scraps of life to make things fit.

I knew something was terribly wrong when I came back into the kitchen after helping Simza with some chores to find Tamiro dozing with his head falling down upon his chest. He never slept in the middle of the day. I went to touch his head and it was burning hot and his hair was clammy. I got him up and helped him limp to his bedroll and brought him tea and broth. I sat with him and held his hand. He shouted occasionally, his febrile dreams haunting him. Once he called out the name of his deceased wife. He opened his eyes and looked surprised to see me, saying, "Oh! I'm so sorry, Jaelle," and slipping back into restless slumber. I washed his head with cool rags and forced him to sit up and drink. When Jana and I unwrapped his bandage later that evening, it was redder and more swollen than ever, with little spiders of red running up his leg.

I went to find Oleksandr and Viktor and I brought them to inspect Tamiro's leg. Stepping far enough away so we would not disturb him, I asserted: "We have to take him to Baba Tsura."

"He's in no position to travel," said Oleksandr. "We'd have to carry him."

"Then we'll carry him!" I said.

"I do not think he would survive the journey regardless," Viktor said.

Jana broke in to say what we all were thinking, "I hate to say it, but we should find a barber to amputate."

"There is one a few streets over," said Viktor. "I can go to find him."

Oleksandr's face was filled with revulsion. "He would despise that. It is no way to live. Better to let him die than that."

"It's not better to die! I will attend to him! What do I care if he has one leg or two?" I asked, my voice pitching up as I almost gave way to total panic.

Oleksandr, as the oldest son, made the call: "We will wait until morning. Perhaps he will improve. If he doesn't, we will send for the barber."

By morning, Tamiro's body lay cold and lifeless, with a yellowish cast to his skin, drab in the dim cold light. I had sat with him all night but dozed off and on. I had missed his passing. Sitting there numb, I was only barely aware when Jana roused. Realizing what had happened, she awoke the brothers. They stood, looking down at their father and then bellowed with great heaving sobs escaping them. Their wives joined in. Simza heard the sound and came running. The whole family, children included, awoke to the wailing and howling of their mourning kin. I sat still.

I was unable to move, to cry, to join in, or to leave. All I could do was sit and look down at the man I had planned to spend the rest of my days with. It was my fault: I had not loved him well enough, I concluded. I had been selfish with my own struggles and had dragged him all over the country. I had not paid enough attention to him as he followed me around, ready to accompany me and assist me in resolving every one of my personal dilemmas. I had not watched him closely enough. I had not healed him properly. I deserved to lose him.

Part Three

Chapter Twenty: The Oracle of Oradea

Oradea was prosperous and dazzling, a modern city built over ancient ruins. Everywhere, signs of contemporary life were blossoming: a star-shaped fortress shielding a massive cathedral, and statues of the Catholic saints and equestrian life were on full display in all the town squares. There was even a gold skull of a king displayed right in the center of everything. It was not clear if the skull had been crafted as an effigy to the king or if his very skull had been preserved in gold. The Citadel of Oradea had been destroyed by the Tatars a century earlier, but that did not stop the current residents from building up around the shattered ruins. The Crişul Repede River ran like a thick ribbon through the center, stone bridges arching over it and wide streets cobbled neatly on either side.

The trades were strong and the guilds powerful, as in Sibiu, but there was a culture of decadence and artful fancy in Oradea that seemed to harken back to the time of the ancient Romans who had first settled there. The city seemed to have two faces: one was devoutly Christian, worshipping their baby god and virgin mother as if this fable were historical fact, tending and tithing the church as if it were a thirsty god itself; the other face was a lecherous and Bacchanalian pleasure-seeker, indulging in passions of the flesh. It was like two sides of a coin. Most clearly the city was divided by its day and night persona. By day, the good people milled about and labored at their respective employment, and by night, the masks came off and respectable citizens became lustful, satiating every whim.

It was a large city, radiating in every direction, with many neighborhoods separated by class. My small shop was just outside the poorest section, where laborers lived a mouthful away from starvation. It faced a thoroughfare lined with shops, where colorful markets and street merchants set up by day. While wealthier people would rarely venture to this part of the city, they often sent their serfs and household staff there to buy cheap wares and foodstuffs. Like in Sibiu, my shop was lined with glass urns of herbs, tucked back and away from the light. Since my training with Baba Tsura, I was much more effective in my prescriptions for ailments. Still, I relied on my old trick of saying with confidence: "This will help," while handing over a packet of dried plant or shredded bark. Customers insisted I had a gift, and many came back week after week for their ills. I never charged much, since they had so little and suffered so much.

The few small coins I made from this venture barely paid for my kindling. I had used Sandor's gold to purchase the building and doled the rest of it out regularly to pay the exorbitant taxes demanded by the rulers of the region. I lived in quarters above the shop and had a small dirt patch of yard in the back to do the washing and hang laundry to dry. In the many months that I'd been in the city, I had made few regular acquaintances, other than my customers. My neighbors were busily tending to their own lives, with little energy left over for the concerns of others. To those who had inquired, I told as close to the truth as I'd ever gotten, that I was a widow who had moved on after the death of my husband.

I still had not reckoned with Tamiro's death. In a daze, I had participated in the funeral process, the burying of his body in a pauper's gravesite outside Rupea, the burning of his few belongings. His sons were distraught, and their wives, children, and other relatives equally devastated. Tamiro was the heart of their lively family, and none could comprehend the meaning of life without him at the center of all. No one seemed to blame me for the infection that had returned to claim his life, but I blamed myself. If I had been any kind of healer, I would have been able to save him, I was sure. The family treated me like his widow, though we had not yet married. I was the only one who felt I did not deserve this inclusion in the family's grief.

It was not discussed what would become of me afterward, but I felt the burden of my presence. Tamiro's kin would care for me as they would have had we been married. I was certain to be given a place in their company when travels resumed in the spring. I was not intended to witness it, but about a week after Tamiro's death, I overheard Simza discussing my prospects with Viktor's wife, Jana. There was another widowed cousin in Turda who might marry a skilled healer, despite her being of Gentle birth. They could head that way when the weather broke to deliver me and see if a match could be made. That night, I packed my few possessions in the small black cauldron Tamiro had made and snuck from the apartments. Stealthily, I hid in the shadows as I departed the city, careful to avoid the drunken bands of soldiers that seemed omnipresent, despite the late hour.

As I got onto the main road, walking out of the populated area and into the countryside, I realized that I fervently loathed Rupea. I focused all my despair of losing Tamiro into vitriolic hatred of that putrid town with its nasty men and dirty streets. I convinced myself that once I put distance between myself and the dread city that I would also leave behind the roiling tangle of anguish that threatened to pull me down into its depths and smother me. I was, in fact, unable to leave the source of my pain behind. It traveled with me to the next town. It stayed with me, keeping me close company on the merchant's caravan on which I bought passage to Oradea. It followed me through the alleys and broad roads that I encountered there. Then it settled in firmly next to me as I set up house in my new locale. A new rent had been sheared in the fabric of my life, and I knew this one could never be mended.

I had never admitted to myself or to Tamiro that I had loved him. Loved him I had, but little good it did me or him to realize it now. I kept reliving in my mind the many days Tamiro and I traveled to Braşov, stayed with Sandor, and went to see Perla. I had never even noticed his discomfort, never checked the healing of his foot, or inquired how he was faring with everything. I barely attended to him at all; I was so preoccupied by my own drama. Now, alone in Oradea, I was sure I was the most selfish woman in the world. I had taken his love for granted. I had grudgingly accepted his presence in my life, and then assumed we'd have the rest of our lives to express our feelings. I never told him that he made everything feel better and make sense, in a life that so often had left me alienated. I thought we'd grow old together, snuggling grandchildren and cobbling together a simple and satisfying existence, surrounded by laughter and family.

Most surprisingly, I felt furious. I was raw from the injustice of being robbed of this small semblance of happiness. I was angry at myself first, for not taking better care of Tamiro, but I was mad at him, too, for not telling me what was going on before it was too late. I felt betrayed by the universe for giving me something just for me, only to take it away– again! Why did it seem to be my lot to lose all that I held dear? It was not fair. Now I found myself in *another* city, all alone. I was upset to find myself a several-week journey away from those left whom I loved. I had been in a fog leaving Rupea, and it had not even occurred to me that I should catch up with Perla and the Badi at Vár Buceci before they started their travels for the spring. I could have gone to be with my daughter instead of being in a city where I did not even know anyone. Even going to stay with Sandor would have been an improvement over being all alone again. Somehow, none of this had occurred to me.

Instead, I went to Oradea. In my disoriented state, I had headed toward Zhulyi, even though in my mind she had rejected me. I was in no shape to be pursuing love again anyway, after losing Tamiro. I just sat alone, building the bare minimum of a life in another new place, without even trying to find out where Zhulyi might be. The city was enormous, and I had seen very few Rroma. While I had set up a home and shop, I had done so automatically, with little heart and enthusiasm. I was just there. I saw little point in anything.

There was some small comfort in helping people in pain. The door rattled and the bells I had placed there jangled with a customer coming in. It was an older widow who lived a few blocks down, in one of the poor neighborhoods. She scraped together a narrow existence by heading to the margins of the city and collecting scraps for kindling. Usually, you could see her coming down the block, hunched over with her torso almost horizontal with the earth, looking like a turtle with her wares piled upon her back. Today, she had set the large bundle that she tied to her back outside the door. She always took a few minutes to be able to stand up straight again.

"Ah, my dear," she said when I went to assist her, lending her my arm to upright herself. "It's a dreary thing getting old. I don't recommend it."

"I am almost there myself," I laughed.

"Nonsense," said the woman, turning her sparkling blue eyes on me. "You still have much life left in you. I know you are grieving now, but you will find another husband someday. A bright young woman like you will surely marry again."

My story of being a widow had come true in Rupea. Although Tamiro and I had not officially married, I felt I told the truth when I said I had been widowed. When I explained my solitary life to others in Oradea—those who cared to ask, that is, as many didn't bother—I described being recently left alone after my husband's untimely death. The old crone, Razel, was one of the few who had inquired. "I am not interested in marriage," I said, and helped her to a stool.

"Not now, perhaps, but you will be again. I would have remarried, myself, if anyone would have had a bent old woman!" she cackled.

"What can I help you with today?"

"It's what it always is, my back and legs. Some days I can get through the work and then I'll make some of the tea you gave me and get right to sleep. Days like today—I don't know how I can make it to the end of the day. I've had a hard life and used my body poorly."

"You sit and I'll make you some tea now," I said. I had just made myself tea, so the water was still almost boiling, but I put it back over the fire and prepared some roots for Razel.

"I have heard from my daughter in Rontău," she said. "She sent word through the smith there who brings his wares to our market. They have two new grandbabies and the sheep have dozens of new lambs. They're doing well. She said I should move there and bathe in the Roman springs. Have you been there?"

"No, I have only heard of them," I said.

"They are warm all year. She said they have magical properties and heal the worst of painful conditions like mine."

"Not a terrible idea, then?" I placed a cup of tea in front of her on a small table.

"I would hate to be a burden. Here, the only one who needs worry about me is me. If I were to go to where my daughter lives, I would become their concern. They have enough worries to be troubled by an old broken woman."

I thought of Perla, and for the first time I was glad I had not gone to her when I left Rupea. She did not need to be saddled with me, despite how I would have loved to spend more time with her.

"This is not what you usually give me," Razel observed, sniffing the wafts of steam coming from the cup.

"No. The tea I have given you before is for nighttime. This should help you to get through the day."

When she was done drinking, I refused her small coins and she gave me a few sticks of wood in trade. "Thank you, my dear. I'll keep my eye out for a good husband for you. There must be someone who would want such a talented herbalist."

Somehow, in other places I had lived, my skills had attracted the attention of the elite of the region. Here, I was virtually anonymous. I did become a refuge for a certain type of client, though. The debauchery that was rampant in the city left more than a few young women in compromising positions. It was not unusual for a timid chamber maid or serf to come in to tell me she was with child and her "husband" could not know. With some encouragement, a story would spill out of an overbearing master, coming home drunk from one of the endless parties, or simply cornering her in a kitchen pantry. In most cases, if it were early enough, a few roots in a bag, brewed strongly before the full moon, would dispel the concern. It happened so often, though, that I started to feel that it was a common plague among Gentle men to feel entitled to the bodies of the women who worked in their homes. While there was an occasional story of a man being too rough or unkind to a wife among the Rromani, this kind of violence was rare.

Yet it was not just the lords of the estates making prey of young maids, I found. Quite often, the girls who worked in the fancy houses fell victim to their fellow workers. I was particularly struck by one young laundry woman who came in, bruised and battered. She said she had a "run in" with a horse in the stable, but later confided that one of the staff of the household had expressed an interest in her hand in marriage. When she refused him, he took from her body what she would not give freely. Every few months she would return, again with child from his vicious rapes. He told her he would force himself upon her until she became pregnant and agreed to marry him. She never disclosed to him that she was compromised, just came to me again and again to request the needed herbs and roots.

She had no family in the city. All her relatives were far away in a distant county. Hers was a good job, and she could not afford to leave it. When she went to confide in the head steward's wife, who oversaw the women of the household, the stern lady told her that she must not encourage him and should be more chaste and inaccessible in the future. It was a heartbreaking sight, to see her return over and over again, head down with fresh bruises each time. I never charged her for the roots I prepared for her. After a while, I did not even ask her what happened. I just brewed the strong tea when I saw her come into the shop. My kindness was a small gesture in the face of such brutality.

What I had learned from Baba Tsura served me well. Soon I had a small following of locals. They came to me for everything from headaches and menstrual cramps to more serious diseases. Those who worked in the stone quarries often had a cough from breathing stone dust for too many years. There was little I could do but calm the spasms in their chest, but it was a slow and suffocating death. I began to hear more and more of the healing waters of the hot springs, and soon began to recommend these to some of my customers who could have little relief from their bodily ills. It was not a long journey, I was told, and for many, there were few other options for their suffering. Those who followed the advice came back heartened and agreed that the soothing waters were magical. Soon, I determined I would need to see this for myself, and so the next time I saw Razel, I proposed that I accompany her to the springs so that I could sample the experience along with her. She would be able to see her daughter and perhaps get some relief from her pain. I packed my pot with herbs and a few necessities, and we started off on a clear day. Without the bundle on her back, Razel could walk faster than the crawl with which she usually ambled, but she was still bent over and the trip took much of the day.

We were welcomed on her daughter's homestead, a rambling country shack surrounded by sheep pastures, and a few close houses with children who had married and settled there with their spouses. There were so many children, with the various households, and there were babies, dogs, and chickens running everywhere. After the lonely city, I found the frenetic life of the little settlement refreshing, if a little overwhelming. Razel's daughter, Mirabel, and her husband Bero were gregarious, sturdy people transitioning from the cusp of middle into older age. Mirabel had been born and raised in the city or Oradea, but had moved upon marrying Bero, whose family was from this region. Razel's husband had been a rope maker, and his work kept him close to the city, so they had rarely visited Mirabel and her growing family. Mirabel and Bero's two sons and a daughter who had settled on the property were similarly hearty and good-natured. The couple had two other daughters, I learned, who had moved with husbands to nearby territories. The children who had stayed were committed to the life of farming and raising sheep and seemed content with the small universe they had made for themselves.

I was happy to be around fresh milk, and began talking cheese with Razel's granddaughter, Lisel, who was the expert in the family. The sheep's milk cheese she made was some of the finest I'd ever tasted, and we compared notes on the processes we'd tried. Lisel was about my age, and had just had her sixth baby, who was a little swaddled lump that kept his mouth firmly at his mother's breast. She kept him tied there by a sling. Being no newcomer to motherhood, Lisel barely seemed to slow as she went about her daily chores with the child upon her. She expressed distress upon hearing of my husband's death, and when she stopped her work to look into my eyes to share her condolences, I felt that she was truly sorry for my grief. This was more medicine than I had received since leaving Rupea, and somehow was a salve on my still open wound.

The thermal waters of this land were concentrated in the nearby large pools and spas that had been popular since the Roman times, but small pockets of warm waters cropped up in the surrounding countryside. Mirabel and Bero's farm was fortunate to have springs that touched the edges and came bubbling up in pockets on the sheep pastures, thawing the ice in the winter and making raising animals easier for the natural warming that occurred around them in the colder months. Razel and I, both early risers, soon made a habit of going to a far pasture in the mornings and sitting in a pool in bathing smocks for an hour or so before drying off and returning to the farm to help with morning tasks. After only a few days, Razel's crooked posture straightened out, and it seemed she could stand more steadily upright and breathe easier from not sloping crunched over her lungs. It truly was a magical transformation to see her bent shape ease upright. She seemed younger by a dozen years in the course of only a few days of taking to the baths.

Razel, who had worried so about burdening her daughter's family, found that she was a help with both the endless meal preparation and attending to her large supply of great-grandchildren. She was terrific at baking bread, they found, and was a source of stories and entertainment for the little ones who flocked around her to hear tales of the city. When a few weeks had passed and it was time for me to return to my shop in Oradea, Razel informed me that she would be staying. She had found a place within her daughter's lively homestead, and the tonic of the baths was exactly what her burdened body needed. She gave me some instructions for the landlord of the small rooms she let in the neighboring district to my shop, and I agreed to pass on the information to him to let him know she would not be returning. When I left the farm, I felt a deep sense of satisfaction at having accompanied Razel into a place where she could peacefully settle into her last days surrounded by family and love.

Upon returning to my house in the city, I was struck by despondence and a sense of homesickness. I could not tell what I was yearning for, but realized it was for the happy little homestead I had left at the springs. It was not loneliness for that specific place, but for the sense of togetherness that had inhabited the space there, filling it to the brim with the happy activity of a shared life well-lived. I had sensed just the tip of that with Tamiro's relatives, when I had inherited, for a short time, his rambunctious and friendly extended family. I wondered if I would ever have anything close to that again or if I was destined to live out my time alone. These thoughts were interrupted by the bells on the shop door tinkling. It was later than I would have expected a customer, but I had just arrived back and had forgotten to lock the door behind me. I turned toward the door and felt like I had seen a ghost: it was Zhulyi.

"Oh good. You are here," she said.

∞

She had been waiting for me to return to the city, she said. The Spirits had informed her I had been taking baths with an old woman. Seeing her was confusing, despite the reality that the whole reason I had come to this region months ago was my connection to her. I suppose I thought if I were to find her in Oradea, it would be after I went looking for her. It never occurred to me that she might come to find me. It had been over ten years since I left Deva in a carriage alone. She had aged somewhat, looking more like a grown woman than the teenager I had met and fallen in love with. She told me she had two boys now, and Aamon had become kinder to her. They were beginning to make plans for the older boy's marriage. The Bihari Circ was settled just outside of the city for its summer performances. They had found a loyal following among the lust-filled nobles and carousers. They were even invited to parties in grand homes to entertain, although they were guarded closely to make sure they did not walk off with the silver or someone's husband.

After hearing about the changes in her life, I relayed a few key features of the past ten years, glossing over much. "Why did you leave?" I finally asked her the question that had burned in my mind for so long, but only after our second cup of tea.

"I am so sorry, Jaelle. I was packed and ready to come with you. I had every intention of leaving with you. Then Aamon showed up. When he came in the door, I knew I was supposed to go with him. I wanted to slip away to let you know, but I couldn't figure out how to do it without raising suspicion. I was still very frightened of him back then. I have missed you, but I have not regretted my choice. I'm sorry, but it's true: I love my boys more than I ever dreamed imaginable, and I would not have had them if I had gone with you."

With her in front of me now, the longing I had felt all these years disappeared and was replaced by anger, simmering below the surface and spiced by feelings of rejection and betrayal. "I am happy you have found marital life satisfying," I said, with cool cynicism. It seemed I could not help these bitter words from erupting.

"It's not like that at all. Aamon and I have found our peace. I have fulfilled my duties as a wife. My only joy has been with my sons. They are the loves of my life."

This stung somewhat, but reflecting on my feelings for Perla, who was not even my own child, I understood what she meant.

"I have missed you, Jaelle," she said, and reached over to take my hand. "I have kept in contact in small ways, through the Spirits and those gifted to speak to them, but I did not know if I would ever see you again."

"I have missed you, too, Zhulyi. I never thought I'd get over you. You will never know how it hurt me to find you gone, to sit in that carriage alone. It stung for years. And then I met someone. I was going to marry him, maybe even have some small portion of happiness. And then . . . he died," I choked.

"Tamiro," she said softly, and I looked up, startled. "He moved on quickly. I have heard of it from Tsura. We have spoken on a few occasions."

I recalled that Baba Tsura knew of Zhulyi. "So, he passed on easily?"

"From what I understand. He had business calling him on the other side."

I was relieved to hear that Tamiro was not a tortured ghost but realized that meant he must have gone to join his wife. "Well, at least one of us was gratified by the arrangement," I said, and laughed a false little chuckle.

"Jaelle, I know you loved him. From what I know, it seems he was a kind man."

"I did love him, in my own way. I thought we would grow old together. But we never . . ." I looked up at her, embarrassed. "We were to be married at the Spring Equinox. We had not consummated our love."

"Do you regret that?" It was kindly asked, and I felt no jealousy from her inquiry.

"No. To be honest, the thought of coupling with him—with any man—has always terrified me. But I regret that I did not express my love for him, at least in words. He died not knowing how I valued him. Maybe I did not know how much I valued him until he died."

"I think he knew, Jaelle."

"I just wish I had told him," I gulped, and a sickened bile came up in my throat. I ran to the back door and spat out the foul substance. I felt her standing behind me, touching my shoulder. Turning, the sobs began to escape me. I buried my head into her neck, shuddering with all the feelings that had struck me numb for the past months. She held me and I sobbed, tears flowing as if they might not stop. I was crying not just for Tamiro, but for all the years separated from her and for all I had lost in life.

"It's okay, Jaelle," she cooed to me, as if I were a babe. "I'm here now."

Chapter Twenty-One: The Fragility of Stone

The years passed in Oradea as I never believed they could. My business grew, but still it remained a relatively modest enterprise. It was somewhat enhanced by the introduction of "Fortune Telling" to my business repertoire. Once a month, at the full moon, Zhulyi came to stay with me overnight. The evening was well-publicized locally, and the turnout was always full of desperate love-struck maidens and sad older widows, looking to know if the future held happiness, or wanting to connect with departed husbands and children through the Cigany soothsayer. Zhulyi became renowned for her passionate readings. Despite her former hesitance with using the craft to entertain the Gentles, she had grown to be an adept performer, pulling out all the tricks of shaking bells, gazing into crystal orbs, and passing on messages with a glazed faraway expression, as if possessed by the messages of the dead. She was able to deliver some sincere truths to her audience, she admitted, and so she found some solace in the legitimacy of her work, however enhanced for effect.

It became a popular event, and the line was long well into the evening. She was paid handsomely for this work, so perhaps this is why Aamon never begrudged her staying over with her "friend" the Gentle who sponsored these lucrative activities. As exciting as it was to have the buzz around the shop—people milling around to buy stones or crystals or herbs for their various complaints—my anticipation was always for when the shop would quiet and we could be alone together. The money I made that one night of the month paid most of my expenses for the rest of the long weeks of tepid sales. The financial boon from the monthly gathering was a blessing, but I only looked forward to it for the precious hours Zhulyi and I spent alone together afterward, wrapped in each other's embrace until dawn.

In winter months, the Bihari took up residence in the destroyed ruins of the Citadel of Oradea. The chapel was still intact and a few other rooms were liveable and housed the families until the spring. This was at the arrangement of the local voivode, to whom they payed dear taxes and allegiance as "slaves" to the Hungarian Crown. To my delight, the Bihari tribe being nearby during winter allowed for even more contact with Zhulyi, and an occasional stolen afternoon visit. I looked forward to those months for my increased time with her. Before I knew it, three years had passed in this manner. As we approached the fourth winter, I began to think of how the following year at that time I would need to travel to Brașov and Vár Buceci to be re-united with Perla. I had already spoken to Zhulyi about it and hoped that she would agree to go with me. In my mind, after heading to the castle together, we would stay there when the tribes departed in the spring. We would spend the next years setting up house together, alone in the crumbling stone that was more home to me than anywhere else in the world. I planned never to return to Oradea: I just hoped she would stay on with me.

She only knew the first part, about my wish to have her accompany me to the mountain castle. She was non-committal, her second son having just married, and the first son's wife expecting their first baby. It was not clear how these changes would affect her and how much she would have to help their young wives, who had moved in with her and Aamon and were learning about the Circ and life as wives who were soon to be mothers. The daughters-in-law had both come from other clans and were unfamiliar with the Bihari lifestyle. "A year is a long way away," Zhulyi said. "We'll have to see what the future holds."

"I thought you could tell that already," I said grumpily, to which she kissed me, ceasing the conversation. When she left the next morning, I escorted her to the street and kissed her cheeks in farewell, watching her walk away. A massive stagecoach was parked nearby. The driver was familiar—I had seen him deliver several guests at once from across the city to our monthly gatherings. The coach was attached to a large turnout with a brace of four horses and imposing, giant wheels. The man had a distinctive scowl upon his unshaven countenance, a contrast to his sparkling livery. I smiled at him and lifted a hand in greeting, but he only met me with a steely stare.

His mouth contorted into an ugly sneer, showing crooked brown teeth. "Cigany lover!" I heard him hiss, and he spat in my direction. A giant hock of disgusting phlegm landed by my feet. I looked at him, shocked, and went quickly inside, watching out the window. To my alarm, I saw him rally his coach-and-four, seeming to follow Zhulyi! I ran back outside but she had disappeared down one of the narrow alleys, and I could see the man looking back and forth to try to track her. Unsuccessful, he spat again and urged his horses into a trot, going too fast for such a large brace on the uneven cobbles of the thoroughfare. My heart was racing as I stood there, dumbstruck. It was the first time I had felt unsafe in Oradea, despite the unsavory side I was always aware was present.

I began to see the evil man everywhere. Sometimes he parked his turnout on my street and just sat there for an hour or so. I saw him when I went to the bakery to rent their ovens: I was baking several long, braided breads to serve to guests as they waited for their readings at our monthly meetings. He was leering at me from outside the window. I spent a great deal of time discussing flour quality with the baker, lingering much longer than I would normally, and looking nervously around when I left. I thought I had evaded him, but then he accosted me in the market. I was picking out eggplants, a favorite of Zhulyi's to roast for her visit that evening. I felt his eyes on me and suddenly he was beside me.

"Witch! How many of my children have you murdered?" His foul breath reeked as he came up into my face to confront me.

I backed up, out of reach of the putrid air spewing from his mouth and the stench permeating the air around his body. "Sir, I beg your pardon. I have no idea what you are talking about." I tried to keep my voice calm and looked around for sympathetic faces to see if I could rely on someone to intervene. The shoppers looked uncomfortably down into their baskets and off into the air as they moved swiftly away from the source of the conflict.

"My fiancé, Rosalie. You've been helping her to dispel my children from her very womb! What kind of sorceress are you? You consort with Ciganyok! I know all about you and your Cigany lover! You are a disgusting wench, a filthy, foul unnatural creature! Witch! Whore!"

I walked away as fast as I could, but he followed me through the market, shouting curses at me, until I was able to lose him by weaving through the crowd and escaping through a back alley that ran along the river.

I told Zhulyi about it that evening: "I have seen this kind of hatred when I traveled with my clan or the Badi. I have never thought much of it except as a marker of ignorance. I know some who have come to harm as a result, but that has been because of superstitions and vague judgments. Gentles can be awful to the Rroma and anyone associated with them. I've had that happen before." I recalled times when my affiliations had drawn suspicion, like in Deva when Liana became distant after learning I spoke Rromani and had lived among them. "This attack was personal, though. I think I know who he is talking about. There is a girl I have helped many times. She is violated over and over by a man in her household. I have helped her to return to her normal cycles after he has forced her to breed. I have probably helped her a dozen times or more now. It seems nothing can stop him from continuing to defile her. I think he must be that wretched man."

"Perhaps you should not assist her next time," Zhulyi suggested. "It seems it can only bring trouble."

"There was more, Zhulyi. He seemed to know about *us*. I have seen him drop off passengers in his coach when we have the Full Moon readings, but he seemed to know about our . . . love."

"We are moving into the Citadel for the winter tomorrow. Perhaps you should come with us. Leave the shop for the winter and let things settle down. It seems no good can come from this man, since he knows where you live and . . . knows too much."

"I can't stay with your family, Zhulyi!" The Bihari were even more closed to outsiders than other clans. It did not seem likely they'd accept me. "Aamon only barely tolerates me because our work together makes money for his family. I can't imagine him or the Bihari welcoming me."

"We need help with the boys' new wives. They are just children, really. They have no idea what they're doing and Aamon is aware of that. I'm sure I can convince him that it would be for the best to have the assistance. Besides, we could use another good healer. Even the Bihari can see the value of an herbalist trained in the traditional Rromani way, Gentle or not."

"I don't think that would be wise," I said, but all I could think of was the stinking filth coming from the man's body and his putrid breath. I might have no choice but to accept Zhulyi's offer.

A few days later, she returned and told me she had spoken to Aamon, and he had agreed. The Bihari elders had met as well, and confirmed I could stay, so long as I followed the traditional laws and assisted in all ways for the health of the clan. This was hardly an issue, as I was familiar with what would be expected. The thought of being close to Zhulyi every day filled me with excitement, but also dread that we would reveal too much and be ostracized. I vowed to myself to be as discrete as possible so as not to jeopardize the life Zhulyi had so carefully built.

Seeing no use in delaying, we packed a few items. I only needed a spare dress and a few headscarves, and my herbs, packed tightly inside my little cauldron. Walking on to the street, I could not shake the sense of dread. I looked around, as we walked the city streets, expecting to see the unkempt face of the man who now terrorized me. The ruins of the Citadel were at the center of Oradea, adjacent to the overflowing markets and near the towering new cathedral. Some of the fortress's exterior walls, thick as a house, were still intact in places, and an uneven barrier existed that prevented others from seeing in to the five-sided complex. No one else would find the complex fit to live there, but all were aware of the Cigany tenants. None dared to enter who did not belong at the risk of angering the ruling Prince.

The Rromani were considered pilgrims, paying homage to the sacred site, as they worshipped the Christian god. All Rromani were familiar with this charade, and at the drop of a feather could play the part of the devout Christian pilgrim when needing to gain passage in a new territory or set up residency. Though most of the ruling class found their appearance and lifestyle distasteful, they were generally accepted as a radical and fringe sect following a divine calling to the Christian faith. It was charitable and righteous to protect these fervent warriors of Christ on their holy mission. The Rroma played right along, agreeing to the role of eccentric devotees. Others, like the evil man, found their way of life evidence of witchcraft. Violence toward Rromani people for no good reason was not unheard of and rarely punished.

We decided to wind through the busy market on the way to the entrance bridge that was dilapidated, but still served to gain careful entry to the destroyed castle. We picked out some fresh vegetables. I finally got the eggplants for Zhulyi that I had tried to buy–but had to abandon–when I was previously accosted in the market near my home. We entered a busy promenade, where hawkers swarmed around and buyers for the great houses balanced wide, round baskets of wares upon their heads or pushed carts overflowing with goods back to the vast kitchens and larders of their wealthy patrons.

"I spoke with Tsura last night," Zhulyi said.

"Oh?"

"She has a new student again."

"Of course, it's that time of year."

"She was very concerned about you. She wanted to make sure I kept you 'off the streets.' I told her I'd be fetching you today, and then I'd be keeping you locked up in my castle for the next several months. She was relieved."

"Yes, I am now your slave and at your service," I joked, bowing.

"I have been worried, too," she said, seriously. "I don't know what I'd do if something happened to you. We were separated for so long. I have to admit, Tsura had me spooked."

"Well, you are rescuing me from any terrible fate," I said. "Thank you, Zhulyi." We stopped and stared into each other's eyes, sharing an intimacy we'd have to guard in minutes once we entered the castle. I wanted to take her hand then. Throughout the market, women held hands or linked arms all the time and no one thought anything of it. As I began to reach toward her, I thought better of it, and brought my hand back to my side as we turned to go on our way.

I heard a shriek then, and a crash and thunderous sound. Turning, I saw with horror the coach-and-four of the terrible man clattering around the corner. People ran out of the way, shouting and screaming as the vehicle picked up frightening speed. It bore down upon us and I saw him, with his menacing grimace determinedly fixed on me. Within, I saw an awful sight: the girl, Rosalie, the one whom I had helped, was standing up in the carriage with arms braced to steady her, a look of terror upon her face. Zhulyi reached for me and I jumped to move from the path of the oncoming horses. I stumbled then on a loose cobble, tripped and fell, my cauldron dropping to the stone. As the hooves rained down upon my body and the immense wheels clamored over me, all I could think was that Zhulyi was safely out of the way.

It seemed like it was happening in slow motion: it took forever for the enormous carriage to travel over my body, both sets of wheels crushing me into the pavement. Finally, it crashed on down the street, and I lay broken in its wake. My eyes fell upon my cauldron, and in my traumatized state, it seemed as if I was looking at the vessel close-up. It was enhanced and crystal clear, every mark on it seeming to fill my eyes although it had been tossed many lengths away. One side of it was dented and the contents spilled across the ground. My hearing was muffled and the sounds of yelling and calls for help seemed very far away.

All went black and stayed so for what seemed to be a very long time. I vaguely recall screaming as I was lifted onto a gurney by several Rromani men who then lifted me into the air. The swaying as they carried me felt almost peaceful despite the terrible pain, and I lost consciousness again. It may have been days later, but I was stirred from the blackness to take sips of water or broth. The agony was so excruciating that I could barely focus, and often blacked out after a moment of consciousness. At one point, Zhulyi was kneeling at my side with a tiny old woman who looked strange and foreign, her tilted eyes speaking into my soul to tell me to calm. She held a pipe to my lips that held a sticky golden resin and Zhulyi urged me to inhale. The smoke burned my lungs and I coughed, which caused white hot pain to shoot through every part of me, but then the pain subsided, and I collapsed into vivid and twisting dreams.

The next thing I recall is being loaded onto a cart. The bumping and unbearable jolts of its movement sent me into blackness again, but I felt Zhulyi at my side, holding my hand. Every time I awoke, Zhulyi held the pipe to my lips and I inhaled again, realizing the substance was the only relief from my torturous existence. Soon the dreams would enfold me, and for a while I would be suspended in time amid a swirling landscape of sparkling and flashing stars and a whole universe of spiraling color. I was forced to drink water, but when crumbs of anything touched my lips, I spat it out, unable to even tolerate food in my mouth. The journey seemed to last forever, in my perpetually altered state from the drug and excruciating misery.

Then, Baba Tsura was there, scolding someone for being too rough with me as I was lifted from the cart. I was on the floor of her cottage, upon the rushes and wool blankets laid out below me. She pushed away the pipe that someone held toward me and instead forced me to drink a foul-smelling tea. I remember the concerned face of a young boy standing at Baba Tsura's elbow. He looked somehow familiar. I held his frightened eyes as I tried to place how I knew him. Then Zhulyi was there again, crying and burying her face in my chest. She placed a kiss upon my forehead and then she was gone. I slipped once again into merciful unconsciousness.

Chapter Twenty-Two: A Broken Vessel

The following weeks–or maybe months–are a blur. Baba Tsura and the young boy tended to me. From one of the early days, I have a disturbing memory of coming to consciousness with Baba Tsura seeming to pull my leg right out of my socket as I screamed in pain. She did the same with one of my shoulders before it all went hazy again. Each time I awoke, I found my body in a patchwork of bandages made from leaves and dripping poultices of crushed leaf pulp. In my distorted mind I tried to sort out what herbs she was treating me with as she fed me different teas and tended to my shattered form, but I could make no sense of it. Frequently, I writhed on the floor and Baba Tsura or the boy would come to assist me, putting a rolled blanket below a part of my body to prop me at a more comfortable angle or giving me another sip of bitter liquid.

I woke one day to snow outside the open door, drifting in before it was closed again, and realized we were in the heart of winter, autumn having passed without my awareness. The fire was always tended, and I felt sweltering despite the cold that creeped up through the reeds and blankets upon which I lay. The boy often sat for hours at my side when he was not fetching wood or water out in the elements. One day, perhaps months later, when he came to spoon some broth into my mouth, I pushed his hand away. I propped myself up on my elbow and grimaced as I sat myself up, the bones beneath me protesting as I sat upon my fragmented bottom. I was practically naked, covered with a short makeshift blouse that went over my front just for decency but was open in the back to tend my injuries. The rest of me was still covered with bandages of layered pulp and leaves, much of which had dried to a stiff crust of brownish hue. Still, I felt exposed and pulled the blanket up over me.

I took the bowl from the boy, my arms and hands shaking from the effort. With much spillage, I tilted it to sip a few mouthfuls, dribbling much of it down my chin before handing the bowl back and collapsing back down. I looked at him then, a fine-looking youth, with bright eyes and a smooth, intelligent face. "What is your name?" I asked him.

"Noem, madam," he said.

"Oh, Noem—I believe no formalities are needed with me, being that you have been attending to my wastes now for quite some time."

He cracked a small smile. "May I call you Mama Jaelle, then?"

"Yes, I suppose that's as good as anything."

"I heard of you before, long before I came here and you . . . appeared."

"Is that so?"

"Yes, you were betrothed to my grandfather before he died." Somehow, this information was not quite clicking. I knew it should make sense, but I could not sort out what he was saying. I must have looked bewildered, because he continued, "My mother is Felice, daughter of Tamiro, who was my grandfather—my Dedu Tamiro."

I sighed with the understanding seeping in. "I see. Well, you come from a good family."

"It is your family, too," he said. "In our way of thinking, you were married to Dedu Tamiro. Only death prevented it from being so, and death is just a nuisance in these matters."

I laughed then, which hurt my whole body. He reached to tuck a blanket under me, which somehow made me more comfortable. "I did not know that Baba Tsura mentored boys as well," I said.

"Of course," he said. "Anyone with the calling can become a healer. We have many male herbalists."

"Do you have the Sight?" I asked.

"No, I regret that I have just the normal capacities," he said.

I smiled again at his funny, careful wording. I liked him, despite feeling as if I was just knowing him after living under his care for months. I could see the resemblance to Tamiro in his features now, which sent a winch into my heart.

"I loved your grandfather very much," I said.

"That is well known," he said, and smiled, reaching for the bowl to feed me some more broth.

The door opened then, and Baba Tsura came in with a wooden bowl, a gust of air following her. I could see the patches of snow on the ground, with some receding to reveal brown, muddy earth. "The hazel is blooming," she said and tilted the bowl to show a pile of yellow spindly star-like blossoms. "I see she is doing better," she said to Noem. "I heard her talking."

"You do not need to speak of me as if I'm not here," I protested.

Baba Tsura looked directly at me with the intense disapproval that I had known too well the year I spent as her apprentice: "My dear, you have *not* been here. You have barely been alive these last months. Now that it seems you are to survive, I would hope you could show me the proper respect for nursing you back to life."

"I'm sorry, Baba Tsura. I thank you. I know I have been close to death. I am barely a person. Perhaps you should have let me die."

"At points, I thought it may have been kinder," she admitted.

"Well, I thank you. I thank you and Noem," I looked at the boy. "You have attended me well. I would have been a lost cause under anyone else's care, I'm certain."

"Yes, I am certain of that, too. It's why Zhulyi brought you to me."

"She is not returning?"

"I do not believe so. She has many family responsibilities to maintain."

I wondered then if Noem, too, knew about my love for Zhulyi. I decided it didn't matter, as I lay back and closed my eyes, exhausted by the conversation and meager activity.

"Crush these," I heard Baba Tsura say to Noem.

"Yes, Baba Tsura."

∞

I sat outside in the wan light of the spring morning. The stumps Baba Tsura usually used as stools did not support me, as I was still not sufficiently recovered enough to sit upright for long periods. Noem had made a cushioned stool with an ingenious sling back that was tied to two trees to hold it firm. I could rest back against the sling, but still sit in a somewhat typical fashion without straining my weakened muscles. I could still only walk a few steps at once and usually required assistance even in that. I could see Noem as a young man now, and not such a boy as he appeared to me in my hazed and injured state. My convalescence was slow, and it was not clear when—or if—I would be able to function on my own.

Baba Tsura was her typical brusque self, dismissing my concerns. "You will live," she said. "What kind of life it will be, there is no way to know."

I always found it amusing when those with the Sight insisted what was to come was a mystery. "But you can see the future, can you not, Baba Tsura? Surely you must know if I can have a normal life?"

She answered sharply, "What is revealed to me and what is in my mind is mine to protect and share only as I see fit."

I took the scolding like I took all of Baba Tsura's rebukes. It was just her way. After she went into the cottage, Noem came and sat by me, handing me some cooled tea in a bowl. "You will never be the same," he said, looking at me sincerely. "You will walk and be able to care for

259

yourself, but you will limp, and the pain will probably never go away." I saw the sadness in his eyes as he shared this confidence with me.

"Thank you, Noem. I need to hear the truth, even if it is unpleasant."

By mid-summer, I was able to walk, and as Noem had said, it was with a pronounced limp. The curve in my hip bulged out and my leg still did not sit right in its socket. The aching in my back, shoulders, and throbbing in my head was ever-present. There were things inside that had shifted and could not be righted, although Baba Tsura had manipulated anything that could be put back into place. She made me move my arms in wide circles twice a day, despite the torture of it, and had me roll forward upon my torso and move my head side to side to loosen my stiff and disjointed neck. The exercise wore me out, but she insisted upon it. Noem helped with gentle reminders and brought me strong tea afterward, since I was always worse after moving.

As the end of summer came, discussions ensued of Noem returning to his people. They would be coming to collect him at the Autumn Equinox. Although I had reflected little upon it with my mind so focused on my bodily trials, I realized that this was the year I was supposed to travel to Vár Buceci to see Perla. Noem's mother, Felice, had settled with her husband's family in the Rednitz valley across the Carpathians. Their path would go through Brașov, and I could travel with them, Noem assured me. Baba Tsura dreaded his leaving. Whereas she had found many faults with me, she never criticized Noem– only praising his skill with plants and with interpreting the messages of the great Earth Mother. His knowledge was flawless, it seemed. He remembered everything and was intuitively aware of the movements of all fauna and the growth of all vegetation in the forest. He knew when the mushrooms should be picked, when each tree would agree to give some fragments of her bark, and when each flower bloomed. He was truly a medicine man.

There would be a new apprentice coming, though. Another from the family– another boy was scheduled to arrive. He was a distant cousin's child who had been gifted with the Sight and needed tutelage. Baba Tsura would take him on as she had taken on a new student each year. I had been her oldest, she told me. "What if one year no one comes to learn from you?" I teased her. "Who will haul your firewood all winter then?"

"As you know, Jaelle, I am perfectly capable of hauling firewood myself. It would be a nice break to be left alone for once. Not with this family. They just keep spawning out healers and oracles, so what can I do? Someone must teach them. I don't suppose that will be you, Jaelle?"

"Oh, no, Baba Tsura. As you know, I was a miserable student and would be an even worse teacher."

"I think you would do fine to teach the basics," she said, which may have been the biggest compliment she ever gave me.

The tips of the evergreens turned orange, telling us that autumn was upon us. The green broad-leafed trees began to tinge yellow with dramatic flashes of red. The grasses turned from chartreuse to gold and the ducks flew overhead. I had taken a short walk down the path. I went a little further each day, but never far enough that I could not call for help if I needed it. When I returned to the cottage, Noem was outside with my cauldron. He had repaired the dent and polished it until it gleamed, its black flesh silken like a dark gourd. I embraced him, the first time I had done so, and he reciprocated. I realized I would miss him greatly. Baba Tsura would miss him, too. She kept saying this in so many ways as she went about her day. "Noem is so fine at drying the herbs perfectly. Now I will have to train someone else, and it will take me all year just to teach him to do it right!"

The boy did arrive soon after, and it was crowded in the cabin for a few days, so Baba Tsura made him sleep on the ground outside. The weather was still warm, so it was not much of a hardship for the boy, who was used to sleeping under the stars with his family anyway. Noem's family arrived right at the Equinox. His mother hugged me, telling me how grateful she was that I had made her father happy in his final days. Noem's father was a stocky, funny man, who joked with Noem and Baba Tsura as we gathered our things. Noem's little sister came, too, and would not let go of Noem, grasping about his waist and barely letting him move without her. As we packed the last of our few belongings into the carriage, Baba Tsura said, "Jaelle, you have forgotten something. Come inside."

I was sure I had everything, as I only owned my pot and a few pieces of clothing, but I followed her. In the dim light of the interior, she brought me to a corner and opened a large wooden chest among the many boxes that stored herbs, grains, and foodstuffs. She shuffled through and pulled out a small cloth package, tied with twine. Opening it, I saw it contained a delicate, long silver chain. On the end hung a flawlessly round, bright silver pearl, the color unlike anything I had seen before in such a treasure. "I have been saving this for you," she said.

"Baba Tsura—it's spectacular! How can I accept this?"

"Oh, but it belongs to you," she said. "Tamiro was planning to give this to you on your wedding night. Simza was aware of it since he had asked her to hold it for him. He had it commissioned by a powerful magician, a truly remarkable sorcerer. After Tamiro's death, Simza was saving it to give you at a time when the loss was not so fresh. Then you were gone." I could not speak as she helped to put it around my neck. Tears sprung to my eyes as I looked down to see its perfect shape upon my imperfect form. Baba Tsura took me in an embrace and held me. "Your journey ahead will not be easy, Jaelle. You may have more difficulties still, and more times of severe loneliness. Know that as long as you wear this, you will not be alone."

"Thank you, Baba Tsura. Thank you for all you have done for me. For the lessons, for the care you have given me, how you nursed me, saved me . . . I . . ."

"I know," she interrupted me. "This may come as a surprise to you, but I have gotten as much from you as you have from me. You are as a daughter to me, Jaelle, and what concerns you concerns me as well. We are connected, as all things are connected in our universe." I gulped back more tears. Never one to tolerate much sentimentality, Baba Tsura shushed me, and said, "Let's not keep them waiting."

The carriage pulled away, with Noem and his father leading the horses in the front so as not to get the wheels stuck on the narrow forest path. I leaned out to wave to Baba Tsura, but she was already scolding her new assistant about something and did not look up.

∞

Once again, I stood before Sandor's great stone archway and the gates before his estate. There was a guard stationed there who let me pass only because he recognized me. It was with great labor that I made it to the door, which was opened as I approached by several more uniformed guards. As we had come in this direction, Noem's family told me of the increased raids and power struggles going on between royalty in adjoining countries and invading tribes from other regions. There had always been strife in this territory, and who was in power one year might not be the same as who was ruling the next. However, this was a particularly tumultuous period.

The Rroma mostly stayed out of it, playing the part of the pilgrims who had no other allegiance except to their holy mission. It kept them out of the conflict in most cases. The only difference was that whoever ended up on top was the next group that needed to be negotiated with for land use or safe passage. It was always a surprise who might end up inheriting the Rromani chattel next. It was really of no consequence to the Rroma: no matter which group believed they owned them, they knew full well that they belonged only to each other. They could gesture in the sign of the cross over their chests, prostrate themselves on the ground, speaking in what the Gentles considered gibberish as they played the role of zealous devotees, and all was usually well no matter who was in charge.

The increased military presence within Sandor's home was noticeable as soon as I entered it, with twice as many uniformed men on duty. In times like this, Sandor could be called upon to defend the territory from invaders at a moment's notice, and he needed to be prepared. When he came to the door and looked at me, I could see the disgust and confusion there. He welcomed me into his arms, but was gentle in his embrace, clearly afraid to do me more damage. "Jaelle! What has happened to you?"

"I'm afraid it is a long story," I responded.

After settling me into a room, which I requested on the first floor, since it was unthinkable for me to climb his great marble staircase in my condition, we ate and then retired to the study. I explained all in a limited way so as not to disclose the assistance I had given the young woman or my relationship with Zhulyi, both of which I was not sure he would approve of. He was saddened to hear about Tamiro's death, despite having come late to giving his blessing.

"This is all my fault!" he exclaimed at one point, hiding his face in his hands.

"What are you talking about, Sandor? None of this has anything to do with you or is anything you could have prevented."

"Yes, but if I had never left Alianor . . . if I had stayed with her and had raised you in my home . . . all of this could have been different. Your whole life could have been different, and you would have been shielded from all that you have suffered. Now you are–hurt, and you have not married. At this point you probably never will."

"I doubt anyone would have me now–even you!" I tried to lighten his dour ponderings, but it did not seem to amuse him.

"Honestly, I still would Jaelle, if only to give you some comfort, but I have recently married someone else."

"Are you serious, Sandor? That's wonderful news! Who is she? Where is she?"

"Her name is Marion, and she is the daughter of a very influential voivode. I must say, I finally folded under the pressure. That and perhaps the fact that loneliness does not get better with age. We have a little daughter! Marion has taken our baby, Abigail, to her parents' estate through Christmas. It is safer there now, as things have become precarious here of late."

"What is it like? How is it to be married? Do you love her?"

"She is little more than a girl–my wife. She is but fifteen! She's lovely, but it is a very strange arrangement after being alone so long. I am but an old man to her, and the age difference makes us quite formal with each other. She is not worldly–and not much of a conversationalist. I think she's intimidated by me still. It has been trying, to be honest. And of course, she's not Alianor."

"No, but Alianor–my mother–is long dead and there is nothing you can do about that. I don't believe even Alianor would have wanted you to be alone the rest of your life."

"No, I suppose not. We are trying for an heir, as that is what I truly need now at this point in my life. Little Abigail is a most precious baby, but we will need a male heir to inherit my titles and property."

"It will be hard to make an heir with a wife so far away," I teased him.

"That's true," he chuckled, "but to be honest, I've been relieved since she's been gone. It's not only because it's safer for her and the child. It's just so draining being so proper all the time! I feel like I'm constantly putting on an act for her, trying to be attentive and considerate, but she is painfully dull to talk to and has little interests of her own, aside from the baby and a new dress here or there."

"You make marriage sound so appealing."

"Well, I'm sure it could be with the right person. I'm sure you would have had a much different experience with Tamiro. I am so terribly sorry, Jaelle. I know how you cared for him."

"Yes, well apparently that was not to be my destiny."

"But this should not have been," he said, gesturing across my body. "You did not deserve to be hurt like this."

"Who knows what I deserve? I don't know if that has anything to do with anything anyway."

"What can I do for you, Jaelle? There are places you could go for treatment. I could send you out of the country–to London even! There are whole schools to study medicine. I hear in France there is a school of doctors studying under master physicians. I could send you there!"

"No, that is not necessary. I just need one thing."

"Name it."

"I will need a small nimble carriage that can get up to Vár Buceci. There is no way I can ride horseback in this condition and clearly I will not be able to walk there myself."

Chapter Twenty-Three: A String of Pearls

"**M**ama, can you please take the baby for a moment?" Perla handed me the bundle, which I held on my lap. I had made a lot of progress over the winter, as such a small thing would have been impossible when I had arrived there in the fall. I looked down into the sweet little face, one that looked so much like my little Perla when I had first run away to the castle with her–now over 20 years ago. The infant girl was the newest addition to the family, born on the Winter Solstice after I had only been at the castle a few weeks. I had assisted with the birth, with some help from another medicine woman less restricted by her body. Perla's little boy, the one who was still a secret when we last met, looked like a miniature Sasha. Kari, who had grown so much in five years was–like this tiny one–an exact replica of her mother. Sadly, Perla had lost another child in between her second and this baby, she told me. This loss was harder than her previous miscarriage as she was further along, and it was extremely painful. She could even see the sex of the boy child after her body expelled him three months early. She had been ill and distraught for a long time afterward.

Now, with the three children, her spirits were restored, and she had settled into motherhood and duties to the clan as she did all else: with her characteristic grace and fortitude. She finished her task and took the baby back from me to change out the dried moss from within her cloth swaddling. I thought back to all the fabric I endlessly washed and hung in the sun to keep Perla dry when she was an infant. I wished I had known the trick of using the thick peat layer and swapping that out several times a day. I might have saved myself half of the trouble. I had to have some sympathy for myself, though, being that I had been around almost no babies up until the point I had absconded with Perla, so had no way of knowing better. Plus, as I reflected now, I was not much more than a baby myself at the time. It was a wonder I had survived and kept her alive at all.

The children called me 'Baba,' although Sasha had at first resisted it, asserting that Ankah was Perla's mother and not me. Eventually, he gave in to Perla's gentle persuasion. I certainly looked like a Baba now with my crooked frame. It had shocked Perla and the others who knew me when I arrived at the castle and had to be helped out of the carriage and to the entrance by the men Sandor sent to deliver me. Perla had cried, both from seeing me again and from my body being so harshly transformed. I shortened the story to explain that a Gentle man became enraged after I helped his wife with some herbs. This was enough to explain the violence that the Gentles sometimes showered down on Rroma healers. Perla had been trying to get me to agree to travel with them when they left in the spring. I was better, but not enough so that I would not slow them down. Even if I were to ride in carts or carriages most of the time, I would take the place of someone else who was infirm and needed the assistance. I continued to decline her offers, telling her I looked forward to time alone in the castle.

Perla had continued to develop her skills with the Sight, even after Selene left the world and could no longer instruct her. Still, when she had tried to scry me, it had not worked, she said. She was worried that once she left, she would not have contact with me for five more years or more. She easily saw the dead, but was less able to communicate with the living in a far-off place. "Everyone's gift is different," she explained. Sasha insisted that she was the most gifted woman anywhere around. He was full of praise for his wife and pride for his children. He had become the wonderful husband that I had always sensed he would be.

"Perla, have you decided what you will call this little one?" Like all Rroma, the child had a True Name, which was a secret. Usually, a nickname or public name cropped up spontaneously sometime after a child was born or when they showed a distinct personality. This little baby was already a few months old and did not have a name yet.

"I'm not sure! I have had such a time of it! I keep thinking something will pop out and make itself known to me, but it has been eluding me! Do you have any ideas?"

"Oh no! I am miserable at naming. It's a good thing the night you were born Ankah saw the bright full moon and it looked like a pearl. Otherwise, I probably would have called you 'Hey, you child!' for the next five years."

"Oh Mama! You're the silliest. I will miss you so much. Please come with us! You will not be a burden, so don't give that argument again. All could benefit from another medicine woman around."

"I am a mediocre healer at best," I said.

"Psh! That's nonsense and you know it," she said. Except I *had* felt worthless over the last few months. Even as my body made progress with healing, it revealed more of how my abilities would be limited in the future. What I knew of herbal treatment required quick responses and wandering far and wide to find the right plants. I was no longer fast and my circle for wandering was smaller than ever.

"I will be the slowest healer that has ever lived," I said, making her giggle. "If you need something, just let me know—then come back in six months and I may be able to help you."

"In six months, most people are either recovered or dead, so that will surely cut down on your customers."

"Precisely."

The snow was beginning to melt, and soon travel off the mountain would be possible. All of our discussion now contained some element of Perla asking me to come with her and me refusing. "We will need to plan for Ankari's marriage in a few years. You should be with us to help with that. I could use your advice to find a good family for her."

"You will have no problem finding a husband for Kari," I said. "She has the Gift, and she is so incredibly bright." It was true that the little dear was smart and had talent. She was physically the copy of her mother, but with less of the overflowing personality that had always drawn people to Perla and helped her to interact easily with them. Kari was more reserved, like her grandmother Selene.

"She could use more training, though, especially with healing. I have taught her how to manage the Sight. I'm still not clear about the breadth of her skills. I sometimes think she holds back so as not to make me feel inferior. I am aware I am restricted with the Sight, but perhaps she is not. She holds her own counsel, that one."

"It is often the best course of action to say nothing," I said. "Then everyone can think you are wise, even though in your mind you are just thinking about the soup you will prepare later."

Perla and I laughed again. I would miss the easy way we had together, but I was aware of how my presence would interfere with her family and her marriage. Sasha was respectful to me, but I could tell there was still resentment there, especially for the attention Perla paid to me. Besides which, most of the Badi Clan still thought of me as the one who had stolen Perla rather than as her mother. As much as it was hard to be parted from her again, I knew it was for the best.

∞

The other clans had departed already and the Badi were the last to leave. Sasha and Perla had been arguing all morning. I had seen them from a distance, engaged in a heated debate about something. It was unusual for them to quarrel. Mostly, Sasha sang Perla's praises and Perla spoke of her glorious husband as if he were the finest man on earth. I was taking care of the baby as they packed and prepared their belongings and the animals and carts to leave. She was a quiet baby and caring for her often consisted of little more than rocking her gently. Perla's son, Petro, was jumping around, with the frenetic enthusiasm of his father, wound up from anticipation of the trip. Ankari stood nearby, occasionally cautioning Petro not to hurt himself. Perla called Kari away to help with the packing, and I engaged Petro in a song about a frog that I had made up for Perla when she was a child. He loved it and began hopping about like a frog to act out the elements of the song.

Suddenly, Perla and Sasha were standing before me with Kari in front of them, their hands on her shoulders. They looked so serious that I sent Petro on a mission to see if he could catch an actual frog from the side of the lake.

"What is it?" I asked.

"Ankari will be staying with you," Perla announced.

"What? Perla, that is absurd. I can't care for a child in my condition! Why would you leave her here?"

"She needs training. You are a skilled healer. She needs the basics of herbalism and medicine."

"There are many who are better suited to teach such things, even among the Badi," I objected.

"Selene would have done it, had she lived. It makes sense for you to do it instead."

I looked at Sasha, but he avoided my eyes, obviously having lost the argument already.

"When will you return for her? Certainly not in five years! She must be married by then."

"We will return in two years. By then I'm sure we will have a family picked out and she will have more services to offer them."

"How can I provide for her? I'm practically a cripple!"

"She can help. She's strong and can make meals from start to finish. As you recall, I was raised on this mountain by a girl little older than Kari."

I could not argue with that.

They left us with several chickens, two goats in milk, and a lame mule who would not be able to make it down off the mountain. The parting was tearful, and I could tell Perla was worried about her choice, despite her pretended confidence in me. Ankari held the baby, saying goodbye to her new little sister. As Perla took the baby from Kari's arms before saying the final farewell, Kari pointed out the clouds reflected in the wide dark eyes of her sister. "Her name is Sky," Kari announced. Perla nodded and took the baby, hiding her face as she jumped into the carriage as

Sasha and Petro walked behind to drive the animals. As the long caravan of the Badi wound down the stony path and out of sight, I turned to Kari.

"Well, it's just us now. Did you ever think you'd be stuck with your old Baba Jaelle?"

"Yes," she said simply.

Chapter Twenty-Four: The Crone

Though the next two years tried my physical endurance, they were some of the most enjoyable of my life. In addition to being in touch with the spirit world, Kari was intuitively aware of all things that grew or crawled through the forest. I saw quickly that her mother was right about her: she knew much more than she let on. Sandor came to see if I had stayed or left with the clans in the spring. "I see you have a . . . new Perla?" he said, to my delight.

He sent supplies up frequently, which were a treat, but we really did not need them. Kari was efficient at milking, which was no longer possible for me, and would be gone into the woods no more than five minutes and come out with a meal ready to be prepared. We harvested the roots of the mallow grasses and Kari even caught fish from the lake to roast in a net she made herself. I was stationary most of the time, and Kari would hand me a root to chop up or some plants to wash and separate leaves from stems. I quickly taught her everything I had learned from Baba Tsura. She took whatever little knowledge I had and brought it a step further. I often felt as though I was her apprentice rather than the other way around. She treated the lame mule with a poultice of meadow flowers and the mule recovered! She treated me, also, and my range of motion improved. She was strict in prompting me to exercise, despite this causing me more pain in the short term. Although she had a serious nature, I would chide her into joking with me. I often told her my suspicion that she had been left on the mountain to watch me rather than the other way around.

One day in our second summer together she said: "Your friend is coming." I asked her what she meant, and she only pointed over the ridge. It was the other direction from where Sandor usually came. A moment later I saw a carriage come over the crest. The getup looked familiar, and I soon recognized it as Tamiro's grandson, Noem, and his family. I had told them tales of Vár Buceci on our journey from Baba Tsura's to Brașov together, and so they had decided to investigate the old castle and see if I had made it there. They ended up staying several weeks, and it was good to have the company. When they left, Kari said: "He will be my husband soon."

When Perla arrived the following spring, distraught that they had not been able to find a match for her yet, I told her about Kari's premonition. Together we traveled to the valley on the other side of the range where Noem's family stayed most of the year. We easily tracked them down through the other Rromani families we encountered. Noem had the same feeling about Kari, and his family was already impressed with her from their stay with us the year prior. It was an easy match. We left Kari with Noem's family to live until they were ready to marry in a few years after her first blood came. Noem's family said that they would join up with the Badi at the castle in three years' time, which might work out to be perfect timing to hold the wedding and see her family again.

Perla and Sasha were heading to Turda to meet up with the rest of the Badi Clan. Yearning for the healing hot springs outside Oradea, I went with them and continued alone from there, with the mule that Kari had healed pulling a small cart for me, since it was still hard to walk long distances. When Perla and I parted ways, I told her I would try to return to the castle when the tribes converged there again, but I think we both knew I would never make it there. She held me for a long time, and I told her that she was the light of my life. "You will always be my one true love," I told her, and kissed her perfect forehead.

From Turda, I meandered the countryside, but eventually ended up in the region I had visited with the kindling woman, Razel, and her family. I found a place out in the rolling plains where a spring popped up to stop with Meshu, my mule. Meshu was more than happy to take all the time in the world to munch the tall grasses while I submerged myself in the warm water for hours. I stayed there for several weeks, living on broths I cooked in my cauldron scrounged together from dried meat rations and whatever greens I could find. I added herbs that were good for healing and repairing the body, especially the bones and muscles. With the combination of the daily soaks and the intensive healing stews, in a few weeks I was feeling better than I had in years.

I had it in my mind to head into the city of Oradea to locate Zhulyi. However, on the way, I passed the small road that led to Razel's daughter's farm. On impulse, I turned Meshu and my cart into the pitted and uneven muddy tracks, and within a few minutes, I was looking at Mirabel and Bero's farm. It looked the same as if I had just left, overrun with chickens and barking dogs and big and little babies and children of all sizes. Lisel came out with yet another baby swaddled upon her. Recognizing me, she ran to greet me with a hug. She informed me that Razel had died the winter before, but that she had ended her days surrounded by love. She was at peace when she left. Lisel was on baby number nine. There were various other new children added from relatives who had come to stay on the property, including a sister that had moved back to her parents' homestead with her children after her husband passed.

Mirabel and Bero were glad to see me, too, and welcomed me to stay on as long as I wished. I did not intend to stay long, but after a few days of working out new cheese recipes with Lisel and telling stories to the countless children, I found myself settling in and staying on into the autumn. The daily baths in the hot springs and helping around the farm, tending to the small injuries and illnesses of the children, made me feel rejuvenated and useful. I slept in my cart at night. If it rained, there was always a porch for me to sleep under. One night, after eating the evening meal under the open sky with the family, Bero and the other men told sordid tales of when they were called into service to a nearby Lord to defend the territory from the invading Mongols. Afterward, I could not get to sleep. I had peppermint tea after our meal, which always kept me up, and my mind was full of the bloody battle scenes. I scolded myself that I should have known better than to drink mint so late. As I lay looking up at the stars, I felt something buzzing on my chest.

At first, I thought it was an insect that had gotten trapped inside my blouse, but when I reached in to grab at it, I felt only the smooth shape of the pearl necklace inside my fist. It was warm and almost hummed. I took it off and looked at it, since I had worn it for years at that point and it had never behaved like anything except a necklace. When I peered into the small orb, it winked and flashed, and then I saw a face there. I squinted, since it was so small, but then the face grew and surpassed the surface of the orb, projecting an image in the air in front of me. It was Baba Tsura! Her lips were moving, but I could not hear anything she was saying. Then I remembered Selene telling me about the trees. I went toward where an old oak grew and shaded a dusty area where the children played. With some difficulty, I lowered myself down and sat among its roots with my back against the tree. I looked at the pearl again.

"That's more like it," I heard Baba Tsura's husky voice as if she were sitting right next to me in the dark.

"Baba Tsura! It's so good to see you! Is all well?" I felt silly speaking out loud to a piece of jewelry, but she seemed to be able to hear me.

"No, it's terrible. I have a new apprentice here. I hate to say it, but she is a dunce. She's already broken two of my pots and she's only been here three days."

"I'm sorry to hear that. I'm sure she'll shape up. She's probably nervous. You can be intimidating, you know."

"Nonsense. I'm an old lady. I only intimidate the worms in my garden."

"Well, be gentle with her. I'm sure she'll get better. What is the meaning of your visit? I assume you are scrying me somehow? Has something happened?"

"No, I just realized after not hearing from you for so long that you probably didn't know how to use the necklace. I had told you that your family would never be far away so long as you were wearing it. But of course, you were never the sharpest, so I suppose you missed my meaning."

I laughed, missing her biting wit. "So how does it work, then?"

"Just as you are using it now! It's best under a dark sky, and you will need the consent of a tree."

"How do you know if the tree consents?"

"You will know if the connection works! If the tree didn't consent, you would not be speaking to me right now! Make sure you thank the one you are sitting by. He is not entirely happy about it, so be sure to make him an offering tomorrow. A little tea pouch buried near the roots will be fine, or some mead, if you have it."

"Indeed, I will do that. Would you believe that Noem—your star pupil—will be marrying my granddaughter, Ankari?"

"Oh, yes. I am aware. I speak to Kari all the time."

"You do?"

"Of course. How else could I keep tabs on you at Vár Buceci?"

"You spoke to Kari while we were at the castle? She never . . ."

"No, of course she didn't. Unlike *some* people who say whatever comes into their heads, your granddaughter inherited some of Selene's restraint. Thank goodness."

"I am going to be heading into Oradea soon to see Zhulyi. The Bihari should be heading to the Citadel for the winter. I should be able to find her there."

"About that . . ."

"Yes?"

"That's not a good idea."

"Baba Tsura? Why is that not a good idea? Have you spoken to Zhulyi? What did she say?"

"There are many complications in Oradea right now. There will be a siege soon. The Bihari are not even going to the Citadel this winter. It's too dangerous. They are heading back to Deva where it is safer."

"Well, perhaps I can meet up with her there! Deva is not so far!"

"Jaelle!" It was the reprimand in her tone that I remembered clearly. "You need not follow Zhulyi to the ends of the earth any longer. That period of your life is over. You must move on."

"But . . ."

"No!" Her voice rang out loud and clear. "You have nothing to offer her and it will only end in misery for you both. It is the kindest thing to let her go, Jaelle."

I did not like or want to believe what she was saying. Soon after, we said our farewells, and Baba Tsura gave me some more helpful pointers for contacting those who might have the ability to receive such messages. Normally, I would not have that potential, being that I had only minimal talents as a healer and no gifts to see the dead or communicate over distances like some medicine women. The necklace was the only reason I could do so, since it was a magical instrument that had been specifically crafted for that purpose. Tamiro had known that, Baba Tsura told me, and had it commissioned specifically so that once we were married, I would be able to contact Perla and relieve some of my worries over her welfare.

I did use it frequently after that to contact Perla, who was thrilled by it. I also scried Kari, who was gracious, but in typical form did not show great enthusiasm. She indulged me, but always seemed as if I had dropped in on her while she was busy cleaning the hearth and was eager to get back to it. I contacted Baba Tsura on occasion, but she had warned me not to try to contact Zhulyi. She said it would do more harm than good. I was tempted to disobey this advice at times, but I trusted her. I understood that she knew more than I in these matters. I found I could also use the pearl to scry people who might not be able to reciprocate and would not be aware of my observation. In this way, I was able to look in on Sandor and his wife, and their pretty daughter. I was happy to see that they had a new baby boy arrive, and Sandor had finally fulfilled his mission to find an heir.

Baba Tsura warned me that there were some things that I should not try to see: there were things that could not be unseen once you saw them, she said. I would only be harmed if I went looking for things that were none of my business. I thought she was just talking about Zhulyi, but I learned the hard way what she meant. I had always wondered what had happened to Rosalie, the girl who was trapped in the stagecoach when the evil man ran over me. I scried her one time: I found her in a miserable hovel, nursing a baby with an older baby and a toddler fighting over a biscuit on the dirt floor. Both of her eyes were blackened, and she jumped when she heard the man, now her husband, call for her to fetch him something. It was one of the saddest things I had ever seen. After that, I did not scry her—or others I had no business seeing.

Although I heeded Baba Tsura's advice about running after Zhulyi, that did not keep me from visiting her in my dreams. Several nights a week, she would be there with me as we did commonplace things—washed laundry in a stream or sat over a fire roasting eggplants together. I would awake and her scent would fill my nostrils as if she had just risen from the bedroll. One morning before dawn, I opened my eyes and she was right there beside me, her head resting only a few inches from mine! I began to speak, but I could not move my lips to say anything. She spoke and I heard her voice as if she were right with me, although I knew I was, in reality, asleep and alone on the ground. I sensed that she was scrying me and only present through the magic of folding the distance between us. The words she uttered–almost whispered– rang with truth:

"My love," she said, "I wish we could have spent all our days together in this life. My body and my heart have ached for you every day. It was only my mind that made me faithful to another path–but that is not your fault, Jaelle! I was built this way: designed to sacrifice my own desires in loyalty to tradition and family. I have often wished I was made like you, following only my own notions. I have envied you–I admit–for your freedom. You have been unfettered by what others have expected of you, throwing off the shackles of the world's demands."

I could not interject, but only thought: "At what price?"

She continued: "You are my heart's match, Jaelle, and I have suffered for lack of you, even in the warmth of my devotion to my sons. I only hope I can be braver in our next incarnation. Or perhaps, we will emerge together again, bubbling up in the same overlapping time, when our love will be better suited. I will yearn for you until then, my love . . ." She said a name then. It was not Jaelle or Sabine, but stored back even further in my memory. I was sure I'd never heard it spoken aloud before–at least not in this life–but I recognized it at once as my True Name. Zhulyi knew that it was safe to speak it in the protected form that was neither wake nor sleep. I could only guess that it was her allegiance with the spirits that led her to know this secret, when I did not even know it myself until then.

I opened my eyes with tears wetting my cheeks. All I felt was all I'd lost. It was true I had followed my own path in life, but where had it gotten me? Alone and broken. I wished dearly to tell Zhulyi that–there was nothing to admire about my inability to do as the world expected. It was my greatest weakness that I could not mold myself to be a better citizen to my tribe. I could be married to Sasha now, living happily among the cheerful Badi, or amusing myself in any way I wished on Sandor's grand estate. I could even be married to one of Uncle Ulric's rich old widowers with nothing more to worry about than pursuing my own interests. I might even have children surrounding me now, ready to care for me in my decline. It was a curse to be married only to one's own selfish tastes. I never compromised, but that only meant that everyone–including me– lost.

After it became clear that going to Oradea was not advisable, I let Bero and Mirabel's family know of my change in plans. They were kind as could be and told me I could stay through the winter, if I wanted. As comfortable as I felt among them, I did not think it was right to impose on their hospitality any longer. Before I left, the men crafted a curved covered wagon with benches inside on top of my cart so that I would have some protection from the weather. It was not unlike the carriages of the Rroma caravans. I was touched by their craftsmanship and generosity. I followed narrow trails back through the plains, with no direction or goal in mind except to travel on my own with Meshu as my sole companion. If I encountered a farm or cottage I would sometimes stop and offer some herbs or medicine in trade for meat or eggs or flour. When I was particularly lucky, I was given fresh milk.

      While my body had recovered tremendously, I still limped and the pain was almost constant. I looked to find a place that might shelter me for the winter, since the nights were getting very cold. I often wished I had not let my pride keep me from staying on at Mirabel and Bero's farm. They would have given me and Meshu shelter and warmth and cheery company throughout the long dark season. It was too far to head back now. On a desolate plain, I came across a small cottage and livestock paddocks next to a trickle of a stream. It was starting to snow, and the wind was going almost sideways, ice crystals striking my face like tiny pieces of glass. An old man came out and saw me struggling to tie up Meshu. Instead, he unhooked her and brought her to the pen where there was a shed, and other animals huddled within against the weather. He gestured me to come inside, and as soon as the door shut, the howling of the wind fell silent. Inside was toasty warm, and an orange fire glowed. An old woman sat by the fire sewing and tried to stand to greet me as I came in. "No, please–do not get up," I urged her.

      They gave me bread and cheese and apologized for not having a hot meal. They had lived there since they had married, raised children, some who were deceased and others who were married and gone. They lived off the small farm and almost never had visitors. They happily gave me a place to sleep on blankets on the floor laid over straw, which was more comfortable than the places I had been sleeping. Despite my physical limits, I was still sturdier than they were. I helped them with their chores and with cooking and cleaning the small house throughout the winter. When the weather broke in the spring, I went on my way, with a little goat kid they gave me to thank me for all my efforts. It was a tawny little doe I named Lumina. I held her across my lap as I drove at first, then she scampered along after Meshu when she got fast enough. That spring and summer, I wandered, picking herbs, and drying them by the roots inside my cart. By the fall, I had a traveling herb shop inside my carriage, and I visited towns and villages selling teas and tinctures and poultices. On the shelves inside my cart, I strapped together thin wooden canisters that held dried roots and leaves and powders. I attached a heavy leather belt with livestock bells to the back of the cart to brace the doors from flying open. We had to go slowly with our load on the deeply rutted roads. The jars would knock together as we drove and the bells would jangle, making melodious twinkling sounds that I loved. They became the background music of my daily wandering life. Those hearing the jingling peals knew that the herb woman was coming through town.

In the winter, I found my way back to the small farm of the old couple, who were more than happy to have the help again, as they were even more infirm than the previous year. This was the pattern for the next several years. Having been raised by a people who travel most of the year, I had found a lifestyle that matched a rhythm that had been instilled in me as a child. I brought my goods to new places in the warmer months, selling tiny handfuls of dried flowers in pouches or trading teas for staples. When I returned the next winter, the wife of the couple had passed; the following year the paddocks were empty and nobody was in the house. I spent that winter alone in their sparce house, feeling their absence. That was the winter the tribes were returning to Vár Buceci and Noem and Kari were to wed. I sent my best wishes through Perla, whom I scried regularly. I had told her far in advance that I would not be making it back to the mountain castle. Though she was disappointed, she did not seem surprised.

All had moved on without me, it seemed, and I was still alone. I had the comfort of my animals, but little else. Each year was marked by greater discomfort in my body and needing to do everything slower and more effortfully than ever. I developed a cough for a season, and when it finally subsided, there was a rattle in my chest that seemed never to fully leave. One summer night, I scried Baba Tsura and found she was not there. She was just gone. Later, I learned from Kari that she had passed on after a brief illness brought in by a new apprentice. The child student had a mild fever and some splotchy cheeks when she arrived, but recovered by the next day. Three days later, Baba Tsura was dead. The girl had to wander out of the woods alone and find her way back to her family. I no longer had anyone to counsel me.

One day I was leading Meshu along a narrow street in a village we had not visited before. I was going slowly and being cautious of the cobblestones. A twisted ankle for my mule would be the end for both of us. We came into a square where a church was being erected, as seemed to be the case in every new town we visited. I went to stand in front of the activity, watching the men lift bricks and unpack loads of mortar. I felt a presence next to me and turned to see what seemed to be an apparition floating in front of me: an old woman looking straight at me with a surprised expression on her face. Her hair wildly escaped her headscarf and had wide streaks of white. Her body was bent over and had been marked poorly by the passage of time and human frailty. It took a moment to realize that the old woman was my reflection. A colossal shiny bell was standing in an open packing crate, destined for the top of the new cathedral. My face had caught the eerie refracted metallic light, making me appear a phantom, and the shape of the bell distorted my already bent form. The specter was me: I had become a crone without even knowing it had happened. After a moment, I shrugged. I had lived the solitary existence of a crone my whole life anyway, so there was virtually no difference.

Chapter Twenty-Five: A Pearl in the Broth

The night air is cold: so cold it hurts my lungs. I can see the bright pearl of the moon, plump in the sky, through the opening at the top of my tent. My animals are breathing, leaning together in their sleeping mass on the other side of the cloth. I can smell their earthy presence. As always, it comforts me to have them so close—my true family—the ones who have stayed with me through all life's journeys. Even when I was a child, my animals brought me comfort.

My cart is nearby, and I can hear the tinkling of the bells as the wind whips through the open plain. It is no longer comfortable for me to sleep between the narrow benches on the planks inside. I set up a tent at night now, and sleep on a rug woven from rags that I roll up during the day. It keeps the icy ground away from my old bones. Winter is coming. I should seek better shelter soon—or should I? Perhaps I should just stay here and let the elements take me. My animals never need to be tied and so they would wander off when the time came. It is a ragtag family: my mule, Meshu; my little goat Lumina and a big meat goat that I rescued from a butcher in a nearby town; also, a silky black sheep and her lamb. The sheep gives me a cup of milk each morning and I ask little else of her. They lay piled close together at night—the lamb in the center—and if any critters come close, Meshu stands and snorts and paws the ground until they retreat.

I look up at the sky: the moon is still framed by the opening above, its creamy ivory face encircled by a halo that lights up the whole sky. It is a clear night, with just the tiniest cottony wisps of clouds. The rattle in my chest has gotten worse in the past weeks. Even the smallest task takes the wind from me. As always, my bones and muscles ache. Pain has been my closest companion in recent years. I have not spoken to Perla in many months but I feel my necklace

279

humming. As I struggle to find the opening in my dress to extract it, I feel eyes upon me. I look up, and the moon herself has eyes! The face above is glowing and familiar: it is Baba Tsura, with all the wrinkles and marks upon her face smoothed out and just her familiar, smiling eyes looking down at me.

There are no trees around this open place, so I struggle to sit up so that I can try to walk to the closest fringe of forest. I find that my body is paralyzed, though. I can feel the purring pearl in my grasp and my wheezing lungs struggling for air, but my limbs will no longer move. My spine suddenly feels very peculiar—as if it is turning in on itself, curling up into a ball—but I am not moving and there is no pain involved. I feel my whole being turning in on itself, like a whirlpool that sucks all water in, but is still only water. I start to panic and look up to Baba Tsura's eyes, gazing down on me with love filling them. I am soothed then, overflowing with perfect calm. I do not see her lips moving, but I hear her voice, resonating throughout my whole being, as if she is inside my body along with me:

"Come, Jaelle. It is time."

Nikki Pison, PhD, is a writer, visual artist, and farmer. She raises
a herd of dairy goats on her small family farm in the Hudson Valley, NY.
She is an avid traveler and a collector of art and stories. In her spare time,
Dr. Pison is a clinical psychologist, although she is still considering
becoming a midwife, a hot air balloon pilot, or an astronaut.

Acknowledgments:

This is a historically-*flavored* novel rather than one that attempts to be factually accurate. It would have taken a lifetime of study to fully understand the time and people I write about in this book. Instead, I was sincere in my efforts to create credible atmosphere without the lifetime investment that would have been required to be 100% historically correct. I consulted many documents and sources in my research to inform choices about culture, language, and contemporary events that the characters encounter.

Some books that were particularly helpful in this endeavor were:

Fonseca, Isabel (1995). *Bury Me Standing: The Gypsies and their Journey.* New York: Alfred A. Knopf, Inc.

Lee, Patrick Jasper (2015). *We Borrow the Earth: An Intimate Portrait of the Gypsy Folk Tradition and Culture.* Ravine Press: Pembrokeshire, Wales.

Lee, Patrick Jasper (2016). *Coming Home to the Trees: Travelling with the Gypsy Spirit of the Past.* Ravine Press: Pembrokeshire, Wales.

Taylor, Becky (2014). *Another Darkness, Another Dawn: A History of Gypsies, Roma, and Travellers.* London: Reaktion Books Ltd.

This was not a Solo Act, thanks to several members of my family:

My content and plot consultants and editors:

Halina Adamski; **Karen Peone Cathers**; and **Elga Antonsen Brown**

Master Formatting Magician: **Justin Peone**

Cover Artist Extraordinaire: **Layla Cummings**

Advisor on Dream Sequencing: **Felix Pison**

Additionally, many thanks to the Almighty Google, who was able to summon at my command a plethora of historical medieval maps and answer such burning questions as:

"Were women allowed to own property in the 14th Century?" and

"What was the head woman in charge of household staff called in medieval times?"

I thank you, Google, for always being there when I need you.

Finally, to my Great Grandmother Media: Perhaps not the first Wild Woman in our family line, but the one setting the precedent for the succeeding generations of Wild Women. She was a psychic medium who wore all black and painted her walls black before it was cool.

I wonder who she is now?

Media Violet Shaeffer
January 9, 1880 – May 10, 1972